Flashman and
the Third Reich

ISBN 9798702774411

www.paulfmoore.com

This is a work of fiction.
Whilst many of the characters existed, the story
is entirely from the imagination of the author.

For Julie, Henry and Hattie

Flashman and the Third Reich

Chapter 1

I was right. I had always known it. He had always been pretty useless but now we had the final proof that this was the case. I had seen the draft statement that he was going to make to the unsuspecting public where he whined about the 'burden of responsibility without the support of the woman I love' and more such tosh. What he should have said was 'that despite all his efforts to keep his flies firmly buttoned closed, he had failed and that he had got some American tart pregnant and would now have to abdicate his exalted position as lord and master of most of the world'. The buffoon Churchill[1] had tried to persuade him not to step down and instead keep the American tart as a mistress and marry someone more suitable that could provide him with an heir or two before retiring into the background. Presumably he also thought that this would allow him to manipulate the palace as required thereby bolstering his own waning political career. But no. In true boche form, he couldn't be persuaded to do anything other than exactly what he wanted and so the selfish bastard abdicated citing his unending love for Mrs Simpson and his desire to indulge himself forever and never do a day's work. Or something like that. I may not have quoted it exactly.

Whatever the truth of it all, it at least meant that he couldn't do me any more harm, not that he had really caused me any major trouble for years. It was the possibility that had worried me. The result of the 'constitutional crisis' was the accession of George VI, the stuttering under-confident Duke of York, prone to towering rages and deep sulks, and his formidable wife, the former Elizabeth Bowes-Lyon. It wasn't promising. But it was what I wanted, and it had amused me enormously to engineer the ultimate downfall of Wales. Y'see, I had caught the bastard leaving my house in Paris some years ago[2] and whilst I was sure,

---

[1] See Appendix.
[2] See 'Flashman and the Red Baron'.

4

well almost sure, that my beloved Victoria hadn't been doing a horizontal quickstep with him, he would definitely have tried. And for that, he had to be punished. Of course, it isn't that easy to punish those born to rule, but I didn't need it to be splashed all over the Times, just a trivial victory would have been enough, but this was superb. I could barely keep the smile from my face.

London of course was awash with rumour and gossip driven partly by the preceding press blackout[3]. Would England become a republic? Who would be President? Churchill? Baldwin? Could we really trust the royals and their German ancestors? We had fought them already this century and the doomsayers amongst us, Churchill being the chief, thought we would soon be fighting them again. There were even darker rumours of other claimants to the throne, some of which were started by my good self, and it amused me no end to see how far they spread before reaching me again.[4]

But I am getting way too far ahead of myself. The memories as always haunting me in my old age. Before you know it, I'll be back in my Spitfire....

---

[3] This was true amongst the Upper Classes who had access to information, but not so for the majority who didn't.

[4] There is little evidence of the British public seeking the end of the Monarchy. When they found out, they initially supported the King along with Churchill, Lloyd-George and others although this may have been driven by the Beaverbrook press. The ruling classes and the Church opposed him for a variety of reasons. The Church cited the need for him to be seen to have a high moral character, the ruling class were most definitely worried about another clash between the monarch and parliament and saw abdication as the way to prevent that. They even cited the civil war despite it being over 250 years since its end.

Chapter 2

Ten years it had taken them. Ten years of struggle, conspiracy, intimidation, violence and more importantly politics.

Prison had made them think seriously about how they could bring their turgid book to life. I had read some of it and the only thing that would put you to sleep quicker was a general anaesthetic. But for them it was a manual, the guiding light for the resurgence of Germany as a nation, the birth of the Aryan master race, a map leading to the end of the rainbow[5]. I believed it when I told Sinclair it was nonsense; it would never come to pass. How wrong I was, and I should have known better having been in their confidence for so long. I suppose I just couldn't see how they were going to get past an electorate who, like the majority of all electorates, didn't care in the slightest about their grand plans as long as they mostly had jobs, food, beer or wine and some money to spend on whooping it up. But then this was the Roaring Twenties[6] when anything and everything went.

It was the Americans that started it of course. At least it was their money that started it. The 1923 putsch had set off a domino effect, or rather the crisis that precipitated it had. As the German economy foundered, the Americans stepped in with the Dawes Plan whereby they would invest heavily in Germany. This in turn allowed the Germans to pay their reparations to France and Britain who could then pay their debts to the Americans.[7] Simple really. Like a mad merry-go-round only this one was fuelled with alcohol, cocaine, jazz and most importantly, credit. The post-war survivor's optimism coupled with the revolutionary new world of technology and innovation began a boom which many, or even most, thought would never end. But it had to, and it did. Some say

---

[5] Presumably 'Mein Kampf', volume 1 of which was published in 1925, volume 2 in 1927.

[6] See Appendix

[7] The 1924 Dawes Plan was slightly more complex than Flashman states. The USA did indeed lend money to Germany to spend on rebuilding the economy. The increased tax revenue was then used to pay war reparations to France which in turn repaid American loans and bought American goods.

that was London's fault. I would narrow it down even further to Hatry. Clarence Charles Hatry.

I knew him vaguely. In early 1929, I had been to a party at his Mayfair house just along the road from Princess Mary[8]. It was that bloated fool Paulet that invited me. I couldn't fathom why at the time, but curiosity had encouraged my acceptance. I realised almost immediately that it was just an attempt to sell shares to the unwary and played on the aristocratic connections of Paulet who as well as being the 16th Marquess of Winchester[9] was also Chairman of General Securities Ltd, one of Hatry's many companies. Hatry was a nobody of course having started out as an insurance clerk, but his shrewd business mind quickly propelled him into the big league and his war profiteering had led to his appointment as a director of numerous corporations. It wasn't just the Americans![10]

It was a strange evening all round. Hatry himself had showed me his house, mainly so I could view his wealth in all its vulgar and gaudy glory. But even I was impressed with the swimming bath he had had installed.

"You will have to come to one of my bathing-suit parties," he had said which sounded jolly.

"Even the ladies?" I spluttered, not because I had any objection to the female form in a bathing suit, it just sounded like the sort of thing that would be more fun in Montmartre. He nodded solemnly and I aimlessly pondered on a fate that meant I would look rather dashing in a bathing suit whereas he, despite his wealth, would look short, bald and ill in his.

---

[8] This is presumably Chesterfield House, a Baroque mansion built in the mid 18th century by Philip Stanhope, 4th Earl of Chesterfield on land owned by the 1st Earl Howe, where Princess Mary, daughter of George V, lived in London with her family.

[9] Lord Henry Paulet led a varied life including military service during the Great War and being made bankrupt in 1930. He married three times, had no surviving children and at his death aged 99 was the oldest ever member of the House of Lords.

[10] This is a very emotive subject. According to a Fortune magazine article in 1934, it 'cost about $25,000 to kill a soldier during the World War'. Many people made fortunes and it is not easy to justify all of them.

It was all pointless in the event because he apparently spent the summer trying to persuade Norman[11] to finance his merger with United Steel and when he turned him down flat, his stock began to fall. Somehow Hatry then managed to coerce Garnsey, the Chairman of Lloyds Bank into trying again with Norman but failed to mention that he had been issuing stocks to cover the deal. What he also failed to mention was that some of the stocks were fraudulent and had been printed twice and given to different banks as security.

At this point Norman told the chairman of the London Stock Exchange that Hatry was bankrupt and trading in his shares was suspended on 20th September. After confessing all to the Director of Public Prosecutions, he and his cronies toddled off to jail.[12]

Officially the exchange had crashed. No one, at least no one outside the banking world, could have foreseen what happened next. The London crash caused the American foreign investors to start panicking and the share volumes being traded rapidly increased. Throughout October the American markets began to slide towards the abyss. Over the weekend of the 26th of October, the American press conveniently fuelled the fire and by Tuesday there were shares for sale that no one would buy. I heard afterwards that $30 billion had been lost in two days.

The merry-go-round came to a crashing halt. Money stopped flowing out of America into Europe and consequently through Europe and back to America. What became known as the Wall Street Crash had just lit the fuse for the resurgence of German Nationalism. And this, dear reader, is where our story really begins.

---

[11] Presumably Montagu Norman, Governor of the Bank of England from 1920 to 1944 and close friend of Hjalmar Schacht, effectively his opposite number in Nazi Germany. He was reputed to be sympathetic to the Nazi regime, a not unusual position at the time.

[12] See Appendix.

Chapter 3

I spent most of my time in Paris. It worked for everybody. Sinclair was happy to have me there as eyes and ears with occasional forays out into the wild, especially Germany largely to maintain my links with Hess and co despite their apparent irrelevance. The Germans liked the delusion that they had more power than the reality should have told them. And Victoria liked being away from her family, especially her Father, something I had no objection to either[13]. Sinclair now had an extensive network of agents most of whom had been in his employ for some time. De Ropp had changed sides and was now the MI6 representative in Berlin and Winterbotham had been appointed head of MI6's Air Intelligence Section.[14]

As for the Germans, the twenties had slid by in the same alcohol and drug induced haze as the rest of Western Europe. The Nazis had revived a little after the ban was lifted in 1925 and Adolf had relaunched the party. By August 1927 they were able to attract an audience of 20,000 members for the first Hess organised Nuremberg Party Day.

"Credulous optimism has befogged hundreds of thousands, in fact millions, of our people. It will take twenty or even a hundred years to establish the National Socialists as the ruling party of Germany." So said Adolf. He was right in one respect and that was that the population was befogged.

Standing in the 1928 elections, the Nazis won 12 out of 491 seats in the Reichstag. It was hardly awe inspiring. But then fate, in the guise of Clarence Hatry intervened. Eleven months after the crash, with unemployment soaring and life in general disintegrating, the German people went to the polls again. This time, Hitler's message was very welcome, and 107 seats agreed, second only to the Social Democrats. Just under two years later, more elections confirmed the general disaffection with the ruling classes and 230 Nazis were returned to the Reichstag, now the

---

[13] See Flashman and the Red Baron. Her alleged Father, Sir Frederick Ponsonby was elevated to the peerage in 1935 as Lord Sysonby and died shortly afterwards.

[14] Appointed in 1930.

9

largest party but without a majority. Weeks of negotiation followed in an attempt to form a coalition government, but the major obstacle was the President, Von Hindenburg, who rightly viewed Hitler as a ranting no good upstart. However, behind the scenes Hess had been talking with Schacht and von Schroder[15] and they agreed with the idea of building up the armed forces and abolishing democracy and so pressured Hindenburg into accepting Hitler.

And so it was that I was there, in the Reichstag, as one of those who had led the Bürgerbräukeller putsch and witnessed the martyrs blood soaking into the Blood Flag[16], to see Hitler sworn in as Chancellor on 30th January 1933.

"I never thought I would see this day," I said to Rudi as we left the building.

He gave me a sidelong look.

"I never doubted him for a minute. I knew it would come to this." He genuinely believed it as well. "I need you to do something for me. But it is Goering's plan. Can you meet him tonight?"

"Of course," I said, my heart beginning to pound.

"It is only a little ruse to speed up the process. It might even be fun!"

---

[15] Presumably Halmar Schacht (see above) Reichsbank President 1933-1939 when he was dismissed. He remained a Minister until 1943, was arrested after the July 1944 assassination attempt and interned. He was eventually tried at Nuremberg but acquitted. Kurt Freiherr von Schroder was a prominent financier for the Nazis and was prominent in Hitler's rise to power. He is rumoured to have funnelled money via Schroders in New York and London to the SS during the war and also assist with the concealment of Nazi finance afterwards. He was tried by a German court postwar and sentenced to three months imprisonment.

[16] The Blood Flag or 'Blutfahne' was that of the 5th SA Sturm carried at the Beer Hall Putsch in 1923 and stained with the blood of an SA man that died there. It disappeared briefly but was returned to Hitler who had it fitted to a new staff and the names of the dead added on a silver sleeve. It was used thereafter to 'sanctify' other banners at Nuremberg by touching them. It was last seen in October 1944 at a Volkssturm induction ceremony. Kept in the Nazi Party Headquarters in Munich (The Brown House) it is rumoured to have either been destroyed by the fire that burnt the Brown House down in 1945 or to exist in a secret location.

Now I was worried. I took my leave of him and spent the afternoon chewing my nails and drinking, never a wise remedy but the only one available. Consequently, I was late arriving at Goering's Berlin abode.

"Fleischmann, where the hell have you been? I was getting worried." He accompanied this statement with a large grin and a tumbler of whisky. "No doubt some charming mädchen?"

"You know me too well," I replied and yawned to hide my look of terror.

"Well, you will need to be well rested for my little plan my friend. As you know, Adolf is going to call another election for the 5th of March. Before that, in two week's time, we are going to burn down the Reichstag."

"We are going to what?" I screeched.

"I knew I could shock you. But it makes sense as you will see."

I couldn't believe my ears. I briefly clung onto the hope that it was his idea of a joke, but he never was very funny. I put my hands behind my back as they started shaking, something that hadn't happened in a long time, and then Goering began outlining the plan.

It had to be just the two of us as it had to be carried out by those whose loyalty was not in doubt – I shivered again at this statement – and it had to be deniable. It was absolutely imperative that the communists were blamed. It also had to more or less destroy the building, so we needed a plan to delay the fire brigade as well.

"So, we are agreed?"

I nodded, for the thousandth time wondering whether there was in fact no God, just a devilish fate waiting for me in the fires below. It seemed apt that this latest addition to my list of unsavoury events was itself a fire.

Needless to say, I took up Goering's offer of more drink and some food with gusto. It had no effect whatsoever other than to provide me with a dreadful headache the next day when I woke up on his sofa. I took my leave as early as possible and wandered around Berlin in a vain attempt to clear my head. It struck me for some reason that the last time I was there had been after the failed Kapp putsch. Why me?

I briefly considered absconding again dismissing this as nonsense as always. I knew what they were like and I didn't have the nerve for it. So, I spent the next two weeks alternately discussing the details with Hermann and trying to think of a way to stop him. There wasn't one of course.

The big day arrived all too soon. I was staying with Hermann for ease and I was up early, my nerves preventing me from sleeping too much. Much to my surprise he was up already and clearly his nerves were jangling too albeit not from fear but excitement. He seemed to think we were about to carry out some schoolboy prank and took great delight in burning some cork and spreading it on our faces to disguise ourselves. Time dragged by as we waited for it to get dark so that there hopefully wouldn't be too many people about to disturb us. Finally, the time came and we set off, Hermann ludicrously tiptoeing along the road and then turning and grinning at me. Perhaps he had been drinking as well.

It took us half an hour to get within striking distance of the Reichstag. Fortunately, most of our approach route had been through the woods of the Tiergarten. Now we were in position with just the last few hundred yards to cross.

"Won't there be guards?" I asked as it suddenly occurred to me that this was likely to be the case.

"Yes, but Adolf has made sure they are a little sleepy by waking them up early this morning and not allowing them a proper break from their duties today."

That apparently settled that dilemma. I couldn't think of any more questions.

"Let's go," he whispered, and a bulky figure appeared in the shadow in front of me.

We crept across the pavement to the edge of the road and then with a glance each way ran across, half crouched with me looking directly ahead and praying silently. Reaching the other side, we kept going straight at the corner of the great building where we stopped, panting as if we had just run a mile or two. Straightening up I shifted the heavy pack on my back to a more comfortable position.

"This way," Goering muttered. I followed him along the wall until he stopped at a window. Reaching up, he pushed at it and it swung open[17]. "You first."

Stifling a momentary snort of panic, I heaved myself up onto the low sill and cocked one leg over into the room. I couldn't see a thing inside, but I could feel there was nothing below me, so I slipped over onto the floor. A few seconds later Goering joined me.

"This way," he chuckled, clearly enjoying himself now.

I followed again as we headed deep into the building.

"Here it is," he announced triumphantly. "The Chamber of Deputies. We'll start here and work outwards. Set the incendiaries and then we can light them together.

I opened my pack and headed into the gloom wondering where exactly was best to set fire to a building. Fortunately for the budding arsonist there was plenty of wooden furniture, so I moved some of the chairs against a wall that had wooden panelling and laid my incendiary underneath.

"Ready?"

"Yes," I replied.

Without another word I saw the flash of something lighting. Almost immediately the flare dimmed and then suddenly burned bright as the fire took hold. That spurred me into action I can tell you. I lit my incendiary, the effect being the same and watched for a second as it caught. I turned to find Goering lighting another and it only struck me then how bright the place was all of a sudden. The firelight danced eerily on the walls of the great chamber. Like most of the population, I was oddly fascinated by fire and the satisfying feeling of burning something to nothing, destroying it for no other reason than seeing it burn.

"Let's go," Goering called and as I joined him at the door, I could see the fire was really getting going. I was glad he knew the way out as for a second I had visions of running in circles trying to escape the hell we had created. We slid back out of the window and when I looked round, I realised there was in fact no visible sign that all was not well inside.

We crossed the road again and slipped back into the woods to await events. Neither of us said a word. For some time, there was no sign anything was wrong, so much so that I began to wonder if

---

[17] Marinus van der Lubbe, the Dutchman arrested and subsequently tried and executed for the fire claimed he entered via a window.

the fires had just gone out by themselves. But then straining my eyes towards the building I noticed a small flicker, like a gas light in a foggy street. Slowly, slowly, the light increased and spread as the fire took hold. Still there was no reaction from anyone. I watched transfixed, the human fascination for burning things well to the fore. There was a loud crash which seemed to reverberate round Konigsplatz[18] for all to hear but nothing happened, and no one appeared to investigate. By now, the windows were quite literally ablaze with light from within and then at last some of the guards appeared and started shouting. It was nearly nine o'clock.

"Come on," Goering suddenly said. "We have to complete the plan."

My innards froze at this statement. He hadn't mentioned any other part of the plan such as it was.

Emerging from the woods we strolled nonchalantly along the road towards the now thoroughly alight Reichstag. Well one of us did, one of us walked as though the fire had spread to the road itself with constant checks behind to see if we were being followed. The shouting had got louder and as we crossed the forecourt the crowd seemed to increase exponentially.

"Was ist los?" shouted Goering. "Was ist los?[19]"

I joined in for no apparent reason. He grabbed a passing man in uniform and shouted in his ear.

"I don't know," he shouted back, "the fire brigade aren't here yet and we are trying to find water but…" He didn't need to say any more, his glance at the inferno said it all.

"Ausgezeichnet[20]," Goering muttered to no one in particular. "Let's help!"

We plunged in. I personally didn't see how running in circles was helping at all but then I suppose that was the point. The fire brigade arrived to a great roar of approval and began extending their hoses. I helped one particular engine that wasn't too near the blaze and suddenly streams of water started playing on the

---

[18] Strictly speaking, the area Flashman is referring to was called the 'Platz der Republik' having been renamed during the Weimar Republic. The Nazis reverted to its original name after taking power in 1933.

[19] 'What's happening?'

[20] 'Excellent'.

windows of the building. It seemed obvious to me that this was largely pointless but having arrived, like everyone, the firemen seemed to want to at least try and do something about the conflagration, mainly I suspected to avert blame should they find themselves on the wrong side. Goering was leaping about like a man possessed. I suddenly noticed his face again with the burnt cork on it and realised it looked rather like we had been in the thick of it. It explained the comment from one of the senior firemen directed at me earlier about whether I had been inside. Naturally, I had denied it for all I was worth with my heart pounding and escape routes blocked but I could see his point now. I realised later that he just thought I had escaped from the blazing building, not been responsible for it. Still, it was nice to know my guilty nature was alive and well.

"Damned communists, they should be strung up for this," I heard Goering shout to a rumble of approval from those that heard him. The rumour spread quickly, mainly because they had recognised him, and before I knew it, I was being told from all sides that "it was those traitorous communist bastards who had started it." I nodded my agreement and carried on getting in the way.

The night continued in similar vein with gallons of water being hosed into the building to little effect, occasional whoomphs as something collapsed with the attendant shower of red-hot debris until at last it appeared to be dying down. At much the same time there was a sliver of light on the horizon and I took a brief opportunity to sit down and hold my head in my hands.

"Fleischmann, there you are." A bear like arm slapped me around the shoulders. "I think our plan worked," he said chuckling. I agreed.

"What now?"

"Simple. We arrest the communists, put them on trial and execute them. Germany is ours."

He was right.

Chapter 4

The Volkischer Beobachter immediately screamed that it was a signal for the start of a Bolshevik uprising[21] and so the rounding up of anyone with real or suspected communist sympathy began in earnest and it wasn't long before the perpetrator was caught. Surprisingly, he confessed very quickly. In fact, he seemed proud of his achievement although he must also have known where this would lead him. He was a Dutchman called Marinus van der Lubbe and he claimed to have acted alone, his reasons being to highlight the plight of the German working classes. Quite why he thought this was a suitable protest baffled me at the time and still does, especially as he had only just arrived in Germany. To add to the confusion, four Bulgarians were also arrested. Ernst Torgler, Georgi Dmitrov, Vasil Tanev and Blagoi Popov were apparently already known to the police as communists. In fact, Dmitrov was the head of Comintern[22] operations in western Europe. Quite what he would have been doing recruiting van der Lubbe to burn down the Reichstag is also a mystery. But then so much was.[23]

By the time the perpetrators came to court, Germany had changed again. Adolf, ably assisted by the possibly senile President Hindenburg, had managed to suspend pretty much any semblance of freedom in the country and by suppressing the communists by any available means managed to win an even bigger chunk of the vote. This meant that by allying themselves with the German National People's Party they had a majority. This was not enough to guarantee their next move which was an enabling act for Hitler to rule by decree, but with appropriate intimidation and the support of various minor middle-class parties they were able to pass this act into law on 27th March. Adolf Hitler was now Germany's dictator.

All that now remained was to try the criminals and execute them. If they were guilty of course. I was there in Leipzig when

---

[21] 'Der brand des Reichstags sollte das fanal zum bolschewistischen aufstand sein. Headline on 1st March 1933.

[22] Comintern or Communist International was a Soviet controlled organisation advocating world communism,

[23] See Appendix.

Bünger[24] opened proceedings. It was farcical from the outset. Bünger apparently hadn't read the script and nor had Dmitrov. Van der Lubbe sounded deranged most of the time, Dmitrov had opted to defend himself and despite being warned about misbehaving in court managed to spend a considerable amount of time arguing with Goering who he accused of setting the fire. I must confess that sent a small shiver down my spine. I needn't have worried of course although Bünger didn't quite get the verdict right as he only convicted van der Lubbe. The Bulgarians were acquitted and deported apart from Torgler who was taken into custody for his own protection. Van der Lubbe was sentenced to death.

Hitler of course was furious. "That idiot Bünger," he ranted when he heard the verdict. "They were all guilty, they were all in the conspiracy."

No-one dared to contradict him even though he knew full well they had nothing to do with it and the actual perpetrators were in fact in the room with him.

"That is the last time they screw it up[25],"

It was. Within days he had set up the 'People's Court'[26] with one Roland Freisler as Judge-President. The verdicts were never wrong again.

---

[24] Judge Dr Wilhelm Bünger of the Fourth Criminal Court of the Fourth Penal Chamber of the Supreme Court.

[25] The term 'screw up' wasn't current at the time and so is probably Flashman using an element of delicate hindsight for what was actually said.

[26] The 'Peoples Court' was indeed ordered to be set up by Hitler as a direct response to the Leipzig trial. It dealt with political and treason cases, the most well known being that of the July 1944 assassination plotters. Dr Roland Freisler was an early Nazi and best known of the Peoples Court judges but Flashman is mistaken in that Freisler was not appointed to the court until 1942.

Chapter 5

The next couple of years in the Third Reich were eventful to say the least. Fortunately for me I wasn't there. Shortly after appointing himself Chancellor, Adolf began consolidating his position, which in the Nazi world meant removing the opposition. First in line were the SA. Röhm and his bully boys had become rather too big for their jackboots and had unwisely begun making unreasonable demands. Consequently, Adolf arranged to get rid of them all. Permanently.

It was the end of June[27] when it began. Hitler flew into Munich and went to the Interior Ministry where he got himself into a rage at Schneidhuber[28] for failing to stop an SA rampage the previous night. He tore his epaulettes off to show him who was in charge but then got really cross and had him executed shortly after. Then, accompanied by the police and a band of the SS, they all toddled off to the Hanselbauer Hotel in Bad Wiessee. Here he confronted Röhm and after a brief chat whisked him off to Stadelheim prison.

The following day, Röhm was given the option to shoot himself but refused so Eicke[29] did it for him. He wasn't the only one. All sorts of miscreants and disreputable characters found themselves on the wrong side, including one Willi Schmid, the music critic of the Münchner Neuste Nachrichten, who the Gestapo apparently believed was a supporter of the opposition. He wasn't, but they apparently couldn't tell the difference between the names Willi and Ludwig. But that was tough. Innocence was no excuse and, in the end, well over a hundred were executed and the SA very quickly lost its prominence to be replaced by the SS and Gestapo, names that would very quickly become feared.[30]

---

[27] Presumably June 1934

[28] This must be Obergruppenführer August Schneidhuber who was chief of the Munich police.

[29] This was Theodor Eicke, Commandant of Dachau concentration camp and eventually commander of the SS Totenkopf division. He was killed in 1943 when his reconnaissance aircraft was shot down.

A month later to the day, Hindenburg died. Luckily, only the previous day, a law had been passed stating that when he died, the Presidency would be abolished and merge with the post of Chancellor. Thus, at a stroke, Hitler became supreme Head of State, Head of Government and Head of the Armed Forces.

The new year heralded an increase in German territory when Goebbels organised a vote for the Saarland to decide whether it wanted to return to German control or remain under the auspices of the League of Nations[31]. Oddly, the vote was massively in favour of returning to Germany. This resulted in the mass arrests of many who had fled there from Nazi Germany. March saw the official creation of Goering's Luftwaffe and Hitler announced his rearmament plans in direct contravention of Versailles. In keeping with the spirit of the times and combined with British military weakness, it was also agreed that the German navy could be increased to 35% of the size of the Royal Navy.

And here, dear reader, I re-enter the frame. Y'see, I had been sent to Britain on Hess's orders shortly after Hitler became Chancellor. Officially I was undercover but vaguely attached to the Ambassador's staff with a roving remit to report to Hess anything useful. Of course, as you will have guessed, it wasn't that simple, not least because I was actually English. I had pretty much engineered the posting myself as I was bored of Germany, bored of France, and wanted to go home. Luckily for me, my real boss, Sinclair, agreed and fortunately for him his boss and relative Hugh was Director of SIS having succeeded Cumming some years previously, all of which meant any awkward questions could largely be deflected upwards. I had moved Victoria and the children back to London as well and for the first time in years, if not ever, we were living as a family. And jolly decent it was too. In fact, it reminded me of the post war years in Paris where I idled my time away pretending to work, partaking of the leisure pursuits available and generally having a riotous time. Back then it had all come to a crashing halt of course but now, after a couple

---

[30] See Appendix.

[31] This was the only part of Germany still outside national administration and home to many opponents of the Nazis having fled there in 1933.

of uneventful years in London, it seemed that life could only get better. How wrong I was.

******

It was 1936. It had a lot of promise and got off to a flying start when Obo[32] almost single-handedly put the All Blacks to the sword for the first time in history scoring two tries, one of which saw him run three quarters the length of the field. I was at the game being an Old Rugger man myself, but the world saw it through Pathé news.

Next up was George V kicking the bucket which propelled my old friend Davy into the hot seat. For reasons known only to himself he was to be known as Edward VIII and he immediately stirred up a fuss by watching the proclamation of his own accession from a window. Of course, he was already of interest to the Yard[33] because of his constant affairs with unsuitable women, most of whom were married, and the consequent lack of security for any state information that went his way. Baldwin[34] and friends were apoplectic at the thought of his current flavour of the month having access to all sorts of secrets. What disturbed them most I think was that she was an American and had been married twice. I took great delight in stirring things up by way of the delectable Freda Dudley Ward[35] whom I had taken up with when I returned

---

[32] Alexander Obolensky, born 1916, was a Russian Prince whose family fled to England after the revolution. He was an Oxford rugby blue and played for Leicester Tigers (the Tigers nickname has been in use since 1885) and Rosslyn Park. On the 4th January 1936 he made his England debut against the All Blacks scoring two tries in England's first ever victory over them, one of which is regarded as perhaps one of England's greatest ever tries. In August 1939 he was commissioned into the Royal Auxiliary Air Force joining 615 squadron. He had just been recalled to the England squad to play Wales in March 1940 when he was killed in a training accident in his Hawker Hurricane.

[33] Special Branch did indeed follow the Prince at various times.

[34] Stanley Baldwin, Prime Minister 1923-1929 and 1935-1937

[35] Freda Dudley Ward was a wealthy English socialite during the 20s, her Colonel Father the son of Sir Thomas Birkin. She was indeed one of the Prince's mistresses whilst she was married to the Liberal MP for Southampton, William Dudley Ward.

to London in '34. She had been thrown over by him a couple of years before for an American woman called Thelma Furness who in turn had introduced him to Mrs Simpson and, having spent eleven years as his mistress, she obviously needed a manly shoulder to cry on, her husband having seen fit to divorce her a couple of years earlier as well. Fortunately, I managed to arrange to be that shoulder, mainly because I hoped to acquire any titbits of information to embarrass Davy.

Reinforcing his unsuitability for the role, he insisted on having his face the wrong way on the coins that would be struck with his ugly mug on.[36] This was apparently so he could have his good side on the coin. He then managed to offend the government by visiting some welsh hovel and talking to the unemployed miners, after which he announced that 'something must be done'. What he meant wasn't clear, but it was obvious he wasn't going to be doing it.

Elsewhere in the world, the Italians incredibly managed to beat the Ethiopians in a battle[37], the winter Olympics started in Garmisch, the Hoover Dam was finished, the Spanish Civil War started, the Summer Olympics began in Berlin, Beryl Markham was the first woman to fly the Atlantic east to west solo and Crystal Palace burnt down. Oh, and one final thing. Davy abdicated. I would love to say I caused it but even I wasn't that good. I did however help him along the way.

---

[36] The monarchs coin portrait traditionally faces the opposite way to their predecessor. Edward VIII insisted that his face left to show his better side and hair parting. George VI restored the tradition.

[37] This must be the Battle of Amba Aradam or Enderta.

Chapter 6

Like all Germans he had a stubborn streak a mile wide and the arrogance of those born to rule who had never done a day's work in their lives. She, as an American, had that innate confidence and desire to pursue the future rather than dwell on the past. It had all the makings of a Hollywood disaster movie and I sat back and watched with fascination. I also added my own twopenn'th occasionally.

It all began with his flagrant disregard for the aristocracy and their penchant for parading around in various uniforms and attending ceremonies that had been going on for centuries, but which had little relevance to the post-war generation, who in turn had glimpsed the good life in the roaring twenties but which for most of whom was still very much out of reach.

He then really set the cat amongst the pigeons by going on holiday to the Mediterranean rather than the traditional but gloomy splendour of Balmoral. Having seen both, I tended to agree with his choice. The foreign press had a field day, gleefully writing about his exploits with Mrs Simpson and scandalising the expatriates who wrote furious letters to the Times, none of which were published. Special Branch were equally busy following them around in the sun, which must have been such a chore. They concluded that Mrs Simpson had a private life that included the 'pursuit of vicious gossip' and identified another secret lover although the report I saw didn't name him. I promise you it wasn't me.

I was transfixed by Freda's story that Simpson had some sort of sexual control over the King. Thoroughly amused I made light of a time where I had seen him in a Chinese brothel for officers in France, and in no time at all the gossip reported that Simpson had cured him of some sexual problem using the skills SHE had learnt in a Chinese brothel. The police also reported that she was involved with a car mechanic called Guy Trundle which had the establishment raging, mainly because he was a mechanic.

It intrigued me how much vitriol was aimed at her simply for being an American, especially by the aristocracy who looked down their long noses and concluded she was unfit. Apart from the buffoon Churchill of course whose own mother was American[38].

The Americans by contrast thought she was great, all apart from Bingham[39] who told me she was a tart.

Politically he was a loose cannon on a rolling deck. He ignored ministerial advice, made speeches contrary to Government policy, called labour councillors 'cranks', opposed sanctions on Italy for their invasion of Ethiopia, then refused to receive the deposed Ethiopian Emperor and wouldn't support the League of Nation's increasing influence.

It was endless. The Archbishop's private secretary wrote that he thought she had some sort of sadomasochistic hold over him and then continuing the Church's involvement, the Bishop of Bradford gave a speech where he commented on the King's need of divine grace. That, however, was the spark that set the country ablaze, much to the Bishop's bemusement. He claimed he had no idea who Mrs Simpson was, but the press disagreed and, emerging from their self-imposed silence frantically started publishing every scandalous thing they could find. Consequently, she went to France to avoid them.

All of which paled into insignificance when I dropped my little grenado into the situation. As Hess' agent in England, I had access to von Ribbentrop[40] although I had to tread exceptionally carefully. Luckily, Ribbentrop was so enamoured with his own importance he took extraordinarily little notice of mere functionaries and what they might be up to. Having seen a dispatch he was about to send to Hitler claiming the opposition was motivated by a desire 'to defeat those Germanophile forces which had been working through Mrs Simpson', it occurred to me a hint in the right ear could cause real trouble for his royal lowness.

It just so happened I was lunching with Archie Sinclair who frankly needed all the friends he could get, given his party was on the ropes[41].

---

[38] Jennie Jerome born in Brooklyn 1854.

[39] Presumably Robert Worth Bingham, US Ambassador in 1936. He was a controversial character who was dogged by allegations that he murdered his second wife, Mary Lily Flagler, reputed to be the wealthiest woman in the USA at the time.

[40] Appointed ambassador to the Court of St James in August 1936.

"What do you make of this situation with the King?" he asked.

"I think it needs careful management," I replied. "Imagine if it became known generally that she is an agent of the Germans."

"That cannot be true," he exclaimed.

"It's only what I hear from the Embassy. Of course, they may be exaggerating or hoping to stir up trouble. But then you know where his sympathies lie."

I didn't need to say anything else. I knew he wouldn't be able to keep his mouth shut as it would be something he knew that the real players didn't, so it wasn't long before Baldwin, Attlee and Churchill also knew. They were naturally horrified, especially given the goings on in Germany. And then came the icing on the cake. The King had declared earlier on in the year that he intended to marry Wallis Simpson. When Baldwin told him that if he did, the Government would resign, the King replied that he was prepared to go too. So, when the whole charade became public in December, everyone had to make up their minds what they really wanted. It couldn't have been better.

******

It was fascinating. On the supporting side were Churchill, Mosley[42], the Communist party, David Lloyd George, the majority of the working classes, ex-servicemen and the Beaverbrook and Rothermere press[43]. The opposition consisted of the government, the dominions, the church, the middle and upper classes and the Times and a few other papers.

At the beginning of December, the King and Churchill, backed by Beaverbrook, proposed an address to the nation. Baldwin blocked it as unconstitutional. At this point the Home Secretary ordered the GPO to intercept the King's calls. At the same time, Simpson's solicitor, one John Goddard, decided to fly

---

[41] Archibald Sinclair, 1st Viscount Thurso, became leader of the Liberal Party at the 1935 election when Sir Herbert Samuel lost his seat.

[42] Sir Oswald Mosley, former Conservative and Labour MP and founder of the British Union of Fascists.

[43] Mainly Daily Express (Beaverbrook) and Daily Mail (Rothermere).

to France to see her. The King summoned him and forbade him from making the journey, at which point he went to Downing Street to see Baldwin who bizarrely provided him with an aeroplane so he could go.

The press went to town. Gleefully noting that Goddard was accompanied by William Kirkwood, a gynaecologist, they made two and two into a bun and speculated that Simpson was pregnant. Rumours flew about Churchill leading a 'King's Party' to take over the Government, but nothing came of it, apart that is from making both of them look foolish, something I was at great pains to encourage.

By the 10th of December it was all over. The King was left with no option but to abdicate. At Fort Belvedere, with his brothers as witnesses, Edward VIII signed the instrument of abdication and became the shortest reigning monarch in British history at 327 days[44]. On the 11th December he broadcast to the nation.[45] He made it sound like he was the aggrieved party, that he was a lost soul unable to carry out his duties because of the great burden placed upon him. Or something like that anyway.

I was listening with Freda and we were both incredulous.

"Well, it serves the selfish bastard right," she exclaimed.

"Indeed it does," I replied grinning inanely. "I couldn't have asked for more." I had a picture in my head of a house in Paris. "At least I haven't offended Albert yet. If he can ever string a sentence together, he might make a decent King. Better then Davy anyway."

"Nor have I, as far as I know. Not yet anyway," she said with a mischievous grin.

The second-best part was the end of the buffoon Churchill's career.

---

[44] Depending on your point of view if you consider Lady Jane Grey to have been Queen for nine days in 1553.

[45] See Appendix.

Chapter 7

"We are sliding inexorably towards war. Churchill may well be correct, but we cannot acknowledge it. We have more important things to see to. Like the coronation. And Windsor's visit of course." This was Sinclair. It was true albeit laced with sarcasm. Personally, I wasn't as convinced as he was of the likelihood of war, but then I often erred on the side of blind optimism in the face of overwhelming odds. Churchill was right about one thing though, and that was a woeful lack of modern weapons coupled with a distinct paucity of antique ones. As a nation we seemed to be relying on that age-old adage that any fighting tommy was worth two of everyone else. I had seen how well that worked in the first lot. And if we were going to be fighting the Germans again it was definitely not true.

"I need you to go to Germany. I know, I know…" This was in response to my fit of spluttering and coughing. "I realise how difficult it will be, but you have to understand the position we are in. Plus, you have the advantage. Edward won't know you are with them. You just need to keep out of his way." He made it sound so easy. "Before that we have a coronation to deal with."

In true British style, with the Germans rearming and taking over bits of Europe they believed belonged to them already[46], we set about organising a coronation for the new George VI. I recalled my father's comments on this sort of thing. Something about given the choice between grafting away at the ammunition returns for a division fighting for its life and taking the King's dog for a walk, most of us would shout 'here Fido'. That's what we seemed to be doing now. With Churchill blustering away in the Commons, society at large was deciding what to wear. Of course, it didn't help that the royals themselves had rather opaque views on fighting the Germans again and would clearly rather we didn't. In fact, they seemed to think that we would be better off being allied to them instead of the French who were of course entirely unreliable. My role in all this was to watch and listen. In fact, both my masters wanted the same thing, and it was quite fun for a change. I generally made myself useful around Whitehall

---

[46] Reoccupation of the Rheinland took place in March 1936.

and the Palace, fetching, carrying, watching and listening. And highly informative it was too. I found out who was sitting where in the abbey, what was going to be served at the state dinner afterwards[47], who was invited and more importantly who wasn't. I reported all this back to my German friends as requested and edited by Sinclair. When I told them the former King wasn't invited they seemed somewhat offended, mainly I suppose as they saw him as an ally of sorts.

And so, time pottered on. Freda was becoming a bit of a handful if I am honest and I wasn't entirely sure that Victoria hadn't got wind of it so for once by mutual agreement we decided to avoid each other. Freda that is, not Victoria. The children were both safely at school, Freddie at Rugby, the poor bastard although not for much longer, and my beloved Vicky at some hideous morally improving establishment for young ladies in London[48]. Victoria herself was heavily involved in numerous societies and social gatherings which I occasionally attended with her. My work kept me busy, my play busier, but whatever the rights and wrongs it worked. I still loved her you see, and I am pretty sure the reverse was true. If it had not been for the promised holiday in Germany, it would have been idyllic. But as Sinclair had said, there was a coronation to deal with first.

I was invited in a lowly kind of way but there was no way I could attend publicly. Even the Germans would see through that. So, I had to arrange a discreet place out of public view. Victoria was furious initially but mollified by being able to use my space to take Vicky with her. Freddy wasn't interested, I suspect for all the wrong reasons if he was anything like his Father... me of course... so that worked out rather well. The Germans were delighted I was involved though quite what they thought I could tell them of any use was beyond me. And so it was on a typically

---

[47] Flashman is slightly mistaken here. The official State Banquet was held on the 10th May although there were numerous other commemorative events.

[48] This is Flashman's first mention of a daughter. His son was born in 1920 just after the Kapp Putsch. He doesn't mention exactly when his daughter was born but this manuscript says she was 14 at the coronation in 1937 so presumably it was 1923.

cloudy, cool, English morning in May that the whole useless charade began. The official German party, and there were lots of them given the royal ancestry, almost didn't come as they were still in shock over the Hindenburg[49]. In the end, the chance of free food, wine and beer persuaded them that their grief could be suspended temporarily.

I was there early as I had to climb up to my exalted position in the rafters. I wasn't alone. Some of Sinclair's other friends from SIS were there to ensure there was no hanky panky[50] and like me to keep an eye on who was talking to who.

A sudden blast from the organ nearly had me leaping like Spring Heeled Jack[51] but I clung on wishing I had brought something to stuff in my ears. People poured into the main body of the abbey, all dressed up in their finery. I spotted my beloved albeit she was confined to the cheap seats in the transepts. Von Blomberg arrived with his entourage looking out of place in their sinister uniforms and shortly afterwards the royalty of Europe, or what remained of it. Most of them lived round the corner of course. Finally, everyone sat down.

If you have ever witnessed the full panoply of royal ceremony you will know what I mean when I say it truly was a sight to behold. I suspect even God would have been impressed had he been there, which if the Archbishop were to be believed, he in fact was.

The chatter and music droned on and then with the preliminaries out of the way, some real rocks appeared. My mind wandered back some years, and I pondered on the anomaly I was

---

[49] The Hindenburg Airship disaster occurred on the 6th May in New Jersey.

[50] The term was used in this context long before it became synonymous with sex.

[51] Spring Heeled Jack was a 19th century phenomenon. Reputed to be a clawed fire-breathing devil capable of astonishing leaps amongst other things, he 'terrorised' London in the first half of the century, making occasional reappearances until the turn of the century. His stories were often used to scare children into behaving. Various theories on his identity were put forward from being Satan himself to a group of wealthy pranksters but no-one ever discovered the truth. He occasionally resurfaces in modern media usually associated with the Victorian era.

watching unfold below me. Y'see, I knew, more or less beyond doubt, that what I was witnessing was nonsense. This wasn't the rightful King. In fact, I had more claim to the throne than he did although I wasn't anywhere near the real succession. But for now, the real heirs lay dormant, waiting again for their moment if it ever came[52]. I also knew that this God that was watching over them, and the myth of his son the saviour, was just that. A myth.

The organ gave me another start and I realised we had reached the crucial moment, when the man in the hot seat was about to be crowned. And he looked hot to me in his ermine robes clutching the orb and sceptre. Quite why they should be symbols of royalty was another mystery[53]. Canterbury lifted the crown from a cushion and held it aloft, muttering something under his breath, before plonking it on the new Kings head. At that moment, I wondered, how on earth did they make sure it fit properly and didn't fall off? Unless monarchs all have the same size head of course.

The ceremony wound on its seemingly interminable course but at last it was over, and the new King and his Queen Consort prepared to leave along with everyone else, the bands got very excited as did the audience and the procession began to leave the abbey. I noticed a couple of people slumped in their seats afterwards and assumed that it had all been too much. I knew how they felt. I needed a stiff drink and a decent meal myself, but I knew it would still be hours before we could get our hands on anything. And so it proved. Just getting to the palace took forever, finding the right reception even longer and even then, a small aperitif and canapés were not what was required. I had made sure I was nowhere near the German delegation so that I could join up with Victoria in comparative safety. I still kept half an eye on who and what were about but there was no one to concern me.[54]

---

[52] See both 'Flashman and the Knights of the Sky' and 'Flashman and the Red Baron' for some notes on the succession and his claim.

[53] Both date from 1661 when they were created for Charles II by royal goldsmith Robert Viner to replace the Crown Jewels melted down by Cromwell. The Orb represents the power of Christ over the three known (at that time) continents. The Sceptre, which has been altered on a number of occasions, the most recent being the addition of the Cullinan diamond in 1910, represents equity and mercy.

"My God, that was tedious," my darling wife spluttered as she indulged herself in a large glass of wine.

"I thought it was rather glorious," my darling daughter replied.

I stared at them both wondering again if I was absolutely sure she was mine and deciding I was. For the moment.

"I have to go to Germany for some weeks. I am to accompany the Duke of Windsor's party in an unofficial capacity. Needless to say, best not to tell anyone."

Victoria looked lovingly at me. In fact, I would say the look was more lascivious than loving and had my loins stirring nicely. Vicky looked downcast for a moment before brightening up when I promised I would return with some memento of my travels and that one day she could accompany me.

The evening wore on with the guests getting steadily more tipsy. Every so often, one of them would be escorted out never to return. I had a hard time keeping Vicky in sight; I knew what all the young blades were thinking, and I was having none of it. She was barely 14 although she looked a lot older in her gown. Eventually I had had enough and rounded them up to return home. Unusually for me I was stone cold sober, not least because I was expecting some action when we got home. Instead, my beloved muttered something about being tired, slipped out of her dress, let me fondle her ever more ample assets and promptly fell asleep. It was the only real disappointment of the day.

---

[54] The Coronation State Banquet was held two days before on the 10th May. There were numerous other events including a review of the Fleet at Spithead on 20th May. It was probably the last real show of power of the British Empire and included ten battleships and battlecruisers, four aircraft carriers and well over one hundred other naval vessels. Foreign ships included the German 'pocket battleship' Admiral Graf Spee.

Chapter 8

It seemed like only days before I was off to Germany. In fact, it was five months. Sinclair had thoroughly briefed me on what he wanted to know, and I had thoroughly forgotten most of it. It didn't matter because the only thing of interest was which side the Duke was on. He had married the love of his life somewhere in France just after the coronation, a wedding the King forbade members of the Royal Family from attending, and then spent his time trying to get money from his brother and persuade him to grant the Duchess the title 'Your Royal Highness'. The perceived insults continued with his exclusion from the civil list[55] and many other trivial slights, all of which meant he was of interest to Sinclair amongst others because whilst not having great access to government, he would know people who knew things which shouldn't be allowed out of the country. At least that was how Sinclair put it to me. My job was to find out what things, what people and what if anything they were planning.

I left a couple of weeks before the royal party, and suddenly what had seemed like a jolly jaunt now became far too serious. It felt like I was going back into the lion's den after some years of freedom, and you can imagine what I thought of that. The worst thing was whether they knew. Why they should I couldn't fathom but every silver lining has a cloud. In the event I needn't have worried. They were delighted to see me when I arrived in Munich and treated me like the prodigal son.

"Thank God you are with us again," said Hess. "It was torture considering you in that place, continually having to hide your true identity." I couldn't agree more. "We must celebrate your return to the Fatherland." Just for a moment I thought he was about to drag Helga[56] out of the closet clad in her favourite sporting outfit and I admit to a momentary pang when he didn't. But it would

---

[55] Whilst true, George VI paid the Duke an equivalent allowance himself as well as buying Balmoral and Sandringham from him. It also appears that the Duke concealed the extent of his wealth derived from his income as Prince of Wales (Duchy of Cornwall revenues) which would normally be available to the new King.

[56] See 'Flashman and the Red Baron'.

have been too difficult, and I made a mental note to avoid her. Assuming she was still alive of course, unlike her brother. So we did celebrate, in Bavarian style with beer and pork in the Hofbräuhaus. I awoke the following morning with a sore head but nothing else. Whereas if I had been in London or Paris celebrating, we would have ended up in a respectable house of disrepute, here they were virtually puritan in their disdain for such things, at least for the officer classes.

"We must get to work at once," Hess announced. And we did like good Germans. I joined in with gusto as to do otherwise was potentially life threatening, but I did make one stipulation and that was that I could not meet the Duke and Duchess as it would blow my cover in England. They agreed wholeheartedly which at least meant I could relax somewhat.

The visit was something of a coup for Hitler and friends despite Davy being an ex-King. The resurgence of German power was very obvious and disturbing but at this time, Hitler's plans had a remarkable coherence. I suspect it was because most of them were in fact Hess' plans, but he seemed happy to be the power behind the throne and in fact that suited me too. I didn't want to get too close to the limelight. It had a tendency to burn.

The plans were quite straightforward. Hitler intended to show the Duke all the wonders of modern Germany and having sold it to him, let him in on a few secrets, like his view of the Russians as 'untermenschen'. It wouldn't be too difficult particularly when one considered the fate of the Tsar and his family who were of course the Duke's cousins. It wasn't too big a leap then to suggest that with Britain as an ally and Europe as a German fiefdom, invading and taking over Russia should be a priority. Once all that was accomplished, the new world order would be simple. Britain would have its Empire to play with, Germany would rearrange Europe to its satisfaction, France would be a mere footnote, the Americans wouldn't be that interested, and the Russians and other assorted Slav nations would become enslaved. The rest of the world was irrelevant, at least for the moment.

We busied ourselves preparing for the arrival.

It all went like clockwork, this being Germany. The Windsors arrived and were greeted by assorted Nazis of varying degrees of importance[57]. They were wined and dined and shown around the wonders of Nazi Germany. In its highly sanitised version, it was easy to show them how far the country had come since the depression of the 20s. There were new buildings everywhere, the roads were far better than those in Britain and the armed forces were impressive. They were also still illegal according to the terms of Versailles, but no one seemed to mind all that much.

There was much handshaking and dining, arms factory visits, dinner at Goering's house, a concentration camp visit which they were told was for storage and finally tea with the Führer at the Berghof[58], all witnessed I might add by myself and a certain W. de Ropp lurking in the background[59]. There were also highly publicised and photographed occasions of the Duke making a Nazi salute.

"We can use him, that is certain. He is more than sympathetic towards us and understands the principles of National Socialism entirely. He agrees we need to supress the Russian menace eventually and should therefore be allies and not enemies. We have offered him the crown in return for his support."

He grinned at me. I had no idea what to make of all this if I am honest, but I grinned back, wondering at the same time how on earth they thought they would arrive at a situation where they could offer Windsor the crown. I shuddered involuntarily at the thought.

"It seems like it has been a success then."

"Most definitely. His wife will also be useful in keeping the Americans out of our business. Churchill must be neutralised also." He paused for a moment glancing round the room. "You must meet Haushofer before you return. He is an old friend and mentor from my university days. He had vision before we had even realised our destiny[60]."

---

[57] See Appendix.

[58] Hitler's mountain retreat near Berchtesgaden.

[59] I can find no evidence of de Ropp being attached to the Duke's party but given his position and interest it would not be impossible. Equally I can find no independent evidence of Flashman being there either.

[60] See Appendix.

It disturbed me somewhat when he spoke like this. For an intelligent man, he had some distinctly odd beliefs, but I nodded enthusiastically and agreed to meet this Haushofer.

The state visit was over, the Windsors gone back to their gallivanting but I lingered nervously in Munich. Germany had changed. There was a surreal air about the place. The populace were quieter somehow, subdued by the rather menacing presence of so many people in uniform. The black of the SS was probably the worst, but the Gestapo had developed a nasty reputation for sticking their noses into the most trivial things. There was no laughter, and it was this that worried me most. I hardly saw Hess as he was so busy. He had so many fingers in so many pies it was impossible to keep up, but I could see the stress was building within and causing him health problems[61]. He appeared out of the blue one afternoon and announced we were leaving to meet Haushofer at his home, Hartschimmelhof,[62] about twenty-five miles outside of the city.

"Willkommen Herr Fleischmann," he announced as I stepped through the door. "It is a pleasure to meet you. Rudi has told me all about you." I assumed the rictus grin I kept for special occasions such as this.

"That is good to know, Herr Haushofer. It is a pleasure to meet you."

We exchanged pleasantries for a few minutes, and it was obvious to me that I was being sized up for something. My hands betrayed me, and I had to sit on them before I spilt my beer.

"We need you back in London." I breathed a silent sigh of relief. "We need a proper contact with connections in the right places. You have those connections." This was Haushofer.

"The next eighteen months will be crucial, especially once the Führer's plans begin to unfold." He smiled. "First, we must unify

---

[61] Hess suffered from various health problems, some or all of which may have been psychosomatic. He was an advocate of alternative remedies and planned to establish a number of homeopathic hospitals. Various theories have been put forward as to why he suffered but the most likely is that he was hugely overworked and deeply stressed.

[62] Hartschimmelhof appears to be in a village called Hartschimmel near the Ammersee.

all the German people in Europe. Schusschnigg[63] will understand, or be made to understand, the sacrifice he must make for the greater good."

The colour drained from my face as I realised for the first time that he was absolutely serious. Y'see, I had heard all their grand plans before, how they were going to expand Germany and incorporate all the disparate parts that had been sliced off before creating the paradise of 'lebensraum' to the east. It had always sounded like pie in the sky up to now, the schnapps fuelled discussions of what ifs and maybes, but this wasn't fantasy, this was real.

"It will begin with Austria."

---

[63] Kurt Schusschnigg was Chancellor of Austria from 1934 until the Anschluss of 1938.

Chapter 9

The most alarming thing about being me is that people trust me with things like information, often secret information, and that was what had happened again. After the meeting with Haushofer, Hess had taken us to his favourite restaurant where we had indulged ourselves mightily. At least I had. Hess seemed to have become almost monk like in his devotion to vegetarianism, but fortunately, as an old original, the atmosphere was enough to loosen his tongue just a little, enough to tell me the outline of the great plans they had for Europe and the world. It was terrifying.

He didn't tell all though. Even he realised that sending me back to England with my head stuffed with their plans probably wasn't such a good idea. He would have baulked entirely if he had known the truth of course. Austria was the first step. It was to have a Nazi government, elected if possible, that would then largely follow Germany's lead. After that, the Sudetenland and Danzig before they struck east. And here was where I came into play. They wanted an alliance or at least an understanding with Britain.

Windsor had convinced them that Britain did not want to fight again. He was right in that respect. We were neither willing nor indeed particularly able to do so. He had also mentioned a peace party. These days it isn't very fashionable to talk about the idea of Britain being allied with Germany and the people in high places who wanted this, but popular or not, they were there. And they had plenty of influence. Windsor was one of course but his influence was somewhat limited. Less well known were the opinions of the rest of his family who were indeed rather German themselves. The King and Queen were not exactly known for their anti-Nazi views and the King had just appointed the Duke of Buccleuch to be 'Lord Steward of the Household'. His sister also happened to be married to Gloucester[64]. Now it sounds archaic and irrelevant but in practice it meant that Buccleuch became a Privy Councillor, an advisor to the King, but more importantly he was the King's liaison to the House of Lords and a very vocal pro-German. The Dukes of Bedford and Westminster along with

---

[64] Duke of Gloucester, third son and fourth child of George V.

numerous other peers had similar views. Monty Norman[65] along with many leading businessmen and industrialists also. Chamberlain. Halifax. I could go on. In fact, the list was exceptionally long. Even Menzies[66] was on it, and probably Sinclair. Along with a name I heard for the first time. Hamilton. Listening to Hess one could be forgiven for thinking that we were already on their side.

What was I thinking you may ask? I was thinking how I now definitely had my essentials well and truly trapped in the mangle. If all these people were to some degree German sympathisers, who could I trust when I needed help? It didn't bear thinking about. And if I had known then how it would all end.... but I didn't.

"And you Fleischmann, you will have the most important job of being our liaison with them so that when the time comes, they will be able to assume the reins of power."

Well, there you have it. I was to go to England and be the filling in a very unsavoury sandwich. I got drunk.

******

I left the next morning for the journey back to England. I didn't exactly rush. I had decided to take the train. It would give me time to think. I needed it but then didn't we all really. With the benefit of hindsight, I realised that this was the time when Europe flung itself into the abyss again. It wasn't alone of course. The world seemed to have taken leave of its collective senses. The Spanish were still viciously fighting each other with Franco's fascists aided and abetted by the Germans although they strenuously denied it. The Japanese were knocking seven bells out of the Chinese with the occasional risky air raid on assorted other foreigners[67], the Russians were content with massacring

---

[65] See above.

[66] Presumably Sir Stewart Menzies. See below.

[67] Flashman appears to be referring to an incident in late 1937 when the Japanese bombed and sank the USS Panay, a gunboat anchored in the Yangtze river despite its prominent US flags painted on the deck. There were a number of fatalities and the Japanese paid an indemnity but the incident

their own population in the name of progress[68] and the flow of Jewish refugees was increasing exponentially.

England, when I got there, was oddly quiet. It felt, and in fact I felt, that we were waiting for something to happen when in fact plenty was already happening. I tried to avoid Sinclair for as long as possible, largely because I didn't know what I was going to tell him, but also for the first time I wasn't convinced exactly where my loyalties lay. It's easy now to say that everyone was raring to fight the evil Nazis. As you know, history is always written by the winners but then it wasn't clear who the winners were going to be. In fact, the most likely winners were the Germans and perhaps that alone was enough to explain the turmoil and divided loyalties in the corridors of power. Hence my dilemma. I was working for the Germans spying on the English, secretly telling the Germans what the English wanted them to hear but the English I was working for were sympathetic to the German view but equally didn't want to be seen as disloyal at the wrong moment. No, I couldn't work it out either. I needed to tread very carefully. Very carefully indeed.

I couldn't avoid him forever though. He finally tracked me down in the Portland Club near Pall Mall[69]. Quite why I was in there I forget.

"Avoiding me?"

"Yes, I was."

Silence.

"Eden is going to resign."

"Really?"

---

severely damaged US-Japanese relations. In true Flashman style, his mention of this incident means a number of months have disappeared in his narrative as it happened in December 1937.

[68] Flashman must be referring to the Great Purge or Terror, an orchestrated political campaign of repression which resulted in the deaths of at least a million people. An unintended consequence of the terror was the lack of experienced officers remaining in the Red Army at the outbreak of the Second World War, many, or indeed most having been executed or imprisoned.

[69] The Portland Club was a card playing club, possibly the oldest in the World and founded before 1815 as the Stratford Club.

"Yes really. The league of nations is now utterly ineffective. That's if it ever was effective. It's because of the Italians."

Now he had lost me.

"Abyssinia."

"What about it?"

He sighed and gave me a look of exasperation. I shrugged.

"Despite Mussolini's protestations, the Ethiopians are still fighting. But seeing as France and Britain have recognised the Italian occupation, not that they were in much of a position to do anything else, they won't get anywhere. There is more to it of course. We are trying to prevent the Eyeties[70] allying themselves with the Germans but as the League of Nations is now defunct, frankly we don't have a cat in hell's chance. All of which has led Eden to conclude that Churchill might be right. It won't change anything, at least not yet. The rest of them believe we can negotiate. De Ropp tells me that Henderson has a plan to get Hitler to take a leading role in a consortium to control Africa provided he agrees not to resort to war on his borders." I snorted with derision at that. "I agree it's a ludicrously out of touch proposal. Herr Hitler isn't interested in Africa. So, tell me, what do you think? Or more importantly, what do you think they think?

It was a good question. I scratched my arse in the time honoured Flashman play for time. I then stared at the ceiling as if deep in thought while Sinclair fiddled with his drink.

"Well, first of all, they don't want to fight us."

"Really? Why? This must be the perfect moment surely."

"Not at all. Hitler isn't interested in controlling Britain. He wants Europe so that he can Aryanise it. He wants to subdue Russia and use it as a vast factory to supply the German nirvana. And he wants a strong Britain to continue its imperial dominance albeit perhaps with somewhat less influence. When I say Hitler, of course you realise most of this is not his idea, he is just the figurehead. Most of it is Hess' plan but he got it from someone called Haushofer." I stopped talking, wondering if I had said too much.

Sinclair closed his eyes and leaned back in his chair.

---

[70] Slang for Italians.

"Of course, it would upset the balance of power in Europe that we have relied on for so long. Napoleon was the last great disturber although Bismarck tried hard. And they would have to get past the Navy[71]."

"Would they? Have you seen their air force? Surely de Ropp and Winterbotham have kept you up to date with that. I'd have thought Guernica[72] would have convinced even the stuffed shirts in Whitehall that we are vulnerable to air attack on a grand scale."

"Yes." He paused for some time. "C's sidekick wants to see you."

"Eh? Why? How does he know me?" My spine dissolved preventing me from carrying out the Flashman No. 1 evasion technique. I resorted to No. 2. "I can't."

"Stop whining, of course you can. He has something important to tell you."

I assumed the look of fear I reserve for occasions when you have just slammed the door in the husband's face, the window is bolted, and you only have one leg in your trousers.

"Here he is."

I very nearly soiled myself there and then. I pointlessly looked from side to side like a cornered animal, then submitted to the inevitable, my hands shaking underneath the table.

"Sir Stewart Menzies[73]. I'll leave you two to get acquainted."

At this point Sinclair, the traitor, made himself scarce.

"Flashman." He stared at me for a minute while I stood staring back. "Rugby of course." I nodded. "At least it wasn't Harrow with that bloody fool Churchill."

He sat down with a thump and a whisky appeared in front of him. He downed it and then stared at the empty glass for a minute.

---

[71] Since the 16th century, England and then Great Britain has been part of the political game of ever-changing alliances. Napoleon very nearly succeeded in dominating Europe and Bismarck did realign the power with the creation of the German state. Whether this balance has ever been successful is open to question given that ever-changing alliances actually led to more or less continual war somewhere in Europe.

[72] The bombing of Guernica in the Spanish Civil War was the first

[73] See Appendix.

"We can't fight them again. It just isn't possible." He paused for a moment. "We don't have to either." He paused again. "Really we need to be opposing the Russians." He let this sink in for a few seconds. "I understand you are in contact with Hess?"

"Yes."

"Good. I am aware of the unusual nature of your position. It is imperative that you maintain contact one way or another. There is a group of us, many of us flyers and some of us in very senior positions, who believe it is possible to find an accord. We need to keep various communication channels open and yours will be especially important, particularly your friendship with Hess. He is a man we can deal with."

I confess it intrigued me that he thought he could deal with Hess. It also intrigued me that his 'group' included flyers but mostly I wondered what he meant by very senior positions. Military? Civil? Something else? I couldn't really work it out. And even if I could, what were they, and by extension I, meant to do about it?

"I'd like you to meet someone as soon as convenient. I will contact you through Sinclair. The less you know now the better."

At this point he got up and left. A moment or two later Sinclair reappeared.

"Best to go back home. We will be in touch."

I did as I was bid.

******

Victoria had welcomed me with open arms back into her own busy life. It was an odd existence really but one that suited us both. I didn't have to do a lot in practical terms as both sides were providing me the information I needed to keep the other happy. What worried me most however was where it was all leading – and who was lying to whom. As the weeks drifted by, it became very clear, no pun intended, that the situation was in fact very murky.

But before I could get too settled, events started to overtake us all.

Chapter 10

1938 started with the momentous release of the Disney film Snow White and the Seven Dwarfs. At the same time, von Blomberg got married and my old friend Goering was best man. It sounded like a dreary party. There must have been something in the air as shortly afterwards King Farouk of Egypt married someone called Safinaz Zulficar. The fun continued when von Blomberg[74] then had to resign when it transpired his jolly new wife had posed for some very risqué photos.

On a more trivial note, on February 20th Eden resigned because he had had a tiff with Chamberlain. He was replaced by Halifax. Oh, and Hitler invaded Austria. I suppose strictly speaking it wasn't an invasion although it was certainly planned that way. And as with anything that the Nazis touched there was an element of farce about the whole thing. Schusschnigg had been summoned to Berchtesgaden to be harangued by Hitler and he more or less agreed to handing over some power to the local Nazis who had failed to gain any in the elections. This agreement lasted about four weeks before Schusschnigg decided to call a referendum to see what the people thought. Like most leaders Hitler didn't care what the people thought because he knew better than them. In this case though, he wasn't on hand to enlighten them. After much toing and froing and bold declarations that the referendum would be a fraud and Germany would not stand by and watch Austria descend into anarchy, Hitler signed an order despatching the troops. Schusschnigg cast about for support from elsewhere in Europe and when he realised there wouldn't be any, he resigned.

Events now took on a life of their own. The Wehrmacht crossed the border in chaos, not that it mattered because the Austrian Bundesheer had been ordered not to fight. The people

---

[74] Werner von Blomberg was Minister of Defence in Hitler's 1933 government and became Commander in Chief of the Armed Forces in 1935, thereby alienating Goering, Himmler and others. When he remarried, Goering and Himmler took the opportunity to destroy him by making sure the Berlin police file on Eva Gruhn, his new young wife, which contained pornographic photos of her arrived on Keitel's desk. (Keitel was Chief of the Armed Forces).

almost universally welcomed the German army, cheering, waving Nazi flags and throwing flowers at them. The invasion very quickly became a sort of Roman triumph. Hitler himself crossed the Austrian border at Braunau am Inn, his birthplace, accompanied by a bodyguard of thousands. He got as far as Linz where a huge crowd cheered his arrival. The triumph continued until he reached Vienna where he made a speech in the Heldenplatz[75]. The crowd, apparently nearly a quarter of a million strong, heard him announce the reunification of Germany. He was planning on the hoof at this stage as the intention had been to create a puppet state, but the reception had convinced him to go all the way and recreate Greater Germany. There were protests both within and without. Those in Austria didn't last awfully long as anyone who dared was quickly arrested and deported. And to be honest those without didn't last awfully long either. The British and French Governments both did some handwringing and harrumphing. Notes were sent about how the Germans had broken the terms of Versailles but that was all. Nothing was actually done. Oddly, the loudest protesters were the Mexicans, though quite why I couldn't fathom.[76]

Aryanisation began straight away with the arrest of Jews and other undesirables, but the majority ignored this and looked forward to a brighter future. It was just the beginning they said. They were right. Emboldened by the failure of the rest of Europe to act, Hitler, like a child who has taken one sweet from the jar and not been scolded, started to take more. Czechoslovakia was next on his list. Or more accurately, the Sudetenland.

On hearing this, Blum, the French leader, declared that France would come to their aid if Hitler carried out his threats. It was probably one of the emptiest promises ever made as within a few weeks Blum was gone, replaced by Daladier who with

---

[75] Square of Heroes.

[76] Flashman's description is largely accurate. Mexico did indeed protest vehemently, far more so than the more obvious candidates, largely because Mexico was already a multi-ethnic population with no racial separation and an unusual for the time freedom of speech. The government had actively supported the Spanish republicans in the Civil War much to the annoyance of the Nazis and eventually fought on the allied side. Diplomatic relations with Spain were not restored until Franco died in 1975.

Bonnet as Foreign Minister was desperate to appease Hitler, thereby abandoning the Czechs to their fate.

The Vatican chose this moment to recognise Franco's government in Spain. Why? Who knows. It was just part of the madness.

May saw a brief crisis when the Czechs mobilized in response to some wild intelligence about German troops on the border. It turned out to be nothing and all settled down again briefly.

There were a few weeks in the summer where little happened, presumably because the politicians were on holiday, but then it was full steam ahead again. The Evian conference in France concluded that no European country was prepared to accept Jewish refugees. The Americans however would take a few thousand.[77]

Negotiations continued apace with various British diplomats and officials attempting to come to some agreement. Eventually, Henderson was told to set up a meeting between Chamberlain and Hitler. Meanwhile, the Russians told anyone who would listen that they would defend the Czechs. The Americans on the other hand stated that they would in no circumstances join an alliance against the Germans.

Chamberlain went to Germany. And then he came back. Then he met the French and between them they decided that unfortunately, due to unforeseen circumstances, they wouldn't in fact be able to fight for the Czechs, at which point the Russians also changed their minds. The Czechs were informed of their fate and with little option gave in to Hitler's demands. At this point, the Poles and Hungarians decided that they wanted some Czech territory as well.

Chamberlain went to Germany again. There was much more hand wringing and teeth gnashing, talk of mobilization and war. But then, almost unbelievably, the Munich Agreement was signed. The German, Italian, French and British governments agreed that Germany could have the Sudetenland. They didn't ask the Czechs what they thought. It was 'Peace for our time[78]'. Time

---

[77] See Appendix.

[78] Usually misquoted as 'peace in our time', possibly because of the phrase's use in the Book of Common Prayer and as the title of a 1947 Noel

magazine were so impressed they made Hitler their 'Man of the Year'.

It was ironic, maybe intentionally, that it echoed Disraeli's speech when he returned from Germany in 1878 having concluded the Treaty of Berlin[79]. The major difference was the speed with which it was discovered to be the fiction it was. In 1878, the Congress of Berlin supposedly settled the continual disputes in Europe. At least it did until 1914. The 1938 agreement fell apart much quicker. In fact, the next day really when German troops entered the Sudetenland prompting the lesser-known ultimatum from the Polish Government stating that the Czechs had twenty-four hours to hand over the Zaolzie region. Unsurprisingly they did.

Now hardly a day passed without some minor crisis. Churchill made a broadcast to the USA in October declaring the Munich agreement a defeat and calling on the west to prepare for war against Germany. Soon after, I discovered that von Ribbentrop had summoned the Polish ambassador and told him to give up Danzig amongst other things. At the same time, he claimed that the French had given him carte blanche to do as they pleased in the east. November saw the horror of Kristallnacht when supposedly the German people spontaneously rose up against the Jewish population destroying businesses and synagogues along with a bit of murdering. The world was stunned, although not enough to take in the Jewish refugees pouring over the borders. It was a lovely Christmas.

Coward play.

[79] 'I have returned from Germany with peace for our time'. Prime Minister Benjamin Disraeli, 1878.

Chapter 11.

I hope you will forgive me the history lessons. I look back from the safety of old age and I wonder how the world didn't notice what was going on. I had spent most of 1938 doing little of any consequence but watching from the side-lines with a growing sense of impending doom. And I don't mean for the world at large, just me. Y'see, whilst it was clear that the crisis caused by Hatry had blossomed immensely and that I was part of it, most of what was happening on the world stage was way out of my league. I would get the occasional call from Sinclair, the occasional letter from Hess. Even Menzies graced me with his presence on two more occasions and left me as baffled as before with his cryptic hints about meeting people. It was hard to know what to make of it all. I should have known of course that I was in fact staring straight into the abyss.

If it wasn't obvious before, the Dutch war scare in January confirmed it. Apparently Canaris[80] leaked a false plan that the Germans were going to invade the Netherlands so that they could use Dutch airfields to bomb Britain. Parliament had a seizure, mainly I suspect because they were so unprepared and suddenly the talk was all of war. When rather than if. At least that is what most history books will tell you. The other topic of conversation in the corridors of power was peace.

It was sometime in March. I can't remember the exact date, but Chamberlain had just made his rather bizarre guarantee of Polish independence in the Commons. I was kicking my heels for a change bemoaning the fact that I hadn't been out of town for weeks being confined to the office on the orders of Sinclair. This it appeared was a minor punishment for having the temerity to invite myself back to one of the Advanced Flying Training Schools where I had been taught to fly the newest fighter in the RAF's armoury, the Supermarine Spitfire Mark I[81]. It had been an

---

[80] Presumably Admiral Wilhelm Canaris, chief of the Abwehr, German Military Intelligence. The incident mentioned did influence British policy at the time when Chamberlain agreed to send troops to France in the event of war. Canaris was executed in Flossenberg in 1945 as a long-time opponent of the Nazi regime.

exhilarating few weeks and I had thoroughly ignored all the intrigue and nonsense of London. Sinclair was not amused for some reason, so I was slightly surprised to be summoned to the office of the great lord and master himself. As I knocked and entered, I realised I wasn't the only visitor in C's office. Menzies was there too[82].

"I daresay you enjoyed charging about the skies, what? You youngsters are all the same, eh Menzies?"

"Yes Sir," he replied rather stiffly I thought. I didn't say anything. There was a brief silence while C looked at some papers on his desk.

"You know we will be at war again soon. I have told them what Herr Hitler is like as they asked but they don't like it. They seem to think it will be easy, that Herr Hitler can be negotiated with. They seem to think they can treat him as one would a member of one's club." He raised one eyebrow at this. "Like you, I believe we can only negotiate with Hess." He paused for a moment to let this sink in. "I doubt I will be here to see this through as it turns out, so young Menzies here will be taking the reins." He seemed to deflate somewhat at this statement.[83]

"Well, we'll see about that but for the moment we need to move quickly. We are going to Scotland for a meeting on the night train. Just pack the essentials."

I didn't say much at all that I recall. I certainly didn't object although had I known what I was being propelled into I would have punched Menzies squarely on the chin and departed never to be seen again. But as you know, the optimist in me sees the best in these things despite mountains of evidence to the contrary and settles for the easy life. What could possibly go wrong in Scotland? It was almost civilised for heaven's sake.

******

---

[81] Entered service with 19 Squadron in August 1938.

[82] Admiral Sir Hugh Sinclair was 'C' from 1923 to 1939. He died of cancer on 4th November 1939.

[83] This report was prepared for Halifax and given to Sir George Mounsey, assistant undersecretary at the Foreign Office. It was ill received because it did not sit well with the current appeasement policy.

We boarded our train at King's Cross. It departed on time and I sat in the restaurant car with Menzies for the first hour or so. A couple of large whiskies had settled my butterflies and Menzies himself had eaten a generous dinner. When the waiter had cleared our table we were left alone, except that is for one solitary companion a couple of tables away.

"My faithful lapdog," Menzies explained. "Not really necessary I suppose. Now, to business. We are going to Dungavel House. It is one of Hamilton's places and he will be there, along with a number of other like-minded individuals. The time has come for action. You will mainly be an observer, but you may contribute should you feel qualified to do so. As our go between with Hess, you have valuable knowledge of the man himself."

I shivered in spite of the warmth in the carriage. The conversation continued on a more mundane level for another hour or so and then having consumed too much malt I retired to my bunk. I stared into space for a long time before sleep came.

When I awoke, light was streaming into the carriage. I lay for some time considering what the day might bring, then realising that was a useless occupation I went in search of breakfast. Menzies was there already smoking. He waved me over to join him. I took a seat, and the waiter took my order.

"Churchill does not know about any of this. In fact, I want to be sure he never does know. He may be more right than he knows but we are here to make sure none of it happens in the first place. Halifax will be there, Hamilton of course, Hoare and an assortment of politicians." He paused for a moment. "Buccleuch will be there as well." He raised one eyebrow and stared at me. "You realise what that means do you not?"

I assumed a non-committal expression largely because I wasn't sure what the meaning was.

"Well, whatever you think, presumably you can see why you will not breathe a word to anyone not already informed."

I nodded dumbly and continued eating. The train slowed and pulled into Waverley station. I hadn't been there for some time. In fact, the last time was shortly before I was shanghaied for the umpteenth time in my life[84]. This time though, nothing untoward happened. We disembarked and Menzies set off down the platform with my good self trailing in his wake. We emerged into the gloom and hailed a taxi.

"Dungavel House."

We got in and the car set off, passing the castle and then heading west out of the city. Neither of us said much and it must have been a couple of hours before we turned from a quiet country lane into a gravel drive. We wound through some trees before pulling up in front of the main house. Before we could do anything else a servant of some kind appeared from nowhere and opened the door. Menzies jumped out and I followed him through the porch.

It was a typical hunting lodge and reminded me of Balmoral minus the appalling tartan decoration. It seemed quiet, almost as if it were watching and waiting for something to happen. What did happen was a servant led us through several doors and corridors before arriving at what must have been a large reception room. In the centre was a large table with twelve seats around it. Two were taken already. Both men stood up as we came in.

"Ah, Menzies. And this must be Squadron Leader Flashman. My name is Aberconway[85]. And this is my good friend Birger Dahlerus[86]. Please sit down. The rest will be here in a few moments."

We all sat down for at least a minute before the door opened and we all stood up again. A number of men filed into the room. I had a minor palpitation when I recognised Winterbotham and I was sure he baulked ever so slightly. But it was the final two that made us all stand up straighter. The first was Buccleuch. The second was Kent.

I assume, dear reader, you will have made the connections by yourself. Buccleuch I have mentioned already but Kent was the King's youngest brother, and I was more than surprised to see him, not least because of my troubled relationship with his other

---

84 See 'Flashman and the Red Baron'.

85 Presumably Lord Aberconway, chairman of John Brown and Co (Shipbuilders) and Westland Aircraft.

86 Swedish friend of Goering and prominent businessman, Managing Director of Electrolux with connections to Halifax.

charming relative[87]. More than that though, it appeared life was about to get just that little bit more complicated.

Aberconway spoke first.

"Gentlemen, welcome first of all to Dungavel and may I express our collective thanks to Douglo[88] for allowing us to meet here away from the, ah, scrutiny shall I say of our perhaps less enlightened colleagues. A couple of introductions as we have a new member of our committee." He waved vaguely in my direction saying, "Squadron Leader Flashman. A man of many talents who will, I hope, be our conduit to number two." He smiled before continuing. "There will be plenty of time for us to get better acquainted with the Squadron Leader but for now I propose we move on. Birger? Over to you."

I doubt I could have spoken if asked. I guessed immediately who number two was but what I think shocked me the most was the idea of being a conduit for some of the people in the room. It didn't bear thinking about. By far the most unnerving presence was that of Halifax, at that time the Foreign Secretary. What the hell was he doing here?

"Gentlemen, I believe we have made some progress. We are still some weeks away from a meeting, but the principles have been agreed. We need to settle a time and place, but I think I have an answer that would be acceptable to both sides. My wife owns a farm, Soonke Nissen Koog, near the Danish border with Germany. The German delegation have agreed it is suitable. Provided you all agree, I can make contact and try to confirm a date?[89]"

Aberconway again. "Thank you, Birger. First of all, any obvious objections?" There were none. "Good, good. Halifax?"

Halifax inclined his head to Aberconway and stood up. "Gentlemen, it is heartening to see and hear that all may not be lost. However, if we are to make this work, we must appear both

---

[87] It is interesting in the context of the events I describe that the Duke and Duchess of Kent were at the German Embassy reception for the coronation of George VI.

[88] Nickname for Douglas Douglas-Hamilton..

[89] Whilst I can find no record of the meeting Flashman attended at Dungavel, the meeting on the Danish border is well documented. See below.

strong and credible otherwise I fear Herr Hitler will not take us seriously. If I may make a suggestion, in light of information recently received I should like the delegation to be expanded slightly to include Squadron Leader Flashman. Whilst I understand his main connection is to number two, he may have some valuable snippet that we can use to influence number three. What that might be remains to be seen but it would be foolish to fail for want of an extra head." There were rumblings of agreement around most of the table, excepting my end where there was stunned silence and a short period of mouth opening and closing, not least because I had I think realised that number three was the fat bastard himself. Goering.

"I think we can safely say that is agreed then. I will chair the delegation accompanied by Sir Edward Mortimer Mountain, Charles Spencer and Sir Robert Renwick. Winterbotham here will fly us over."

I missed quite a bit of what was said in the next minutes. How was I going to get out of this? I couldn't meet Goering. He would smell a rat in seconds, put two and two together and conclude that one Fleischmann was in fact one Flashman and, and…. what exactly? On the other hand, perhaps I could pull it off. Perhaps he wouldn't in fact smell a rat. If you know anything of my history, you will understand why I had stopped listening. It didn't bear thinking about. I glanced at Menzies in the hopes that he would ride to the rescue, but he didn't the bastard. I had to try. There was a suitable pause in the conversation.

"Gentlemen, are you sure I should accompany you on this delicate mission? Whilst I agree I probably know Hess best of all of us, I am also known by Herr Goering who thinks I…" I paused for a moment as it hit me I wasn't sure who was in on what. I glanced at Menzies again to see him with one eyebrow raised very slightly. I confess it put me off my stride somewhat.

"…. who thinks I am a supporter of their Aryan crusade."

"Excellent," said Aberconway. "Even better than I thought if one is known to both of Herr Hitler's right-hand men. You must indeed accompany us." He grinned around the table.

"And what if he denounces me, drags me outside and shoots me, where's your blasted peace mission then?" I wanted to shout. I didn't of course. Habit? I don't know even after all these years.

There was more inconsequential drivel and then someone mentioned Haushofer. I realised it was Hamilton himself, or rather Clydesdale[90] if we are to be correct.

"Indeed," he was saying, "Albrecht himself was here last year and we discussed at length the resurgence of German power and the 'Greater Germany' theory. In fact, he drew it in my atlas. I can show you later if you wish."

"Very interesting. I would like to see it if you would be so kind." This was Hoare. It struck me then, and only then if I am honest, the power in that room. Hoare was Home Secretary although curiously he had been the Air Minister[91] in the 20's, Halifax, Kent Buccleuch and so on. If ever one wanted to be in on a conspiracy, I suppose this took the biscuit.

"Well gentlemen, shall we reconvene for dinner?" Numerous chairs slid backwards and the hum of conversation increased. Menzies collared me. "You're used to all this of course but don't underestimate either the difficulty or the importance of this meeting. We need to give your cover some thought with regard to Herr Goering, but I will come up with something plausible enough."

He left me gaping at his back as he disappeared to ready himself for dinner. I retired to my room and stared out of the window at the gloomy heather covered landscape. I resolved never to come back of my own free will as I had had my fill of Scotland. How wrong I was. Again.

---

[90] Douglas Douglas-Hamilton was indeed Marquess of Douglas and Clydesdale at this time, succeeding his father as the 14th Duke of Hamilton in 1940.

[91] As mentioned earlier in the text, there was indeed a curious aviation connection amongst many of the peace group on both sides.

Chapter 12

The meeting broke up the next day with little further discussion and we returned to London. Menzies briefly had the bloodcurdling idea that I should pop over to Germany to see Hess. Fortunately, I didn't rave and shout about it as I didn't find out straight away and when I did, it was followed almost immediately by Menzies changing his mind. He rambled on a bit about keeping in touch and I promised to send him a postcard. It was odd really. I hadn't heard much from the man himself anyway. I guess he was busy expanding Greater Germany but at the end of May I received a cryptic letter. In it he politely enquired after my family which nearly had me running for the hills until I remembered it was just a standard phrase we had agreed on to say everything was alright. He hinted at what I knew already about Germany acquiring further bits of mainland Europe and then guardedly asked about the existence of a group in Britain that were interested in a peaceful resolution to potential difficulties. No names were mentioned but it did refer to his aviator friend from the Olympics. There was only one candidate for this position. Hamilton[92]. It was signed Wolf which was our secret code name[93].

Reading between the lines, it was clear there was a meeting arranged with some eminent British figures, but he wasn't entirely sure of them and wanted me to check them out. I breathed a sigh of relief at that point. Not only did I not need to check them out, I could honestly say I was part of the group and would be attending the meeting to which I thought he was referring. I showed the letter to Menzies and I am glad I did because judging by his reaction he had seen it already. He seemed pleased as punch with himself, almost as though he had set the whole thing up singlehanded.

---

[92] Hamilton claimed he never met Hess at the Berlin Olympics, Hess claimed he did. The evidence and common sense suggest it is more likely they did meet given their mutual interests.

[93] Presumably after Hess' son, Wolf Rüdiger Hess born in 1937.

"We are struggling a little with the detail. Given your letter, I don't quite understand the reluctance to settle but this should resolve things. You can mention it in your reply."

I did just that. And before we knew it a date was settled for August. I now had a couple of months to chew my fingers off and start at shadows including my own. The weeks slipped by albeit every day there was some new hammer blow to the illusions of peace.

Along with the strange guarantee to Poland, a similar offer was made to Romania and Greece. The Spanish civil war, which should really be considered as something of a German warm up, came to its bloody conclusion. Hitler tore up the Anglo-German naval agreement whereby the Germans had agreed the British would always have a much bigger Navy, and the King and Queen visited Canada.

With his finger right on the pulse as always, Chamberlain and his Government decided to severely restrict Jewish immigration to Palestine. With hindsight it seems especially callous, although perhaps not so bad as the Americans turning away a ship full of Jewish refugees which then had to return to Europe where many of its occupants were never seen again.[94]

But my war really started on June 6th, a date seared into the memory of most of western Europe and the USA but for quite different reasons. I was having breakfast alone at the Lyons' Corner House on the Strand after a somewhat exhausting evening out, when some sixth sense made me look up. Glancing round, I noticed the absence of waiters. I realised I was well and truly alone. Apart from one man looking straight at me. Alarm bells rang, in fact I would go as far as to say it was more like an air raid siren in my head. With my fork poised halfway to my mouth, I inspected the newcomer. His demeanour screamed German which was worrying in itself. His raincoat and hat pulled too far down on his head screamed Gestapo but that surely couldn't be possible in the middle of London.

My brain and legs appeared to be disconnected at this point because one was screaming at the other to act but there seemed a certain reluctance to comply. For a moment I pondered on where

---

[94] See appendix.

the back door might be, not that it would have done me much good at this juncture,

but one never knew I suppose. He was coming towards me now and I was on the point of screaming for mercy but instead I jammed my fork in my mouth. Even through the terror it was good kipper. He came right up to my table, pulled out a chair and sat down.

I swallowed, immediately regretting that action as a fit of coughing overtook me, my face burning red in the process. Through all this, my new companion watched without saying a word.

"Herr Major?" he whispered.

"Ja," I wheezed through the kipper.

"Our friend Wolf sent me." He paused dramatically. I barely noticed after my brush with death by fish. "He needs information. About the meeting."

I nodded, hardly daring to speak lest it set off another coughing fit. I hoped my new friend took this to be cautiousness.

"Not so much who is coming, but who exactly they represent. And what peace terms would be acceptable. You can reach me here. It is perfectly safe."

I glanced at the card he had discreetly left on the table. I rather doubted his assertion about its safety as I was sure that MI5 had its grubby fingers in all sorts of pies including private members clubs like this one. Still, their entertainment wasn't at all terrible so I would probably enjoy a visit[95].

And just like that he left, and as if by magic a waiter appeared.

"Coffee Sir?"

I nodded again and he disappeared, returning a few minutes later with a pot. He poured some for me and I drank it eagerly at the same time digesting my visitor's request. Y'see, I was beginning to get somewhat jittery. I had been shanghaied into some sort of British peace delegation by Menzies and his friends who all believed that we should not be fighting the Germans.

---

[95] Without a name it is hard to say where this might be. There were and still are dozens of gentlemen's clubs in central London. Flashman has mentioned 'The Rag' previously but clearly this is not it.

They knew that I was also the eyes and ears of Hess and yet still believed there was a deal to be made. Me? I was beginning to think the whole lot of them should be in a padded cell.

I waited another half an hour before leaving and took a stroll down the embankment to collect my thoughts before I headed for the office. I immediately requested an audience with the Almighty and was slightly taken aback when I was told to ascend there and then.

"Flashman," he announced to no one in particular. For a moment I thought he knew about my Gestapo friend and was on the point of launching into an explanation. Luckily, he beat me to it. "Nothing to worry about, here are the travel arrangements for August. Remember and destroy." He winked at me for some reason. "No warrants I am afraid, not strictly Government business. If I were you, I'd make myself scarce until then."

I took him at his word.

Chapter 13

We left from RAF Hendon on a warm misty morning that promised to turn into a fine day. Nevertheless, I shivered as I boarded the specially converted Wellington and strapped myself into a very uncomfortable seat. I could see Winterbotham in the cockpit preparing things and looking around me the very unmilitary group of businessmen. I shivered again. It was noticeably quiet, no one seemed very keen on talking, content with their own thoughts. The engines started and we bumped slowly over the grass before turning into wind. Checks completed, the engines roared and we began rolling faster over the field. We got airborne and seconds later we popped out of the mist and climbed into the blue sky over London. We flew down the Thames, the taller buildings appearing to thrust through the low cloud giving the city a rather ethereal look. We continued climbing virtually all the way down the estuary levelling off at about ten thousand feet. I peered out of the long thin windows pondering everything that had happened recently, not least my little excursion to the RAF club in Piccadilly where somewhat bizarrely I had met my Gestapo friend. Quite why he thought that would be a suitable location escaped me at the time but on consideration I supposed it was unlikely that MI5 would be spying on the RAF, however much it might want to.

It had been a strange meeting. Menzies had told me to more or less tell the truth assuming it would get back to those in high places unvarnished although quite frankly it didn't need any varnishing. And any military planner worth his salt would be able to see right through the less than overwhelming summary of British military strength. So, I had done as instructed. I told him that the British establishment at the highest possible levels, with a slight emphasis on highest, desired peace with Germany. This wouldn't be at all costs of course, but there was room for manoeuvre provided they didn't invade Poland. Well, not yet anyway. I hinted again as my cheery friend left that he could rely on support at the highest possible levels. He gave me a slightly puzzled look but refrained from asking the obvious question. I wondered what he would tell his superiors. I wondered what he would tell Hess.

The flight droned on and on. The view was not inspiring but then Holland isn't exactly an inspiring view on account of it being flat. Neither was the sea. Someone produced a flask of coffee and sandwiches. They were in plentiful supply as not everyone partook, and it used up at least fifteen minutes before I returned to contemplating the view. At last, the coast hove into view and we started descending. We joined the circuit at some airfield or other and landed. The engines stopped and I took a deep breath before clambering out of the aircraft.

Dahlerus was there to meet us and after handshakes all round we climbed into three cars for the next stage of our journey. Fortunately, it didn't last all that long, and we arrived at the Soonke Nissen Koog within the hour. Lunch was laid on and then the meeting would commence. I could only assume that Goering knew I was going to be there.

It was half past two. I know because I looked at my watch when I heard the distinctive crunch of large vehicles arriving on the gravel drive. I shivered again and for the umpteenth time wondered what I was doing there. Doors slammed and then we were summoned into a large dining room where a large table had been prepared for both delegations. I tried to look inconspicuous shuffling in at the back, but he spotted me straightaway. I like to think he winked at me but at this distance in time, it could just be my memory playing tricks. I had been given the somewhat dubious role of air advisor, just blurred enough to not fool anyone I thought. But then they all believed I was on their side. I wasn't of course. I was only on one side. Mine.

The talks began innocuously enough. No one said anything controversial and the whole thing was adjourned after an hour or so for dinner. We would reconvene in the morning. I spent the next couple of hours quivering in my room before finally summoning up the courage to dress for dinner which it turned out was exquisite. I was nowhere near anyone important which suited me fine. It was only afterwards, when the cigars and cognac came out and everyone started moving around that he cornered me.

"Flashman," he boomed pumping my fin. "A pleasure to see you again." He grinned around his audience like a larger and more lethal version of the Cheshire Cat. The audience took the hint and found other more interesting things to do, leaving us isolated. "Are they serious?" he asked. I nearly disgraced myself.

Resisting the temptation to apply my usual evasion techniques, hopeless as they may have been, I answered seriously. "Yes. I believe they are. They do not want war in Europe but neither do they want a Germany that can challenge them at sea or in the empire. They have little interest in Eastern Europe other than the balance of power. Why they should support Poland I really don't know." Well, it was what I thought albeit perhaps not quite the official line. He smiled again.

"Ausgezeichnet. You will be staying in England." It sounded like a question, but it wasn't really. I nodded in response. He clapped me on the back, took a large gulp of cognac and walked away. I breathed a sigh of relief. I hoped I never saw him again. It was a vain hope.

Next morning, we got under way early. It wasn't a lot more interesting. Someone trotted out the party line about standing by Poland but in return we would ensure financial and industrial prosperity. Quite how we were going to do that was not mentioned. Lebensraum surfaced again. A four-power meeting was proposed to sort out the Danzig problem. Hints of support in high places were made again. No one mentioned the Jewish question which was lucky I felt because we had been ready to say that Britain had never been preyed upon by them to the same extent that Germany had. This was our reason for not persecuting them apparently. Quite what this utter nonsense was meant to convey was therefore moot. Finally, Goering made a little speech where he emphasised that Germany would never attack Britain. And that was that. The odd thing, to me at least, was that no one mentioned following any of it up in any way at all. I presumed that everyone had Dahlerus' phone number.

We flew home that night. Everyone seemed quite cheery although there didn't seem to be an awful lot to be cheery about. Maybe it was just me. Perhaps I was becoming a pessimist.

Chapter 14

Nothing. Nothing at all happened, at least not to me. Unless you count being promoted of course. Mind you, it had taken long enough. Hoare told me later that some Labour Lord or other went to Germany and met Hess a week or so later[96]. Hess never mentioned it, and nothing apparently came of it. Two more weeks slipped by at the end of which Dahlerus met Goering and then telephoned Chamberlain to pass on the glad tidings. But still nothing happened albeit one could slice up the atmosphere with a knife. The advent of September changed everything of course.

Reading between the lines some years after the event, our much-vaunted mission had served only to convince Adolf that Britain would not honour its obligation to Poland. He was right of course because Britain never did however much we like to think otherwise. And there are many other anomalies about that period. The most obvious of course is why, after Germany invaded Poland and then Russia followed suit, Britain only declared war on Germany. What was the difference? Of course, if one cares to delve a little deeper into the Machiavellian politics of the time, it becomes obvious that Great Britain had form and plenty of it. For example, if you will forgive me the digression and history lesson again, why when Poland and Hungary both annexed parts of Czechoslovakia in 1938, did we not even send a snotty letter? We also didn't bother supporting Poland in its war with Russia in 1919 even though Versailles obliged us to do so. I could go on.[97]

However, one of the other rather glaring issues was that of the Jewish question and Nazism in general. Hindsight being a wonderful thing it is easy to look back and say it was all for a

---

[96] Lord Charles Buxton went on an ostensibly unofficial mission which nevertheless had the backing of Halifax.

[97] Flashman is broadly correct in this statement, although the support of Poland seems to be a wider League of Nations policy to intervene to prevent wars. Politics between the wars, especially in central Europe and the continual change in borders and nations is complex enough to need an entire book of its own. The League of Nations, trumpeted as an organisation to end wars had a major flaw. America, whose idea it was, refused to join. Germany and Russia weren't allowed to join. And therein lies one of the seeds of the Second World War.

great cause. But in 1939, the holocaust was not even on the horizon. The Nazi regime was keen to remove the Jews from its lands by deportation and intimidation. Rather like its neighbouring government in Poland, which had for some time officially treated the Jewish population as inferior and already had concentration camps. Pogrom is a Polish word[98].

So, to summarise the position, when the Schleswig Holstein[99] shelled the Polish naval arsenal in Danzig and German troops poured over the Polish border thus triggering a day or two later Chamberlains famous clipped radio broadcast announcing that 'I have to tell you now that no such undertaking has been received, and that consequently this country is at war with Germany', we were apparently charging off to support one anti-Semitic dictatorship against another.

Another little flaw in the plan was what exactly we proposed to do about any of it. Again, popular myth says that our armed forces at the time were extremely feeble. Churchill was right in that we had not heeded until much too late Germany's rearmament and much of our hardware was outdated or obsolete. But the Royal Navy was still the largest by far and the expansion of the RAF had exponentially increased its strength. France had the world's largest standing army albeit a lot of it was hiding in the Maginot Line. It also had a lot of armour and so Hitler's reluctance to take on Britain and France was somewhat understandable. When the British and French Chiefs of Staff said what they would do in the face of German aggression, they weren't particularly unrealistic, at least on paper. Gamelin stated that the French army would cross the Maginot Line and attack Germany. Ironside said the RAF would raid Germany on the same scale as German raids on Poland. Both of which were possible, neither of which actually occurred.

---

[98] It is in fact more of a Slavic language term but its original meaning refers to attacks on Jews in the Russian Empire in the 19th century.

[99] SMS Schleswig-Holstein was a Great War battleship that was allowed to be retained at the end of the war. It was the flagship of the much reduced navy until 1935 when new armoured cruisers became operational. On 1st September 1939, Schleswig-Holstein fired the first shots of the Second World War.

On the other side, Hess told me that when the British ultimatum was received in Berlin, Hitler reacted with utter dismay. He probably couldn't see the logic in it either. Ribbentrop had been wrong with his assurances although Hitler only had himself to blame for that.[100]

So here we were then. What to do next? It was 1914 all over again. And I wasn't sure I could bear that.

---

[100] Ribbentrop was completely out of his depth in London. A more experienced diplomat might have convinced Hitler that at some point, Britain would react if it kept getting pushed. It is more than likely that the British guarantee to Poland was an excuse to intervene rather than a promise to actually help given the logistical impossibility of Britain intervening on Germany's eastern borders. British diplomacy through the centuries is littered with unrealistic broken promises.

Chapter 15

"Lord knows how we are going to sort this mess out." This was Menzies. He paused to stare at the ceiling for a moment. "The government feel we can fight for a few months and then negotiate some sort of peace deal. Personally, I'm not sure that will work. We must pre-empt that. That's where you come in." I assumed my customary look of fear. "Don't tell me, I know." My fear turned to puzzlement at what he thought he knew. "Getting you into Germany will be almost impossible at the moment. We have to think of something else." Puzzlement became temporary relief. "Hess is the key, for you at least. Are you sure he has the ear of Hitler?"

"Indeed I am. That has always been his modus operandi. Power behind the throne and all that. He will be keen to do some sort of deal if only because he is a realist."

"Well, we need something to give him before it gets too far out of hand and public opinion prevents any kind of deal being made. Especially if Churchill has anything to do with it."

Churchill was doing the rounds with an 'I told you so' kind of look on his face. Largely because he was right of course. Maybe it was because he was part yank. Either way, the British had stuffed their fingers in their ears and looked at the sky whilst the world disintegrated around them, hoping no doubt that it would all go away. And so far, they had been proved right. Hitler was preoccupied in Poland and other parts of Eastern Europe; the Russians were making a nuisance of themselves as well but in the west the 'Phoney War' was well and truly under way. Apart from the loss of HMS Courageous and the sinking of HMS Royal Oak in Scapa Flow, both with heavy loss of life, not much else had happened. British troops were dug in in France, the RAF had shot down a couple of Ju88s near Edinburgh and dropped thousands of leaflets telling the Germans how bad they were, and it would be best for everyone if they could desist. Me? I had drunk tea, looked busy around the offices, done the rounds of the fashionable clubs in London and occasionally popped home to see my dearest Victoria. It couldn't last of course.

"I have the beginnings of a plan in mind. We have an agent in Holland. Payne-Best. He is our man. He has a contact. They have met a few times already and he claims to represent a group of generals who think they can depose Hitler. Get over there, give him this and report back."

It sounded innocuous enough, enough for me not to be in the slightest bit concerned. Y'see, despite my position I had realised quite quickly that, provided I played my cards carefully I could probably sit the war out in Whitehall. It was clear the Germans weren't that interested in fighting us and I could use any influence I might have to further that cause. The best place to do that was London. Menzies seemed keen for me to stay put as well, possibly because of my connections with Hess. Who knows? It suited me anyway, short trips to the continent notwithstanding.

And so it was I found myself on a flying boat bound for Holland in the first week of November. More precisely we were headed for Woensdrecht via Bergen-op-Zoom. It wasn't that cold, but as always I shivered as I settled into my seat. German fighters had been reported daily around the coastline and just the thought was enough to set the old gnashers off. And frankly, in this bone shaker we were unlikely to survive an attack by two old dears with their handbags, let alone the Luftwaffe's finest. I closed my eyes as the engines roared and we accelerated along the Solent, bouncing through the waves. I had the beginnings of sea sickness but fortunately I knew it wouldn't last long. We got airborne for the final time and began climbing slowly along the coast. We reached our cruising altitude and the noise diminished somewhat. I undid my harness to stretch a little and peered out of the porthole at the grey sea below.

We flew past a pair of warships looking menacing but that was the only encounter with the actual war before we began our descent into neutral Holland. We landed somewhere completely nondescript and then drove slowly towards a disembarkation ramp. I had been assured that there would be someone there to meet me. It was at this point I rather unhelpfully recalled my last visit to Holland some years previously[101]. I shivered at the thought and tried to forget about it, but it didn't seem like a particularly good omen.

---

[101] See Flashman and the Red Baron.

The engines finally clattered to a stop, there were some muffled shouts, the aircraft swayed around somewhat and then the door opened. The Flight Sergeant wished me good luck and saluted. Quite why I wasn't sure as I wasn't in uniform, but I returned the favour with a tip of the tile and stepped out onto the ramp. There was a car a few yards away and almost immediately the door opened, and an attractive woman emerged. My blood warmed a little for the obvious reasons and she half waved at me. Considering I was the only passenger, it seemed strange, but I smiled and waved back and walked quickly up the ramp.

"May Payne-Best," she announced holding out a hand for me to shake.

"Enchanté," I replied raising the delicate gloved hand to touch my lips. "Flashman," I continued in my best Dutch.

"Welkom in Nederland, Meneer Flashman. We don't have much time."

At this she turned on her heel and I followed her to the car. She got in the front and I in the back, only to find another man already there.

"Dirk Klop," he said holding out a hand and without further ado we set off.

"Venlo," she said turning round after about fifteen minutes of silence. "It is on the border. Siggy and Richard will be waiting for us."

That was the limit of the conversation apparently and we lapsed into silence for the rest of the journey. I looked at the view, but it was still as boring as the last time I had seen it. I must have nodded off because I awoke to the sound of the door slamming. I got out of the car myself and followed May into a small café. The only occupants were two men sitting in a corner cradling mugs. They looked up as we came through the door and stood up as we approached.

"Sigismund Payne-Best," said one.

"Richard Stevens," said the other.

"Harry Flashman," I replied trying not to stare at Best and his ridiculous monocle[102].

---

[102] Payne-Best served in the Intelligence Corps during the Great War and was sent to the Netherlands in 1917. Recalled to London after a scandal, he

"We don't have long. We have just met Schaemmel. He is coming back tomorrow and thinks that may be our last chance to meet the General as there is to be an attempt on Hitler. And no, I don't have any more details." This was presumably in response to my raised eyebrows. "What's the latest from London?"

"No change in policy so far. Peace, not at any cost, but there is a lot of room for manoeuvre. 'C' believes we can do it if the will is there on both sides. The palace is keen as is Downing Street. It is just Churchill and friends in the way. Obviously, we mustn't look ridiculous, but momentum is there if we can find common ground."

I wasn't sure if I believed all this, but it was what I had been told to say. The problem was largely what the Germans thought and unfortunately, I had not been able to find out anything from the other side for some time.

"Who are we meeting?"

"Schellenberg. At least that's what Schaemmel said."

"Bloody hell. I didn't realise it was that high up?"

"Yes. He has the ear of the Führer I think."

"Where are we meeting?"

"Here."

If I had been a lady I may have swooned at this point and had I not been sitting down it was still touch and go. As it was, my mouth fell open.

"Yes, the border is just down the road." Luckily, they seemed to take my reaction as surprise rather than anything else and clearly revelled in shocking me.

"When did you say we were meeting?"

"I didn't. At least not a time anyway. We agreed on four o'clock."

---

returned to Holland after demobilisation in 1919. He was presumably an SIS agent by this time as he set up a business in The Hague, married Margaretha van Rees and occasionally confided in others that he was a spy, partly because to the Dutch, he looked like a British spy in his spats and monocle. An Intelligence officer in the Indian Army until 1939, Stevens became the passport control officer in The Hague, always a faintly ridiculous cover for SIS agents. Both spoke multiple languages, but neither seem to have had any specific European intelligence gathering experience or training.

That just about concluded proceedings for the day. We left the café and walked to a small hotel in the town. We met again for dinner but nothing of interest really happened except it was decided that we would drive to the Café Backus for the meeting the next day in Best's Lincoln Zephyr[103]. There would be four of us. Best, Stevens and Klop with myself taking the place of one Jan Lemmens[104]. I retired having consumed more whisky than strictly necessary and consequently didn't sleep very well.

The next morning came all too quickly. I don't know what I was worried about really. Despite being at war, we were in a neutral country with no intention of leaving it. The mood was decidedly cheery, and my nerves subsided as I stuffed my face with something more akin to breakfasting at home. None of that European rubbish.

We managed to make it last until almost midday before Best decided we ought to get ready. I did this by staring out of my window and having a double. What the others did I have no idea.

At three thirty, we met in the hotel foyer. There was a palpable air of excitement. Best kept fiddling with his monocle and at one point showed me his gun, a Browning automatic. The only effect that had was to make me wish I had one. Then I reminded myself, we are on neutral territory. Fat lot of good that did me I can assure you.

Finally, we trooped out to the car. I got in the back with Klop and Best started the engine. We pulled slowly out of the hotel and drove the short distance to the café car park. As we pulled in, I glanced over to the other side of the street where another car was sitting. It looked like the engine was running but it was hard to tell. What I could tell was that something wasn't right. My head turned with the motion of the car and as I saw it through the back window it started to move towards us. Time slowed down.

"Behind us," I managed to blurt out. Klop took one look and pulled out his gun. It seemed I was the only one without one. Best jammed the brakes on which at that point didn't seem like the best idea to me. There was a bang and one of the windows

---

[103] Schellenberg maintained the car was a Buick. Best owned a Zephyr and states in his memoirs that it was the Zephyr used at the time.

[104] Klop's Dutch driver.

shattered spraying glass around the car. I took this opportunity to duck behind Stevens' seat. I saw that they both had their guns out as well and were aiming them through the windows. Klop fired his and then the noise was deafening as they all let rip. I felt a sharp rap on the back of my head and for a second I thought I had been hit. I added a scream to the cacophony before I realised that it was Klop's gun that had struck me. I screamed again when I felt and smelt the familiar tang of blood and then something heavy was on me and I couldn't move. There was a groaning noise and, in my panic, I tried to get up. That was when I realised the weight on my back was Klop and he was leaking from the head.

"Nicht schiessen, nicht schiessen," I heard Best shouting from the front of the car. It was a good idea I felt but it took a moment or two for the message to get through, a moment that I spent supporting Klop as he made a convenient shield. The shots fizzled out and I tentatively pushed Klop upwards. He wasn't helping so I assumed he was either dead or unconscious. Having got him upright, I looked out of the windows. There was no one around apart from the goons from the car and they were now surrounding us.

"Throw your weapons out of the car," a voice instructed.

There was a clatter as both the Brownings hit the floor.

"Now get out, slowly, and with your hands where we can see them. What's wrong with him?"

An answer was unnecessary as they looked in and saw for themselves. We got out as instructed. One of them then approached us and handcuffed us before pushing us over to the nearest wall where we were briefly searched. Having found nothing, we were bundled into their car, which I have to say was not as comfortable as Best's, and definitely not built for three grown men in handcuffs plus a couple of guards and a driver. As the car pulled away, I saw Klop's face looking decidedly grey as one of them got into the back of the car and another in the front. A few seconds later it appeared behind us on the street. It was only then that I realised we were in Germany.[105]

---

[105] Flashman's account is largely accurate, the only difference being his replacement of Klop's driver. See appendix.

Chapter 16

We stopped in Dusseldorf. It occurred to me somewhere along the way that no one had actually enquired as to what was going on. I mention this because until that afternoon I had to all intents and purposes been on a peace mission and yet somehow, we had been shanghaied from a neutral country without so much as a by-your-leave. I mentioned this in passing to Best who gave me a hard stare through his monocle that he had somehow managed to retain. It must have struck a nerve though because when we stopped, he asked what on earth they were playing at and where Major Schaemmel was? The German merely chuckled.

"Who is Major Schaemmel?" he said which was a trifle worrying. "You are spies and will be treated as such. But first you must answer for the attempt on the life of the Führer."

"What attempt?" Best said. He sounded genuinely baffled. I on the other hand was more concerned about being treated as a spy. That way led to the wrong end of a firing squad.

"Last night, in Munich. The Burgerbraukeller. The bomb."

"What bomb? We had nothing to do with a bomb."

He was wasting his breath. The German neither knew nor cared what we knew. He had orders to follow. For some reason at this point they decided to search us thoroughly. Having found nothing of interest we resumed our journey. Stevens asked where we were going.

"Berlin. Prinz-Albrecht-Strasse.[106]"

---

[106] 8, Prinz Albrecht Strasse was Gestapo Headquarters in Berlin.

Chapter 17

I don't recall much of the journey. We must have stopped along the way but where I have no idea. However, I do recall arriving feeling and no doubt looking somewhat shabby, and whilst this wasn't the most important factor it certainly didn't help my gloom. Best and Stevens had hardly said a word to me all the way and I assumed they felt somewhat aggrieved by my performance in the car. They were right in some ways. It wasn't a highlight of my career and I still look back and wonder. Of course, my dilemma wasn't the one they imagined it was.

It was difficult to know when to play my trump card really. The trouble with the Germans, and the Gestapo in particular, was getting them to believe your story. They had a disconcerting tendency to disbelieve everything until they had hammered it out of you. Even then it was often dressed up to make them appear victorious in the eyes of their superiors which was all that counted. It worked all the way up to the top. Consequently, I had to tread very carefully. Panicking, yelling and screaming would have no effect whatsoever despite that being what I felt like doing. So, I waited, chewing my nails.

When we arrived in Berlin, we were escorted smartly to separate cells which was something of a relief to be honest. Whatever plan I came up with, it didn't necessarily include Best and Stevens. Or Klop as he had unfortunately kicked the bucket.

Your true coward dies a thousand imaginary deaths and so for someone like me, it was the subliminal terror that was the worst. The distant screams and groans as well as the occasional muffled gunshot. At least I imagined that was what it was. They let us stew on all of this for a couple of days at least before I was hauled out of my cell, trying desperately, against all my better instincts, not to scream and plead. They took me to a small room that had a table and two chairs in it, one of which was clearly for me. I was forced to sit down and handcuffed to the arms. I waited for what seemed like hours, letting my imagination run wild which was all too easy I can assure you. Then the door opened. I daren't look round. Whoever it was didn't say a word although I could hear him breathing.

"It is really you isn't it!" Hermann had found me. I didn't know whether to laugh or cry.

"Yes, it is me." I felt a huge slap on the shoulder and then the big buffoon was in front of me.

"Now then, what have you been up to, eh?"

"Well, first of all I tried to assassinate the King, then when that failed, I thought I would get them all in Munich." It sort of slipped out. With hindsight, it probably wasn't the cleverest thing to say, particularly as that was apparently one of the reasons we had been detained.

"Ha," he exclaimed. "I told them it was you all along." There was a brief pause while I considered the penalty for trying to bump off the Führer and then he fell about laughing. "Of course, you will be shot." This elicited a further bout of merriment. "Nein, it is too much."

He composed himself and then pulled up the other chair.

"Any chance you can take these off?" I said.

"Only if you promise not to escape."

I did promise but once again it was lost in the howl of laughter. It occurred to me that laughter was not really something that was heard very much in Prinz-Albrecht Strasse.

"So, what do you know about Schellenberg?"

"Who? Nothing."

"Well now you know something. He was behind this. Him and that bastard Heydrich." Him I had heard of. "Did they mention Major Schaemmel?"

"Yes, they did. Said they had met him the day before the, er, incident and that he wanted to meet them again." I was on risky territory again, not least because as I knew all too well you never knew quite who was working for whom. Apparently, Hitler liked it that way.

"Well, that was Schellenberg." He gawped at me in triumph as though that revelation should have had me proclaiming the second coming. Instead, I sat mute. "Surely you realise what that means?"

"I have to confess that unusually on this occasion I have no idea what that means."

"Nor do I! Ha! Except that they are trying to get one over on me and Hess and make us look foolish with the Führer. But, now you are here, we will get them back."

I will say it again but how I have not had some kind of fatal seizure when confronted with the plans of madmen is beyond me. Here I was again. He hadn't even asked me what I was doing in Venlo.

"Let's get out of here," he said suddenly. "I have booked you a room at the Adlon[107]. It is near the action and we can get up to some of our old tricks eh." He winked at me and I shivered as I remembered a night in 1933. My God, it was over six years ago. At that, he finally took the cuffs off and we left for the short drive to the Adlon.

---

[107] The Hotel Adlon, opened in 1907 by Lorenz Adlon with the Kaiser in attendance quickly became the social centre of Berlin. It remained so through the Nazi era and despite surviving the bombing and shelling it was burnt out in 1945 after Russian soldiers set fire to it. With the reunification of Germany, a new hotel was built on the site.

Chapter 18

It was as luxurious as I had heard. No expense spared, at least for the leaders of the Third Reich and their minions. I had a suite all to myself. It even had a chair without handcuffs. We hadn't been in the room for more than a minute before Hermann found the drinks cabinet. He poured us a large scotch each and collapsed onto a comfortable looking sofa.

"So, fill me in. What on earth have you been up to?"

Well that was a tricky one really. I sat down and assumed the pensive look of the profoundly disturbed. I briefly studied the ceiling but found nothing inspirational there.

"Nothing much really. You know, getting on with life, trying not to be too conspicuous in a foreign country." I stopped as I had very nearly set off on a story about the wife and children which certainly would have had him wondering. Luckily, he just laughed.

"Oh, I know, you can't tell me everything." He winked at me and I stared back. "For once though, I am ahead of you. Hess will be here shortly and then we can see about stopping this pointless war with England. It's just a waste of everything."

I had never heard him oppose war in any form before. I always imagined he just liked it as well as believing that as a German he was predisposed to winning any that he happened to take part in. The Great War notwithstanding of course, but then according to the Nazis they hadn't actually lost, they had just been stabbed in the back. I took another swig from my glass. Then it dawned on me what he had actually said. We should see about stopping this war. We? As in the three of us?

As I pondered this, there was a knock at the door. Goering jumped to his feet and opened the door. Hess came in. I stood up as he approached me with what I can only describe as a tortured smile on his face. Fortunately, he didn't bother with the required Nazi greeting and just shook my hand and smiled again before taking Goering's place on the sofa.

"At last. I couldn't believe it when I heard it was you. How did you manage to get here? No, tell me another time. We have much more important things to discuss.

Chapter 19

"How powerful is Churchill?" This was Hess. We were alone in my room.

"Becoming more so all the time, but only because the others are perceived to be weakening."

"What would it take to persuade them to negotiate do you think?"

What did I think? I had no idea. Yes, I had sat in on meetings and moving in the upper echelons of society one heard much information pertaining to the current crisis, but what it would actually take to get the Government to negotiate a peace deal when they had only just declared war was a different order. However, I had to say something.

"Well, it is exceedingly difficult to say at the moment. Churchill is manoeuvring for something and forever bombarding Chamberlain with memos. He thinks it is so he can write a book after the war has finished. Part of the problem is that Chamberlain and many others don't believe the war will be long anyway as the Royal Navy will blockade Germany. Obviously, Scapa Flow hasn't helped that belief[108]. But in the end, he will have to save face. Germany will have to concede something so that everyone can say that they won."

Hess looked suitably perplexed by this statement and there was a moment of silence while we reflected on what I had said.

"The Führer believes…". He paused again. "He believes that Britain will only respond to strength. That by giving proof of Germany's military strength, it's opponents will be cowed into submission."

"And is that what you believe?"

---

[108] Scapa Flow was an excellent natural harbour in the Orkney Islands and home of the British Home Fleet. However, it had only just become operational again and needed defensive improvement. It was more or less empty when U47 entered and found the battleship Royal Oak at anchor. Firing three torpedoes only one struck causing minimal damage. Turning to fire again, the second salve of three all hit. The explosion ignited a magazine and a fireball engulfed the interior. Listing badly, the ship sank in thirteen minutes taking with it 835 men and boys.

"I believe continuing a war with the British Empire for any length of time would be unwise. I am not sure that even Chamberlain would be cowed by a show of strength. Let me describe a scenario to you. The Führer does not wish to cross the channel. However, if he were to be in a position where that was an option, how would the British Government respond?"

I was about to answer when I realised it was a rhetorical question.

"I doubt very much that they would respond by surrendering without at least some show of force. The Royal Navy is very strong as you say and a cross channel invasion would be fraught with difficulties, but the threat would be real. But what would the same Government think if in this situation, the offer was for the Führer to stand aside to allow a more moderate view to prevail? They might think that this was enough especially if there were guarantees for the Empire. And as for the French? Well, they would recover in time. They aren't really particularly useful allies of course."

It took me a moment to realise that he was serious.

"This is of course, er, hypothetical."

I didn't agree. Knowing Hess, he had dreamed up his scenario and as he had more or less unfettered access to Hitler as well as being the architect of the Nazi regime, he was well aware of the reality. I had of course already worked out where the conversation was going next.

"When you return to England, you will have to make contact with the appropriate people. Tell them what I have told you and then we can arrange to meet. But you can't go just yet."

An icy chill ran through me settling in my lilyish liver. Was he hinting at something, something utterly unthinkable? Had he seen through me at last? How I didn't bolt for the door at that moment defeats me even now. I was in Berlin with possibly the most powerful man in Germany who had hinted ever so slightly that despite all we had been through, he wasn't convinced I was quite the ticket. I stared into space. The silence became even more unnerving if that were possible.

"Is the hotel comfortable? If not, we can move you, but it is such a convenient place to stay for the moment."

"Oh yes, it is fine, very convenient."

Now I was profoundly disturbed. There was nothing I could do though. He hadn't said anything directly, in fact he had merely given me an outline plan for further action. But this was Hess, probably the most sane and intelligent of all the Nazi leaders. The conversation continued in a desultory fashion for a few minutes.

"I must leave unfortunately. I have so much urgent business to attend to. If possible, I will join you for dinner later in the week."

And with that he left. I pondered long and hard on whether he had in fact hinted at anything, or whether my imagination was making more of it than necessary. I couldn't make up my mind. I ordered some dinner in my room and then didn't eat much of it, preferring a feast of fingernails. Eventually I went to bed, hoping to wake up and find it was all an unpleasant dream.

Chapter 20

It wasn't. But neither was it a nightmare. In fact, what it mostly was was boring. Life trundled on. It took a few uneventful days to get used to my new situation, but as always, I did. The fear I had experienced with Hess subsided as I persuaded myself that it was all innocuous and that he was just a man under pressure. My optimism resurfaced and slowly I took to exploring, first the hotel and then the city. Both were enlightening.

The hotel treated me like some sort of unstable bomb which might go off at any second. This could only be because they knew I had arrived with Goering and been visited by Hess. In fact, the hotel manager visited my room personally entreating me to assume this was my home and behave as such. I took him at his word. The food was excellent, the beer also along with a comforting array of other facilities. I got to know some of the clientele in the smoking room and slowly worked out who was who. Obviously, there were quite a few characters in this play. The first on the scene was the house detective[109]. I fell into conversation with him early in my stay, mainly because I had caught him watching me. It was pure luck because he was very professional. But it was particularly useful to have him, if not on my side, then at least not against me. I suspect he was aware of my links high up the food chain and so saw an opportunity to potentially ingratiate himself. It was my conversations with him that really made me realise how dangerous the situation was.

Not everyone was a fan of the Nazis. But to admit that was a very risky business indeed. It wasn't that the Gestapo were listening. They weren't. It just wasn't possible. But it was what they wanted you to believe and highly successful they were. It only took a few high-profile arrests of enemies of the state, a few denouncements by informers and the majority of the population clammed up. It was easier to go along with it than fight it. Practically of course, most of it was just a minor nuisance.

---

[109] Flashman clearly doesn't name him but there is an interesting 'fiction' series by the late Philip Kerr that follows the cases of detective Bernie Gunther, at one point the house detective at the Adlon. The series gives a fascinating insight into pre-war Berlin.

Attendance at the occasional party function, celebration of the successes of the regime, but also of course the fact that many believed that they had been unfairly treated and whilst they probably weren't keen to go to war, there was a belief that it would restore their standing in the world. I suspect also that the military were itching to try out their skills on the battlefield. The Luftwaffe of course were raring to go.

It was with all this swirling in my head that shortly after Christmas, which was very jolly I have to say, what with spending most of it with my new friends from the hotel, especially Lotte whose skills were many and varied, Goering appeared one day and invited me to join him at a Luftwaffe station just outside Berlin. He was his usual larger than life self, expounding at length about all the developments in the war so far and how it wouldn't be long before it was over one way or another.

"Come and spend a day flying with me. You will see how far we have moved on."

I had a good idea of course. The Spitfire had convinced me of that, but I couldn't help but be interested. We drove out of Berlin to Gatow, which I knew was the location of one of the Luftwaffe's training schools. I expected an enormous fuss when we arrived with Hitler salutes and bands and the like but there was none. A junior officer whose name escapes me now met us at the main guardroom. Goering didn't seem bothered at this apparent lack of ceremony.

"Is Hanna here?" Goering enquired.

"Yes, she arrived an hour ago."

"Good, tell her I am here with someone I'd like her to meet."

We strolled off into the base led by the officer and found the officer's mess where we indulged ourselves in a whisky or two.

"Ah, Hanna," Goering suddenly exclaimed. "This is Major Fleischmann. He was one of us in the war."

As an example of Aryan womanhood, she was perfect. Slim, blonde, blue-eyed, she smiled at me and shook my hand.

"Hanna is one of our test pilots." I must have looked stunned. "She will show you how to fly the Bf 109 and then you can pop up and have a play[110]."

"Excellent," I said, just about stopping myself from saying I would see how it compared to the Spitfire.

And off we went, Hanna leading the way. I got changed into more appropriate flying attire and then we set off to a hangar where I was introduced to the Bf109E. It was a formidable looking machine. We looked around the outside. It seemed squat and powerful sitting quietly, unlike the Spitfire which looked graceful in repose. This one had a cannon that fired through the nose cone thus removing the need for your target to be at the point where the fire from wing mounted guns crossed[111].

We climbed onto the wing either side of the cockpit and Hanna showed me the inside. There was nothing I didn't recognise and after a few minutes she announced we should try it out.

"Follow me," she said cheerily. For an instant, my mind returned to the conversation with Hess. 'Killed in action', the headlines in Germany would say. 'Traitor', I imagined those in England would say, assuming they ever heard about it.

"Well get in then," she said. I daren't hesitate for any longer so I did. "Follow me into the air and then we can have a practice dogfight. Wonderful, I thought.

The actions were more or less automatic even having never flown it. We started our engines. Someone pulled the chocks away and we trundled across the field. I heard her check her

---

[110] This must be Hanna Reitsch, darling of the Nazi propaganda machine, pioneer in so many ways of women in aviation. She became a test pilot in 1937, was the first woman to fly a helicopter and tested many of the Luftwaffe's aircraft including the Stuka, the Do17 and the rocket propelled Me163 Komet. She survived the war going on to be a record-breaking glider pilot and heavily involved in aviation in India and Ghana where there is a suggestion she had a relationship with President Nkrumah. She died of an apparent heart attack in 1979. Eric Brown, former Royal Navy test pilot said he received a letter from Reitsch saying 'It began in the bunker, there it shall end', speculating that it was possibly a reference to a suicide pact with Ritter von Greim and that she had finally taken the cyanide capsule given to her by Hitler.

[111] The Bf109, colloquially known as the Messerschmitt 109, was probably the best fighter aircraft of the early war years. See Appendix for a comparison with the Spitfire and Hurricane.

engine and I did the same. It occurred to me that I had no idea if the cannon was loaded. More importantly I had no idea if hers was loaded.

The engines roared and we began moving. The tail came up and it seemed mere seconds before we lifted off. I selected the wheels up and we climbed away, me tagging along beside her. We climbed through 3000 metres and then she slowed up to pull alongside me. She waggled her wings and then suddenly hauled her aircraft upwards. Instinctively I rolled left and down to gain some speed and try and get behind her. I noticed immediately it was better than the Spitfire, not least because the acceleration was far superior. I came round almost full circle before pulling upwards to see where she was. Nowhere. Damn her. I frantically rolled left and right, searching the sky behind for the speck of dirt that would be death if this were for real. An aircraft roared up in front of me climbing and rolling at the same time. I nearly had a seizure and tried to follow but I was too slow so immediately changed my mind, pushing forward and applying full power to accelerate. I tried to get into what I imagined would be her blind spot. I thought she might be flying some sort of Immelmann and if I followed suit, I might get behind her. But of course, she didn't and in seconds I knew she was on my tail. I jinked hard left and then right and she followed, anticipating my every move, closing in for the inevitable kill. My heart was properly racing now. I briefly wondered what the range was and how far it was to England but dismissed it as ludicrous as I waited for the blast of cannon fire that would signal my end. It didn't come.

Without thinking about it, I throttled back suddenly pulled up and over and rolled into a spin. I lost 500 metres in seconds before I recovered and now, much to my surprise I had a very slight advantage. She was above me that was true, but I had the low afternoon sun behind me. I saw a glint and that was enough. I shoved the throttle as far as it would go – it wasn't my aeroplane after all – and keeping the sun behind me headed straight for where she was most likely to be. The Gods were smiling on me clearly as her machine appeared ahead and above, searching the sky for me I assume. It was a matter of seconds as I closed in for the kill. Well, I did knowing that there wasn't going to be one obviously. I decided against her little manoeuvre and instead came up below her tail before suddenly appearing behind her no more than a few metres away. She immediately rolled away, but she knew I had got her back. I grinned to myself for a second before she appeared on my wingtip again and waved for home.

I followed her back to the field and landed. I was sweating buckets, but it was only as I turned the engine off that my hands started shaking again and I had to sit for a moment to calm down. I clambered out and jumped down to the ground, trying not to fall flat on my arse. We strolled back to the mess where Goering greeted us with a drink.

"Whisky?" he said as he handed me a large one. I gratefully accepted and knocked it back if only to make sure my nerves were back under control. Reitsch had a Schnapps. She didn't appear to have any nerves.

"How was my old comrade?"

"Good, very good. I think he almost got me."

I looked at her for a moment thinking it might be a little joke, but her serious face told me it wasn't and that she was a proper fanatic. I couldn't decide if I had just made an enemy or not.

More drinks appeared and vanished followed somewhat later by some good old German schweinshaxe. We were joined by a few others as time went on, none of whom I recognised, but it promised to be a rip-roaring party. Someone started singing and before I knew it, I was joining in. Luckily, it wasn't the ridiculous party approved stuff, more the old songs from the war that usually involved a lot of drink and the removal in some more or less accidental way of an unfortunate lady's garments and her subsequent embarrassment. At one point I noticed the Reitsch woman staring at me, but I was too far gone to care.

At one point, Hermann appeared at my shoulder and muttered something about sleeping before he looked at his watch and with the impeccable timing of a music hall act tipped his entire stein over my lap, much to the amusement of all concerned. That seemed to me to be a cue to do the same, particularly as the party was thinning out anyway. It occurred to me at that point that I had nowhere to stay. I wasn't particularly bothered by this, it was more of a fleeting thought, but no sooner had it passed then a batman of sorts appeared at my arm and muttered "this way, Herr Major," in my ear. I was more than happy to oblige.

We staggered over to some stairs. I say we because I was using him as a human crutch. Climbing them proved troublesome but we managed after a couple of false starts and accidental reversals. He guided me along a corridor and stopped at a door. It was partly open, but oddly he knocked and muttered something unintelligible through the gap. Getting into the spirit of it, I held my finger up to my lips and tried to slide through the door quietly. Having got through, I heard it click shut behind me and I began a survey of my surroundings, looking mainly for somewhere to park my exhausted carcass. Halfway through this I noticed something was not quite right.

Chapter 21

It was the jackboots I think that gave it away. They were standing neatly beside the bed, ready for action. I was puzzled for a long moment wondering why I would have to share my room with some bloody Nazi. It was an outrage, and I was about to remonstrate and call for the batman to have the intruder removed when I realised the said intruder was already in the bed. As I stared, the covers began to lift as the occupant sat up and looked at me. I looked briefly into the blue eyes and then my attention was drawn somewhat lower at the rather lovely bouncers that had just revealed themselves.

Now, you may or may not have found yourself in this situation before. My late Father was an expert of course and I had tried to maintain the family tradition. When confronted with such obvious charms, it was best not to consider over long the political leanings, mental shortcomings or impossible relations of the voluptuous firecracker in question. I promise you it is not as easy as you think, mainly because most gentlemen are inclined to enquire whether they are in fact in the wrong room and should absent themselves forthwith. This is not what the voluptuous charmer requires. What she requires is action, and that in one form or another was what I had trained myself to deliver.

Another useful skill is disrobing on the move. It can only be achieved with practice, such that even under the influence, I was a master at it. I reached the bed as the last of my clothes came off. I heard a gasp and realised she was now examining my expanding accoutrements. I didn't give her the chance to say anything else before my mouth clamped over hers, I grasped a tit and sounded the charge. It wasn't going to be a long drawn-out affair I could tell. But there was plenty of time for that in the morning. She gasped again and with a yell of 'tally ho' we were away.

******

As promised, round two took place shortly after we were awoken, partly by the sun streaming through the curtains, partly by the noise of engines and aircraft. It lasted a significantly longer

84

time with greater satisfaction for all concerned. Round three was the same. After that, Hanna decided breakfast was required.

It was days like this that made me wonder what all the fighting was about. It was midday before we surfaced and went down to the mess again. It was mostly empty. Goering had long gone but had left a message to say he would contact me soon at the hotel. We had some lunch – she was definitely a hungry blighter – and then a driver appeared to return me to the Adlon, but not before my firecracker had made arrangements to drop by occasionally. She said this with more than a twinkle in her eye and I wondered how long it would be before Hess made me leave. Mind you, that wasn't a subject I really wanted to contemplate too much. It seemed that crossing the lines had not improved as an occupation since the first time way back in 15 by parachute. I tried not to think about it.

******

My detective friend was waiting for me in the bar that evening.

"Any good gossip?" he asked with a hint of a smile.

"Lots," I replied and proceeded to regale him with my tales of derring do.

"I know her," he said when I talked about Hanna. "She is on all the posters."

He was right as well. It seemed wherever I looked after that, there she was smiling out at me and extolling the virtues of Nazi womanhood which was an enigma in itself given that Hitler and friends rather saw German women as nothing more than providers of blond cannon fodder for their imperial plans. Still, nothing really made sense in this city and after a few days my exploits had faded into the background somewhat as I resumed my routine in the hotel. She did drop in from time to time, and we had some energetic bouts, but she was too much the Nazi for me and I feared I wouldn't be able to hide it forever.

January drifted into February and I was still kicking my heels. But then so was everybody, at least on the face of it. Except maybe the Finns and the Russians. Why anyone would want Finland was beyond me. I had never been there I suppose but most of it was just ice as far as I could tell. But then the Russians always were a strange bunch. Despite experience telling them for at least two months that they were not up to it and that the Finns liked fighting (and living presumably) in sub-zero temperatures, they finally invaded the place. I hope they liked it.

I was getting properly bored. I had explored almost every inch of Berlin, day and night. I had discovered, largely thanks to my detective friend, that not everybody stuck to the wholesome mantras of the Nazi regime and that there was vicious fun to be had just like everywhere else albeit with a somewhat Prussian formality to it. But frankly I was sick of it. But if I had known of course what the spring would bring, I would have happily invaded Finland and spent the rest of my life there.

April 4th, 1940. That was when it started properly. Chamberlain made a speech to the Tories. It was probably one of the most misguided he ever made. He said he was confident of victory and that Hitler had 'missed the bus' by not taking advantage of Germany's military superiority at the start of the war. Everyone then decided that Norway was the place to be and they all rushed off to be there. It was a bit like invading Great Britain via Cornwall. But it was no less lethal for all that. Although the fighting was somewhat disjointed and sporadic, numerous ships were lost on both sides before both German and British troops arrived. It was doomed of course, mainly because the Luftwaffe largely had air superiority and this became obvious as April trotted along in the wake of Chamberlain's ridiculous pronouncements. Within weeks of landing, evacuation plans were being made and considered. It was a busy time and about to get much busier, mainly because the Germans were about to go French but also because the British government was about to implode. They couldn't have timed it better of course.

Chapter 22

Guderian. Rommel. No one really knew these names at the time, but they soon would. Within hours of Hitler issuing the go order, they were off with their tanks heading for the Channel coast. They didn't bother with attacking the Maginot Line where the French Army were hiding in their supposedly impregnable defences having failed to move on since Verdun. Our lot weren't much better. Gort who was commanding the BEF apparently thought he would have a few weeks of preparation before having to face the Germans in battle. Nowadays, everyone assumes the Germans just had more and better troops and armour. But they didn't. Nothing like it in fact. They were simply better organised, better trained and led by officers and NCOs who had learnt the lessons of modern warfare and were not hidebound by a class system that had condemned so many second sons to a gruesome end. The all arms warfare that resulted was something to be seen. Unfortunately for many, their first encounter with it was also their last.

Momentous events were also taking place across the channel and it was in fact this that now prompted my German masters to change their plans for me. I had been wondering what to do myself in fact, not because I wished particularly to join in, more because the thought of living in a hotel for too much longer did not appeal. Especially not in Berlin. Equally the thought of somehow hightailing it into the hills uninvited had me hiding behind the furniture. So, it was with some surprise that Goering appeared one evening. He appeared to have been drinking.

"Fleischmann, how are you?" he cried with a loud guffaw and a hefty slap on the back.

"Absolutely spiffing what!" How he laughed at what he took to be my humorous impression of how an Englishman would respond.

"A drink with you before you go." He guffawed again, just as I registered what he had actually said.

"Go? Where?"

"To war my friend." I nearly spat my drink in his face. "But you have to move quickly. Events are moving fast. And they have taken an unexpected turn with Churchill. We anticipated Halifax taking over. It will be much harder to end the war in the west now. That is why we need you to get to England as soon as possible so that we can avoid unnecessary confrontation. This letter is from Hess. It explains everything."

So, yet again, I was to be the postman for the Germans.[112]

"There is a car downstairs. It will take you to a fighter squadron. There you will be assigned an Me109. You will then need to get across the lines, but you will need to be quick I think." He chuckled again at this, then took another great swig from his glass. I poured myself one, if only to hide my fear and give myself a pause for thought. Not that there was anything I could do about it as always.

There was indeed a large Mercedes[113] waiting for me and without so much as a by your leave I was off. It was a long way. Goering showed me on a map before I left. It had an outline of the German invasion plan on it. I was appalled. It was nothing like what I had been led to believe by the upper echelons of our own politicians. They, having learnt nothing in the twenty years since the last lot, believed the French when they said the Maginot line was impregnable. They believed the Belgians and the Dutch would put up a stiff resistance. They also believed that once the BEF was in the field it would also hold up the Germans and then force them back. How deluded they all were. Looking back, I realise they were still fighting some sort of Napoleonic campaign.

******

It took me more than two days just to get to the border. The roads were full of military traffic all going the same way. It did occur to me that they could have chosen a nearer airfield, but they didn't. At last though, we found the squadron we were looking for. It had been moving forward so quickly we had not been able to catch it up. But finally, I was there. It was dusk. Aircraft were landing, back from combat sorties, some with damage but mostly they looked unscathed.

---

[112] See Flashman and the Knights of the Sky. It was in fact the Austrians.
[113] High ranking Nazi officials tended to use the Mercedes-Benz 770.

I went into the Mess and ordered a drink. Slowly the pilots -drifted in. Somehow it reminded me of a similar situation not too far from where we were now but a long time ago. The same black humour, the same somewhat artificial merriment. I was introduced to most of them but few of the names stuck in my mind. I was to fly shotgun for a pilot called Rall for the brief time I was with the squadron[114]. He was the only one who knew that my mission was special and that I would shortly disappear. Where to he wasn't told. He probably didn't care either.

Eventually the evening broke up and we drifted off to bed. It was a short night. Being probably the most civilised arm of the German military, I was woken far too early by a batman of some kind. Breakfast was taken on the hoof and before I knew it, we were heading for the aeroplanes. In my head I had an idea that I was just going to get airborne, fly around for a bit and then tootle off to the other side. Of course, these things are never as simple as one would like. We had had a morning briefing on what were the last known front lines, but it was emphasised that they would have changed overnight. I seem to recall it was the 15th of May or thereabouts, and I heard afterwards that this was the day that Renaud telephoned Churchill to tell him all was lost[115]. Five days to defeat a nation. "Encroyable," as the frogs might say. To be honest, with hindsight they were defeated before they began, mainly because their hearts weren't really in it and they didn't have Rommel and Guderian. Without these two, who were both prepared to interpret orders to suit themselves, things may have developed differently. But who knows?

We were airborne over the Sedan area with orders to escort some Stukas[116] whose orders were simply to hit roving targets at

---

[114] Presumably Gunther Rall of JG52, eventually one of Germany's top scoring aces. He survived the war going on to hold senior positions in the German Airforce through the Cold War.

[115] French Prime Minister Paul Reynaud did indeed call Churchill and tell him that France was beaten. It was however another month before France surrendered.

[116] Junkers Ju87 Stuka was a dive bomber used with great success in Spain and initially in France. It had a lethal flaw in that as it pulled out of its dive it was very slow and very vulnerable and many were shot down in this way

will, something they were particularly good at. I was also looking for a convenient spot to jump ship, but it was nigh on impossible to tell who was who. It didn't help that the last time I had done this was in a much slower machine.

Suddenly, Rall was chattering on the radio and the Stukas had identified an armoured column as a target. It seemed to be completely stationary. I watched in fascinated horror as the Stukas began their attack run and dive. I wondered what it would have been like to be underneath.

"Bandits, 10 o'clock low," shouted someone. Without thinking too much we pulled up and round. We were in the sun and the French had not learnt the most basic lesson. Or not remembered it. They were Morane 406s[117] and therefore largely useless against the 109. It was appalling. I lost count but there seemed to be lots of them. The German pilots plunged into the melee from above, selecting their targets and then executing them. I did the same. I had no option. I would have looked ridiculous if I hadn't. I tried to fire at the tail in the hopes that the pilot would get the message and jump out, but it was nonsensical to expect that to happen really. What actually happened was within seconds, at least six of the French fighters were on fire, at least two exploded including the one I had shot at and the rest were trying to push their throttles out of the mounting hoping against hope that it might produce more power than ever before.

We let them go. Our job was to protect the Stukas and that we had done. I don't think a single one was even damaged and the 109s were the same. A cold shiver ran down my spine as I realised what we were up against. If the army was like this, our bumbling Colonel Blimps[118] didn't stand a chance.

In the excitement I had all but forgotten my actual mission and running low on fuel it seemed the only option was to return to the base. When we got there, it was chaos. I turned the engine off and jumped out to see what was going on.

---

[117] The Morane-Saulnier MS 406 was the most numerous fighter in French service. It was no match for the Bf109.

[118] Colonel Blimp was a cartoon character invented by David Low in the Daily Telegraph. He was a rotund ex-army officer who hated innovation and new ideas.

"Moving again," someone shouted.

Apart from the first few weeks of the first lot I had never seen anything like it and even that comparison wasn't really valid given the much reduced speed of everything then. Engineers dashed about, aircraft were fuelling and arming, the ground crews were shoving everything into any vehicle they could[119] and before I knew it, we were starting up for the short move to the front. That at least was uneventful, but it meant our operations were pretty much over for the day.

I was exhausted. But it was nothing to how I would feel in a couple of weeks' time.

---

[119] Despite most film and propaganda of the time portraying the German military as extremely mobile, reality was that they were in fact quite limited and many units still had horse drawn transport.

Chapter 23

The next day was more of the same. And the next. Early start, bomber escort, shoot up the French and go home. I hadn't seen hide nor hair of the British. Neither had I knowingly seen any kind of front line. I realised then that I was simply going to have to work out a better plan and go through with it. I would have to somehow detach myself from my squadron, in itself not particularly difficult, then fly into the allied area and either land or bail out. Neither option appealed. I had rather rashly assumed that everything would be a little more obvious and that I would be able to find somewhere innocuous to leave the war behind.

Reports arrived that the army were nearly at the coast. It must have been about the 18th or 19th[120]. My options were quickly evaporating. At this rate, the war would be over in a couple of weeks anyway. I contemplated the meaning of that thought and what the consequences might be. Surrender? Not the buffoon Churchill. Peace? The same was true. Unless someone else was holding the tiller of course.

I realised that I needed to get out, not necessarily because I thought I would make any difference or even that I thought I was in danger. So far, I hadn't had a single shot fired at me. Mainly, it was because I had no idea what was going on.

We took off after lunch and headed towards the coast. Everywhere stuff seemed to be on fire. I can't actually remember what we were meant to be doing but we were fairly low level.

"Spitfires!"[121] someone screamed in my ear. And they were. From nowhere, about half a dozen of them appeared their wing guns blinking at us as the tracer rounds zipped past. I reacted perfectly properly as a Flashman should. I jammed the throttle open, gripped the controls for dear life and started flying as

---

[120] Guderian's panzer corps reached the coast late on 20th May having advanced 250 miles from their start points. By doing so, they completed the encirclement of about 1.7 million allied troops including the Dutch Army which had already surrendered, the Belgian Army, one French Army with parts of four others and most of the BEF.

[121] Spitfires were only sent from bases in England, they were never based in France.

though my life depended on it. Which it did of course. Suddenly I was back over the Somme with Immelmann and Boelcke and Richtofen and Ball and Mapplebeck and Strange and Hawker and all those other dead heroes[122].

The 109 was quite a bit more powerful than the Spitfire[123] in a straight climb and I used that advantage now. I had no intention of hanging around to get shot up by my own side. Where the others went and what they did I had no idea. Knowing them they probably turned straight into the scrap. All well and good because it meant no one was going to pursue me. And so it turned out. I levelled off at about 5,000 metres as I had checked and rechecked and checked again that there was no one on my tail. I was on my own. For a moment I automatically began thinking about getting back to the base before realising that this was my chance of course.

I climbed higher. The view was superb and for once I got a good view of the area. I knew Guderian had made the coast near Abbeville, but they couldn't have taken much of it. Now it was obvious what to do. I could see the river mouth on my left. The allies must be to the north. If I followed the coast towards Boulogne, Dunquerque and Calais, all my problems would be over. I shiver now to think of it, but it seemed like the perfect plan at the time. What would have been better of course would have been to fly across the channel. If only. At that point, there was a loud bang and oil started streaming over the windscreen. In seconds I couldn't see anything and then I noticed the unmistakeable whiff of smoke. There was no one around me so a lucky shot had hit something that then took a few minutes to manifest itself.

---

[122] Except Louis Strange survived and by coincidence had just arrived in France on the 21st May. He was a 50 year old RAFVR Pilot Officer and 24 Squadron's aerodrome control officer. Shortly after arrival at Merville and 24 Squadron having already started evacuating, he was the only pilot available with an unarmed and part cannibalised Hurricane still on the ground. He got in it, got airborne, climbed to avoid flak, was attacked by two 109s but escaped across the channel at low level earning himself a bar to his DFC. Strange remained in the RAF until June 1945. He died in 1966.

[123] See Appendix.

I pulled the canopy back and felt the blast of air. I also felt the blast of heat as smoke turned to flame. I shut the throttle and immediately slowed down, released my harness, had a brief panic about whether I had anything incriminating in my pockets, put my hands on the side of the cockpit and tried the dignified roll out of the cockpit that was advised in these situations in order to avoid decapitation by the tail. To my surprise, it worked rather well. As a pioneer of the use of parachutes[124], I was expecting worse. I began plummeting earthwards. I spotted the 109 continuing on its merry way, noticed the fire and smoke now streaming from the nose and then once I reached ten, I pulled the cord. Out popped the chute, there was a disconcerting jerk in the essentials and I was floating. The silence was serene, the view was wonderful, the smell slightly singed. I just needed to hope I was in the ever-diminishing allied territory, find some friendly locals and then thumb a boat back to Blighty.

---

[124] See 'Flashman and the Knights of the Sky'.

Chapter 24

Of course life, mine anyway, isn't like that. As the ground approached, I stopped gazing at the countryside and prepared for my arrival. I thumped down in the approved manner, rolled in a less than approved heap and came to a halt. A few seconds to get my bearings, then I undid the harness, rolled up the chute as far as possible and then left it for some fortunate farmer to find. I was in the middle of a field. I glanced towards the sea but the 109 was long gone. Nothing for it but Shanks's pony. I decided to head in a north-easterly direction as home had to be that way. Hopefully somewhere I would be able to cadge a lift towards civilisation.

I trudged over fields for what must have been several miles before I found a road and followed it. It was half an hour before so much as a bicycle passed by. And being a bicycle meant it was useless unless I mugged the owner. Another fifteen minutes or so slipped away and then I heard something motorised approaching. I turned to face it and stuck my thumb out. For a moment I thought it wasn't going to stop but it did.

"Bonjour monsieur." I smiled. Silence. "Allez-vous Arras par hasard? More silence. "Pouvez vous m'y prendre?" It wasn't that I particularly wanted to go there, I just couldn't think of anywhere else.

"Pah," he said and thumbed towards the back. Half expecting him to drive off I walked to the rear and clambered aboard. I thumped the back of the cab to let Monsieur Joyeux know that I was safely aboard then made myself comfortable amongst the vegetables.

I had had worse rides and some of them had been along these very same roads. They appeared to be in the same state they were in in 1916. But the sun was shining, I wasn't walking, and I was out of the Fatherland. We clattered along for some time. I had made myself comfortable and was stretched out enjoying the sun on my face. I must have dozed a little because I awoke as the brakes screeched and we rolled gently to a halt. I guessed correctly that this was my turning and indeed I glanced up at a convenient signpost announcing the road to Arras. It was at this point that I heard the distinct but distant crump of high explosive. A cold shiver ran down my spine, but I had little choice but to head towards the action. I watched my ride creep off into the distance, more or less southwards away from the noise but apparently oblivious to it. I started walking.

I supposed as I was approaching from the west it was unlikely that I would see much action. It was only as I passed into the outskirts of a town whose name escapes me now that things started to hot up. There weren't many locals around. I guessed that most had found an excuse to go and see some relatives anywhere but here. What I did see was an increasing amount of military hardware and military people rushing about. I ambled in towards what I imagined to be the town centre. The frenzy just seemed to increase. I stopped a passing junior officer and asked where I could find someone in charge. He stared at me popeyed and pointed behind himself before disappearing at high speed in the opposite direction. Something wasn't right. I could tell.

Eventually I managed to find what seemed like the main square. No one had asked me what I was doing despite my informal get up and in fact no one seemed in the slightest bit interested in me. It was a little disconcerting I must admit. It made me wonder if getting back to Blighty was going to be more difficult than I had imagined when I was sitting in my 109.

"Who the devil are you?" said an animated voice from behind me. I turned to see a somewhat dishevelled infantry officer.

"Flashman, Wing Commander Flashman actually."[125]

"Over there. Air force in that green building I think." And with that he ran off.

"You know they're behind you don't you," I yelled after him hoping to spoil his day.

I sauntered over to the building in question, wondering if I really wanted to see the air force as such. On the other hand, it would be somewhat churlish not to at least say hello. I poked my head in the door to find a scene of chaos. There were people everywhere and more people rushing to be somewhere else

---

[125] Flashman's rank seems somewhat lowly given his total time in the service. He doesn't mention it anywhere, but I suspect he was, along with many others, demoted after the Great War. He also spent a lot of time away from the service which could be a factor.

clutching reams of paper and so on. I stood in the doorway wondering what to do.

"Who the devil are you?" said another animated voice.

"Wing Commander Flashman," I replied hoping that this might elicit a more helpful response.

"Squadron?"

"Well, I don't actually have one at the moment..."

"Pilot?"

"Spitfire was the last thing I flew." I nearly said 109 but luckily refrained, not that I think he would have noticed. His face lit up though.

"Desperately short. There is a driver outside. He can take you to the nearest mob. Hall. Group Captain Hall" At least I think that's what he said. I wasn't listening carefully.

"But I have to get back to England." It sounded lame even to me.

"All in good time, what! Jerries to polish off first. All hands to the pumps I'm afraid. Good luck." With that he shook my hand, winked at me and hurried off.

Well, as you can imagine, that left me with a terrible conundrum. I had foolishly given my real name and whilst I thought it was unlikely he or anyone else would remember it, one never knew. I went outside.

"Sir," said an oik saluting. "Car is ready to go."

And without so much as a by your leave I was in it and off. I considered these events as we drove away and decided that once we got to wherever we were going I would have a stern word with the squadron CO and requisition one of his aeroplanes to get me home. Yes, the more I thought about it, that was the easiest way. It would also be a lot quicker than the boat and I was unlikely to be sick.

I peered out of the window as we sped out of town again. I suddenly noticed that my driver was wearing a tin hat.

"What's the hat for?" I shouted.

"Well Sir, if it's all the same to you, them Jerries is dropping a lot of bombs everywhere."

It was only then that I noticed the spiralling columns of smoke in the distance. And then the noise. It wasn't particularly loud, but it was intense. It was like there was a real war going on. And we seemed to be heading directly for it.

The tyres squealed as we took a corner a little too fast and then I nearly hit the roof as we bounced into a field. In the distance, I noticed a few aeroplanes, Hurricanes mostly, surrounded by people frantically pulling at them. We pulled up beside a camp table and the driver turned round and grinned at me.

"Here we are Sir," he said. Apparently, he wasn't going to open the door for me, so I got out.

"Who the devil are you?" It was beginning to grate somewhat.

"Flashman, Wing Commander."

"Can you fly?"

"Well, yes."

"Yours." He pointed at an aeroplane surrounded by various people fiddling with it.

"What do you mean…" I stuttered taken aback.

"No time to explain. Flight commander's over there. Follow his lead. Good luck!"

He turned his back on me as another man in flying kit ran up to him.

"Lost a couple. Seems like hundreds of them over Calais and the front."

I can tell you I was thoroughly disturbed now. Quite what I was meant to make of all this I didn't know. What I could categorically state was that none of it sounded like good news.

"Oi," shouted a voice in the distance. "Yes, you," as I looked towards its owner. "Are you my replacement?"

"Well…"

"Good. Ten minutes then we're off." He came over to me. "Name's Cane. Stay on my wing as long as possible. Then it's every man for himself. Take some of them with you if you can. Tally ho!"[126]

---

[126] It appears to be too far north but it is just possible that this is the New Zealand ace, Edgar 'Cobber' Kain. He was with 73 Squadron at the time. He was the first fighter pilot to become an 'Ace' in the war and also the first DFC of the war. He claimed a total of 14 victories and was ordered home on the 7th

I think at this point my mouth must have dropped open. But he didn't notice, and nor did anyone else. He was gone. The worst thing was they all seemed so bloody cheery when clearly that was not appropriate for the situation. What I couldn't understand, and I was not alone it would seem, was how in such an apparently short period, everything was so chaotic. I had experienced enough war to know it was often like this, but there was an undefined sense of disorder, of frenzy even.

"Hurri's ready sir," said an airman who looked about twelve.

"Thank you," I replied, the incongruity of that statement ringing in my ears. It also occurred to me that I hadn't flown a Hurricane for some time.

Someone handed me a parachute and I clambered into it feeling not a little discomfited. I climbed onto the wing and into the cockpit, my mind racing. The twelve-year-old strapped me in, hooked me up to the oxygen, slid the canopy forward a bit, shouted something incomprehensible and was gone. I fumbled through the routine and almost without realising the engine burst into life with the unmistakeable roar of the Merlin. Checks complete, someone pulled the chocks away and we were off. I turned into line following the flight commander as we trundled over the bumpy grass.

"Bandits!" screamed someone in my ears. My head started revolving and out of the blue, literally, appeared the entire Luftwaffe, heading straight at us. I couldn't be absolutely sure, but they looked rather like the 109 I had just abandoned along with some other odds and ends. Somewhat obliquely I wondered whether the one that was probably now at the bottom of the channel counted as a victory for me. I didn't wonder for long.

There was an explosion and about five tons of earth flew into the air. I glanced to my right and noticed the muzzle flashes but couldn't see the results. Closer, closer, closer and then with an enormous bang the Hurricane beside me flew into the air slowly coming apart. I was frankly speechless. The leader kept going as the 109s roared overhead. I seemed to be unscathed[127].

June. To say goodbye to his colleagues, he took off, started some low-level aerobatics, misjudged a flick roll, crashed and was killed.

[127] The Bf109E variants did have a rack capable of carrying bombs.

"Let's go," a voice said in my ear. I followed the Hurri round and then opened up behind him. There were two aircraft ahead of him. How they had got there was anybody's guess but apart from me no one cared right at this moment. And thank God they had. Out of the corner of my eye I could see black specks getting bigger again. It was going to be really close. Faster and faster we trundled over the field and bigger and bigger grew the Luftwaffe's finest. I saw the two ahead get airborne. I was close, the tail was up and I had bounced off briefly once already. I saw more muzzle flashes from the corner of my eye. I had no idea where it was all going until I saw the slightly higher of the two Hurricanes ahead suddenly spew smoke and flame. I felt sick. I watched horror struck as the aircraft continued climbing for a few seconds before slowly rolling over onto its back and descending. It hit the ground almost upside down. If the pilot was alive before the crash, he certainly wasn't now. I roared overhead passing through some of the smoke from his funeral pyre. The chatter on the radio increased in intensity and confirmed at least that some of the squadron had made it into the air. What exactly we were going to do now was another thing altogether. I followed the leader into a steep climb as we tried to get away from the carnage below. I was frantically scanning the sky around me searching for the 109s, but they seemed to have vanished.

"Tally ho!"

I nearly had a seizure as my companion rolled away. I followed instinctively wondering what on earth he had seen. I soon discovered. Below us were several black smudges that very quickly turned into Ju88s. He was going straight for them. I looked up and behind for their fighter cover. There was none, or at least none that I could see.

"What about fighters?" I couldn't help but ask.

"Probably still busy with the airfield. One pass and then we head for the front."

The 88s loomed larger and larger. I had glanced round to discover there were five of us and three of them.

"Leader's mine," said our leader.

It was obvious which one was ours. We had split into two pairs and a singleton without thinking about it. Again I saw muzzle flashes followed by an almighty clang and a whistling noise as a couple of holes appeared in the canopy. We both opened up at the same moment and almost immediately the 88s started to turn. It was probably their downfall as they managed to present a bigger target just at the crucial moment and we took the opportunity to fill the bastards with .303 bullets. Smoke began trailing from our target and then I saw another almighty explosion as the third in line exploded. Presumably someone had hit a bomb. Of the remaining two it was obvious ours was in its death throes. Someone jumped but they were far too low for parachutes. The leader was trailing a lot of smoke and down near the ground but apparently under control.

"Let's go,"

We rolled hard and headed east at low level. I glanced down occasionally and every time I looked there appeared to be hordes of ants swarming over everything. I suspect this was an exaggeration but at the time it seemed apt. There was also a lot of smoke in the air from burning things. What they were was hard to tell but the sight didn't fill me with confidence I have to say.

"Here we go," a voice said.

I looked around me but couldn't see anything vaguely resembling a target. Then I noticed we were following a river and ahead was a bridge. On it were more hordes only this time recognisable as humanity. German humanity. My mind flashed back twenty years to a station, probably not too far from where I was now, and the carnage we had wrought. And the carnage we had suffered.[128]

The noise was incredible. I hadn't closed my canopy so there was a mixture of the airflow, the engine, guns, explosions, voices yelling in my ear and someone screaming for mercy. All of us were hurling our aircraft around the sky now in an attempt to put the German gunners off. I could see men crouching behind the bridge parapets, others attempting to get off the bridge, vehicles everywhere, some stationary, some moving, and then one crashing into a gun pit at the bridge end flinging a couple of bodies into the air, both of which landed in the river.

My guns were singing their deadly song as I aimed at anything I could. I saw bodies fall and vehicles catch fire, but the

---

[128] See 'Flashman and the Red Baron'.

worst thing was seeing the Hurricane just to my left, guns blazing, dip suddenly and crash directly into the centre span of the bridge. There was an enormous explosion which rocked my aircraft and then I was past the bridge and following the leader into the clear blue sky. I ripped my oxygen mask off and was sick in my lap.

It took me a few seconds to recover any sort of composure. I glanced at the fuel gauge. Why I did just then I will never know but I got the shock of my life when I realised I was almost out.

"Home," said the leader. There was no more conversation until we landed about ten minutes later.

Chapter 25

I sat in the cockpit for some time. It was only when someone jumped onto the wing and slid the canopy fully back that I rejoined the real world, albeit real was hardly the right description. I was drenched in sweat but the cooling effect of standing up made me shiver. At least that was what I told myself. I climbed slowly down and noticed the frantic group of airmen pulling at the remains of my Hurricane. When I saw the holes, I was nearly sick again. Suddenly I was very thirsty. I headed over to the shed that passed for the squadron (ha!) headquarters. There was a sink and a tap and I tried it.

"You'll be lucky. Might be some water round the back."

I went round the back and there was as suggested some jerry cans with water in and tin mugs beside them. I drank as much as I dared and then feeling no better whatsoever returned to the hut.

"Is it always like that?"

"Well, only for the last two weeks or so since the Jerries began attacking us. Won't last long now though."

"What do you mean?" I spluttered.

"Where have you been then?" he replied with a confused look on his face. "We don't stand a chance. As soon as they came over the border, we started retreating and we haven't stopped. In case you hadn't noticed, the channel is just behind us."

I opened my mouth to say something then closed it again. What was there to say? He was right but it was only when he said it that I appreciated the enormity of the situation.

"I thought we had a whole army here?"

"We did." I considered that statement for a moment.

"Where's it gone then?"

"Up in smoke mostly I should imagine. There are rumours of an evacuation. I'll believe it when I see it."

"Evacuation? Then what?"

"Hopefully that's what our lords and masters are carefully considering at the moment, although I somehow doubt that whatever is left of the army and air force will be anything like enough. I've seen the future and it isn't pretty."

This disturbing conversation was halted by a shout through the door.

"Let's go."

My unnamed companion ran out of the door grabbing a semblance of flying kit on the way. I was still clutching mine from the last lot. I hesitated for a few seconds desperately trying to think of a situation where I could sit this one out. In the lottery of life that hesitation saved mine.

"Take cover!" someone yelled at the top of their voice as I stepped outside. I glanced round frantically looking for non-existent shelter. I heard sirens from somewhere and my mind immediately flashed back to a few days previously when I had wondered to myself what it would be like to be underneath. I was about to find out.

Almost instantly there was an enormous bang. I flung (or was thrown – I am still not sure really) myself behind the shed praying that it wasn't a target. From my prone position I peeped round the corner of the building. Where once there had been two Hurricanes there was now a large bonfire. Lying nearby on his back was my shed companion looking for all the world like he had just decided to have a little rest. I could tell however, that this rest was his last.

The Stukas had gone. The sirens had stopped. The cacophony of war subsided. In less than two minutes, apart from one flight that oddly didn't belong to this squadron anyway but got away with Cane leading, the remainder of the squadron had been destroyed on the ground. Casualties had been limited to one of the airmen who had been too slow to abandon his charge and my friend who, when I went over to where he was lying to assist, was clearly dead. I could tell by the large hole in the front of his face. I was very nearly sick again. I stood up and walked away, looking like a man deeply affected. I was of course. But I doubt my thoughts were similar to the other surviving squadron members.

"Well, that's it then." This was the CO who had managed to survive as well. "Nothing for us to do here now without any aircraft. My orders were to resist as long as possible then try and get home. We have reached that point I believe. Leave the kit. Load up those lorries and head north for the port."

Chapter 26

It didn't take long to load. No one really had much kit, me included. Essentials. And us. I imagined that it wouldn't take that long to get to the port. How wrong I was. We had been going about half an hour when someone shouted, "Take cover!" the lorries stopped and there was an immediate exodus from the back. As one of the first in I was also one of the last out. This allowed me a grandstand view of a couple of Messerschmitt 109s attending two Ju 88s in what could be described as a low fly past with bombs and bullets. My eyes were fixed on the leader as I scrambled over the tailboard and down onto the road just as the first explosion lit up the sky taking a truck with it. It wasn't one of ours, but I realised instantly that travelling along a road in a truck with numerous others was simply inviting trouble. Walking in France was most certainly the best option. Apparently, I wasn't the only one to arrive at this conclusion.

"Where's the bloody RAF?" I heard someone shout. It was very tempting to reply. It would appear that most of it was either wandering towards the port or dead in a field of burning wreckage.

Once the initial excitement was over, we gathered by the trucks. Both were intact but in front and behind were burning vehicles. Even if we had fancied continuing by road, we couldn't have. The CO gathered us together again.

"Gentlemen, it has been an honour to serve with you all. However, judging by that little escapade, we are now down to the fundamentals. It seems unlikely that we will be able to stay together and also unlikely that we will all make it. I think now is the time for every man to make his own decisions. I will lead any who wish to accompany me to the port. But should you prefer to make your own way, then you have my permission. Good luck!"

This was an unexpected dilemma. I could feel the situation spiralling ever more out of control. And chaos is never conducive to effective escape. On the other hand, hanging about by the side of the road was equally useless. I didn't particularly feel the need to follow the boss as I hadn't been with the squadron long enough to care – so much so I still don't know which one it was - and, slightly disconcerting though it was, being alone had its advantages. Not least was not being obliged to help anyone else.

I set off before the rest had decided what to do. No-one noticed me leave, and within minutes I was just an anonymous straggler amongst many others. One of the first things I noticed was the absence of officers and uniforms. It became clear fairly quickly that the former were largely dead and the latter ruined by the ravages of war. This meant that no one really noticed that my attire was a little unconventional to say the least. There was a somewhat bizarre atmosphere everywhere. No one had the faintest idea what was going on.

We trudged along in the direction of the biggest smoke plumes on the understanding that if this was the biggest target then that was where we needed to be. It was a slightly odd assumption of course and anathema to me but there seemed no other option. If we, or more importantly I, was to extract myself from this mess I needed to find transport over the water. I rued the day I had had to jump out of my 109.

It was hard to tell how long it lasted, but it was more than a few hours. As countryside walks go, it was hideous, punctuated by bombs, bullets and other assorted hardware. I had decided early to parallel the road, but I wasn't alone and this slowed everything down. At last, the outskirts of some town or other hove into view. Dunkerque it said. Nearly there I thought.

Of course, amongst many French names, now Dunkerque, or Dunkirk as the English liked to call it, is seared into that English catalogue of heroic disaster. It's one of the things we are good at as a nation. Last stands. I remember my Father telling me about Gandamack where there was officially only one survivor from the army that left Kabool. Brydon I believe his name was[129]. Unofficially there were two as the parent made it out as well with the help of his ability to disguise himself as a local. If you have read his memoirs, the parallels are obvious. Underequipped, under established British Army is sent with various unsuitable

---

[129] Surgeon William Brydon was indeed the only official survivor of the disastrous retreat from Kabul in 1842. See 'Flashman', the original work edited by George MacDonald Fraser. 'Return of a King' by William Dalrymple is an excellent recent reappraisal of the campaign.

idiots in charge to upset the locals. Lacking intelligence but brimming with overconfidence, as aristocratic second sons so often are, they soon find themselves at a loss as to what to do next and resort to convincing themselves that all is well and that what is needed here is some well-earned rest and maybe a game of football for the underlings. Guidance from above is sadly lacking as the equally useless politicians are convinced that, despite all the evidence to the contrary, a Guards officer with the benefit of hundreds of years of pedigree and an Eton education, will know exactly what to do when the critical moment arrives. Consequently, when it does, chaos ensues. It turns out that being the 85th Duke of Dumbleby hasn't endowed the owner with the gift of foresight and charging around on a horse at the Guards Club isn't suitable training for opposing a highly trained Panzer Division.

This was exactly where we found ourselves now. There was no one in charge. There appeared to be no order to anything. Everyone was heading the same way and consequently the approach to Dunkerque was a huge crowd of people wearing all sorts of uniforms. The horror I experienced at this moment equalled almost anything I had seen previously. It was not the immediate problem of staying alive that worried me. Just the fact that so many people crowding into one small town made an appetising target, a target which was apparently getting smaller by the minute. Well, smaller in area, bigger in numbers.

Of course the other problem was the people going the other way. The locals, bless them, had decided that they mainly didn't like being shelled and bombed and were leaving the scene in ever greater numbers. All in all, a recipe for utter disaster.

I trudged on with all these charming thoughts crowding my head. I was amongst houses now. The atmosphere was odd. A few local people were still around but I did wonder if they were just the potential looters. I carried on heading towards the port. It couldn't be far away now. I don't know how much longer I walked on for, but it must have been some time. There was little chatter amongst the hundreds of stragglers that I was trying unsuccessfully to stay away from. It was impossible now. And then there was a collective gasp. I stopped in my tracks as did many others. It was only now that the enormity of what was happening sunk in.

Chapter 27

I had emerged with so many others on what was probably once a pleasant seafront promenade. One could easily imagine people strolling in the summer sun. Families, the elderly, young children playing getting under one's feet. The current scene was so far removed from that it was like comparing heaven and hell. There were people everywhere. Most were in some semblance of uniform, but the mixture was incredible. Oddly it didn't seem particularly noisy, war generally being a particularly noisy pastime. There wasn't much shouting, just the odd call, mainly of people trying to find their unit or someone they knew. We clambered down onto the dunes and there we found numerous others lying down having a rest or a smoke or in a few cases dead.

I heard someone ask where we should report to which seemed both strange and appropriate at the same time.

"Navy running the show," someone said. "Over there."

I looked where he was pointing and out on the beach there did indeed seem to be some sort of command post. As a group we started shuffling towards it. I glanced upwards as I had heard an engine. It got louder quite quickly and then multiple voices started shouting 'take cover'.

I spotted the offenders. Stukas, diving on us with their ridiculous sirens. Now it is an eternal mystery to me why when someone shouts take cover in a film, everyone seems to run straight ahead along the intended line of the bomber. Have a look next time. I guess this provides a spectacular outcome as the bombs fall and the heroes have a narrow escape unlike the extras who are blown to smithereens. Or not actually because films don't really show the reality of course.

In real life, everyone scatters attempting to get out of the way of the assailant. This generally means people running into one another causing more chaos. I have decided after a life of running from these situations that a useful ploy is occasionally to turn and run straight at the problem. On this occasion I did just that. It had the desired effect. No one else thought of it so I was on my own. And the Stuka pilots weren't going to drop a bomb on a single man running although what hadn't quite made it into my mind was the possibility of people behind me. Luckily, I had dallied over heading for the command post and was at the back of our group so fortune smiled on me a little.

I judged the moment to hit the sand perfectly. I found a tiny ridge and dived behind it just as the first bomb detonated. The explosion was deafening and followed by several others. I looked up involuntarily and wished I hadn't as all I saw was mangled humans in the air. They hit the ground along with the mountain of sand that had been blown upwards with a strange whooshing noise. There was a moment of comparative silence as the Stukas climbed away and then all hell broke loose again, anyone who had a weapon firing it madly into the sky, the injured screaming, the uninjured shouting. I pondered for a second where all the ammunition was going. As always, there would be significant casualties caused by our own side. Then, slowly, calm returned. The medics did their jobs, the guns were put down.

We resumed strolling to the command post where a bearded naval officer was holding court.

"Who the bloody hell are you?" he enquired politely amongst the madness.

"Flashman, Wing Commander."

"How lovely. And all these people?"

"No idea really, we didn't get round to introductions on our way to the party."

He raised an eyebrow at this, unsure if I was being insolent or not.

"Well, Flashman, not much to tell you really. Join that group over there. They have a naval rating with them so they know their place in the queue. When we are ready for you, we will let you know."

With that he turned away and summoned a rating standing nearby.

"Go and fetch group fifty-five 'A'," he said. Or something like that. I can't really remember after all this time.

I turned round to find my group of stragglers staring at me waiting for direction.

"This way," I said and led them off to join another group of stragglers lying in the dunes. I can honestly say I have had better holidays on a beach.

There was nothing to do but wait. Those who had cigarettes smoked. Those who didn't wished they had. Some had things to read but most just lay in the sand, hungry, thirsty and exhausted. Of course, we barely had any idea what was going on just a few miles away where the 51st Highland Division[130] were fighting to allow us all to get away. We also had no idea how touch and go it was. Now of course everyone knows. And at the time, those in England had some idea. But being there was a vastly different experience.

Night fell. It got cold quite quickly despite the time of year. Quiet descended as more of those around fell asleep. We hadn't seen any more aircraft, but we had heard the sound of guns and bombs alright. Then out of the blue, our Navy minder appeared.

"Come with me, come on, now."

There was a great shuffling as we roused ourselves and followed him into the gloom. It wasn't really dark, partly because of the stars but mainly because of the distant fires in the town. We followed him down to the water's edge where he stopped.

"There's your queue, join it," he said pointing into the water.

"In there," I heard someone exclaim, realising quickly it was me.

"Yes, in there. Boats can't get right in to the shore."

That was apparently all the explanation we were going to get. We all paused for a moment wondering if it could get worse. I stepped into the water and realised it could. It was freezing.

Slowly I walked into the sea, like someone not entirely sure about ending it all by drowning. The others followed me. I could see a darker patch ahead and as I approached it, I realised it was more men. I waded up behind them and stopped. The water was just under waist deep. Either it got warmer with depth or one just got numb with familiarity.

---

[130] Why Flashman mentions 51st Highland Division is a mystery. They were in fact attached to the French Tenth Army on the Maginot Line and withdrew to the Somme thus avoiding Dunkerque. They fought on until the 11th of June when they were due to be evacuated from St Valery. Fog prevented this and with the surrender of the French the next morning, they had no choice but to follow suit. 'Dunkirk' by Hugh Sebag-Montefiore is an excellent source.

"Ow do," said a voice in front of me.

"Good morning," I replied. "Er, might I enquire how long you have been here. In the water I mean?

"About six hours."

"Good God," I replied.

"Too late for tha'. If 'e's thar at all, e's not looking down on tha kindly."

I considered this information. I couldn't disagree with his comments on the almighty. I had long since given up on divine intervention unless as a last resort, but this was not good news at all.

So we stood, bored, freezing our goolies off, wondering what would happen next. I pondered whether the cold water had any long-term effect on the crown jewels. I also pondered how I had ended up here, the long road I had travelled to end up queueing in the channel for a boat. Life is full of imponderables apparently.

The column of men was mostly quiet, resigned to whatever happened next, nothing to talk about, nothing to do but endure the cold. There was a moment of cheer when the sun appeared on the horizon, but this swiftly went a little sour when someone reminded us that the Jerries would be along shortly in their aeroplanes, unhindered by His Majesty's Royal Air Force who were lazing around doing nothing, having bacon and eggs for breakfast and ravishing the local lasses. I didn't like to say but that was exactly what I would have been doing given half a chance.

I heard the buzz at the same time as everyone else, only this time there was nowhere to run to. We frantically searched the skies until someone pointed and shouted. It didn't particularly help to know where they were coming from to be honest. The only decision to make was what if anything one was to do about it.

Most of those ahead of me in the queue just watched. I did the same, wondering whether it was safer under the water or not. 109s they were. Screaming along the shoreline at high speed with their cannon and machine guns spitting lead. They were four abreast which made it hard to assess where their bullets were going. Of course, what also made it hard was that like my own Spitfire, the machine guns weren't particularly suited to ground strafing as they were aimed directly ahead of the fighter and converging. This added a somewhat lottery like element to who was actually in the way as it was only as the ammunition lost its battle with gravity that it descended onto a target.

I heard screams and decided that now was the moment, took a deep breath and dived under. It was still freezing and now I could barely see anything. The seconds stretched away, I thought a saw a shadow race overhead and stood up again.

There was carnage on the beach and in the water. We had been lucky as we were standing more or less between two of the aircraft. But thirty yards either side there was screaming, blood and floating bodies. The worst thing was the injured being dragged back to the shore to be treated and to stop them from drowning.

"Don't lose my bloody place," I heard more than one man shout.

"Boats!" someone else shouted. And indeed there were. Tiny boats that would fit in your garden pond. I stared in disbelief.

"Tha'll do no good staring with tha' mouth open. Tis all there is. Tak' it or leave it."

Only in Great Britain, with an empire covering a third of the world, would we send the Serpentine Rowing Club[131] to retrieve our stricken army from France.

I watched in awe as these wonders motored, or rowed in some cases, up to the heads of the various queues and started hauling men aboard until they were so full they were in danger of capsizing, then ponderously turning round and heading out to sea where I could see numerous bigger ships waiting. Some of them were even warships.

And so it continued all day. All of it. The boats, the screams, the blood and gore, the queue edging forward until one was neck deep, broken occasionally by cheers as one of the Luftwaffe's finest met a watery end flying through the murderous hail that greeted their every foray down the beach. Some of them had taken to attacking the warships further out which seemed hellishly

---

[131] I am not aware of the existence of such a club, but the Serpentine Lake in Hyde Park was and is a popular place for hiring a rowing boat for an hour, so Flashman's comment is presumably facetious.

dangerous to me as they opened up with everything they had and blew the occasional Stuka or 109 from the sky. I did however see one of the warships attempting to get away with smoke pouring from it on all sides.

I was beginning to get delirious I think. Perhaps it was just exhaustion. I had at some point fallen face first into the sea when I dozed off standing up. It woke me up but only to return me to the hell that was the beach at Dunkerque. And then suddenly, I was being hauled over the gunwale of a boat. There were far too many of us in it, but I, along with everyone else, was too tired to care. The light was failing as we turned around and headed out to sea. I don't remember much else. I must have climbed the side of a bigger ship and then somehow gone below. I was reminded of a similar journey many years back when I had sailed the channel in a warship of some kind[132]. That journey seemed a lot more civilised. There was a bar for one thing, not that alcohol really helped my feelings of sickness. But I also found a safe place to hide on that occasion, if there is a safe place on any boat of course. I attempted to do the same now but was largely thwarted by the sheer numbers of men on board and I eventually gave up, settling for a place to lean near the forward rail. The whole place stank of the great unwashed, vomit and piss, mainly because there was absolutely no chance of performing those functions anywhere near the side or the heads as our navy friends like to call them. As I said, very uncivilised.

But at last, we saw cliffs in the distance. I think someone cheered until he was told in no uncertain terms to keep quiet. They crept closer and closer until we finally steamed into the harbour at Dover. We inched towards a dock of some kind until there was a muffled clang and then some shouting. A naval rating came through the boat shouting instructions as to what to do next, something that hadn't actually occurred to most of the men on board. It was quite odd really. There were very few whole units. Most were just stragglers like me. But they were also largely regulars so they took it in their stride assuming that the army would eventually find them. Which it did of course.

---

[132] See 'Flashman and the Knights of the Sky'.

114

"RAF? No idea sir," was the greeting they reserved for me. Apparently not many RAF personnel had been lifted from the beaches. I was sent into a large shed where some office wallah took one look at me and said he only had army warrants for travel. It was at this point I had finally had enough.

"I don't care who signs the bloody warrant, but I have been standing up to my neck in the channel for days only to find that the bloody mess was closed for the crossing, so I haven't had a drink, or anything to eat for some time, so if I were you, and I wanted to retain all my faculties intact, I would sign it, give it to me and forget it ever happened. Or send it to the King. I'm sure he would understand."

Just for once it worked and I left a minute or two later clutching a warrant for travel to London. Now I just had to find the station.[133]

---

[133] See Appendix.

Chapter 28

London was abuzz. The talk was all of invasion. Now our army had come home with its tail firmly between its legs I was quite glad I was in the air force. The navy had managed to largely appear heroic and the RAF had made a bit more noise about how it had been in combat over the beaches, and Churchill had made his speech about how 'we were going to fight them everywhere apparently'. So everyone was happy. For now at least. The Germans weren't in England yet. No one had invaded since the Conqueror and the Home Guard[134] would make sure they didn't now.

Me? I considered the possibility of just vanishing and becoming a statistic of war. Missing in action, presumed dead. Victoria could wear black for a bit before continuing her society life with a tale about her heroic late husband before succumbing to the charms of some other bounder like me. No, it wouldn't do. I liked life too much. But the problem was that once I admitted I was alive and well, I would be right back in the firing line. And of course I had the letter. Quite how I had managed to keep it in one piece I didn't know. And as I thought about it, I realised that was my way out.

It seems strange now in this age of instant communication[135] that I could arrive in London with nobody knowing I was there, pop home to catch up with the wife and family, spend an energetic weekend mostly horizontal although we did use other positions, then on a bright Monday morning tootle down to Whitehall to present the aforementioned letter. "Traitor!" I hear you cry for delaying delivery. Well maybe. On the other hand, Whitehall was largely closed at the weekend and Victoria was most appealing.

---

[134] On 14th May 1940, a radio broadcast announced the formation of the Local Defence Volunteers. A quarter of a million men tried to volunteer in the first week. On the 22nd July, the LDV was renamed the Home Guard.

[135] Flashman's obituary dates his death to 1988, so assuming his manuscripts were written before that he would be astounded at the difference between then and now regarding instant communication.

Menzies did give me a severe stare when I presented myself early. I handed over the envelope in its sailcloth packet without a word.

"Who?" he enquired.

"Goering. With Hess behind it."

"I thought as much." He fell silent while he continued contemplating the contents. "Of course this will be much harder to arrange now that Churchill is in power, albeit his position is less than solid. Still, in some ways, Dunkerque will have helped us. Army and Air Force home. Navy patrolling the Channel. French surrendered. There is a deal to be done, Flashman!" He fell silent again looking at the ceiling. "I have it!" he exclaimed suddenly. "602 Squadron. Based in Glasgow. Far enough away to be discreet, but close enough to..". He stopped suddenly. "Best not to say anything at this stage. Come back here Friday. I will have everything settled by then."

It wasn't hard to work it out really. Glasgow. Clandestine meetings. Royal Auxiliary Air Force Squadron. Hamilton. I was being sent as an emissary for Menzies and all the other plotters to Hamilton, where presumably I would be general dogsbody. Well, that was just nuts to me. Nowhere near the potential fighting especially as it seemed to be the consensus that the first thing that would happen would be the Germans trying to destroy the RAF and you can imagine how near I wanted to be to that.

I spent the week in London with Victoria. We had decided that she and our now nearly adult daughter would stay there initially, at least until I had arranged suitable accommodation in Scotland. She was used to me going away of course but seemed genuinely keen to accompany me on what I imagined would be a rather cushy number. I felt I deserved it having seen far too much of the war already, far more than most. And whilst Scotland was the home of my more severe relatives, or step relatives I should say, it was civilised enough to spend the rest of the war making myself useful whilst others faced the bloody krauts.

I can't remember much of what we did that week, but it was jolly and boded well for our jaunt to the north. I met Menzies on the Friday as requested and he gave me some more information about what he expected of me, which wasn't much fortunately, and then I left. I couldn't help smiling as I ambled into Euston for the train journey, First Class, to the wilds of Glasgow. I should have known better.

Chapter 29

It was slightly awkward. I outranked the new squadron commander and I was significantly older. He was an Auggie,[136] a weekend flier who had been called up just before the outbreak of war. He was 24 and his name was Sandy Johnstone. Luckily, I have the charm of the Arabs and I quickly made it clear my appointment to the squadron was political and I had no wish to step on his toes. I also hinted at times when I would be absent on other service which gave me carte blanche to disappear at awkward moments. At least I hoped it would.

"It's an honour to serve with you, sir. I know you won't like me mentioning it, but I know something of your exploits in the last lot."

He grinned at me and I looked suitably modest.

"Well, it's kind of you to say so. They were interesting times of course."

I left it at that. I was fairly certain it would be common knowledge round RAF Drem in hours.

RAF Drem. It wasn't where I had originally imagined I would be, but the squadron had moved to the estuary coast as its air defence. They had briefly claimed fame as the second squadron to shoot down a German bomber during the Luftwaffe's first raid on Britain in October 1939 when they bombed the shipping in the Firth, 603 squadron being the first during the same raid. Since then, it had gone quiet. Even the krauts had realised that the war wasn't going to be won by bombing Scotland. Consequently, 602 were generally kicking their heels at the same time as straining at the leash to get to grips with the enemy. I sympathised with them and fuelled their fantasies with stories of the epic battles in France. I didn't give them all the details of course, leaving out the frantic relocations and regular destruction of the aircraft on the ground, flying with machines full of holes, generally outnumbered and more worryingly, often outflown. It hadn't really occurred to me before as I had had a busy few months, but the similarity between France 1940 and Bloody April was a little unnerving.

---

[136] Slang for a member of the Royal Auxiliary Air Force.

What was encouraging however was the quiet. The squadron flew most days on patrolling and training sorties. It was deadly dull, but largely safe. I flew most days too, partly to keep my hand in but partly because I enjoyed it. We practiced dogfighting over the North Sea, A flight against B flight, and it became clear that most of them had no idea. Even Johnstone was an amateur. But then that's exactly what he was albeit one with a couple of victories to his name[137]. I suppose that was the point though. They were all reservists and needed plenty of training and that was what they were doing.

Down south things were hotting up of course. The official start date of the Battle of Britain is now recognised as the 10th July for some reason. I'm not sure why as the Luftwaffe were over the channel before that engaging the fighters. I suppose it was when they started bombing the ports and the 10th was when they first did that in force.

It's strange really. If you were underneath, I am sure it was horrifying. But given what happened later in the war, the German bombing campaign was puny, and the destruction was fairly limited. But they kept coming. Ever more and more of them, Ju 88s, Heinkel 111s, Stukas, Dornier 17s all accompanied by the omnipresent 109s.

One thing that the Spitfire and Hurricane pilots discovered quickly was how close and how accurate they had to be for their Brownings to be any use. If they did manage, the 17s and the 88s just fell apart. As for the Stukas, they were most vulnerable as they pulled out of their dives as they were so slow with only one way to go. That was all assuming one could avoid the 109s which, as I had discovered personally, were good and whose pilots were experienced killers.

We carried on training and patrolling the north east coast. I didn't see a sausage let alone a sausage eater. It was perfect.

Churchill made another rousing speech on the 14th July in which he said this would be a war of the unknown warriors, following that on the 18th June which pre-empted the naming of the coming battle and claimed that this would be 'our finest hour[138]'

---

[137] He did indeed, a Heinkel He111, a Junkers Ju88 and damage to a Dornier Do17.

. I can only assume he actually thought the war would last more than an hour. Then it was the turn of the bomber boys who had been sitting about doing nothing for some time[139]. Apparently, they bombed Essen that night although in their Wellingtons and Hampdens they probably did about as much damage as the 88s did. In terms of war, it was a bit like throwing rocks at each other.

However, the most interesting thing that month was Hitler's speech in the Reichstag. Earlier in the day he had promoted Goering to Reichsmarschall at the Kroll[140] presumably with all the savage comic opera that only a proper dictatorship can display. Then in his speech he reviewed the course of the war so far. He missed out the useless Italians getting their warship sunk in the Mediterranean that day, mainly due to their lack of air cover[141] but he did make an appeal direct to Churchill. Not many people noticed the significance of it. I quote it here because of that.

"Mr Churchill, OR PERHAPS OTHERS, for once believe me when I predict a great empire will be destroyed, an empire that it was never my intention to destroy or even to harm. I do realize that this struggle, IF IT CONTINUES, can end only with the complete annihilation of one or the other of the two adversaries. Mr Churchill may believe this will be Germany. I know that it will be Britain."

Later on, he said he could see 'no reason why this war must go on'.

There you have it in black and white. Hitler didn't want it. Why did we? Yes I know it's easy with hindsight, but knowing all

---

[138] See Appendix.

[139] Bomber Command dropped thousands of leaflets initially over Europe but largely refrained from bombing until early 1940. When they did, it was largely ineffective and the aircraft were obsolete, particularly the Fairey Battle which frequently suffered losses of more than 50%.

[140] The Kroll Opera House was situated opposite the Reichstag and after the fire in 1933 was used for sittings of the Reichstag until 1942.

[141] This can only be the Espero, a somewhat antiquated destroyer of the Regia Marina which was in fact sacrificed to save the other two destroyers sailing with it. About 1600 shells were fired by 7th Squadron RN in two hours of fierce fighting before the Espero sank taking most of its crew of 225 with it. It was the first Italian naval loss of the war.

that I knew then from both sides, there seemed few reasons to continue and many to come to terms. Not least of course that we had just been flung ignominiously out of France.

There were also the Mass Observation surveys. The government didn't like to say it but morale in Britain was rock bottom. The general feeling after Dunkerque was that this war was 'one of high up people who use long words and have different feelings' which of course it was. Wars always were. Whatever happened next it was going to take some clever manoeuvring to get the people to fight[142].

I wasn't even sure that Churchill himself believed it. After his speech on the 4th June where he promised to fight them everywhere but the garden shed and that we would never surrender, someone, I daren't say who, told me that as he finished, he muttered 'and we'll fight them with the butt ends of broken beer bottles because that's bloody well all we've got'[143].

The point really was that he was right. We had very little to fight them with. We could defend ourselves alright, provided the Navy could be persuaded to bring their ships out of Scapa[144] and use them for fighting rather than as giant yachts, and what fighters we had were good. But only as good as the man in it. And as I had just seen, and my years of experience had taught me, it took time to train a fighter pilot so that he survived long enough to make a difference. Which brings me neatly back to the squadron. That same night, the Germans bombed the Rolls Royce factory in Glasgow.

---

[142] Mass Observation originally began in 1937 to record every day life in Britain through a panel of about 500 volunteer's diaries or responses to questionnaires. It was used by government in various ways during the war but did have some importance as a barometer of public opinion. Unsurprisingly, morale was recorded as rock bottom after Dunkirk with about half the population expecting the war to continue. The quote is from an MO survey.

[143] This is well documented but as far as I can tell, who he said it to has never been revealed.

[144] The Royal Navy were notorious for not committing their ships to anything and the chain of command via the Sea Lords made for a somewhat autonomous service, but the reality was that if required, the Home Fleet could sail in plenty of time to get to the Channel to confront an invasion force, albeit outside the service this was not well understood.

Someone called the squadron ops room and told them. Quite what we were meant to do about it was unknown. Flying at night was all very well. Flying and trying to find and destroy an enemy were all but impossible. I shivered when I thought about a night over London many years before[145].

The next day, there was a lot of huff and puff in the mess. I kept out of it. The youngsters of course were all for having a crack at finding them next time. I left them to it after a while. I doubted my thoughts on not seeking sorrow unnecessarily would have gone down very well. Not that they would have believed me anyway. It was after this that I was sitting on my own in a deck chair away from the mess having a smoke when Johnstone appeared out of the blue.

"Ah, Flashman," he said in that way people use when they have bad news to impart. "Orders."

I smiled thinly.

"Looks like we are heading south in a couple of weeks. Place called Westhampnett[146]. In Sussex. Do you know it?"

I shook my head. I was unable to speak at that moment.

"In the thick of it at last. Just off to tell the chaps."

I grinned as he turned and strolled off back to the mess. What on earth was Menzies thinking?

---

[145] See 'Flashman and the Knights of the Sky'.
[146] RAF Westhampnett near Chichester in West Sussex was a satellite station for RAF Tangmere.

Chapter 30

Apparently nothing. He wasn't aware, and when I made him aware, he muttered something about everybody doing their bit.

"But didn't you hear what Hitler said?"

"Of course. We all know what needs to be done, but unless we can persuade Churchill, then short of assassination there won't be much we can do. And believe me we have considered it."

"So what now? And what should I do?"

"Do? Go back to your squadron until we sort this mess out."

"Go.... where?"

"You heard me. We need every man we can get. They started bombing the airfields yesterday. There's only so much of that we can take!"

"There must be some mistake. Hitler said 'perhaps others', surely now is the time for those others to make their views known, especially if the population agree. And if the Duke of Ke.."

"For God's sake Flashman, you know better than that."

I stared above his head at the wall. He was right of course. Walls had ears and all that baloney. I glanced around me, searching for inspiration, a way out, anything really that would keep me away from 602 Squadron. There was nothing. I knew it. He knew it.

"When then? When are we going to do this? If not now?"

Menzies stared at the floor now. He knew I was right as well. The entire war stood on a knife edge. As did the peace, or the chance of it. If we didn't take it now, then we would either be destroyed when the Germans invaded, or we would commit ourselves to a desperate and long fight. I say that of course with the benefit of hindsight.

The silence stretched from seconds into minutes. Menzies paced around the room. I kept my own counsel, knowing that I had said enough.

"You are right, of course." He paused again. "Look, you will have to go back for the moment. I will talk to... the group and decide on a course of action. We need to move quickly. I will send a message as soon as I can. You need to be ready to act."

At that he turned on his heel and left his own room. I stood open mouthed. I didn't move for a couple of minutes as I digested what he was expecting me to do. I had had enough of all of it. But what was I to do? If I refused to go back… well it didn't bear thinking about. LMF[147] was a proper disgrace.

******

There was no time to get used to our new home. The raids were getting bigger daily. Ports, airfields, radar masts, all targets. We arrived on the 13th August. We had one day to settle, then the 15th arrived. The day had dawned clear and hot. It was ideal for picnic lunches, strolling in the meadows and fornicating in the bushes. Instead, I was sitting in a deck chair outside the ops room at Westhampnett airfield near Chichester. It was just before eleven in the morning. I had been staring silently at the sky for some time, occasionally following the vapour trails in the distance, wondering who and what. Then the telephone rang. Numerous faces turned to the hut.

"Squadron scramble!"

My heart leapt into my mouth and it took a few seconds for it to register what was going on. Men had jumped up and were running to their aircraft. I automatically followed. As a senior member my aircraft was near the ops room, so I was there in seconds. I jumped onto the wing and climbed in. My crewman started connecting me up to the oxygen and the radio as I did my straps up. My hands were shaking although no one would have noticed as there was so much going on. He jumped off the wing as I pulled the canopy over my head. The trolley acc[148] was ready and with the customary spluttering and groaning the merlin burst into life.

"Chocks away," I signalled and in seconds I was rolling over the grass. I wasn't alone. In fact, the first aircraft were already accelerating over the field. Only seconds later I was airborne as well and climbing to form up on the flight commanders.

---

[147] Lack of Moral Fibre was indeed a serious matter and treatment hadn't advanced that much since the days of the trenches.

[148] Trolley Accumulator. Essentially a set of batteries used to start the engine.

We were at maximum normal power and climbing frantically. Whatever it was, the enemy had been reported at about fourteen thousand feet. It was only a few minutes to climb above them, but they were long minutes. The radio was alive with orders from the fighter controllers, vectoring us and other squadrons onto the Luftwaffe formations, themselves only minutes from the coast.

"Bandits, 10 o'clock low." Johnstone.

"Roger, tally ho."

That was it. I saw them. 88s. I glanced upwards and saw another gang of spitfires a thousand feet or so above us. They must be going for the fighters. My heart lurched as I followed the flight towards the bombers. There was a brief silence on the radio. I flicked the gun button to fire.

"Tally ho," someone shouted again, presumably one of the youngsters.

"Jesus save me," someone yelled in my ear.

And then we were there. I saw the black crosses on their wings get bigger as the range closed. I picked a target, aimed and began firing bursts. Nothing seemed to happen and I hurtled through the formation, passing under them then pulling up into a rolling climb to get back on top. My two wingmen[149] were with me though I had no illusions about how long that would last. Another target presented itself. The Brownings spluttered again and this time I could see the de Wilde[150] bullet strikes on the engine and around the cockpit. There was a puff of smoke and the engine was on fire. The 88 immediately began descending as bits started to fall off. I gave it a final burst before pulling out to look for another target and more importantly not become one myself. We seemed to be on our own, surrounded by Germans. I felt rather than heard the jolt of bullets striking the Spit and immediately took some kind of evasive action. Hard to say what

---

[149] Standard RAF battle formation was a tight V whereas the Luftwaffe used two pairs in a 'Finger Four'. Neither lasted more than a few seconds in a dogfight.

[150] De Wilde bullets were a form of tracer ammunition that flashed on impact giving pilots a much better idea of where their ammunition was going. Originally hand-made, by late 1940 most tracer ammunition was still called 'de Wilde' but was actually a completely redesigned and more effective incendiary ammunition. It still lacked the punch of a cannon shell.

it was because it was instinctive, the Flashman survival technique. I glanced over my shoulder to see if my wingmen were still there, just in time to see one of their engines puff smoke and he fell away. It didn't look fatal, but it left just the two of us.

I took a second to listen to the radio but that didn't help an awful lot, it was just yells really. I was bouncing around the sky trying to avoid the German formation, but it was now breaking up as numerous individual battles took place. I watched with a sort of fascinated horror as an 88 shed a wing, rolled over and plunged straight down taking an 88 below with it. I had seen that sort of thing before of course but it was still terrible. Another 88 appeared in front of me, more or less head on and suddenly I could see its crew aiming at me. I fired a long burst at it and the gods of aerial combat were with me because the nose disintegrated in a shower of glass, metal and assorted body parts before it began a long dive to the ground. I doubted anyone was getting out of that.

I'd like to say that was it. But it wasn't. Unlike the dogfights of the previous war, these ones went on and on because the numbers of bombers were so big. We also had more ammunition and more fuel. Nevertheless, I tried, I promise.

I pulled up after the destruction of the 88, forgetting that the fighters were most likely above me. And sure enough, no sooner had I climbed, a gaggle of them appeared, mixed Spitfires, Hurricanes and 109s, all in a mad whirl of metal. I fired a couple of bursts at passing 109s but didn't hit anything. In fact, I was now concentrating on not colliding with anyone. That always struck me as such a useless way to die.

I tried diving again and almost instantly found myself back in the bomber stream. A Dornier 17 loomed ahead, its top gunner immediately opening up. I had the advantage though and dropped below it, pulling up towards its belly, slowing down briefly as I fired, raking it left to right and having the pleasure of seeing its right engine flame as I swept past. Its crew were now too preoccupied to pay me any attention.

At that point I ran out of ammunition. I had long since lost my second wingman so now seemed like an opportune moment to depart. I rolled away from the bombers and dived at full speed and in seconds it was suddenly quiet. I opened the canopy and felt the cool air flood in drying the sweat that was pouring off me. I glided gently down towards Westhampnett, joining the circuit from the east before landing and rolling back to dispersal where I was instantly joined by various ground crew. I sat in the cockpit contemplating the world for a few minutes before I had the energy to haul myself out.

I nearly fell down when my feet took my weight as I was so drained. But I didn't, and I staggered over to the ops hut to report. A quick glance round told me half the squadron was back including one of my wingmen. The other wouldn't be back for a while I assumed. Most were chattering excitedly about the battle, a few seemed to have hit the occasional German, most had no idea if they had done anything at all.

I stuck my head in the door and the duty grunt took the details of my action. Neither had been confirmed as yet but I imagined the 88 would be when they found the wreckage. The 17 not so sure.

Johnstone appeared looking hot and sweaty.

"Well Flash? Thought I saw you bag one of the buggers?"

"I think so. How about you?"

"109 I think, got a bit shot up for my efforts though. Nothing serious damaged."

"What fun!" I exclaimed and got a slightly mystified stare for my trouble. "Still, back in the thick of it tomorrow shouldn't wonder." With that I left the ops room to find a quiet place to be sick.

The Germans appeared to have given up for the day so we got the stand down call an hour or so later. They would be back.

Chapter 31

They were. Every day. And every day we sat outside the ops room waiting for the bloody phone to ring. The most annoying thing was that everyone used the same phone, so it would ring, everyone would sit bolt upright, I would start to shake and sweat, and it would be the canteen telling us sandwiches were on the way. It was nerve shattering.

The squadron flew almost every day although I didn't necessarily. Apart from being a trifle unhealthy, you would lose your edge very quickly as tiredness overwhelmed you. A day off was apparently all that was needed. I spent mine trying to get to London to see Victoria and succeeded for an unsatisfactory hour and a half. I spoke to Menzies which just confirmed that nothing useful was happening with regard to stopping this nonsense, and then I was back in the thick of it. The talk now was all of invasion and when it might be. It was truly terrifying. Now of course, with the benefit of hindsight, it was all very unlikely. The Germans greatly overestimated their ability to destroy the RAF and Goering couldn't decide whether to bomb the airfields and the factories or something else. They also tried luring the Spitfires and Hurricanes up for a gigantic fighter battle, but again they underestimated the effectiveness of the 'Chain Home' radar which combined with the Royal Observer Corps could largely differentiate between the fighters and bombers meaning we didn't get flung into action with hordes of 109s, which was a blessing of sorts.

I think it was the 18th August that was the most fun so far. The worst thing was that we were in the south, because the squadrons still in the north had the joy of hordes of unprotected bombers coming over, largely it appeared because the Germans thought the RAF was running out of fighters. It was a massacre. Down south it wasn't quite so much fun because the fighters were still there.

It started in the east. A large raid was spotted forming up in the Pas-de-Calais around midday before it set off across the channel. We didn't know this at the time of course. We were just sitting in the sun praying to the gods it wasn't our turn. Well I was. I wasn't sure everyone felt the same. Of course, most of them were only five days into the battle and no one had been killed yet so it all seemed like a fabulous game still. There was no doubt that would change. I just didn't appreciate how soon.

Lunch came and went with the attendant alarm and I was just snoozing in the sun when the phone rang again. This time it was real.

I hauled myself out of my seat and staggered rather than ran towards the spitfire that was sitting armed and ready a few yards away. I jumped onto the wing, clambered in and started the engine. The chocks disappeared again and off we went, rolling slowly over the field before turning into wind. I pushed the throttle and bumped forward, the tailwheel coming up almost immediately. Accelerating, it took only seconds to get airborne and climb into formation before we set course for the coast. The raid was apparently heading for Worthing, that well known military stronghold, and we were going to intercept them just over the channel. We needed to get higher and we strained the aircraft to their limits. We weren't alone either. I heard callsigns for 43, 152, 234 and even 213 coming over from Exeter. It looked like it was going to be one hell of a scrap. I felt my arse clench in my armoured seat, my throat went dry and then I started to sweat.

Minutes passed as we continued climbing. The radio was quiet for a minute. All I could hear was the roar of the merlin and my heart pounding in my ears. Then all hell broke loose.

Chapter 32

"Bandits, bandits," someone yelled. I was already frantically scanning the sky and I saw them instantly. "109s and Stukas," they yelled again.

"Jesus Christ there's hundreds of them!" That was my helpful contribution. But there was. I didn't know at the time how many Spitfires there were, but it wasn't as many as that. The only blessings that I could see were that quite a lot of the 109s were in close escort, some were too far away, and the Stukas were sitting ducks. As I watched I saw the Stukas begin their dives. They were about twelve thousand feet as they nosed over. It was too tempting for most of the Spitfires and they started to follow them down. We were near enough overhead Ford airfield and as I followed the rest of them, I could see aircraft on the ground although judging by the shape they were biplanes. I picked a target and followed him, my wingmen doing the same I imagine.

It only took seconds to lose about ten thousand feet, the bombs were away and pretty accurate they looked to me, and then the doomed Stukas started pulling out, straight into a maelstrom of lead. I saw my Stuka take a long raking burst, a plume of smoke shot from its nose and then I heard a scream on the radio.

"Christ those 109 bastards are on us!"

They were but all I could think of at that moment was the dressing down whoever had said that would receive for his shocking abuse of radio discipline. You could blast the bloody Jerries to Kingdom Come but God forbid you should swear out loud so everyone could hear.

Anyway, back to the fight. I pulled up hard and glancing in the mirror saw I had acquired a tail. There was no sign of the other two, not that I really expected them to be there. I hurled the Spit around the sky, desperately trying to anticipate what Hans was going to do. I was running out of ideas when a flash in my mirror revealed he had blown up. There was just a cloud of smoke and falling wreckage where once there had been a man and machine. I breathed a sigh of relief, thanked the Gods of fighter pilots and pulled round in a hard climbing turn. A Spit flashed in front of me followed by a Hurricane; what the hell he was doing there was anybody's guess; then a 109 chasing them both. I fired a burst but it was ineffectual.

Looking round nearly gave me a seizure. There were aircraft everywhere. Spitfires, Hurricanes, 109s and the occasional Stuka although they didn't last long. Either they scarpered or they were destroyed. I was sweating profusely as I tried to stay alive. It was a manic version of the dogfights of the Great War. At least I had a parachute.

I glanced in my mirror again. Nothing, well at least nothing threatening. There seemed to be no way out though. Wherever I turned were more and more fighters in a swirling maelstrom of extreme violence laced with a sort of murderous chivalry. The more I looked the more I saw aircraft trailing smoke or on fire and then the parachutes as some at least bailed out.

There was a sudden bang and the Spitfire shuddered. I knew instantly I was in trouble but again checking the mirror I had no idea where it had come from. Smoke started seeping from the engine and I could smell it in the cockpit. The seep became a stream, the shaking got worse and I felt the controls turn sluggish. I wasn't very high as the fight seemed to have slowly descended below eight thousand feet. I was over water, but I could see the coast no more than half a mile away. Turning towards it I glanced in the mirror again to see a 109 filling it. I nearly soiled myself. He opened fire and I felt the Spitfire shudder again with the impact of the cannon shells. Clearly he meant to kill me.

I slammed the throttle shut and pulled up with full right rudder. For a second he thought he had me, but he was going too fast. Without power, the damaged Spitfire slowed instantly and the rudder flung me over into a spin. The 109 shot by and I assumed, or hoped at least, that he would lose interest. Of more immediate concern was recovering from the spin. And then getting out.

I reversed the rudder and pushed. The Spitfire stopped spinning but was now heading downwards at frightening speed[151]. I pulled the canopy release and luckily the airflow snatched it

---

[151] Spin recovery in a Spitfire was standard but it used up at least two thousand feet, partly because the speed needed to be at least 150mph before attempting to pull up or it would stall again.

away. Here I was again I thought, other side of the channel this time, undoing my harness, struggling out of the seat, and then rolling over the side. The tail narrowly missed me as I fell and I grabbed for the 'D' ring and pulled hard. The chute blossomed above me and only at that moment did I look down and realise I was going in the water. Yet again, a nice dip in the bloody channel. I had a moment or two to reflect and I glanced up at the battle which was still raging above me.

I splashed into the water, inflated my mae west[152] and wondered what to do next. It wasn't that far to the coast, but I was exhausted already. On the other hand, the water was cold as always. No choice. I started swimming in a kind of dog paddle breaststroke having relieved myself of as much drag as possible. It was hard to tell but wherever it was appeared to be getting bigger albeit very slowly. I guessed it was mid-afternoon. The battle overhead had suddenly finished as they did and the world had gone quiet, apart from the squawks of seagulls and the occasional sound drifting out from the coast.

Then, out of the blue, a boat appeared. It was motorised, heading along the coast and obviously military of some kind. I frantically waved my arms and shouted. Almost immediately it turned towards me and approached, slowing down as it got to me. They had boathooks and other charming stuff to haul one out of the water and in mere seconds I was laying on the deck.

"Flashman! What the hell are you doing here?" It was the lunatic Finucane.

"Just out for an afternoon swim old boy. You?"

"Same. 109 bounced me when I went down after those Stukas. Didn't last more than a minute shouldn't wonder."

How we laughed at this in true stiff upper lip style. No choice of course, couldn't have the hoi polloi thinking we were absolutely terrified, although I did wonder if friend Paddy was quite the ticket. Irish of course[153].

---

[152] Life jacket, so called because inflated it made the wearer appear to have the same chest characteristics as the actress.

[153] This presumably is Wing Commander Paddy Finucane, DSO, DFC though I cannot find a record of him being shot down on the 18th. He came to England in 1936 and joined the RAF in 1938 and was posted to 65 Squadron.

"We'll be out for a little while longer. Still one of you chaps missing." This was a navy type who appeared to be in charge of the boat[154]. "Quite a scrap it looked like from down here."

"Yes it was," replied Paddy. "Did you hit anything Flash?"

"I thought I hit a Stuka and maybe a 109 but then got shot up by someone I didn't even see." I shivered again at this thought. "Then one of the bastards had the nerve to have another go when it was obvious I was going down."

"Bloody cheek!" exclaimed Paddy. "This isn't an uncivilised free for all. There are rules!"

He seemed quite indignant and I drifted off as he and the navy bod compared relatives. As with all Irishmen, they knew everyone.

We continued our jolly ride along the coast for another hour or so before we headed for port. We landed somewhere near Lee on Solent where the Fleet Air Arm had a base. They seemed to have their own little jetty so we were dropped off and sent to the front gate to organise transport and hopefully something to eat and drink. I realised I hadn't eaten for hours.

After the Andrew[155] had had their fill of mickey taking, they found some transport and we set off home. It took ages of course because getting anywhere took ages and it was nearly nine before we got to the main gate. The guards recognised us and within minutes we were sitting in the mess where I intended to get drunk.

His first victory was on 12th August. In January 1942 he was posted to 602 Sqdn as a flight commander not long after this being promoted Wing Commander. His last mission was one of the controversial fighter sweeps over France. He was hit by ground fire, attempted to get back across the Channel but didn't make it. Saying 'This is it Butch' to his wingman Alan Aikman, he ditched and was never seen again. He was 21.

[154] They were both lucky. The RAF Marine Craft Section had 13 high speed launches at the time. There was a distinct lack of coordination in rescue operations and only about 20% of aircrew who landed in the channel were rescued. About 200 pilots were lost in the channel during the Battle of Britain.

[155] Slang for Royal Navy. Short for Andrew Miller, reputedly a notorious member of a Press Gang.

Chapter 33

I woke the next morning with a stinker of a head. I had been a virgin until the day before of course. They say the first time is truly terrifying. After that, it's just terrifying. I'd like to say one gets used to it. But you don't. Being shot down I mean. I think the record was five times in the Battle of Britain[156]. Of course for the RAF it was an occupational hazard but for me floating down to earth was akin to losing a feline life. Fortunately, I wasn't down to fly that day. Even the air force realised that having the kind of day I had had was not great preparation for another day in the sky. I wasn't alone. Three 602 Spitfires had been destroyed the previous day and one other damaged. Luckily, no one was dead and everyone had got back to the base eventually[157]. We weren't short of pilots as a squadron. Experienced pilots yes. On the other hand, every day raised the levels and we could only hope the Luftwaffe had the same problems. Of course, their other problem was that anyone shot down would be taken prisoner whereas we were fighting again quickly. Unfortunately for me.

The next few days passed slowly, particularly up to the 23rd as the weather had turned with low cloud and rain. It was respite for us and pure frustration for the Jerries. Churchill made another speech. We had heard it all before of course but there was one line that would resonate through history. "Never in the field of human conflict, was so much owed, by so many, to so few."[158] We would become 'the Few'. It was a name that would buy immortality. Not literally obviously because dead was still dead,

---

[156] Many Battle of Britain pilots were shot down multiple times. As far as I can tell the record was five. For Flashman this was the first time being shot down, although not his first time using a parachute.

[157] As far as I can tell this is accurate. FO CJ Mount's aircraft was damaged in a fight with a 109 but he managed to land at Westhampnett. Flt Lt J. Dunlop-Urie's aircraft was irreparably damaged in a fight with a 109. He also landed at Westhampnett having been shot in the legs. Sgt E.P.Whall ditched his Spitfire after shooting down two Ju87s. He was subsequently killed in a crash on 7th October. The fourth pilot I have been unable to identify.

[158] This is possibly one of the most famous speeches ever made in the English-speaking world. Churchill is said to have coined the phrase on leaving the Ops Bunker at RAF Uxbridge a few days previously.

and it wouldn't help them at all. But for the survivors, it was being able to say, 'I was there'. And like the survivors of Trafalgar, or Waterloo, or Crecy, or Agincourt, or Blenheim, or the Armada, or The Charge, or Isandlwana, or Rorke's Drift, or Ypres, or…. well there were so many where government had sent too few men into battle with a superior and better armed enemy and closed its eyes and hoped for the best, only those that were there really knew.

Then normality resumed. And the Luftwaffe made what with hindsight was possibly their biggest mistake. The bombers came over, the Spitfires and Hurricanes launched to fight them, the 109s fought the fighters, the bombers tried to bomb the ports and installations and then the airfields as well. And one flight made a critical error. Navigation without reference to the ground below was extraordinarily difficult to get right and that was without taking evasive action to avoid being killed. Whatever the reasons, they decided they were over their target and dropped their loads. The bombs exploded in the City and West End. It was Saturday 24th August 1940.

The casualties mounted, especially amongst the newer pilots. I think we were lucky on the whole. We lost aircraft but not a single pilot. Everyone bailed out or force landed their aircraft. And it became obvious that even if every squadron was experiencing the same thing, or even slightly worse, the Luftwaffe was not destroying the RAF which we had all realised was their aim, particularly if they needed air superiority over the Channel.

Our own bombers had hit the Channel ports on the other side to try and disrupt the invasion fleet as well. And one assumed the navy might deign to join in at some point. But the biggest factor at this point was Churchill's apparent outrage at the bombing of the imperial capital. His retaliation was to order the RAF to bomb Berlin. The results were pathetic except for one thing. Hitler.

Chapter 34

I could imagine his rage. He would have been apoplectic. The arrogance of it. The sheer impudence of it. The best thing would have been Goering cowering under his spittle, pretending that it wasn't that bad, and that the Luftwaffe would now destroy everything and it would never happen again.

It took a few days for it to manifest itself, days full of action I assure you. I didn't manage to shoot down anything, at least nothing that was confirmed. I had a couple of close calls myself. Biggin had a particularly bad day but even then, it was only closed for a couple of hours. We were helped by the 109s apparently changing their tactics to close escort which meant they were slower and near the bombers instead of hunting for targets and everyone knows that's not the best way to protect slower aircraft. Everyone except the bomber crews of course who think fighter pilots are just prima donnas flouncing round the sky showing off.

On the 4th of September, Hitler apparently made a speech in Berlin promising that the Luftwaffe would drop a hundred times as many bombs on London as the RAF were dropping on Berlin and that he would raze England's cities to the ground. It was utter fantasy of course but none of us really knew that at the time.

In higher places they realised pretty quickly that if he did as he promised, it was tantamount to admitting defeat. But then friend Hitler knew best. It was a couple of days before the strategy really got going but on the night of the 7th, a Saturday, what became known as the Blitz started. The RAF quietly breathed a sigh of relief whilst watching in despair as London started taking the brunt. Hitler could not have known it but at this point fighter command was in fact stronger than at the start of the battle. Someone told me much later that the numbers of pilots increased throughout the battle albeit their ability to shoot down the Germans perhaps didn't.

Anyway, following that raid the weather turned nasty again and it was the morning of the 15th when I was next on duty. The day dawned bright as expected. I nervously assumed my position at the ops hut and sat in the sun smoking, hoping that by some miracle or other the Germans might have surrendered, or lost all their maps of Britain or some other unlikely but uplifting scenario.

It was silent. The phone didn't ring at all, but somehow news got through that the Germans had launched a big raid. Park[159] had apparently scrambled most of the group from his Uxbridge bunker where apparently the Prime Minister had turned up to visit and stayed to watch the drama unfold. It was nearly midday before the engagement began. The news that reached us was confusing and there was nothing decisive.

There is a famous photo somewhere of a Dornier 17 that was downed over London that day[160]. Apparently, it had had engine trouble or something that had caused it to lag behind the main formation. Consequently, it became a sitting duck and was surrounded by fighters. Having all had a go, it was still flying until Flight Sergeant Ray Holmes, having run out of ammunition decided to finish it off by flying into it. It was quite a feat really when you think about it. It's hard enough to hit anything moving at speed if one of you is stationary, let alone to hit it when you are both moving at hundreds of miles per hour, but he managed it, his port wing shearing off the tailplane. As the stricken Dornier plunged out of the sky the wings came off and the photo shows it just before impact on Victoria Station. It was also that same raid when some bombs fell on the palace prompting the Queen's comment about being able to look Londoners in the eye now their house had been bombed.[161]

Holmes' adventures also continued shortly after the collision as he quickly realised his Hurricane had had it as well. In a vertical dive he bailed out, hit the roof and tailplane of the Hurricane before finally getting his chute open and losing his boots.

He landed in a dustbin near Victoria station from where he was retrieved by the locals and subjected to numerous women adoring him. Life wasn't so good for the Dornier pilot who also

---

[159] Air Vice-Marshal (later Air Chief Marshal) Sir Keith Rodney Park, 11 Group Commander during the battle. See Appendix.

[160] A copy of this photo is posted on my website.

[161] Not quite right. The Palace was hit for the first time on the 13th September, prompting the Queen's remark.

138

bailed out but died from his wounds. It was never clear if they were battle wounds or inflicted by the enraged population.

But I digress. The morning went by painfully, nerve shatteringly slowly. I ate half a sandwich and had more tea. It was getting cloudier steadily which was good news. But then, at twenty past two, the blasted phone rang like the town crier[162]. I knew what was coming.

"Scramble," he shouted and I was up and trotting before I knew it. Usual procedure. Engine started, checked, throttle up and airborne in moments, setting course for Biggin and a holding pattern. The chatter had started and there were aircraft everywhere. It sounded like there were two streams of bombers with hundreds of fighters, but there were also hundreds of RAF fighters harassing them and it wasn't long before the first aircraft had been shot down. We were ordered to engage but with the deepening cloud it wasn't easy to find anyone. We cruised about looking for trade but found none. It wasn't until the bomber streams turned round and tried to get home that we bounced them.

There were still aircraft everywhere you looked, bombers retreating, fighters arriving to escort them home and the Hurricanes and Spitfires almost getting in each other's way in their eagerness to get at the bombers. But our chance came.

"Bandits, bandits," someone screamed and we rolled over in a descending turn to come down on top of them. It was a mix of bombers and fighters, all heading for the coast, the fighters probably low on fuel especially because they had burnt a lot of it in close escort, the bombers shot up and also desperate to reach the Channel as well as fighter cover sent over later to cover the retreat.

They were sitting ducks really. The entire squadron pounced on them from above, the .303s tearing into the fragile aircraft and it was only moments before bombers started to fall out of formation smoking or on fire followed by parachutes blossoming below. I did see some 109s, but they were pretty ineffective. There seemed to be private battles everywhere, con trails criss-crossing the sky, smoke from burning aircraft, floating wreckage.

---

[162] Town Crier's usually rang a bell so perhaps this is what Flashman is referring to.

I emptied my guns in less than five minutes, mainly because there were so many targets. I thought I saw a Dornier break up after I had emptied the last of my ammunition into it, but to be honest I was more concerned about colliding with someone. There had been a couple of collisions that day according to the rumours as well as the one over the palace and as I have mentioned before I did not want to be that statistic.

Guns empty, sweating like a pig but for once not particularly shaking in my boots I returned to Westhampnett with my wingmen. It looked like everyone made it.

We didn't know it at the time of course but that was pretty much that. The battle was over bar the shouting. The next day was quiet and we didn't even get airborne. There were a couple of skirmishes with lone raiders or small groups over the next few weeks, but I didn't get near any of them. There was a raid on the 18th and as far as I know, that was pretty much the last big daylight raid of the war. The Luftwaffe had changed to night bombing, or more correctly, exclusively night bombing. There was little defence against that. Neither the Spitfires nor Hurricanes were any use. I had palpitations at the thought, again remembering the night over London many years before. The Defiants[163] had a go but they were equally useless. They had to do something I suppose otherwise public opinion might have something to say. In a way I am surprised it didn't as the casualties mounted in London. The bombing became relentless and probably the worst thing, according to Victoria anyway, was that the sirens seemed to go off regardless of where the raid was headed meaning no one got a decent night's sleep. The barrage balloons were still largely ineffective and the anti-aircraft guns that had appeared everywhere were more for show than anything,

---

[163] The Boulton-Paul Defiant was a 'turret fighter' and something of an anomaly. It was thought the turret would allow it to intercept and destroy slow moving bombers but the lack of forward firing guns was a serious weakness. It's effectiveness was thus erratic. If enough aircraft could be positioned in an effective firing position, the destructive power was hard to counter and occasionally it was mistaken for a Hurricane giving the following 109 a lethal surprise, but more often than not, the casualty rates were huge with entire flights being shot down. It was eventually moved to the night fighter role before being superseded completely.

most of their ammunition ending up back on the ground. No one would ever admit it, but I imagine a fair percentage of the civilian deaths were self-inflicted.

Once it was certain the RAF was safe and any invasion was at least delayed, I got my marching orders again. Summoned to Menzies office, it appeared there was to be a strategy meeting to decide what to do next. I couldn't help but wonder what the point was but at least I was off operations and back in London enjoying myself. If I could wangle it, that was where I intended to stay as well. Some hope.

Chapter 35

Menzies was considering what was to be done. Apparently, those who thought there was a chance of a negotiated peace were going to join us shortly. I hadn't so far contributed to the meeting.

"Stalemate," he said. "I think the chance of invasion now is over although obviously we don't want the general public to think that. But beating him will be a long hard road and just not possible on our own. Even with the Empire we don't stand a chance. So, what do we do to convince Marlborough to negotiate?" Marlborough was Menzies' pet name for Churchill[164] and the question was clearly rhetorical. I kept mum. "Nothing, because he won't. We have to find a way to convince a majority of other influential people on the inside. It shouldn't present that many problems, what with Kent openly on our side. I think the bigger conundrum is how we convince the Germans. It's all very well fighting the Luftwaffe to a standstill and we know the Navy is superior in general, but neither of those things are any good for fighting in Europe."

All good points really, although I doubted the Germans needed that much convincing given Hitler's stated position. The biggest problem as I saw it was who would end up with egg on their face. No politician would risk that if they could avoid it by sacrificing a generation of young men instead.

"What if one of them came over here?" This was me. I don't know to this day why I said it.

"What on earth do you mean?" Menzies.

"Well, say for example, someone like Hess or Goering came over here and met with the influential people you talk of. If it could be done secretly maybe, and then present Churchill with a fait accompli."

There was a moment or two of silence while he digested this.

"It's a long shot," murmured Menzies. "But it could be done." I could almost see the cogs in his head whirring. "If we could contrive to get Kent to appear publicly with the Germans, with a plan for an honourable peace, and do it on Churchill's front porch, it just might work. A kind of palace coup."

---

[164] Churchill's grandfather was the 7th Duke of Marlborough.

You see, I should just keep my mouth shut really. I had set a train of thought running that he hadn't considered and before long he would be coming up with some kind of plan. And that, as I should have known all too well, would involve me in some ridiculous and no doubt dangerous role. It was too late now though.

"Dungavel," Menzies exclaimed. "Of course!"

"What about it?" I said.

"Red Cross." I stared at him none the wiser. "Well, don't you see?"

"No, not really."

"Neutral ground. Dungavel." He stared at me as if that would be enough. "There is a Red Cross station at Dungavel. That effectively makes it neutral territory. There's also a runway that the RAF use for emergencies. And the occasional Blenheim[165] lands there so it's long enough for most German aircraft. At least that's what Hamilton told me."

"Excellent. That's so perfect as to be almost unbelievable." He began pacing the room. "Hedin[166]. We need to get in touch with the Germans. And Hamilton. And we need to do it soon." He was virtually foaming at the mouth with excitement. "Flashman. Get yourself up to Turnhouse. Hamilton is there. We need to start getting some details on this plan and we can't do it without Hamilton. And we need him to get Kent involved properly. And everyone else he knows. How do we get in touch with the Germans these days?"

"Lisbon. Violet Roberts. We have already had a letter from her of course[167]."

---

[165] The Bristol Blenheim was a light bomber that came into service in 1937. Like so many WWII aircraft it was obsolete almost immediately. On 14th May 1940, a combined force of 71 Fairey Battles and Bristol Blenheims lost 40 aircraft, probably the highest ever loss on any RAF operation in history underlining the obsolescence of both types.

[166] Presumably Sven Hedin. A Swedish academic, explorer and admirer of the German empire, there is some evidence that he was in contact with Hamilton and had agreed to mediate a peace deal, largely it would seem because he supported the idea of crushing the Bolshevik menace which in turn meant avoiding conflict with Britain.

[167] Violet Roberts with her late husband had met the Haushofers before

"Have we by God? When did that arrive?"

"A couple of days ago."

"What the hell was it about?"

"She said Hamilton had already asked her to contact his friend Haushofer. She didn't say why but I think we can guess."

"So, Hamilton has got the ball rolling already! Excellent! I was at school with her nephew of course[168]. Flashman, what are you still doing here man?" He grinned at me which was somewhat disconcerting given his usual demeanour. "I have a good feeling about this."

******

For once my rank actually meant something as Menzies ordered someone somewhere to allocate me a Spitfire for my personal use. I used it to fly from Northolt to Turnhouse. It was late when I arrived so I didn't see Hamilton till the next morning. He seemed somewhat on edge, but I knew how that felt. Plotting against governments was an unnerving experience as I well knew.

"It's a pleasure to meet you again Wing Commander Flashman." If he had winked at me I wouldn't have been surprised but I wasn't sure he meant what he said. "I would offer you some tea, but we can't talk here. Come with me."

We left the room, he mumbled something to a WAAF[169] girl and we left through a side door where there was a car waiting.

"Hop in," he said before getting in the driver's seat himself. "Dungavel. About as safe as we could hope."

The journey was quiet, but it didn't take too long. There wasn't much traffic and the road was empty by the time we drove in the gates of Dungavel. It was quiet at the house. Hamilton let

---

the Great War. Her father was a prominent landowner in Renfrewshire and would have known the Hamiltons. There was a PO Box address in Lisbon that was used for correspondence to and from Germany.

[168] Walter Roberts worked for the recently established SOE as their finance director. He was at Eton with Menzies.

[169] Women's Auxiliary Air Force, predecessor to the Women's Royal Air Force.

us in, glancing behind him as he did so which gave me a quick palpitation.

"There's no one here. Servants are all away or at Turnhouse. My office is this way."

I followed him in silence through a corridor, past the meeting room from before the war. That already seemed like an age ago. He stopped at a solid door, took out a key, unlocked it and I followed him in.

"Take a seat." I did as he bid and he sat down behind a large desk. I waited for him to speak again. He contemplated the ceiling for a couple of minutes. "This is going to be appallingly difficult. Churchill is a tenacious opponent." It was the first time I had really heard him described as such. "He is ruthless and he won't worry about a few innocent victims along the way." By that I assumed he meant me. "I suspect he is already well aware of us, but he doesn't feel strong enough to take us on openly. Not yet at least. And we do have numerous powerful allies, albeit he has managed to get some of them sent abroad. Not that we really need Halifax and Hoare here. In fact, they are useful where they are[170]. So, what did Menzies suggest?"

"Get them over here. Organise a palace coup. Something like that anyway."

"Yes, that could work." He pondered the ceiling again. "When you say here, do you mean right here?"

"Well yes actually. Sinclair mentioned the Red Cross."

"Exactly. Dungavel is two things. An emergency landing ground with a long enough runway for most medium aircraft and a neutral Red Cross post. If we can fly a German delegation here, Churchill would be risking a lot to flout that neutrality. He would do it without thinking, but he would need to be very sure that he would win. There are plenty in the Commons ready to assassinate him. Lloyd George for one. Who I wonder?"

I wasn't sure if he was looking for an answer, so I kept quiet.

"Got to be Hess really."

---

[170] Hoare had been sent to Spain as Ambassador. Halifax was still Foreign Secretary at this moment but shortly to be sent to Washington as Ambassador.

I suddenly realised that more or less my whole life had led up to this moment.

"I have written to Haushofer already. It will be some time before we get a reply but if I know my man, we will need to meet him somewhere else to thrash out the details. Sweden probably. Churchill's cronies will have seen the letter, but they won't stop it. Not yet anyway. Plus, they won't actually know everything it says."

That finished the conversation. We spent some time working out details of how, when and where but that wasn't particularly difficult.

"I can get a weeks leave easily enough. We just need to give ourselves some time for the letter to get there and back. A month or so should do it."

And that was that. I went back to Turnhouse and flew south and waited. It was a strange period of the war. The threat of invasion was receding even in the minds of the public at large although the government didn't say anything much about it. Each day it didn't happen was enough and people generally get bored of preparing for something that seems less and less likely to happen. The RAF carried on bombing Germany and the Luftwaffe carried on bombing Britain. On the face of it the raids seemed large and devastating, but the reality was they were like pinpricks on an elephant. Most of the ground fighting seemed to be between the Greeks and the Italians and the eyeties came off worst. But then they hadn't really been interested in fighting since the end of the Roman empire whereas the Greeks probably saw it as a chance for revenge for the empire inflicting so much indignity on them. Whatever it was, the Greeks largely won.

British troops were fighting too, mainly in North Africa. Luckily, they were also fighting the Italians so despite looking handsome in the heat, the eyeties got a thrashing there as well. Churchill even made another speech at some point imploring them to give up, kick Mussolini out and join us. He was wasting his time. They were too busy sitting awkwardly on the fence and most of the population were unaffected so couldn't care less.

Autumn was beginning to cast its gloomy pall over everything, and then suddenly things got exciting.

Chapter 36

I know what you were thinking. Something warlike. I promise you that was never as exciting as a female showing up. I was waiting at Northolt for delivery of a new Spitfire as I had nothing else to do. Mine had been mostly written off by some mad Pole in his Hurricane when he landed with his wheels up, slewed across the grass and buried his wing in the tail of my Spit[171].

Consequently, I was sitting outside the mess staring at the sky and smoking endlessly sipping the occasional gin and tonic when the unmistakeable growl of a merlin interrupted my reverie. I watched it join the pattern, saw the wheels come down as it turned onto a short final approach, hop over the fence and touch down beautifully. The canopy slid back, and it rolled over to the dispersal area where much to my surprise a woman jumped out. I automatically ran a hand through my hair and stood slightly taller whilst adopting the pose suitable for a first meeting with someone I may become intimate with.

I watched her walk towards me and there was an air of familiarity that I couldn't place. There was also a confident swagger that had my loins stirring. She reminded me of Hanna, not least because I hadn't had another woman since. Well apart from Victoria of course.

"I'm looking for Wing Commander Flashman. Know him?"

I smiled. "You found him."

"First Officer Amy Johnson[172]." Suddenly I knew why she seemed familiar.

"Drink?"

"Lovely. Mines a double."

We retired to an empty mess and I ordered two doubles. Well why not! It was after midday.

"A little different to your previous exploits is it not?"

---

[171] Presumably 303 Squadron, an all Polish unit based at Northolt until the 11th October 1940.

[172] Amy Johnson was the first woman to fly solo from England to Australia in 1930. She joined the Air Transport Auxiliary on its formation. The ATA moved and delivered aircraft around the country. See Appendix.

"Just doing my bit. Plus, it's the only way I get to fly that."
She nodded towards the Spitfire that was sitting outside tinkling
to itself as it cooled. "And everything else of course. You?
What's your history?" Direct. I liked that. So I told her.

"They tell me I am an ace. Again."

"What's it like? Combat that is. And please don't tell me how
glorious it is."

"Terrifying. Utterly terrifying. The hardest thing is trying not
to collide with anyone. They tell you there are tactics and ways of
defeating your opponents. There are. But most of it is completely
irrelevant once you are in the thick of it. You need to be quick to
react, quick to decide and never, ever stop looking at your tail. Do
that and you are dead." I took a slug of gin while she considered
what I had said. "Fancy a go?"

"What?"

"Fancy a dogfight? Just you and me of course but it would be
interesting."

"Of course. Lead the way." She smiled.

It took an hour to arrange. I had to borrow a Hurricane from
the Poles, but they were always ready for a bit of fun and in fact
decided to come and join us. The airfield reverberated to the
sound of the merlins starting. I grinned at Amy as she slid her
canopy shut and rolled across the field. I followed her to the end
of the runway, checked everything and trundled on behind her[173].

"Let's go." a Polish voice said sounding far too excited. I
powered up, following the lone Spitfire down the runway. The
tail lifted and seconds later the aircraft lifted off. I put the wheels
up and we climbed away. We passed through five thousand feet
and turned towards the coast, forming up in a finger four. We
carried on that way until we crossed the coast and then with a
shout of tally-ho we split up into two pairs, both with a Polish
wingman.

I climbed initially before turning back to find her. For a
moment I had a minor panic thinking I'd lost her until Polski or
whatever his name was screeched through the radio that she was
twelve o'clock high. How on earth she had got above us I had no

---

[173] Northolt was deemed important enough to have a concrete runway
added in 1939.

148

idea. For a moment I had no idea what to do. But she wasn't a fighter pilot so it should be easy enough to get on her tail. I suddenly grinned to myself and lifted the nose to point straight at the Spitfire. She was coming straight at me now. I had a momentary flashback to the last lot. Christ that seemed a long time ago now. I had been in a DH2 heading straight at some German bugger shortly before I killed him. I shivered at the memory[174].

We were closing fast and I wondered what she would do. There were a few seconds to go and I felt she was taunting me as the Spitfire loomed in the windscreen. I counted to three then shoved the stick forward, saw the Spit go over and pulled hard. I came over the top and as I expected she had been too slow. I rolled right way up and she was directly in front of me slowing slightly and caught right in my sights.

"Gotcha!"

"Yes, this time. Go again?"

So we did. Six times I think. She was a fast learner. Each time she evaded me for longer before I got on her tail. The sixth time she caught me out like a bloody wet behind the ears novice straight from flying school. Our Poles were having a jolly time chasing each other so we were on our own. We had started from a head on pass and I pulled up into my old favourite, an Immelmann[175], expecting to find her below me but she had vanished. I grinned to myself for a moment whilst frantically scanning the sky and my mirror, all the while flying straight and level in astonishment. As the seconds passed, my search became more and more frantic. Realising I hadn't turned for some time, I rolled hard to port and pulled right round in a full circle. Nothing. Not a sausage. I tried the same to the right. Still nothing.

"Gotcha!" a female voice said on the radio. I nearly propelled myself through the canopy.

"Where are you?"

"Look behind you."

I did and saw nothing.

---

[174] See 'Flashman and the Knights of the Sky'.

[175] An Immelmann turn was a reversing course manoeuvre made famous by the man himself.

"I can't see you."

"Keep looking."

I did and as I stared the Spitfire rose from below me into view. I was dead.

"How…" I spluttered.

"Outside loop just after you pulled up." I could almost hear her chuckling.

"Let's go home. Well done."

I didn't begrudge it. It was well done. Never even occurred to me that she would push hard down just as I couldn't see her and go right under, coming out underneath and then climbing straight at me into my blind spot. She had guessed I wasn't keeping quite as good a watch as I should have been and so sat underneath me matching my every move until she admitted she was there.

I got back to Northolt in about ten minutes, landed, shut down and slid back my canopy. I was sweating as always and sat in the cockpit for a couple of minutes cooling down. She landed a minute or so after me.

"Dinner?"

"Why not." She smiled. There was a twinkle in her eye.

"When do you need to get back?"

"I think I can put it off for a day or so."

If you look at photos of the time, she was handsome rather than attractive but there was something about her. Maybe it was the fame. We went up to London. I knew a discreet restaurant hidden in the back streets of Piccadilly where the maitre'd kept a table for me if I should ever need it. This was one of those occasions. It was an interesting evening. I wasn't normally one for hearing about others exploits but I made an exception for her. After all, she was probably the most famous woman in aviation circles, not least for her recent divorce. We talked for hours really, also unlike me. Eventually, having demolished a significant amount of average wine and most of a bottle of Macallan. I believe it was a 25-year-old, always a pleasure of course, but my plan was for a 40-year-old. I think she was thinking the same.

The RAF club always had a room and a little grease for the porter to turn a blind eye meant we were not noted in the log. There was a raid somewhere that night. We ignored it because quite frankly, she was using her experience to good effect and I didn't get to sleep before about three in the morning. All in all, I had had a rather good day.

You may be wondering why I tell you all this of course. Simple really. I needed someone to perform an unusual task. It involved moving some rather heavy boxes discreetly. And if someone had an aeroplane and carte blanche to fly it around, well that would be a real bonus. And I never saw the point of making life too difficult so a bit of fun on the side would be a nice bonus. All I needed to do now was make sure Amy agreed. And we were half-way there on that front.

Chapter 37

"I do like a conspiracy!" She was sitting astride my thighs gently riding almost as if she was trotting around the countryside. I had my eyes closed. "And there are royal people involved as well. How charming! Do you think breakfast will be long?"

I hadn't given it much thought to be honest, distracted as I was. Clearly the thought inspired her to the gallop and she cleared the final fence with aplomb before collapsing beside me just over the finish line. Breakfast appeared, was demolished and then we got dressed. I did briefly consider an extra furlong or two but decided against it. Besides, she was up and about and contemplating mischief of a different kind.

It was a fairly straightforward job given all that had happened so far. I needed her to get something a bit bigger than a Spitfire, meet me at RAF Lincoln in a week's time and then take me north. She promised me it would be simple. For once it actually was. I was, for the first time in quite a while, actually enjoying myself.

It was a Friday evening when I arrived at Lincoln. I parked my Spitfire and popped into the mess who were expecting me. I had a couple of drinks at the bar and then retired. I was anticipating a busy day so went to bed.

Sleep was a little fitful, but I woke up feeling refreshed with the sun streaming through the window. I washed, dressed and went down for breakfast which I ate alone. My first rendezvous was due at midday. I strolled around the station alone. It was quiet but that was commensurate with its unusual status. You see, the first meeting of the day was to take delivery of a large parcel. It was coming courtesy of the Luftwaffe directly to RAF Lincoln. I can hear you gasping of course but it is true. Even in war, there was a need to communicate with the enemy and just after midday a Dornier 217 appeared on the horizon, slowly got bigger and then landed[176].

Once it had parked and shut down on a remote part of the airfield, I drove over to it. Its pilot clambered out.

"Leutnant Schmitt."

---

[176] These flights were fairly regular at least until Germany invaded Russia, then it would appear they stopped.

"Wing Commander Flashman."

"There are four boxes. We will need to unload them together." He spoke perfect English as he led me over to the aircraft side and opened a hatch. Inside were the four boxes marked with the name Messerschmitt. He dragged one to the edge and we both lifted it out and carried it to the edge of the apron. We repeated this three times, he shook my hand and saluted, climbed back in and started up. It was very strange.

I waited until he was no more than a speck on the horizon again before examining the boxes. I don't know why but it seemed prudent to open at least one and see what we were getting that was so important to the operation. I fetched a screwdriver and a hammer from the car boot and wedged the screwdriver under the lid of a box. I tapped it lightly in and then levered it slowly upwards. I repeated this all round until the lid was loose and with a final flourish, I removed it. For a second I thought they were bombs and was about to run for the hills, my cheery mood vanishing but a second glance told me they weren't. They were somewhat bomb shaped, but I realised they were drop tanks. These were something of a new idea to extend the range of fighters[177]. It only occurred to me afterwards that the Dornier itself must have had some and dropped them somewhere over the North Sea.

Relieved I wasn't about to be blown to bits, I hammered the lid back on, got back in the car and returned to the mess to await the second arrival of the day. I had some lunch and then sat outside in the sun dozing and smoking.

It was about three o'clock when I heard the drone of engines again. I spotted the aircraft on the horizon and wondered what it was. It quickly became apparent that it was a Blenheim. I hopped back in the car and drove out to my favourite part of the airfield. The Blenheim landed and taxied to our prearranged rendezvous. Quiet descended again as the propellers stopped. I waved and then walked over to the entry hatch. I opened it slowly and before I knew it, I was being dragged inside, hands reaching for my nether regions.

---

[177] First used during the Spanish Civil War on the Stuka and Bf109. These sound like the 900 litre fin stabilised version for the Bf110.

153

It took me a moment or two to grasp the nettle so to speak but once I had I joined in enthusiastically. It occurred to me that I still hadn't managed to do the business in the air, and I was beginning to wonder if that moment may be approaching. I pushed that thought away to concentrate on the task in hand which was quickly reaching its climax. Two minutes I reckoned from shutdown to ecstasy. Marvellous.

We adjusted our attire and Amy hopped out of the Blenheim. It was just the ticket, plenty big enough and would in fact kill two birds with one stone. We loaded the boxes and probably less than fifteen minutes after she landed the engines were running and we were bumping over the grass. We took off turning north and climbed up to about five hundred feet. Our flight was somewhat unauthorised. Apparently, Menzies had had to pull many strings to arrange for the delivery flight. Amy had known how to arrange to fly it and it had been up to me to be at Lincoln to meet the inbound Dornier. It was just the stop at Lincoln that wasn't in the plan. Fortunately, all it meant was we were a little late and I was pretty sure Amy could come up with some story about headwinds and so on. Of course, the second stop would add a little more delay, but I wouldn't be there to see the aftermath. That was her problem.

The flight north took forever. She was taking the aircraft to Lossie[178] but we were going to Dungavel first. There were two reasons for this. First obviously to drop off the boxes. Second to prove that an aircraft that size could land there. We knew it already really but there were always people who would throw up excuses to try and prevent things happening so the easiest way to stop that was to land something big there.

I was bored. Really bored. Even low level had become tedious. She had thrown the thing around a bit to see what it could do, and it was sluggish. Nothing like a Spitfire or Hurricane. But at last, it was coming to an end. We had skirted round Carlisle then more or less overhead Dumfries before following the Sanquhar valley straight to Dungavel. It wasn't the easiest place to find but I was hoping for some direction from the ground. I

---

[178] RAF Lossiemouth. At the time, 107 and 110 Squadrons were based there operating Blenheims.

154

saw the house and pointed it out. We overflew it and almost immediately lights came on. I thanked the Lord, Amy turned onto a final approach and we landed, rolled over to a hut at the edge of the field and stopped. The hut door opened and a man came out. For a moment I wondered who it was as he was in civvies but as soon as he turned round, I was relieved to see it was Hamilton.

"Flashman, welcome. Miss Johnson I presume. Glad of your help." She smiled in return. "Better get these boxes out."

We opened the hatch and hauled them out. I must admit I then felt a brief pang when Amy climbed back onboard and started up. Hamilton and I were just moving the last box onto the back of a small truck as she took off for Lossie. I turned and watched her disappear into the blue then we got in the truck and drove the short distance to what looked like an old barn where we unloaded the boxes. I'd like to say we then hid them, but we just left them stacked to one side.

"I'll take you back to Turnhouse. I'm sure you'll be able to get a flight back to Lincoln tomorrow."

Chapter 38

I did nothing for a few days and then all hell broke loose again. November had started and the weather had turned cold when I was summoned to Menzies office.

"Go to Turnhouse, collect Hamilton and then go to Stockholm. Haushofer will be there. Hamilton has the authority to work out the details. Things are moving fast, and we need to strike while the iron is hot so to speak."

"How…?"

"Northolt. A Wellington will be waiting for you. The crew are on our side but the less they know the better."

I stood looking at him. It's possible my mouth fell open.

"What are you still doing here?"

I turned and left. A car was waiting to take me. It didn't take long but I rather felt like I was struggling to keep up. The Wellington crew gave me some kit and I strapped in and closed my eyes. It was unlikely but I felt like I needed to sleep so I closed my eyes and gave it a shot. The flight was over in a flash. Of course, it wasn't. The bloody thing shook like a virgin on her wedding night. All the way there. I didn't get a wink and my head was pounding by the time we arrived. Hamilton was waiting again. He took me to the mess and found me a room and once I had dumped my bag, I met him in the bar.

"Whisky?"

"Only if it's decent." He raised an eyebrow.

"You know you are in Scotland don't you?" I acknowledged this fact and he ordered two doubles. "This could be it you know. The end. Or at least the beginning of the end as Mr Churchill said."

"Tell me, what the hell are we actually going to do?"

"Haushofer. He is the power behind the power behind the throne. Hitler is just a figurehead really. You've seen him speak of course. But he isn't the ideas man. That's Hess as you know and then the real power behind them all, Haushofer. He is the man of influence, the one we need to make some agreement with. Although I don't think making an agreement will be that difficult. The hard part will actually be convincing our own side. At least those who think we stand a chance fighting them. But I digress.

156

Haushofer was a prime mover in the birth of the Nazi party. He's as convinced as the rest of them that the Aryan race are destined to rule the world. The difference is that he is not an anti-Semite. His wife is half Jewish.[179] He is also an admirer of the Empire, so that is where Hitler's idea of leaving us alone comes from. He told me he got involved right at the start of the Thule society and from there the Nazis invented their own version of history. None of that matters of course. All that matters is that he and Hess have enough influence in Germany to broker peace."

It was a fine speech, albeit he thought the problem was the opposite to Menzies. It was also true. These days, of course, everyone thinks we won the Battle of Britain, the Germans were astounded by the superiority of the RAF, they retreated into their shells and despite various setbacks, we slowly overcame the boche, culminating in the invasion of Normandy, a stroll through the fields of northern France, a somewhat unwise but heroic defeat at Arnhem, followed by final victory and huzzah all round. Oh, and the side issue of the Japanese. As I may have mentioned before, the reality was we had no chance. We could just about defend our island, but the very idea that we would somehow get back into Europe and free it was laughable. Churchill seemed to think the Americans would ride to the rescue. They might of course, but it wouldn't be for some time, time that would essentially involve him sacrificing thousands of our own people for his own grandstanding. Still, he was a politician so that wasn't a major problem.

By this time, we had made a large hole in the bottle and my head was starting to spin. Hamilton was looking decidedly ropey as well, so we called it a night.

******

It was an early call the next morning. Breakfast was hot and delicious and over too quickly. I packed my bag again and left the mess. It was still dark when Hamilton met me on the steps.

---

[179] Karl Haushofer's wife Martha was indeed half jewish. It seems that Hess arranged for some sort of protection for her, a not uncommon strategy used by senior Nazis.

Neither of us was in uniform. This was unofficialdom at its finest. No orders, no identifying papers, nothing written, no chance if it ended in disaster. Situation normal.

We walked in silence out to the apron. There was another Wellington sitting there though this time it was white. Where that had come from overnight was a mystery. Hamilton didn't seem surprised though, so we opened the door and clambered in. The pilot looked around, Hamilton gave him a thumbs up and he started the engines. A gust of warm air passed through the fuselage and then it went back to being freezing. We trundled over the field before swinging round. The engines roared and in seconds we were airborne. I glanced out of the window at the darkened land below us. There was still just a moon of sorts and the coast was quite clear as we crossed it and set course across the North Sea.

I settled back into the seat as far as that was possible in a bomber. There was no chance of conversation of course. The noise was deafening, the smell was appalling and the tea I had brought, despite being laced with brandy, tasted disgusting. The journey seemed endless. There wasn't even a decent view of course. On and on and on it went until I thought the only way out would be suicide. But eventually it did end with a bumpy landing somewhere near Stockholm. It was gloomy, cold with hints of snow in the air and there was a grey looking man to meet us. He didn't say much but Hamilton seemed to know him and we set off in what must have been a car built by the same people who built the Wellington. This didn't improve my mood.

"Sven here works for Birger. He will take us to the house for tonight and then I believe the meeting is set for tomorrow. As I understand it, Haushofer will be bringing a draft treaty. Essentially, it says that we can keep hold of the empire largely intact less a couple of minor former German colonies and in return, they will have a free hand in eastern Europe. Of course, they are allies with Russia in theory but that won't last long. They need the food to start with[180]. But possibly the biggest difficulty

---

[180] Rarely mentioned, but a major plank in Nazi thinking was the provision of raw materials and food, both of which were imported to a large degree. Conquest of large parts of Eastern Europe would address this

for them will be the change of leader. Hess told me once that even Hitler agreed that the National Socialist ideal was bigger than any one man and if it were ever necessary, he would stand aside. That would be important for any peace deal as it would be unlikely that any government could deal with him, especially after Munich. The converse of that is that we need to remove Churchill. Now, whilst that is ideal from our point of view, it will be a much harder sell to the masses, particularly as he has only just assumed the reins. Once they know a bit more about him it shouldn't be too difficult, but you know how fickle the general public are."

That ended the lecture for the time being. We lapsed into silence for the rest of the journey. The odd thing was travelling through a place that was behaving normally. There were no soldiers hanging around, no random guns pointing into the sky. People looked like they were enjoying life without the threat of being blown to smithereens any moment.

We pulled into a driveway and stopped outside a large wooden door. As we got out it opened and a man stepped out, shook our hands and bid us follow him. This we did and he showed us to our rooms. These were something else. The whole house appeared to be made of wood as was everything in it. The rooms were enormous and unpacking my travel bag didn't really fill any of the space. I realised instantly that I had forgotten to pack my dinner jacket and so was unable to change appropriately. Fortunately, Hamilton was in the same boat so we turned up looking like a couple of scruffs. The Swedish hosts didn't seem particularly upset by this, so all was well. Apart from the food. The food was disgusting. After months of wartime rationing mixed with the extras given to heroic fighter pilots, I was hoping for something exciting. It was not to be. If you have ever been to a Swedish restaurant, which you won't have done of course, you'll know what I am talking about.

We started with some rubber herring spiced with the smallest scraping of some herb or other, followed it with a couple of dishes that appeared to be salmon and meatballs mixed with beetroot in them and finally some sort of rice pudding. About the only thing that numbed the pain was the akvavit[181]. Being

---

problem. Frankopan's 'Silk Roads' discusses this in more detail.

Swedes, they had plenty of it and drank it by the pint. The best thing was it improved the dinner although after a couple of hours I wasn't capable of eating any more anyway. Probably because my mouth was numb along with most of my body.

At some point in the evening, I had a brief flashback to an air force mess in Germany a quarter of a century earlier. There, the locals had forced a shocking dinner down my throat before helping me drink copious amounts of schnapps and just like the swedes, they steadily anaesthetised themselves with it. This was the situation now. The conversation got steadily more random and eventually it came round to more serious subjects. Like women. After some discussion of the women we had known, the cigars and nuts appeared. The Swedes were impressive when it came to their conquests and judging by the Swedish women we had seen already it was a pity we weren't staying longer. I hadn't much experience of blondes but that would certainly change given half a chance. Sadly, it was unlikely and we broke up as the clock struck two.

I slept the sleep of the dead, or the dead drunk but much to my amazement woke in the morning feeling full of the joys of spring. Breakfast was a random wander in and out as you please affair. Hamilton didn't show his face, so I was left to my own thoughts. The meeting was scheduled for eleven so having eaten my fill I wandered around the grounds for an hour or so. I was just returning to the house when a small convoy of cars pulled up. They were unmarked but it was obvious they were Germans. After so long amongst them I could just tell.

There was a flurry of heel clicking and bowing, the Swedes being just a sort of peaceful version of the Germans. They had the blonde hair and blue eyes of course. Eventually everyone went in. I followed them through the door, bumped into Hamilton and together we went into the conference room and sat down.

Once everyone was seated, Birger stood up. The chatter died away and he began by introducing everyone. It's hard to remember now who was there, partly because I am not convinced many of them used their own names. The Swedes did however.

---

[181] The Scandinavian equivalent of whisky or schnapps. It is produced from grain or potatoes with the flavour provided by various herbs and spices.

Birger himself, his sidekick Sven and another chap who appeared to be taking notes which surprised me and was called Harald, presumably after some Viking hero or other.

Haushofer obviously used his own name as he was known to all and sundry as did Hamilton. But when Birger introduced me, I noticed an immediate swiftly hidden flash (ha!) of recognition pass across Haushofer's face. I thanked the Gods that my real name could almost be an anglicised form of my German name as clearly he had been briefed, presumably by Hess.

"I believe we can get down to business now," said Birger. "I anticipate some hard negotiating but let us all give thanks we are of the same Aryan races and thus we can leave out the emotion attendant on any discussion including the Latin races."

"Hear, hear," said Haushofer or something like that. He had a point really. Imagine the Spaghettis being involved. Not only would they complain about the weather and the food, both valid points of course, but we would get nothing done unless it looked like they had suggested it and also that they had in fact won. A ripple of polite laughter rang round the table.

"Herr Haushofer?"

He stood up and without notes briefly expounded the Nazi ideology of lebensraum in the east, their wish to essentially be uncontested rulers in Europe and their parallel desire to leave the British Empire alone and even to let it flourish. He referred to Hitler's speeches and the undeniable fact that Hitler had let the British Army escape at Dunkerque. This was news to me and having been there it hadn't really felt like they just let us go, but what did I know?

He carried on. It boiled down to the world being run by three powers. Us, them and the Americans across the ocean who no one really cared about and would almost certainly be happy to stay across the ocean. Simple, effective, everybody would be happy. Except for Churchill, his friends and I suspected large swathes of people across the world who didn't matter because they didn't get a say in the great plans of the great powers. It was ever thus.

"I have here a draft treaty for you to consider. Obviously there will be many questions and I would suggest that we adjourn to digest it in full. We can then return to discuss any major points before reporting back to our principals. I believe the next meeting is scheduled for the end of January, by which time we can but hope the major details are settled."

The meeting broke up. The only thing I remember about the brief afternoon session was a discussion about the respective leaders and how whilst Hitler was probably not acceptable to the British, equally Churchill would not be acceptable to the Germans, but that neither of these were a problem. Hitler would stand aside voluntarily, and Churchill would be forced out by Parliament. That is the way of democracy.

The next morning, we flew back to Turnhouse clutching our draft copy. To say we were optimistic was an understatement. I felt like we had the fate of Europe and the Empire in our hands. Plus, it would be pleasant to get one over on the big buffoon Churchill.

Chapter 39

Hamilton was equally enthused by our journey. He could barely contain himself although for such a senior aristocrat that largely amounted to the occasional unprovoked chuckle. We had both read the treaty and it was much as described. Britain kept its empire, Germany had a free hand in Europe particularly to the east, everybody became friends again except the Russians, Hitler was consigned to history as was Churchill and everybody was happy. Perfect revenge for me.

London was frantic. I never seemed to keep still or in one place for more than a few minutes. I saw Victoria and spent Christmas at home. There were sporadic raids on London, the worst on the 29th December when they set fire to a huge area of the City[182] but largely we ignored them. We had by this time rented a house out to the west where there were very few targets. Maybe it was complacent but in general I think the vast majority of people just got on with life, mainly I suspect in case it ended abruptly.

The new year dawned. It was freezing. Life was still a frantic round of meeting people who were sympathetic to the cause and convincing them that peace was the answer. I was a mere functionary in most of this and spent a lot of time with Hamilton shuttling back and forth to Edinburgh. He in turn regularly met with Kent to keep him up to date with progress. This wasn't too difficult as they were based at Pitliver House in Rosyth, just across the river from Turnhouse.

It was in the middle of all this a minor tragedy occurred. I had seen Amy a couple of times since our jaunt north, mainly when she dropped in to Turnhouse to refuel or just stop. It was just after

---

[182] An American journalist described this as the 'Second Great Fire of London' and in fact the area covered was larger than that devastated by the Great Fire. The fire was caused by dropping thousands of incendiaries and exacerbated by the area being largely non residential along with damage to the primary water main causing drops in water pressure for the firemen plus low tide on the Thames making it difficult to draw water from the river. The raid is primarily remembered for the iconic photo of St Paul's Cathedral rising from the smoke.

one of these stops when she had left to cross over to Prestwick to pick up an Oxford[183] to take south. I heard afterwards that she got lost in terrible weather, not an infrequent occurrence and possibly ran out of fuel. In her distress, she apparently failed to identify herself twice and so an anti-aircraft gun opened fire on her and shot her down. That in itself was a miracle, worse however it appeared that she survived this and bailed out landing in the freezing waters of the estuary. A ship nearby came to her rescue and they claimed they threw ropes to her, but she couldn't hold them. For reasons unknown the Captain then dived in to help, reached the body but then let go of it. When a boat got to him, he was unconscious and died of the cold. Amy, possibly having been run over by the ship, was never recovered. It put rather a gloom over the new year for a few days.

A couple of weeks after this I was summoned by Menzies again.

"I think we have broad agreement on the main heads. Sinclair has agreed to let Hamilton have the week off and go to Stockholm again. You can go with him."

So off we went again. Hamilton seemed inordinately pleased that he had recorded this in his diary as a visit to Lesbury where his brother-in-law the Duke of Northumberland lived. There were other machinations going on in the background and I got the feeling that things were about to get doubly frantic. Lloyd-George, the former PM from the first lot was apparently getting ready to take over the government. Clearly the Government suspected this and tried to get rid of him by sending him to Washington as ambassador. Being Welsh and a bastard he refused to go, an enormous snub to Churchill who retaliated by appointing Halifax instead. Halifax being an old school

---

[183] The Airspeed AS10 Oxford was a twin engine trainer. It was notorious for being impossible to recover from a spin. This was discovered by four crew trying it out at 18,000 feet and when finding it impossible attempted to bail out. On releasing their harnesses they were flung to the rear of the aircraft beyond the exit and were unable to move forward due to the centripetal force. They were extremely lucky. When the aircraft hit the ground it was spinning in such a flat trajectory that it largely skidded across the ground. The tail broke off and the four occupants walked away. Following this, a rope was fitted to assist crew in a similar situation reaching the exit door.

gentleman couldn't refuse. It seemed something of a blow to the peace party, but they brushed it off saying there were plenty of others in places of influence.

We spent ten days in Stockholm this time, most of it bored out of my mind while faceless men in suits pored over the meaning of documents and whether the word 'if' was suitable or would it be better to say 'maybe' or 'but'. Most of us didn't care and continued sampling the local food and drink. Sadly, the local women were largely absent.

Finally, we came home at the beginning of February.

Chapter 40

It was obvious that things were coming to a head. I spent most of my time at Turnhouse, occasionally flying but mainly running errands for Hamilton. Menzies had ordered me to stay there. Why became suddenly obvious when Menzies appeared out of the blue at the station, summoned me to his presence and announced we were going to Dungavel. The journey was quiet, Menzies and Hamilton both seeming preoccupied. On arrival there were no formalities and we went to a quiet and private room.

"The time is near," announced Menzies. "Halifax is going to Madrid shortly to meet Hoare, Haushofer and Hess[184]. The plan will be finalised and a date set as soon as possible but likely to be April or early May." He paused here for effect. "As far as we know, what I am about to tell you is known only to a handful of people, but we have to assume that some or all of it will leak out. There are spies among us. Churchill is not a complete fool. Hess has been training on a long range Me110. He will fly in on the appointed date for a final meeting. The meeting will be here at Dungavel. He will be coming to meet Kent and they will prepare a joint proclamation for transmission the next day. In essence, it will say that the war can be concluded peacefully. Hess will announce that he will take over power in Germany and Kent will invite Lloyd-George to assume the reins of power here. Churchill will be invited to stand down as will Hitler. In the meantime, our ground crew here will attach the drop tanks to the 110 and fuel it up. Hess will then return to Germany and make the same proclamation to take immediate effect. Bombing will cease just before Hess flies over."[185]

He stopped talking so that we could absorb what we had been told. It all made sense now, even the boxes in the shed at

---

[184] Halifax had already been posted to Washington at this stage and there is no record of him leaving to travel to Spain. That doesn't mean that it didn't happen of course.

[185] There is some evidence that this happened. The last major raid on England by the Luftwaffe took place on the 10th May, after which they all but ceased. The same was true of Bomber Command.

Dungavel. It also occurred to me that pretty much everything I had done recently was high treason for which the penalty was the rope. I doubted my exploits in a Spitfire would save me if it came to it. My blood ran cold. You can guess what I was thinking. Or maybe actually you can't. Because what I was thinking was actually unthinkable. Whose neck was I prepared to substitute for mine if it came to it? I vowed for the millionth time that I was never going to get caught up in these peoples plans again, assuming I survived this one.

Obviously I didn't actually say anything at the time. I nodded along with Menzies while he explained the details. Our job, or rather my job, was going to be reception committee at Dungavel. The plan was very detailed as I would have expected from someone like Hess. He was going to fly a long way north to start with before turning west following the Kalundborg radio beam. This should give him a landfall at Alnwick. Suddenly, Hamilton's visit to his brother-in-law made sense. Alnwick would show a signal light as Hess passed over and from there, he would continue to Dungavel where our little reception committee would be waiting. Hamilton would be at Turnhouse where he would add to his list of treasonable actions by preventing interception of Hess by any RAF units.

Once he had landed safely, Kent would be alerted and would travel to Dungavel to begin proceedings. Dungavel, he reminded us, was neutral territory. There was a lot more detail to absorb, none of which was written down and we finally broke off for some refreshment about three hours later. I was exhausted.

******

I spent the next few days nervously watching for the arrival of the rozzers. But they didn't show up and I carried on making my treasonous preparations. My main problem was arranging for a fuel bowser to be at Dungavel on the appropriate night. Obviously there wasn't one kept there because it was only for emergencies and the chances of needing fuel were small. Somehow, I would have to arrange for one to arrive from Turnhouse but avoid the shock to the driver of seeing it hooked up to an Me110. I decided I would have to do at least the refuelling part if not the driving. But that meant the bowser arriving in the afternoon and then disposing of the driver for the night no questions asked. I pondered on this whilst I was at Turnhouse with a couple of airmen showing me how to work the aforementioned bowser. It wasn't as easy as it looked of course.

Other details came to the fore such as lights showing Hess where to land, arranging accommodation for the Duke of Kent near Dungavel so that he could get there quickly and most importantly doing it all in secret.

The strain was immense, especially being to all intents and purposes alone at Dungavel. More than I could have imagined. Dealing with royalty or their minions was the worst but then it always had been. The days turned into weeks and then suddenly it was all go. The phone rang at Dungavel where I was living. It was Hamilton.

"He's coming."

It was all he said. I put the phone down and reached for the whisky. Two good slugs helped steady the nerves. Then I got on the phone to the ops room at Turnhouse and using the agreed story explained the need for a fuel bowser at Dungavel. That done, I wandered out to the shed where the drop tanks were and checked them for the thousandth time. I turned the lights on and off also for the thousandth time and then went back into the house. I considered more whisky but decided I would need my wits about me. I lay down and stared at the ceiling. It would be hours before anything happened.

Chapter 41

Nothing happened. Nothing at all. Except at about three in the morning the phone rang. It was Hamilton to tell me he wasn't coming. Some technical problem apparently according to the Swedes[186]. Saved from the gallows for another day at least I went out into the clear night and stared at the stars. It was the 1st May. After half an hour of concentrated staring I went back to bed to stare some more. Sleep was a rare commodity at this time.

Looking back now from the safety of old age it should have been a pleasant interlude. I was away from the war, which was still going badly as I recall, particularly in North Africa which was pretty much the only theatre where the Army was fighting. They did manage to take over some places in Ethiopia although the significance of that escaped me then and still does now. Churchill didn't see it that way of course. He kept wittering on in the Commons about the Americans supplying us and the Germans hadn't invaded so that meant we had to win in the end although it would be pretty grim for a long time or something like that. Personally, I thought he sounded a little desperate.

And then it came. Saturday the tenth of May. The phone rang. I can't remember the time, but it must have been late afternoon or even early evening.

"He's coming. Definitely."

That was it. I leapt into action. I went outside with a glass of whisky, medicinal I assure you, had a smoke, then came back inside and picked up the phone to Turnhouse. Having made the now familiar arrangement for a fuel bowser to come over, I went and checked the lights again, looked at the drop tanks nestling in

---

[186] Hess made several flights with drop tanks in his specially converted Me110. Some were probably training or practice flights but this one on the 30th April appears to be the first attempt at flying to Britain. Hess did not in fact take off but sat in the aircraft with the engines running whilst his adjutant telephoned Berlin. After a short delay, Hess shut down. According to Helmut Kaden, his instructor and Messerschmitt test pilot, Hess told him that the Führer had decided not to give his May Day speech from the Me factory in Augsburg, itself a break with seven years of it traditionally being given from Tempelhof in Berlin, but that Hess was to give it instead. It is hard to claim as the establishment does that Hitler was not aware of what was going on.

their boxes then returned to the house to wait for act two in the drama.

Somewhere over the North Sea was a lone Me110 following a radio beam towards Scotland. Things were about to hot up. I was waiting by the phone at Dungavel. Hamilton was waiting by the phone at Turnhouse. Kent was waiting by the phone in a shack up the estate road. Northumberland was waiting by the phone at Alnwick.

What I didn't know was that there were quite a few others also waiting by their phones for something to happen. Not all of them wanted the same things to happen though.

The phone rang at Turnhouse. Obviously I wasn't aware of this immediately, but I note it here because it triggered a number of events, the first of which was to make me jump out of my skin when Hamilton called me.

"Fifteen minutes." He put the phone down. I shivered, took a few deep breaths to steady myself, grabbed my coat and went outside.

Back at Turnhouse, Hamilton had contacted the local anti-aircraft units and warned them about an aircraft passing overhead telling them they were not to fire on it. Radar units had also contacted him with reports of an incoming lone raider or small raid which he had acknowledged and ignored. The Royal Observer Corps had done the same. They were also acknowledged and ignored. He also told me afterwards that he had had a hell of a job stopping two Czech pilots trying to intercept Hess. When you look at that list, there was enough to get him a silk rope.

Back to my predicament. The fuel bowser was ready, the driver firmly installed in a village hostelry and by now three sheets to the wind. Just the lights. I hurried out the door and over to the airstrip where there was a small control room. Hess had about 150 miles to travel from Alnwick to Dungavel so there was plenty of time from him being spotted to arriving. The trick was to not have the lights on for too long, just long enough for him to identify them correctly, not so easy at night when you haven't been somewhere before although in theory there shouldn't be any other lights showing brightly, and then make an approach and

170

land. Obviously turning them on too late would have been disastrous as well.

In the darkness I stumbled along the well-worn path. I had done it enough times that I could probably have done it blindfolded. But with the nervous excitement of the night, it would have been easy to blunder about and get lost. I was almost at the control shed when I heard a strange noise. I stopped instantly and listened. Nothing. I waited another couple of minutes as I had plenty of time. I don't know why really but suddenly the hairs on the back of my neck were bristling. I looked around me again. Still nothing. Or was there? I was almost sure I could hear a faint rustling, but it could be anything.

I carried on to the shed, opened the door and fell inside. Everything was as I had left it. How much time had I wasted outside? Too much I decided so I pulled the light switch and the lights came on. I went back outside and walked across to the short runway and waited, listening intently for the noise of an approaching aircraft. Then the lights went out.

I nearly bolted as my imagination joined up the dots but then stopped and thought about it. The lights could easily have blown a fuse. There was an overload system that had tripped off before. I hurried back to the shed breathing heavily and looking around for intruders, but I saw nothing. I got to the door and went back in to find that that was exactly what had happened.

A feint buzzing noise attracted my attention. Jesus he was here. I shone my torch on the control panel and found the reset switch and pulled it praying it would stay up. It did. I stared at it for a moment and then hurried outside back across the strip. Now there was the unmistakeable noise of aircraft engines and they weren't British. They got closer and closer until I thought I saw a shadow approaching. It was him. I imagined him up there, the relief of finding the lights after such a long flight alone. He flashed low across the strip and I imagined him timing his turn to come back and land. He would have been around the turn and descending towards the runway when the lights went out again. I swore loudly, they had never done this before and began hurrying over to the shed. I was halfway there when I stopped dead and stared. There was a light in the shed and the unmistakeable sound of a sledgehammer smashing everything in its way. My blood ran cold again. How I didn't faint I don't know.

Frozen to the spot I realised it was over. He couldn't land but he didn't have enough fuel to get anywhere else safe. Hess flashed over again in a climbing turn as far as I could make out. Hamilton had told me Hess would have some sort of abort plan, but I didn't know what it was. Jesus, I would have to let Hamilton know. But what if my friend with the sledgehammer decided to use his expertise on the witnesses? I wasn't armed but there was a gun in the house. I ran.

In seconds I was inside and scrambling for the drawer where my pistol was. I grabbed it and spun round expecting him to be on me. But there was no one there and as I looked frantically round, I realised the only hammering sound was my heart going much too quickly. I gaped around for a little longer, realising that completely unbidden I had crouched behind the most substantial piece of furniture I could find. Still nothing. The seconds dragged by turning inexorably into minutes. Then the phone rang.

How my heart didn't give out I shall never know. I grabbed the receiver.

"Is he there?" Hamilton.

"Christ, no."

"What, what happened? He was definitely on the way."

"The lights."

"What about the bloody lights?" I could tell he was getting slightly ruffled now.

"I put them on and waited on the runway. While I was waiting, they went out and when I went to investigate there was a group of armed men there smashing up the control shed."

Quick thinking I am sure you will agree. If it was only one man, Hamilton would have expected me to take him on. Had I had the pistol on me I would have considered it for half an hour or so.

"Christ almighty, betrayed!" There was a brief silence. "Wait there, I am coming to get you." The phone went dead.

I hovered by the phone wondering if it would ring again or whether I should phone anyone, deciding against this course of action. However, I did decide that Hamilton would want to know about the shed, so, like it or not, I realised I would have to go and

172

investigate. Reasoning that whoever had been there would have gone by now, I crept out of the door and crawled along the path. The night was silent and dark.

I was halfway along the path when a flash of light caught my eye. It was in the opposite direction to the shed but at that moment I assumed it was the hammer man, in which case he was some way away. I stood up slowly, looking around me. Nothing else caught my eye so I carried on slowly towards the hut. I realised later on that the flash was probably Hess's crashing aircraft about fifteen miles north of me on Eaglesham Moor.

I reached the shed and slowly looked around me. There was nothing. I stood up slowly and switched my torch on. Still nothing. The door was hanging open and as I shone the torch in, I realised whoever it was had done a proper job. There was truly little left in one piece and even had I shot him I could not have turned the lights on.

Satisfied there was no future in hanging around I walked back to the house and sat down to wait. It was a long drive from Turnhouse.

Chapter 42

Hamilton finally arrived. He was seriously agitated and ordered me into the car.

"We have got to find him. If Churchill's gang get him, we are done for."

"What do you mean Churchill's gang?"

"SOE. They have been on our case for months. Luckily, most of them are rank amateurs but they do have some dangerous people."

"How dangerous?"

"Very. But then so do we."

For about the fifth time that night my blood turned to ice. It wouldn't be the last.

"Where are we going now?"

"God knows. The abort plan was to get to Aldergrove, but I don't think that happened. After I spoke to you, I checked with a number of allies. No one saw an aircraft but there was a report of a possible crash somewhere on the moors south of Glasgow. There was even a report of a parachute. If that's true, we have got to get to him first."

"I saw it. A flash. It would have been no more than fifteen minutes after he flew over."

"That makes sense. It's not far. But that is also some time ago."

We fell silent as Hamilton pushed the car as fast as it would go. It was somewhat disconcerting racing over Eaglesham Moor in the dark, hoping for the life of me we didn't meet anyone coming the other way. After several hair-raising minutes, we shot into the village of Eaglesham.

"There's an ROC unit here. If anyone knows they surely will."

Another couple of minutes threading our way through the village and we saw a sentry outside a building.

"That's it. You go in and find out. They might recognize me, but they won't know you."

"What a fantastic idea," I didn't actually say. I could already see the route this night was going to take.

174

I approached the sentry who saluted. He didn't ask me for any identification and I didn't offer any, so I just pushed open the door and went in.

"Good evening," I announced. "Who's in charge?"

"That'll be me," a voice answered from the gloom. I waited as the voice's owner came over and threw me a hasty salute which I returned.

"Flashman," I said.

"Donald," he said.

"I've just come from Turnhouse," I said, emphasising the Turnhouse bit. "I've been sent to find out about this reported aircraft. Any news?"

"Weeel, aye there is. First reports say it crashed on a farm. Home Guard are there and have the pilot in custody. Taking him to Giffnock[187] now. Come along if you wish."

"Will do. We have a car outside. Lead the way."

I went back outside and got in the car.

"Well?"

"They've got him."

"Who has?"

"Home Guard apparently."

"Oh Jesus, they'll want to follow every procedure ever invented plus some of their own." He held his head in his hands for a moment.

"They're off."

Hamilton started the car and followed the ROC transport.

"Do you know a Major Donald? He seems to be in charge here."

"No. I have heard of him but never met him."

Silence again as we followed the car ahead. It was only a mile or two to Giffnock and we were there in moments.

"Same procedure. See what you can find out. See if there's a way we can commandeer him and get him out of here." I gasped. "Let me worry about how I'm going to square it with the authorities. Don't forget we have Kent in the wings."

We pulled up outside the Home Guard headquarters. That rather glorifies what was in fact the village scout hall, but it didn't

---

[187] Local Home Guard HQ was in Giffnock.

pay to offend the locals too much just yet. I was dreading the next few minutes, mainly because I wasn't sure how Hess would react to the surprise of seeing me. He most definitely wasn't expecting me and he would immediately wonder why. And more importantly whose side I was on.

Donald opened the door and we went in. Rather incredibly the room was packed.

"Who the hell is in charge here," he barked. There was a moments silence and then a confused babble. From out of the melee a police inspector appeared.

"Hyslop," he announced. "Not entirely sure to be honest. Home Guard chaps arrested him, but they don't have the authority. They say they can't get hold of the army. Argylls should be available especially as all leave was cancelled for all military and police personnel today, but they're not[188]."

"Where is he?"

"In the kitchen. Apparently he wanted a beer earlier. There are two soldiers in there as well. They were the ones who found him in the McLean cottage and they seem to think they are responsible for him[189]."

There was a short silence while we all considered what to do next. No one knew of course because there wasn't a plan for Hess bailing out and being collected by a bunch of farmers playing at soldiers.

"Where is he?" another voice said.

"Who the hell are you?" Donald.

"My name is unimportant, but I am on Sikorski's staff.[190]"
Why? I pondered this at the time and occasionally have done so

---

[188] All leave had indeed been cancelled that night which begs the question why?

[189] One of many strange anomalies that evening was that the first soldiers on the scene were Sergeants Daniel McBride and Emyr Morris. Both were unarmed and based at a top-secret signals establishment in Eaglesham House. Hess had landed near ploughman David McLean's cottage and David himself helped him to the cottage. When Morris and McBride appeared, Hess asked if they were friends of Hamilton. They then had an odd conversation about beer and at some point, Hess gave McBride his iron cross. This was just the start of a very unusual night and Flashman's description seems accurate.

[190] Roman Battaglia was a clerk at the Polish Consulate in Glasgow. The

ever since. Why was there a senior officer from General Sikorski's staff in a Home Guard hut in the wilds of Scotland? I have never been able to answer that question. "I need to see him urgently."

"Feel free," said Donald. "Everyone else has." Quite why he felt able to allow all and sundry to chat to Hess escaped me.

However, I was delaying the inevitable.

As the Pole, at least I imagined he was a Pole, entered the kitchen, I followed. Hess looked up and his eyes immediately widened. Thankfully, it was his only reaction. Two other of the room's occupants snapped to attention and threw a smart salute my way. I returned the compliment.

"McBride, Sir," one of the soldiers said. "We were first on the scene. Mr Horn here was the only crew. He's unarmed."

"Horn eh," I mumbled glancing at Hess who nodded imperceptibly. "On his own you say? And you know that how?"

"Yes Sir. He told us Sir."

"Good. I have a colleague outside who needs to know about all this. Keep a close eye on him for the moment."

I glanced at Hess and left them all to it. The last thing I heard was the Pole asking him who he really was. I walked out of the kitchen into a barrage of questions from Donald and Hyslop. I didn't really listen to any of them, just nodding and making noncommittal noises before scurrying out of the door and over to the car.

"It's him," I said.

"Jesus Christ," said Hamilton. I knew how he felt.

Polish connection is most intriguing. Sikorski, Polish leader of the exiled government based in Scotland, at one point offered the Duke of Kent the Polish throne. It is also worth noting that Michael Bentine, the British comedian and himself a slightly shadowy character with links to the intelligence world and liaison to the Polish government, made the point that whilst many Poles hated the Germans, ALL Poles hated the Russians. It is worth making the point again, why did Britain declare war on Germany and not on Russia when they invaded Poland? Officially it was because the agreement only mentioned Germany. Was that deliberate because there are many occasions where officialdom, especially British officialdom, interprets documents in any way it sees fit.

I stood by the open door breathing heavily while Hamilton appeared lost in thought.

"They also said they had tried to contact the RAF to take him but both stations refused."

"Yes. I ordered them not to accept any strange requests this evening. Amongst other things."

"There's some Polish chap in there who says he is on Sikorski's staff. I left them talking."

Hamilton just rolled his eyes. Then he seemed to come to a decision.

"Right, we need to contact the Cameronians in Glasgow. Get them to come and get him."

I trotted off again into the hut and found a telephone. After a short argument I managed to get them to put me through to the appropriate barracks at Maryhill. I had wondered how I was going to persuade them to send a detachment but whoever I spoke to seemed oddly aware of the situation. I put the phone down and stared at it for a moment or two before going back out to the car.

"They're coming."

"We won't be able to keep him just yet but at least they are neutral. But mainly I need to talk to him alone. When they get here, we need to intercept them and arrange to stop somewhere on the road to Glasgow and talk to Hess."

Chapter 43

The wait was interminable. Eventually a staff car arrived containing a Cameronian Major. Hamilton had a short conversation with him and then we all stood and waited for a truck to appear. This was the escort apparently. Once they had arrived, a couple of kilted soldiers got out of the truck and we all, except Hamilton, went back into the hall. Right on cue, the Pole appeared from the kitchen, mumbled something and disappeared into the night. Hyslop and Donald were still inside talking quietly. Hess was still in the kitchen with McBride. When I went in, I noticed McBride jump and slip something into his pocket. The Cameronian officer didn't say much but gestured for Hess to follow him which he did, glancing at me as he followed him out.

He didn't say a word as he climbed into the car with the Cameronian. I slid in beside Hamilton and we set off ostensibly for Maryhill barracks. The truck and car followed. We drove for about ten minutes before turning off the main road, pulling over and turning the lights out. Hamilton took a deep breath, opened the door and stepped out. I followed. The car behind had stopped as well and both its doors opened. Hess climbed out and came towards us.

"It is so very good to see you Douglas," he said holding out his hand.

"And you. What on earth happened?"

I think at this moment the blood drained from my extremities.

"The lights. They were on then they failed. Then they came on again. Then failed again and didn't come back."

There was what one would perhaps call a stunned silence. Luckily, it being dark neither of them could see my face.

"There was someone else there," I said. "They turned them off, I turned them back on again. I thought it was a fault, but they got to them again." Obviously I didn't take the next step of admitting I was too terrified to go looking for these people. I could almost feel the heat from Hamilton. And Hess. There was another pregnant pause.

"I couldn't stay for too long as even with the drop tanks I didn't have long and certainly not enough for Aldergrove. I think the wind was stronger than expected over the sea. Then I got bounced by two fighters and realised I didn't have long to do anything. I tried to fix my position as close to Dungavel as possible and then bailed out. I realise of course that makes my return rather difficult."[191]

Hamilton glanced at me again.

"Yes it does. Lord knows how we are going to sort this mess out. We have powerful allies as you know but whether they choose to acknowledge the situation is far from clear. As the senior officer on the scene, I will have to inform Churchill one way or another. Quite how that will turn out is also hard to discern. Obviously he is no friend of ours."

"Indeed. But I have faith in you my old friend. And also in Fleischmann here."

With this they both looked at me significantly. Quite what I was meant to do with that information was a mystery.

"Do not lose that faith. We may not be visible all the time, but we will be there."

We all shook hands and returned to our vehicles.

"How did they know about the lights?"

"Hard to say."

"I suppose so. Who was it though?" This was more of a rhetorical question I imagined so I kept mum.

We lapsed into silence again for some time.

"What the hell are we going to do now? Everything depended on the meeting with Kent. Somehow, we have to get them to meet, even if it is only in passing, just to show Hess we are

---

[191] Yet another anomaly in a long list. Two Defiants tried to intercept Hess but they weren't scrambled intentionally to do so, they were already airborne. At least two Spitfires were scrambled but too late to do anything useful. Two Hurricanes from Aldergrove were scrambled but were recalled when Hess turned back east. The Czech pilots stated that they were in range when they were recalled. The official reason for the recall was that they were entering another area of responsibility. This is nonsense. Despite reports from the ROC, no other fighters were scrambled although Hamilton and the Air Minister made it sound like numerous fighters were sent to intercept. There was apparently some confusion over the identity of the aircraft but that would normally be enough to warrant investigation. All Anti-Aircraft units in Glasgow that requested permission to open fire were refused. For more detail see 'Double Standards'.

serious. At least while he is in Scotland, we have some control."
He thought for a moment. "I have it. Craigiehall. Near Turnhouse.
If we can get Hess there on some pretext or other, it would be
strange if I can't arrange for the two of them to get together."

Chapter 44

Things assumed something of a surreal tinge. The journey continued in a brooding silence. We pulled up to the gates of Maryhill barracks. They were expecting us by this time and they swung open as if by magic. We glided to a halt just inside.

"Guardhouse sir?" said the Cameronian officer to Hamilton.

"No, I think the mess will do. But make sure it is guarded well."

It only occurred to me later why Hamilton insisted on a guard. Not to prevent escape of course. Where would he go? To prevent abduction! News was spreading fast.

We trooped into the mess and then upstairs to find a suitable room.

"You will be safe here for the moment. I will come and see you tomorrow. But for now, I have to start trying to fix this."

"Thank you, my dear Douglas. For everything."

That concluded the formalities for the evening and we went back downstairs leaving a heavily armed officer and two soldiers outside his room. We stopped at the bar where Hamilton helped himself to a large whisky. He offered me one which I took and gulped down.

"Let's get out of here pronto. Jesus what a bloody mess."

He said it with feeling and I couldn't help but agree.

Chapter 45

I woke up early in the mess at Turnhouse. I tried piecing the previous evening's events together to make some sense of it all, but it was impossible. Hess was here but under guard. His aircraft was a mangled wreck, so the drop tanks so carefully stowed by my good self were now useless. Hamilton had his doubts about many things, one of which was me. I chewed my nails for breakfast as the enormity of what we were doing began to sink in. Surely having Hamilton and Kent on my side would count for something? That assumed they were on my side of course. Royalty being royalty they would cut and run for the hills at the first sign of trouble. They had too much historical familiarity with the chopping block I suppose.

Hamilton appeared early as well.

"Car outside. We've got to get over to Maryhill early and then fly south. I have an appointment with Churchill."

The car journey dragged somewhat I have to say. But it was over eventually. The barracks was oddly quiet. We were met by the same officer from the night before and he took us to the mess. There was no fuss and fanfare, not that I expected any.

"Good morning," Hess said.

"Good morning," we replied.

"I have some news," Hamilton said. I glanced at him because I wasn't aware of any news. "I have arranged a meeting for the day after tomorrow. It will confirm your faith, I hope. Until then I have to go to London. You will be collected at the appropriate time. There were no papers found in the wreckage I understand?"

"No, I didn't bring any. The document is ready though. I have arranged for it to be sent in the usual way in about two weeks time."

"Excellent. Till Tuesday."

We left and drove back to Turnhouse. Hamilton briefed me on the way.

"This situation is not entirely disastrous. We have to see Churchill and we have to see Menzies. There is a nasty little power struggle going on that we have to win. At the moment, we are slightly ahead as we have Hess. But that could change in an instant. On the other hand, I have arranged for Hess and Kent to meet in secret on Tuesday."

This sounded more promising. There was so much going on now that I was beginning to hope the lights fiasco would be forgotten. Hamilton didn't mention it at least. We flew south. A car collected us at Northolt and took us to Ditchley.

"This is where Churchill goes instead of Chequers. More secure apparently. It belongs to the Trees[192]." I did wonder for a moment whether I had heard him correctly. "Sinclair will be there. The Air Minister. I believe you know him."

"In an oblique way I suppose I do. He is related to some other Sinclairs I know."

"I have no idea how this meeting is going to go. I would suggest refraining from contributing if you can."

He didn't need to tell me that. I had no particular problem with meeting so called great men. Often they turned out to be as ordinary as you and I. It was more what they were capable of doing. Or ordering to be done more correctly. That was definitely something to fear.

A butler led us into the house and installed us in a drawing room where we waited. Eventually a door opened and we were beckoned forwards.

"Ah, Hamilton," said a gruff voice.

"Prime Minister," he replied. "This is Wing Commander Flashman."

We all shook hands, Churchill staring into my eyes as we did so.

"Shall we dine? I believe the Trees dine well."

We sat down to dinner.

It was a strange kind of meal given the circumstances. Churchill didn't mention Hess at all, and Hamilton was strangely reticent as well. It was akin to being invited into the wolf's lair

---

[192] Ronald Tree was elected MP for Harborough in 1933, the same year he bought Ditchley. Already moving in establishment circles, he became friends with Churchill and offered his house as a place to meet for those of like mind. During the war, Churchill used the house as a retreat since the security services considered Chartwell, his family home, and Chequers, the official PMs residence as too visible to bombers.

for lunch and then watching as the wolf ate some other poor sheep. The conversation was desultory with Churchill wittering on about the heavy raid on Sunday evening. Even I thought that was strange as there hadn't been a raid on the Sunday, only Saturday. It was almost as though he was trying desperately to cover something up. Which he was of course[193].

Only when we reached cigars and Churchill lit up his trademark Cuban[194] did the conversation turn more serious, albeit very briefly.

"Well Hamilton, now tell us this funny story of yours."

"Indeed, sir. I was on duty at Turnhouse as you are aware when I received numerous reports of a lone raider. Various attempts at interception were made, none successful and I thought little more of it until I received a report that the raider had crashed near Glasgow. The local army units were on the scene quickly and the pilot was captured and eventually taken to Maryhill barracks. It wasn't until this morning I was made aware of the possible importance of the prisoner and that was when I presented the matter to higher authority."

I rather stopped listening at this stage because it was all a complete fiction. I noticed Hamilton glance at me at one stage as if to say keep your big mouth shut so I continued smoking, drinking the rather fine Courvoisier and contemplating the ceiling. At least I did until I heard Churchill say, "Well, Hess or no Hess, I'm going to see the Marx brothers!"

For a moment I wondered if he had completely lost his mind. And to the world at large, this was reported as Churchillian repartee, calm in a crisis, bulldog spirit and other such nonsense. It was only after Churchill retired that Hamilton let me in on a little secret. To Churchill, the Marx brothers were the King and his relatives.

---

[193] There is significant evidence that Churchill deliberately obfuscated the official version of Hess' arrival to make it appear he had no knowledge of it on the 10th.

[194] Churchill visited Cuba in 1895 and from there developed his taste for 'Romeo y Julieta' and 'La Aroma de Cuba' cigars. He was regularly sent boxes by various people and dealers.

We were shown to rather comfortable rooms and told to be ready to leave early. Breakfast would be served at eight sharp. Given that it was already two in the morning, I felt that was a little unfair but apparently it was typical of the PM. And who was I to contradict the great man.

Consequently, eight sharp saw me sitting at the breakfast table looking seedy. There was no sign of good old Winnie of course. He was breakfasting in bed with a cigar and whisky no doubt, being the undoubted alcoholic he was. I did feel somewhat better after ham and eggs with a kipper thrown in for good measure. Hamilton hardly touched a thing, but nerves have never prevented me from eating and they certainly weren't going to now, especially as this was presumably being paid for by the government. Eventually the PM deigned to get out of his pit and it was sometime after nine that we set off for London. I wasn't of sufficient rank to travel with him, so I had a lonely ride in a staff car carrying his private secretary who looked down his nose at me and refused to communicate. He was terribly busy shuffling great reams of paper, most of which I imagine no one would have missed if I had opened the window and hurled them out. I didn't of course but the daydream was pleasant enough.

As we drove through west London, I started to notice the bomb damage. I hadn't really paid much attention before but the further in one went, the worse it got and as we approached the centre it seemed to be everywhere. Transfixed by this, I only noticed when we stopped. My innards froze as I stepped out of the car and into the main headquarters of SIS where we were taken almost immediately up to a private office.

"Good morning Prime Minister," said Menzies.

Chapter 46

"Good morning to you," he replied, "though I suspect the jury is out on that particular question just now." He grinned at all and sundry. Menzies face betrayed nothing at all.

"In here. Take a seat."

We all sat down in what was clearly a private meeting room that I had never seen before. There was a shuffling of chairs and paper and then a brief silence. It seemed no one particularly wanted to go first. In the end Menzies cracked.

"We need to bring him south."

"Who?" said Churchill feigning ignorance with a smile on his face.

"Hess. As you well know." Menzies who was used to dealing with Prime Ministerial truculence. "I have the very place. It won't be ready immediately, but in the meantime, we can keep him in the Tower."

I nearly spat my teeth out at this statement.

"Why the Tower?" I heard myself ask.

"Where else?" Menzies replied. "He can't go to a standard prison camp, he can't go to a civil prison and we need him close by."

That apparently settled that.

"Well Menzies, on your head be it," said Churchill, a loaded statement if ever I heard one.

When I write it down like this all these years later, the conversation seems ridiculously short and pointless. I am sure I have forgotten some of the detail but that was the gist of it. It didn't strike me until afterwards that Churchill was just weighing up the opposition. He left abruptly leaving the three of us to stew over it all.

"Flashman, get back to Scotland and bring him south. We will provide a train with guards and so on. Hamilton, we have to make sure he meets Kent as arranged if only to reassure him there is a plan, although Christ knows what it is at the moment."

Hamilton and I left and drove in silence back to Northolt for the flight back to Edinburgh. It was going to be a busy couple of days.

Chapter 47

Time has a strange way of blurring at moments of extreme emotional turmoil. This was one of those. And now when so much of it has passed it is hard to separate the days and the events on each of them. I know that there was a flurry of statements to the people. The Germans went first even though they didn't know what had happened to Hess, their initial statement being ambiguous enough to allow them to alter their story if necessary. It also meant the agreed signal from Hess to Hitler had not been sent. As I found out somewhat later, one of the reasons Dungavel was so important was the Red Cross presence, not just because it was neutral, but because they could have legitimately sent a signal confirming Hess' arrival. But as he had vanished, they were unable to do so.

Next the British government made a statement. It was bland to the point of being meaningless. Until that is you consider that had Churchill told the people that Hess had come on a peace mission, it is just possible many of them would have been heartened by that and the appetite for more unending war diminished. That would never do.

Then the Germans had another go. This time they mentioned that Hess had believed that he was to be met by a peace party. They then pointed out that he was delusional and believed in hypnotism, astrology and other such nonsense and also declared it could have been a trap. To sum up, it was noted that Hess' ideas on peace were misguided and well-intentioned, but Hitler would continue the war until they won or the British were ready for peace.

Now that doesn't sound much, but I can assure you it was meant as a hint to the British. Obviously it was never taken up. Then the Germans dropped another bombshell. They announced that Hess had come to see Hamilton who belonged to a group that opposed Churchill and the war. They also stated that Hess believed there would be fuel available for his return flight, which of course there was had he landed at Dungavel.

The Government were caught on the hop and had no choice but to at least admit that Hess had asked to see Hamilton. Officially at least that was it. They, or Churchill, didn't make another statement until 1943 by which time it was largely irrelevant.

None of this stopped them doing what British politicians spend their expensive educations learning. Lying without being caught, whether that be by omission or in this case by hinting that something might be true to the press who then diligently report it so that by default it becomes fact. In this case, they briefed the press that Hess had 'not brought any peace proposals with him'. This was in fact true when looked at purely from the contents of the wrecked 110 or the contents of Hess' pockets. At this point I should like to ask you, dear reader, to take a look at whoever is in power right now and ask yourself this. If Churchill was, as history likes to pretend, the greatest Prime Minister Great Britain ever had, and he was capable of such downright lies that led indirectly to the deaths of hundreds of thousands of British men and women, what are the pygmies in charge now capable of? I am sure you can think of something appropriate. But I digress.

Hamilton was apoplectic. Even Churchill could see that something needed to be said to support him. By devious parliamentary means, a question was asked of the PM which denied that Hamilton and Hess had met at the Berlin Olympics and also allowed him to state the following: "Contrary to reports that have appeared in some of the newspapers, the Duke has never been in correspondence with the Deputy Führer. None of the Duke's three brothers, who are, like himself, serving in the RAF, has either met Hess or had correspondence with him."

This masterful piece of understatement managed to give the impression that all was well. But by being so carefully worded, it begged a number of questions which were never asked, at least not publicly. The most obvious point was that Hamilton may well have not contacted Hess directly, but he didn't need to when he had Haushofer. And by denying they met at the Olympics, they suggest that they did meet elsewhere. Mentioning the other Hamilton brothers was just an attempt to blur the view of course. While all this was going on, events were proceeding in the north.

I arrived back before Hamilton with orders to arrange a guard detail suitable for a brief but discreet royal visit. He emphasised the discreet and I didn't even question it. I called one of the Squadron Leaders based at Grangemouth[195] and told him to

189

organise a dozen of his fellow trainees into a guard detail, smarten themselves up and report to Turnhouse the next morning. I commandeered a truck and held it on standby with two drivers. I had somewhat lost track of the passage of time but when I stopped and thought about it, I realised that only two days had passed since Hess' arrival. A lot had happened since then.

Hamilton arrived back at Turnhouse at about two in the morning. I know this because he hammered on my door to wake me up. I opened it without thinking. Normally I would have told whoever it was to bugger off.

"What the hell…"

"I have arranged a meeting for tomorrow. The Duke will meet Hess. I need you to collect the Duke from Pitliver[196] in civvies and take him to Craigiehall[197] for midday. Tell the guard detail to be there at eleven. No arms. Royal salute indoors when the Duke arrives. Hess will be in an upstairs room. I am sure they can work out where best to stand."

"Of course, Sir," I replied. Or I may have grunted instead, I can't remember really.

I went back to bed and lay awake staring at the ceiling until the light started to penetrate the curtains. Then I got up, dressed, shaved and fished out my best civvy outfit as befits meeting a royal nobody again.

I breakfasted in the mess where I bumped into Squadron Leader Day, the leader of the guard detail. I repeated Hamilton's instructions and left him to it to arrange. Sausages were the order of the day and I had six before the mess steward gave me a knowing look. I then went to the bar and made the attendant there give me a large brandy. I telephoned the motor pool and arranged for Hamilton's official car to be brought to the mess for 10.30, where I climbed in and drove slowly through the airfield gates.

---

[195] 58 Operational Training Unit was based at RAF Grangemouth from December 1940.

[196] Pitliver House in Rosyth was the Duke's wartime residence.

[197] Craigiehall was the seat of the Earl of Annandale from 1699. In 1933 it became a golf and country club and in 1939 was requisitioned for the duration. The Army stayed after the war, eventually purchasing the house to be used as Army Headquarters Scotland.

Turning right, I headed for Queensferry. It took no more than a few minutes to get to the landing where I waited for a quarter of an hour for the next crossing. Once across, it was no more than a few minutes to Pitliver.

The house seemed deserted when I arrived but a sharp rap on the door attracted a servant of some kind. He gave me a haughty stare for a moment until I announced I wasn't there to deliver the coal but to collect his royal numbness.

"Yaaas indeed. Perhaps you would wait in the parlour."

He showed me into a small cupboard and left me there. He didn't offer me a drink.

It was some minutes before Kent appeared, minutes where I started to fret we would be late as we had to get back across the river, but one couldn't hustle one's betters. He did finally appear in his Group Captain's uniform as agreed. He looked down his nose for a moment, decided I wasn't something the cat dragged in and headed for the front door.

Maybe it was because I didn't show any real deference, mainly because, as you know, I had previous with the family, but after a few minutes and as we approached the river again, he suddenly turned to face me.

"Have you met him?"

"Yes sir, I have."

"And what did you think?"

His piercing blue eyes bored into me. I wondered how much to say.

"I have known him for.... some years. Here and in Germany. After the first lot. He is an intelligent man, he has some unusual beliefs, but they are not central to his thinking. He is a believer in peace."

I don't know why I said so much really. It just seemed right. Maybe it was the feeling that I didn't want to fight any more and this was a possible way out. Plus, I couldn't stand the drunken buffoon Churchill.

"Very interesting. Very interesting indeed. I remember you of course. At Hamilton's place. You went to Sweden."

"That is correct sir."

"And what did you make of that?"

"It made sense sir. Not fighting them I mean. Keeping the Empire and so on. We've never been much good at interfering on the mainland. Waterloo of course. And he's right. About the outcome if we do. We will be bankrupted, the Americans will be the dominant force in the west and communism will dominate Europe and increasingly Britain. Is that a price worth paying for victory? Is that even victory?"[198]

I still had no idea why I was talking so much.

"Indeed. Not much room for my family then either."

We continued the journey in silence, contemplating what all that meant.

---

[198] This was indeed Hess', and it must be said Hitler's, view of the outcome of a long war with Britain. The British Peace Group would have realised this as well. The real question is what would the population have thought? See Appendix.

Chapter 48

He was right. There wouldn't be much room for a royal family. I was reflecting on this and other important issues as we turned into the drive at Craigiehall. As we approached the house, there seemed to be an awful lot of people about. This didn't strike me as particularly necessary given the circumstances. I pulled up outside the door.

Before I could move, the car doors were opened and Kent was on his way out, salutes being thrown all over the place. I hopped out quickly and ran round to follow him. I had no intention of being left behind at this stage of the drama. I tagged on to his shoulder looking official and barged my way through the front door as the guard saluted. There was no sign of Hamilton, but I guessed he was avoiding trouble.

Kent headed straight for the stairs and trotted up them. At the top, Squadron Leader Day was heading the guard who also threw a stiff salute which Kent returned with that familiar royal half wave half salute raising of the gloved hand. Day then opened the door and in we went and for the second time in so many days there he was again looking the picture of a German officer[199].

He glanced up and stood as we entered. Kent immediately approached him as I closed the door and held out his hand. Hess shook it warmly and invited Kent to sit at the small table. He smiled at me and I took a seat on the convenient bed.

"Well, something of a pickle we find ourselves in," said Kent.

"Indeed," said Hess. "But I am sure we can find our way out in time. I think it may be more than a couple of days though." They both grinned at this.

"Yaas. Hamilton is working flat out. Churchill knows you are here, as do the major interested parties, including the King.

---

[199] Day reported afterwards that he had been posted on the first floor beside a door. Two men in khaki arrived escorting a tall German officer, mounted the stairs and entered the room. Five minutes later, an RAF ranking officer arrived with a civilian and both entered the room. A servant told him that the RAF officer was the 'Duke'. Asked next day in the mess whether he had seen Hess, he replied he had for about thirty seconds. For some years after the war, there was supposedly a photo in the mess at Craigiehall of Hess arriving at the house. It has long disappeared.

Churchill won a confidence vote in the Commons a few days ago, but that is essentially meaningless as our supporters won't vote against him until we are sure of winning. The Lords are all but rebelling. And I believe we have Beaverbrook on our side. Of course, he removed Asquith in the last lot."[200]

"Militarily surely he must see reality?"

"I'm not sure he does. At least publicly he gives that impression, preferring to make much of the Battle of Britain and glossing over the fact that, as you say, we are essentially losing everywhere."[201]

"The U Boats will not stop. In fact, there are more and more coming into service all the time."

"We are aware of that."

There was a brief silence during which, considering the conversation that had just taken place, I contemplated the nature of treason yet again and whether being with the King's brother was sufficient excuse.

"There is the ultimate royal prerogative. The King can force Churchill from office. A Prime Minister without royal support is unlikely to survive in office for long. But we can't get away from the fact that Churchill has support amongst the people and if he refused to stand down, it is not beyond the bounds of possibility that there would be civil disturbance. To what degree is hard to determine. My brother would do it, but it would only be in extremis."

"Of course." I could almost hear Hess thinking that things like this were better ordered in Germany.

"Lloyd-George and Hoare would I believe form the backbone of a new government. Lloyd-George in particular is still popular which would undermine some of the Churchill sentiment."

"Ja, ausgezeichnet."

---

[200] Churchill himself called a confidence vote on 7th May. Potentially a risky move given that his position was not strong and the peace group, led in the Commons by Lloyd-George was very vocal in its criticism. He won easily but mainly because few MPs would risk voting against unless they were sure of the outcome.

[201] North Africa, Atlantic, Greece. Until mid 1942, Britain was losing catastrophically.

"I hope, Herr Hess, that my coming here has reassured you that all is not lost. There is a long way to go. I believe Menzies is going to arrange to have you moved to the Tower of London. I realise that sounds daunting but in reality, means we can be in much closer contact. Not many people have the privilege of being imprisoned in the Tower." Kent grinned at this statement and even Hess seemed a trifle pleased at joining an illustrious band. "We have to go. Good luck and I am sure we will meet again soon."

"Thank you, sir. I am most grateful for your visit and I too believe we will meet again soon."

Hess stood, clicked his heels together and made the strange palm forward salute that the senior Nazis used. He then shook Kent's hand again and I opened the door for us to leave. Day and co immediately snapped to attention and saluted and Kent trotted down the stairs to the car. Someone opened the door, he got in, everybody saluted furiously, I got in the driver's seat and we drove away.

Chapter 49

If you think the story so far is confused, well, this was just the beginning. After I had dropped Kent back at Pitliver, I returned to Turnhouse. Hamilton was waiting for me. He looked worried as well he might.

"There is a train arranged for Hess. Go with him. You can't use your own name though. You are now Captain Barnes. Menzies idea before you ask. The situation is extremely complicated. I am not my own man. Churchill has, how can I put this, agreed that there may be some merit to at least considering a negotiated peace. But it must be kept secret for the moment. That is why there have been no details released in parliament. I have to brief all the members of the group. For the moment at least, there is a truce."

He raised his eyebrows at this from which I deduced that he wasn't being entirely honest with me. Why and what about I couldn't fathom and I daren't ask. Instead, I packed. I had a feeling I wouldn't be coming back for some time.

The train was late of course and took forever to get to London. There we decamped into a blacked-out bus for the journey to the Tower where the guard that met us recognised Hess and asked for a signature. He obliged and was then taken to the officer's quarters in the Governor's house. I left him to settle in and found my own room for the night. I had never slept in the Tower. I couldn't help wondering which of the more ethereal residents would drop by in the night. None of them as it turned out.

I woke up early next morning and availed myself of breakfast in the mess. It was somewhat surreal and quiet. The occasional ancient fusilier officer[202] appeared and passed the time of day but apart from that I ate alone. Around ten o'clock I went to find Hess.

He was quite happy. His audience with Kent had cheered him up no end and oddly he seemed to think that being held a prisoner in the Tower was a good thing. I didn't disabuse him of that

---

[202] The Royal Fusiliers Regimental Headquarters have been at the Tower since 1685.

notion by pointing out such national landmarks as Traitor's Gate, the White Tower and the Bloody Tower. We passed the time of day saying nothing and I left him to it. I spent the afternoon wandering around the Tower and along embankment. Dinner was in the mess and then I retired to the bar and helped them reduce the stock of brandy. They seemed quite keen to help so eventually I stumbled into my bed long past midnight. Consequently, I missed the morning's drama. All of it. Right up to when they called me in the afternoon.

My head was pounding along with the door. It was the chief yeoman warder or whatever they called him.

"Captain Barnes. Herr Hess wishes to see you as soon as possible."

I nodded and shut the door, only for him to batter it again with a hammer and reaffirm his assertion that I was needed as soon as possible. I opened it again and made dressing noises whilst he stood there and watched. Once I had succeeded in this, he led me to Hess. He was lying on the bed groaning.

"They drugged me," he moaned.

"What?" I replied.

"They drugged me," he said again.

"Who did?"

"How should I know? It was in something I drank."

"Why?"

At this point I think he got bored of the conversation. At least I assumed that was what he meant by throwing himself back on his bed. I left, wondering through the haze what on earth that all meant. Why would someone drug him?

I decided to wait until I felt a little more alive before investigating further. Although that said it occurred to me that it might be best not to know. But then what was going on? I climbed onto the battlements to think. I was under no illusions that there were a lot of people interested in Hess, but which ones would drug him and for what reason were a mystery. I decided to see Menzies.

It took me a while to walk over to Whitehall, but it did give me an opportunity to think some more. Not that it helped in the slightest. I went up to Menzies office and waited. It was an hour before he turned up.

"Flashman."

"Sir," I replied unusually formal for me. "Hess says he was drugged." Normally I would avoid that sort of direct statement but in this case, I couldn't think of anything else to say.

"Yes, he was."

"He wants to know why?"

"Well he can't know. Not the real reason anyway."

"What is the real reason?"

"We needed a copy of his uniform."

"What? Why?"

"Contingency."

"In case of what?"

"Emergency."

"What the hell is going on?" At this he stared pointedly at me.

"The situation is on a knife edge. Churchill is bizarrely feeling somewhat stronger despite having little support. But then that's the kind of obtuse bastard he is. We have to be sure of our position before we act, otherwise we will fail and all end up in the mire. Control of Hess is crucial, but Churchill has wrongfooted us by agreeing there may be some merit in peace. I don't believe a word of it, but I also can't act alone. I think there may be some connection to the Yanks that he is using to his advantage. Of course, he's half yank himself.[203] Hamilton is doing the rounds to see who stands where. Hess is being moved to Aldershot shortly. He will be interrogated by Simon and Beaverbrook. What then is anybody's guess. I need you to stay with him incognito. You will be party to some of the interrogations. And my eyes and ears. Report when you can."

******

Mytchett Place it was called. It sounded so innocent really but in reality, was impregnable. It was bugged so that every word spoken in the place was recorded. It was surrounded by well over a hundred Coldstreamers[204] and the enormous garrison at

---

[203] Jenny Jerome, daughter of financier Leonard Jerome. Jerome's father was of Huguenot extraction and emigrated to America in 1710.

Aldershot was just down the road. Hess was placed on the first floor.

It was about this time that rumours started to circulate that he was unhinged. I don't know who started them, but it was someone official, presumably in the Churchill camp. I didn't see him for some time and not before he had managed to throw himself off the balcony in an apparent suicide attempt.[205] Apparently, part of the reason the rumours started was his persistence in asking to see the King who knew he was coming and would provide a safe conduct as a peace envoy. The strange thing was I knew it was true because I had seen the safe conduct letter in the King's name signed by a Grenadier Colonel called Pilcher[206]. But Churchill typically made some glib remark about Hess' disordered mind and so it took root.

The days slid by inexorably. I sat in on a couple of the interviews or conferences as they were officially called. Hess obviously appreciated me being there although he clearly wondered why I was referred to as Captain Barnes. He expanded at length on the U Boat war and how Britain would be starved into submission if necessary. He mentioned Russia and how the plan for expansion east would involve more negotiation, even negotiation with coercion. What he didn't mention was invasion, either of Russia or Britain. It seemed, to me at least, that there was never any intention of invading Britain. What Hitler needed was peace such that he would be in a strong position to dictate to the Russians exactly what he needed. And one of those things was

---

[204] Coldstream Guards, the oldest regiment of the British Army formed in 1650.

[205] This was on the 16th June when Hess apparently called for the doctor and when the door was opened, he was in full dress uniform, ran past and threw himself off the balcony breaking his leg.

[206] Lt-Colonel William Spelman Pilcher, Grenadier Guards. His career was unremarkable except for the fact he served at the same time as the Duke of Buccleuch. He was in Poland from 1920-21 and retired in 1936. Who's Who states he was recalled in 1939 but then in 1943 he disappears from the records including Who's Who. The oddity of that is that supposedly every single person should be listed in the general index. Pilcher appears to be the only exception. He died in 1970. If he did sign the safe conduct, he took that knowledge to his grave.

wheat. No one mentions it now, but one of Germany's main reasons for expanding east was to acquire food. With hindsight, I realised that Churchill wasn't quite the buffoon I imagined as he had worked all this out too. And realising that far too late, meant that despite being utterly confused at the time, looking back I worked out his plan. It was thoroughly cynical and worthy of a true upper class Harrovian politician. Now of course it is virtually heresy to suggest anything other than that Churchill was a hero. Of course he was.

However, back to the present. So much was going on it was hard to keep up. There were three strange incidents that occurred in quick succession. I didn't find out about them immediately as the first was only a couple of days after Hess arrived. Literally out of the blue, or black, a Czech called Richter landed north of London. The police were their usual efficient selves, bumped into him and arrested him for trespassing or something equally trivial. At the time he was just some random spy but later on, a lot more came to light. Secondly, and something I was familiar with, a Dornier 217 landed at Lincoln where the pilot, Heinrich Schmitt, handed over a large package. It was the peace document in its entirety.

Finally, at the end of May, two more parachutists arrived near Luton Hoo. Menzies told me that 11 group had received a message that they were coming and that there was a fierce but silent tussle over what should happen. Consequently, they were arrested. And then vanished[207]. Sir Harold Wernher who owned the place was livid. He was Chairman of Electrolux of which Dahlerus was Managing Director. He was a friend of Queen Mary and married to a niece of the last Tsar who was related to virtually every Royal Family in Europe. To say they were a large part of the peace group would be understatement of the year.

Anyway, the struggle continued in the background and it was only another month before all became clear. June 22nd to be precise.

---

[207] The only evidence of this comes from a Major John McCowen who was on the staff of 11 group. Leigh Mallory, AOC 11 Group, received a message about the drop of two SS men and told him about it and ordered him to intercept them. This he did. They were arrested and never heard of again.

Chapter 50

One hundred and twenty-nine years. Any ideas? I didn't know either, but it was the anniversary of Napoleon's assault on Russia. The date resonated with Hitler although one would have imagined his defeat might have done as well. And just like that it all suddenly made sense. I knew of course from Hess that the Germans wanted 'lebensraum' in Russia. I also knew that they wanted food, or at least the space to grow it. They also wanted to rule Europe one way or another. But what they needed most was security behind them. This was where Churchill had made the connection. If you change 'security' for 'peace', it is easy to see where the peace proposals came from. The Germans didn't really want to fight us. They considered us brothers in arms as well as master of large parts of the world. There was little or no point in upsetting that particular applecart as it was unnecessary for their plan. So, for many years in fact they had been making the connections that would allow a peace deal. The Royal Family, being German, were the most influential part of that. What they perhaps didn't allow for was that the royals were somewhat in hock to whatever politicians were in charge at the time. With the likes of Chamberlain and Halifax who were all part of the royal circle one way or another, it was relatively easy. Had Halifax assumed the reins of power in 1940, I am quite sure peace would have followed whatever the general public thought it wanted. They would have been sold a deal that may well have been humiliating on the face of it but after a short period would have been accepted as it prevented invasion and more loss of life. What the Germans didn't consider was the ability of Churchill to get himself into the seat of power. It is still a mystery how he did it.[208]

If one extrapolates that little power struggle a little further, one can see that Churchill had no intention of surrendering. He was himself beholden to his vision of his own destiny. A modern Marlborough if you will. An exaggeration I hear you cry! Really? Have a study of his completed works.

---

[208] There is indeed a lingering mystery over how Churchill managed to become Prime Minister. Numerous theories have been presented over the years, but I suspect only a few people knew and they are all dead.

Churchill was an imperialist through and through, which is probably the biggest contradiction in all of it when you consider he was willing to sacrifice the Empire and British sovereignty and power for his own ends. Surely you ask, he can't have been that self-centred? Well, let me set out the facts for you as described by Hess himself.

If Germany and Britain signed a peace deal, Russia would be pushed back well within its European boundaries, its influence non-existent. Hess well understood how weak Russia was at this point in history, largely of its own making. Stalin's purges and collectivisation had destroyed the ruling classes and whilst many of them made no difference, many did. The people that really matter, not the politicians or the wealthy, but the workers, the middle management, those that really run things, all gone. The system was fundamentally broken not least because of communism's obsession with being better than everything else which manifested itself as one long continually reported increase in harvests and production, all of which was made up to please the party. Reality was starvation, stagnation and decline. Russia was in no fit state to fight a war.

That being the case, the Germans could walk in and do as they pleased. The one thing that would really stop them was fighting on two fronts. Not us of course, we were no more than an irritant. What they feared was the Americans. The Americans weren't interested in fighting a war for us or anyone else. They never have been and never will. And why should they really? The Germans knew this.

The Germans therefore needed to break the British link with America. The problem was, whilst the Americans didn't want to fight a war, they were desperate for Europe to have one so they could manufacture the weapons for it and sell them to the British Empire. That was the key.

Churchill realised that Britain on its own was finished. Even with the Empire it wasn't going to do that much as it was all far too thinly spread. He knew that the only way Britain would 'win' was with American arms and he was prepared to beggar Britain to do it. Hess described what Britain winning would look like. He thought the Empire would disappear, British influence everywhere would decline and fall, we would have American debts that would take decades to pay off and we would become a shadow of our former selves. America would be in the ascendent in the west and Russia in the east. Europe would be a Russian satellite.

It is interesting to note, with hindsight of course, that the only point Hess missed was that the Americans would stay in Europe after the war, thus limiting the Soviet Union's influence to everything east of Germany and preserving the 'freedom' of western Europe. Further of course, one could analyse the 'United States of Europe' concept engendered in the EEC and how that furthered Hitler's ultimate aims. But that is another story.[209]

---

[209] When Flashman wrote his memoirs between 1957 and his death, the now EC was called the 'European Economic Community'. It is all too easy to link the EEC to Hess' plans for Europe post war and wonder who influenced its creation and how. Controversial throughout its history, in 2020, the break-up of the EC along with the decline in European power has become all too possible. The East is rising inexorably.

Chapter 51

Here you have to forgive me for jumping forward a year or so. I assure you it is necessary for the end of our story. The whole Hess debacle went quiet. In fact, it went utterly silent. The bombing had ceased, something that is rarely mentioned of course. The Luftwaffe 'blitz' stopped on the 10th May, the night Hess arrived. Equally strangely, the RAF pretty much gave up bombing Germany. It has been described as a secret armistice. Part of Churchill's plan? Who knows now? Portal, Chief of the Air Staff sent Churchill a memo asking why the plan had changed and 'Bomber' Harris, when asked about the effect of bombing later in the war by an American journalist remarked that 'he didn't know and perhaps we ought to try it sometime'.

Churchill had effectively silenced the opposition, first with his claim to be considering peace, then with threats although it still mystifies me quite how as he wasn't exactly in a strong position himself. I had seen through his pretence of considering a peace deal, so I assumed everyone else had too. In the end I suppose it was political and societal self-preservation, which was far more important than a mere war. I had suddenly found myself with little to do but before I could get too bored Menzies managed to send me to Washington. Oddly enough it suited me at the time, and it is possible the Americans would have stayed out of the war had I not gone, but that is also a story for another day.

It was June 1942. Suffice to say I was home and breathing a large sigh of relief for a couple of reasons. First of all, it looked likely that my fighting days were finally behind me. Secondly, my cockup with the landing lights at Dungavel seemed to have been forgotten. This was important to me if not to anyone else. Whether Hamilton had told Menzies I am not sure, but he was too occupied with self-preservation and libel cases[210] anyway to think too much about me. Consequently, I began to relax and enjoy the pleasures of wartime London. Not for long though. I had tried to sneak in quietly, but Menzies got word somehow and I was summoned to the presence.

---

[210] Hamilton fought and 'won' two libel cases. The most important however was the one he didn't fight against Beaverbrook. See Appendix.

"Flashman."

"Sir."

"I have a job for you. It is extremely important. It is extremely secret although you know a lot about it already." My heart began its ascent and my mouth went dry.

"Really Sir?" I said.

"Yes, really." He paused for dramatic effect. "Hess."

Well that silenced me effectively I have to say. I opened my mouth to say something, but I couldn't think of a single thing.

"It is our last chance. We have a small window of time to get him out of the clutches of Churchill and his gang. We can't stop the war now I imagine but who knows what would happen if that buffoon were unmasked."

"Churchill?"

"Of course, Churchill. Who else would I mean?"

"No-one."

"They have a plan which I am party to. This plan involves switching Hess with a double. This double will then become Hess at a place called Maindiff Court in Wales. The real Hess will be held somewhere secret. That I am not party to."

"What? Why?"

"It's very complicated and I am not completely sure everyone involved quite understands the significance. There are a number of interested parties shall we say. Obviously Churchill wants to keep Hess as a prisoner for the moment. He realises that there are others that would use him for other purposes should they manage to acquire him. Sikorski for example. The Poles realise now that they have been effectively betrayed by the allies and that there is almost no way they will regain any sort of effective independence without Russian influence. Had the war halted in 1941, they could have been party to negotiations and their view is that at least the Germans would listen. The Russians on the other hand they regard as savages. And then there is our own party. Kent and so on. There are several reasons why it would be useful to acquire control of Hess. Exposing Churchill would be attractive but ultimately pointless at the moment. After the war, the situation changes. And that could be sooner rather than later."

I didn't say anything again. I was flabbergasted to say the least.

"Anyway, the point is that Churchill is convinced the Poles wish to act. He seems to think they might assassinate him. At least that is the story he is peddling around and to be honest, we are not denying it either. He has been convinced by... people, shall we say, that if Hess were to be moved to Wales where security is less tight, it would flush the Poles out, especially if the move were to be publicly announced in some way."

"People like you no doubt?" He gave me an evil look.

"If you wish. However, it would be a lot better if Hess didn't make it at all to Wales."

"You mean, kill him?"

"No of course I don't mean kill him. I mean, if Hess were to be diverted along the way and replaced with someone else. Churchill thinks this is a wonderful plan. It appeals to his inner child. This is where you come in. Churchill wants to arrange for SOE to make the swap. I have agreed with this because it puts me at a remove from what is actually going to happen. I just need one more thing. You."

Chapter 52

Why me? Why do 'they' think 'I' am available for their seedy plans at a moment's notice? I have never had a satisfactory answer. Maybe it's in the genes. Flashman family available for dinner parties, opening fetes and lethal party games. I knew all about SOE of course. Menzies had filled me in on their selection process and training procedure, all of which was approved personally by Churchill. He thought it was all part of some big game. I didn't even bother arguing and pleading gout or age or even just pure terror. Menzies had me by the goolies and he knew it. I would rather be fed to actual wolves.

Having accepted fate, he told me what was going to happen and when. It was as he said, complicated.

"You will need to get to Mytchett Place to collect Hess. From there, you will be driven to Wales, ostensibly to drop Hess at a place called Maindiff Court. It's a mental hospital that was taken over for the duration. More usefully, it is just along the road from another place called Cae Kenfy house, which is owned by the Herberts[211]. Do I need to explain the significance of that?" My puzzled look convinced him I did. "The son is Kent's equerry. Before you reach Maindiff, you will have to 'convince' our SOE friend that a diversion to Cae Kenfy is required. There, the swap will take place and arrangements have already been made to get him to Scotland. You will then accompany him to Braemore Lodge. That is on Portland's estate of course." He raised his eyebrows. "Good God man, do you know nothing? Portland is the Queen's Uncle. Braemore is where they kept the Kaiser after the war."[212]

---

[211] The Herberts were the Earls of Pembroke. The heir at the time, Sir Sidney Herbert was indeed an equerry to the Duke of Kent.

[212] Apart from local stories there is no evidence whatsoever that the Kaiser was held in Scotland after the Great War. In these days of instant news, it is hard to imagine a time where hiding someone with a high profile was possible. It would appear that the Kaiser was given a chateau in Holland that belonged to Count Godard Bentinck but while it was being prepared, he was accommodated at Braemore Lodge on the Duke of Portland's estate. The 9th Duke was the chairman of the wartime Joint Intelligence Committee, other members of which included Sir Stewart Menzies. Portland's family name was

"How fascinating." He stared at me for a moment.

"Sometimes…." He paused for effect. "Sometimes I wonder. Still, that is what will happen. And I need YOU, to make it happen. Needless to say, the SOE man is expendable in the circumstances."

"Expendable?"

"Yes. Kill him if you must. Persuading him would be less trouble. You are booked on a train to Aldershot in about two hours. The car will collect Hess sometime tomorrow afternoon. I suggest you are there in good time."

With that, he handed me an envelope and shoved me out of the door. I decided to spend an hour on research. This I did at the Rag and Famish[213] and consisted mainly of inspecting the contents of a bottle of single malt. I did open the envelope to discover that at least there were some travel warrants and more importantly a short anonymous page of other instructions.

It seemed that Hess was to be driven to Wales by his doctor, one Captain Johnston and another officer. The other officer was clearly the SOE man. The driver was a Private called Hamilton which amused me slightly. He was to collect the appropriate vehicle from the main MT pool in Aldershot and then proceed to Mytchett Place. As neither Johnston nor Hamilton had the faintest idea who I was, they wouldn't question whether the driver was in fact who he said he was. The instructions made it clear that the driver wasn't to be harmed in the substitution. That, I realised, was the easy bit.

Slightly befuddled by now, I left the Rag and headed for the station. Had I known what the next day, and the next few weeks, were to bring, I would have bought another bottle or two, cashed in the warrant and bought a ticket to anywhere that wasn't Wales or Scotland. But I didn't.

Cavendish-Bentinck. The story emanated from the estate gamekeeper who told an RAF maintenance crew who were clearing a wrecked aircraft from the estate. The upper classes have always assumed their servants were both deaf and dumb.

[213] The 'Army and Navy' Club.

Chapter 53

What could possibly go wrong? Nothing at all, I convinced myself.

I was waiting at the MT pool just before midday when Private Hamilton turned up for his duty. I think I made his day when, dressed as an officer for the moment, I told him to go back to his barracks as he wasn't required. No one else needed to know. It was a bit hush hush. He didn't need telling twice.

Once he had gone, I acquired the vehicle and drove out of the main gate and a couple of miles down the road where I stopped and changed into a Private's uniform. I then continued to Mytchett Place. I was early so I waited a few hundred yards from the gates. I must have dozed off, but I woke up quickly enough. Gunfire[214]. For a second or two I was back in a Spitfire but then I realised it was coming from beside me. Slumped in the seat I couldn't see what was going on and nor did I want to. It was only when I realised that the shots were going both ways that I considered what to do next.

A gun battle though? How? Why?

Well why was obvious enough. Menzies had mentioned the Poles and it didn't require much deduction to put two and two together. How was a different matter although I had seen and heard enough of their pilots to know they were suicidally brave and reckless at the same time. For someone like me, being with Poles was an unnerving experience.

A bullet pinged off the roof and into the trees. Something had to be done and fast. I opened the door and performed something of a parachute roll into the trees, nearly colliding with a soldier in the process. He whipped round expecting trouble and I immediately put my hands in the air.

"Where is your officer?" I said in Polish. I hadn't wasted all my time with them. They were very resourceful chaps and I had

---

[214] There is almost no evidence for this except an MI5 report written by Kenneth de Courcy that talks of a gun battle between Polish troops and the Mytchett Place guards. There is no other detail. De Courcy was an unusual character with aristocratic relations who swam in the murky waters of both military and civil intelligence organisations.

spent many a night being entertained by them and the bevies of beauties who found them both exotic and attractive. More than a few young ladies had had the pleasure of Captain Flasmanski.

"Over there," he replied pointing. "Major Palak."

I crouched down, half ran and half crawled calling out for him as I went. It only took a moment before I found myself grovelling at his feet. He of course was standing, oblivious to the .303 rounds shredding leaves all around.

"Major Palak?"

"Yes. What can I do for you?"

"Actually, I think it is what I can do for you." He looked puzzled. "Hess." He crouched down instantly.

"How do you know? We told no one."

"They all know. You realise there is a battalion of Coldstream Guards in there don't you?"

"Yes. But they are English. We are Polish."

"That's all very well but even being Polish, one requires a little help some time."

"How?" An almighty crash told me that the Guardsmen had found something more lethal than their rifles.

"Easy. I am collecting him to take him away. In that car. Later today, although I imagine I can postpone it until tomorrow now given your little party. I'm driving him to.. well somewhere else. I don't care if he gets there or not. You can have him. Just let me get a few miles from here. How far away do you think you can get overnight?" He was sceptical as the look on his face showed.

"Ten miles, perhaps more."

"Look, you aren't going to get him out of there like this."

He was convinced because he wanted to be. And with a lifetime of practice and my family being who they are, I am a very convincing liar. It took us another ten minutes to come up with a plan and then I said we must be getting on because I knew reinforcements would be on the way.

It was fortunate my parking spot was out of sight of the gates. I got in the car and started the engine, gave the Major a thumbs up sign and took off like a shot. I rounded the bend and saw the gates ahead. Right on cue, a huge volume of fire started up and I saw heads go down amongst the defenders. At least two bullets hit the

211

car from behind as the Poles tried to add to the realism. There were already several holes in the front and rear windscreens although it would take a detective to notice they had been made from the inside at close range.

As I approached the gates I started waving frantically out of the window, keeping my head as low as possible. They were clearly wondering, and I could imagine the dilemma in the probably junior subaltern's head. Just a few more seconds was enough. Within a hundred yards of the gates, I screeched to a halt, leapt out of the car, ran round the front and dived headlong into cover. There was a final flurry of bullets from behind and then a noticeable diminution. Another couple of volleys came from the buildings and then the firing stopped. I stayed where I was.

It was about three hours in my head before I heard footsteps approaching.

"You alright mate?"

"I am."

"Crikey, aren't you a bit old to be a squaddie?" I glared at the Coldstreamer.

"Recalled, home service only. Wounded in the last lot. Enjoyed it so much I couldn't resist." I had no idea if it was plausible, but it wouldn't matter. No one was going to question him or me about it, least of all some Eton educated, puffed up Guards officer who had better things to do with his time.

"You'd better come with us."

"Not on your bleedin' life mate. Well not without this 'ere car anyway."

He laughed and waved at me to carry on. I drove in the gates and stopped outside what was clearly a makeshift guard house. I explained my mission to the duty officer, and everyone agreed it was best to stay the night while they checked out the grounds and made the buildings secure again. There was no sign of my passengers but presumably someone let them know they were delayed.

After all that, they took me to their mess, found me a bunk and fed me some unspeakable slop that only a soldier could eat. Someone gave me some brandy and I retired for the night where I stared at the ceiling and listened to the snores of twenty more guardsmen.

Morning came. More slop, tea and a summons to the guard room again. The aforementioned Eton clone appeared, sweeping the floor behind him as he went. I threw him a salute calculated to be just the right side of insolence and stared at a point on the wall a fraction above his over large forehead.

"Yaas," he said in the affected drawl beloved of Guards officers and other helpless animals. "Something of a surprise, what? Hush hush of course. You know how it is. Orders from on high. Applies to us all." I assumed he meant me.

"Sir," I said in that reply common to all soldiers who wish to say nothing without saying nothing.

"Yaas, I understand you are here to collect the ah, German?"

"Sir."

"Good, good. I believe Captain Johnston[215] and his sidekick are coming with you. They are in the main house and I believe they are aware you are on the way. You can collect them from there."

He turned away and from that I assumed the interview was over and I was free to go. I just had one more thing to do and that was find somewhere to change. I needed to promote myself again.

It didn't take long. I thought Major was enough. I just needed to outrank Johnston. I pulled up outside the front door of the main house, stopped the car and went in. Johnston was waiting for me.

"Ah," he said in that English way of starting a conversation without knowing what to say. "Good. Our friend here is accompanying us." He turned to look at a rather nondescript man. He was my problem.

"Yes indeed," I said. "May I speak to you in private?"

"Of course, Sir. In here. My office."

"Excellent." We entered. "We have a small problem. You are aware of the incident yesterday?" He nodded. "We have not been provided with an escort of course. Apart from us and your friend. He's SOE isn't he?"[216]

---

[215] Captain M.K. Johnston RAMC had recently taken over medical care of Hess.

[216] This is correct. Given everything that had happened, the movement of the Deputy Führer with no military escort over a long distance rather beggars belief, especially when you consider the battalion of guardsmen at Mytchett

"I understand that to be the case, yes."

"Right, excellent. There is something of a concern that those responsible for yesterday may try again. I doubt they would harm us, but they might try and stop us. So, I have an ingenious plan." I grinned at the Captain to reassure him that I was in fact a genius capable of such a plan. "Your SOE friend can wear Herr Hess' uniform. Throw them off the scent. Perhaps you could tell him and arrange the change before they come out. Excellent." I turned away as he was about to voice his objections, but I wasn't having any of that and by turning away forced him to acquiesce regardless. English officers. Jesus Christ. I despaired. Again. "I will see you in the car in a moment."

I knew it would work. As always, bluff and confidence, whether one felt it or not. Plus knowing how the English upper classes work.

They appeared about ten minutes later. They were about a head difference in height, so they had kept their own trousers, but it made little difference overall. The main point was to convince a Polish officer who had, and this was important, never met Hess. I had checked in case you are wondering.

We got in the car and set off, Hess giving me an incomprehensible look.

Place. It leads one to assume there was more to it.

Chapter 54

I was relying on several things. First of all, that nothing would actually be done about the gun battle outside Mytchett Place. And nothing was done. No one ever heard about it. The house was remote enough and secure enough for there to be no observers. It was also close to enough garrisons and firing ranges that the noise of rifles and so on would be dismissed as nothing more than the usual disturbances. There was a war on.

I didn't know any of this at the time obviously, but knowing how the bureaucratic mind, and in particular the British bureaucratic mind, worked as well as the obsession with not telling anybody anything and never admitting there had been an almighty cockup, I was as sure as I could be that they would kick me out of the gate as soon as possible. Anything to pass the responsibility to some other sap.

Sandhurst. It wasn't far which was the beauty of it. It was surrounded by troops so no one would wonder what we were doing. Plus, it was the last place they would expect a band of marauding Poles. Of course, the other thing was that I knew they had given themselves up. Well, most of them. Major Palak had laughed when I suggested it, but he considered it worth it. They wouldn't execute them, they would just hand them over to the Polish authorities, give them a sharp rap on the knuckles and make them promise not to do it again.

The best bit? My favourite part? The whole thing wouldn't even be my fault. How? Well, this is how.

I drove slowly through the country lanes. Johnston sat beside me looking sceptical. Hess behind me looking equally puzzled and the SOE chap just looked like the Cheshire Cat. I had thought he would go along with it because they were that sort of organisation. They reflected Churchill and his ridiculous Boy's Own[217] view of war. Intrigue for intrigues sake. Don't make

---

[217] Boy's Own was a magazine for boys published between 1879 and 1967. It was a mix of adventure stories, public school stories, notes on sports and games and instructions on how to make useful things like canoes or puzzles. It reflected the times in its unquestioning support of Empire and thus British superiority, particularly with serials like 'The Stirring Days of the British

anything easy when you can over complicate it. He had leapt at the chance to dress up for the sake of his country and much to Johnston's surprise as well. It couldn't have been better.

And so it was that in the woods near Sandhurst, where so many of our great military leaders learnt their trade rushing around in the mud, I accidentally took a wrong turn.

"Bugger it," I said to no one in particular. "A roadblock. Thought I took a wrong turn back there."

I pulled up to the makeshift log across the road and stopped. I opened the window as the sentry approached. It was an officer but not my new friend. Glancing round, I could see soldiers appearing from the trees to surround us. He stuck his head through the open window.

"Him," pointing at our SOE friend who now looked a little concerned. "Out."

He looked at me silently pleading for help. I just nodded and shrugged. The door opened and he was helped out of the car. I daren't look at the others who were sitting staring at the drama unfolding.

"Thank you," said the officer before he turned and vanished into the woods with the soldiers. We sat for just long enough to let them get out of sight before I restarted the engine, turned the car round and drove away before anyone asked too many questions.

Chapter 55

"What just happened?" Johnston.

"Orders," I replied.

"But what about… him?"

"What about him? This is a war. He's expendable for the greater good." I smiled at my own callousness.

"Who are you then?"

"My name is irrelevant. I am a senior officer in the RAF. My orders come from Whitehall. We are going to Wales and you are going to drive."

He didn't reply and at the next opportunity I stopped and swapped seats with him. Hess said nothing and I just winked at him when I got a chance. He almost smiled. And we drove for hours and hours. I had forgotten how far away Wales was, both in distance and civilisation. I had just about had the presence of mind to bring some sustenance in the form of sandwiches and brandy.

It was late evening when we arrived. It had been a struggle to find the place but fortunately I knew Cae Kenfy was next to the River Usk, and being summer it was light 'til late. Menzies had drawn me a map that helped, crude as it was.

"Ah Flashman, you made it," said the very man. "Herr Hess," he said with a slight nod of the head, "and this must be Captain Johnston?"

"Yes sir," Johnston replied looking bemused.

"And?" he said looking at me.

"You said he was expendable." I paused to let this sink in as I had a sneaking suspicion that Menzies thought I wouldn't have the necessary balls to get rid of him. I didn't but he didn't need to know that. "The Poles have him. They think he is Hess."

"Oh my God, there will be hell to pay. Sikorski is not a rational man. How?"

I related the story and watched his eyes slowly widen, Hess was still there, and he seemed equally amazed.

"One more thing. I would like you to meet someone." He grinned and led us out of the room, along a hallway and quietly opened a door. Sitting in a chair in front of a fire was a man. As we entered, he stood up and turned round. He was tall, as tall as

Hess. He was wearing a German uniform that looked suspiciously like Hess' and when Menzies turned on a light, three of us gasped because it was Hess. Well almost.

"Was ist…" Hess began.

"Rudolf Hess is going to a place called Maindiff Court tomorrow. He is also going to Scotland. From there, the real Rudolf Hess will be taken to Sweden and from there perhaps we can breathe some life into negotiating our way out of this mess. Captain Johnston, you aren't coming to Scotland. You are going to Maindiff. By the way, I am the head of the Special Intelligence Service. If you breathe a word of this to anyone, you will find yourself persona non grata. For the rest of your life. Anyway, we can't hang around here. Rest tonight and we start for Scotland tomorrow."

******

It was another long, long drive. We took it in turns. It was much quicker by Spitfire. It was so long it was about as far as you could go without driving into the sea. It was beyond the edge of civilisation. But we got there in the end. Hess seemed pleased when he found out it was where the Kaiser had stayed after the war and he quickly made himself at home. There was enough space for both of us, and we settled in for a prolonged stay. Menzies had said it might be some time before he could organise a flight. Apart from anything, he had to judge the repercussions from the swap and who would take the rap for it. I didn't care about any of that. I was happy to be away from whoever was going to take the rap for it. It wasn't me for a change.

What I didn't know was what was going on behind the scenes. Apparently a lot. I had always known I was part of some much bigger plot and that I had hitherto only been on the periphery. But when Menzies appeared again about a week later, ordered dinner for three then dismissed the staff, I knew something was brewing. The talk over dinner was desultory, but there was an atmosphere that was sliceable. It wasn't until we reached the cigars and brandy that Menzies finally told us.

"You won't know this, but Churchill and his gang signed a new treaty with the Russians a few weeks ago[218]. It commits them, us even, to a prolonged alliance of twenty years or more. Why he thinks that is a good idea is beyond comprehension, but I guess it is the only way to go for him given the deteriorating situation. Singapore was bad but Tobruk could be the final nail. We are about to be presented with a golden opportunity. Churchill is going to Cairo and then on to Moscow to tell Stalin there will be no second front in Europe this year. He thinks telling him about 'Torch' will placate him[219]. We can make sure that is met with the contempt it deserves. He doesn't trust us of course. Even the pilot for his aircraft is American! It is quite something when the Prime Minister doesn't trust his own air force[220]. All the other players are ready. Hoare and Halifax are ready to form a government. Beaverbrook is being his usual self, but he will back us if we look like we are going to win. And that is crucial. What we need is the catalyst. That is where you come in."

I opened my mouth to protest that I had done my bit, that I liked living in a remote lodge in the middle of nowhere, I wasn't interested in fighting anymore and that I had a prior engagement. But Hess beat me to it.

"Excellent. I knew we would overcome the warmonger eventually. What do we do?"

"Stockholm. You will fly over on the 25th. Kent will be with you. It will be a neutral flight. The crew will be handpicked. You will be met and next day, you will make an announcement together that peace has been agreed as per the terms flown over last year. The King will be at Balmoral the night before to

---

[218] On 11th June 1942, Eden announced in the Commons that seventeen days earlier, the British and Russian governments had concluded a twenty year alliance and committing to closer post war co-operation. It was signed by Churchill, Eden, Attlee and Sinclair, thus tying all the main political parties to it.

[219] The largest surrender in British military history occurred in February 1942 with the loss of Singapore. The fall of Tobruk in June was equally devastating. At the time, any by-election candidate supporting Churchill was utterly routed in the polls and Sinclair, leader of the Liberal Party, felt it necessary to implore his MPs to support the Government. 'Torch' was the planned US/British North African offensive planned for November.

[220] Odd indeed. The American pilots name was Vanderkloot.

approve the scheme with Kent and confirm that he is acting with his authority. The Lords and the Commons will approve."

"Incredible," said Hess. "I couldn't have done it better myself." Menzies gave him a raised eyebrow but then continued.

"You will be picked up at Loch More. A Sunderland from 228 will come over from Oban a couple of days before[221]. You can join it there and then Ho! for Sweden and victory!"

I didn't say anything. What was there to say really? For once it was an entirely safe mission. Entirely.

Menzies departed soon after leaving us to discuss our forthcoming holiday. Hess was ecstatic.

"All this has been worth it," he said. "What do you think?" There was a sudden edge to his tone. "Wing Commander."

"Well, it's excellent news, we can all go home and stop fighting and so on."

"Home? Which home are you thinking of my dear Fleischmann?"

"Well, I hadn't really thought about it, I have lived in so many places." I was fast assessing what weapons were available and more importantly what escape routes there were. None of course. He had me cornered in a room with the door behind him. It was an amateur mistake. I must be getting slow in my old age. A lifetime of bedroom escapes had taught me nothing apparently. Could I kill him? He was older than me I thought and must have been affected by a year of confinement, whereas I had maintained a lithe, fit form with alcohol, cigars and womanising. So about evens then.

He laughed out loud. A long, loud guffaw that lasted for at least a minute. I stood rooted to the spot.

"You think I didn't know?"

"Know? Know what?"

"That you were English?" I didn't say anything. "Oh. Mein Gott don't worry. No one else knows. I only realised last year when I flew over. It explained many things. But then I think you were a very clever agent to work both sides at the same time. And

---

[221] 228 Squadron were based at RAF Oban, a flying boat station on the west coast of Scotland. They were equipped with Short Sunderlands.

220

perhaps, this will be our finest hour. When we finally stop the Aryan races fighting each other and turn against the true enemy."

Chapter 56

I awoke feeling out of sorts. My head was spinning and not just from the half-drunk bottle of whisky beside the bed. I went outside. It was a glorious day but with a bank of cloud approaching albeit at least a thousand feet high. And that is important, in fact especially important given what happened later. I walked down to the edge of the loch to contemplate life and clear the fug away. I was there long enough that Hess joined me. He was full of the joys of spring, mainly I suspect because he was out of the clutches of Churchill and also because in his view, he was about to complete his delayed mission to bring peace on earth. Well, to some of it anyway.

We didn't really talk. We had said probably all there was to say over the previous few days, having discussed our mutual history, the rise of the Nazis, the future of Europe in German hands and so on. He had told me most of it before anyway when he believed I was on his side. He still chuckled at that, how I had fooled him for so long. As I said, it was nothing compared to fooling everyone else that one was an officer and a gentleman. The similarity was that everyone wanted to believe what they heard.

The morning slipped slowly by. It wasn't cold but once the cloud had hidden the sun it was distinctly cooler, and we went back inside to await events. It was just after two o'clock when we heard the faint throb of engines.

We went outside as a white Sunderland flying boat came over the ridge at the end of the loch and flew low over the water before touching down a few hundred yards away. It slowed immediately and headed for the lodge where there was a small jetty. Once it was close it turned round and sat outer engines idling waiting for us to row over to it.

It took no more than a few minutes to climb in and close the nose door. Once in, there were some necessarily brief and cramped introductions. Kent was first but we knew him already. Oddly, he had a briefcase handcuffed to his wrist. Frank Goyen was the commander despite his lowly rank[222] and the presence of

---

[222]26 year old Flight Lieutenant Francis (Frank) Goyen was a well-

his CO, Wing Commander Thomas Moseley. There was another pilot, Pilot Officer Syd Smith, and a navigator George Saunders.

Kent had a small but impressive entourage with him. First an RNVR Lieutenant, John Lowther who also happened to be the grandson of Viscount Ullswater and PO Michael Strutt, son of Lord Belper. He had a valet, John Hales as well.

Finally there were the NCOs, Flight Sergeants Charles Lewis, William Jones, Andy Jack and Ernest Hewardine, Sergeants Edward Blacklock, Arthur Catt and Leonard Sweet who were amongst other things the gunners. I rather hoped we wouldn't need them. We didn't. But not for the reasons I imagined.

All four engines running again, I took my seat as near to the tail as I could get. Hess was somewhat forward of me and Kent and his entourage were out of sight completely. I could hear the crew running through checks and so on on the intercom. Ready at last, we turned to point down the loch facing the way they had landed. Hess smiled at me for some reason and then put his head back in a gesture of relief. I heard a brief conversation about the throttles and then the noise made conversation impossible and the Sunderland began its take-off run, slowly at first but steadily increasing speed. The water was calm which meant it would take a little longer, but this was not unusual on a lake.

I felt it lift off and touch again a couple of times before we finally broke free of the water's grip, and then we slowly climbed away towards the ridge at the end. The aircraft began to turn and then suddenly I heard a gasp of pure fear.

"No more elevator, nothing!" It was Moseley I thought but couldn't be absolutely sure.

"Will we make it?" another voice chimed in. Paralysis gripped me now as I was suddenly aware of being a mere passenger in whatever was unfolding.

"Too low, too low, no elevator." What the hell did he mean 'no elevator'? I wondered in one of those moments where your

---

regarded Australian Sunderland pilot having flown over 1200 hours on type and having been selected to fly Stafford Cripps, the Ambassador, to Moscow in 1941. He was the commander regardless of anyone else's rank, a principle still extant on any RAF flight.

mind diverts itself from impending disaster to think about something trivial.

"We're going in." It was a bald statement, no more. And then we did.

Chapter 57

There are times in one's life where one knows death is imminent. This was one of them. Not the only one for me. In fact, it was an all too frequent occurrence. But this had an added element of finality. I had crashed aeroplanes before and survived, but I had always had some semblance of control. At this moment, I was in someone else's hands.

The first impact wasn't that big to be honest, and for a fraction of a second I thought that might be it. The second however was enormous. The women in my life flashed before my eyes. As this took longer than a few seconds it was interrupted by the destruction of the aircraft and my being knocked into unconsciousness.

I don't know how long I was out and I never will. When I opened my eyes, I was laying on my back. I didn't move for a while as it seemed like that would be a painful thing to do. I was dimly aware of movement nearby though and after a short period of reflection I decided that moving might in fact be a wise choice.

I rolled onto one side first of all. There was little pain apart from a lump on the back of my head and my wrist feeling fragile. I rather wished I hadn't rolled though because the first thing I saw was the wreckage and strewn around it, the bodies of the crew. I say bodies because none were moving although at this point, I couldn't have been certain they were all dead. And they weren't as it turned out.

Suddenly I remembered why I was there. Hess. Where was he? I leapt up, or rather I tried to leap up, but it turned into more of a geriatric stagger onto my knees followed by a slow ascent to my feet. I stood swaying for a minute or two taking in the scene. I noted the patchy cloud in an otherwise glorious blue sky, the remoteness of the hill on which I now stood, the gentle crackle of burning aeroplane and the man standing staring at me.

This finally sank in and I stumbled towards him. He was clearly in shock as I suppose I was.

"They're all dead," he said gesturing around him. " 'Cept you and me Sir."

"Indeed. I'd better just check myself though." He looked at me but didn't question my statement. "Can you show me?"

"Follow me Sir."

We set off on our gruesome tour of the hillside. He was absolutely correct. Each body was unmoving and unlikely to do so again. I made a point of inspecting them all, but my only real interest was in Kent, who was lying on his side oddly surrounded by his entourage, and Hess who for possibly the first time since I met him looked at peace. That is apart from the unusual position of his legs.

The flight crew were still in the burning cockpit. If they did survive the initial crash, they certainly would not have survived the fire now consuming the aluminium fuselage.

Now what? I had absolutely no idea what to do. Standard operating procedure following the loss of one's aircraft was to remain with it if at all possible. But it wasn't possible. Well, it was physically possible. Just not sensible at this point. All I could think of was that last comment on the intercom.

"Jack, we've got to get the hell out of here." As the yanks might say.

"But sir, shouldn't we stay with the wreckage?"

"You know who was on board, don't you?"

"Yes sir, the Duke of..."

"Not the Duke, Hess."

"Well, I did guess something was going on."

"Then you appreciate that this is not as simple as it might at first appear. There are people out there who would be more than happy to see the demise of all on board. That includes you and me as witnesses. And don't for a second assume they aren't capable of finishing the job." He stared at me for a minute, his face a picture of disbelief in the very idea of what I was suggesting. "So, we need to get a move on and skedaddle. Someone will have heard that crash even out here."

Not quite convinced, we collected everything we could find that might be useful and set off across the valley. As we walked, I started to get an idea of what might have gone wrong. We had turned slightly after take-off and then again before I heard the comments about the elevators and felt more bank as they tried to turn harder. There was what I can only describe as some sort of optical illusion at the corner of the valley. We had taken the obvious route only to find the ground rose to the point where we

226

hit it. Had we turned harder initially, we would have made it into the valley proper which looking down it led to the sea and safety. Which meant of course it could just have been an error of judgement. But that elevator comment still nagged at me.

The sky was clearing as we set off into the valley. It was slow going. Jack was clearly in some discomfort from the burns on his hands, but he kept quiet about it luckily. As a general rule, I only want to tell others about my misfortune, not hear about theirs. We trudged on, the ground imperceptibly starting to rise ahead of us. At some point, we stopped and turned round. The burning wreckage was there for all the world to see and by now it also had a number of people in attendance. We drank our fill of water plus a slug from my flask which had survived the accident before continuing our stroll up the hill.

The fire died away slowly and as the dusk came down, we both curled up in the heather on the hillside. We had a good nights sleep, probably because of the shock and woke to a glorious dawn. We had nothing to eat so eventually conceded that at some point we had to find civilisation again. We headed for the coast on what would have been the Sunderlands flight path had it made it over the ridge until we saw a crofter's cottage ahead.

After a short debate, we approached the cottage and knocked on the door. A minute later it opened.

"Aye?" said the owner.

"Good morning," said I. "We have just come from the hills there," pointing vaguely behind me, "from where our aircraft crashed. We were wondering if you could help us at all?"

"Aye," said the owner. "Ye'd better come in."

And yet again, from here, events overtook us both.

Chapter 58

Elsie Sutherland her name was. She immediately phoned for the local doctor in Dunbeath. This done, I asked her if I could use the telephone, hinting at various dark reasons and so on. She consented and I telephoned Menzies. It was an odd conversation.

"Is that really you Flashman?"

"Yes it really is."

"How on earth did you survive?"

"No idea. But there were two of us. The tail gunner survived as well."

"Jesus Christ." That said a fair bit about the official reaction. "We've got to get you out of the area. Not much we can do for this gunner chap though. Can you get to Turnhouse? Or Dungavel?"

"I suppose so."

"Then do so. I will be there as soon as possible. And tell anyone you have spoken to to keep quiet, including your gunner friend." With that he ended the call.

Mrs Sutherland provided some tea and a couple of eggs for a belated lunch. Jack struggled with it because of his burns which were beginning to tighten everything up and were clearly painful. I was starving and wolfed down everything provided. I had just finished when a car pulled up at the cottage and a Dr Kennedy appeared. He took one look at Jack and said hospital was essential immediately. I thanked Mrs Sutherland for her hospitality, bought her silence with some money I had collected at the scene and got in the car. We drove to Lybster hospital where Jack was admitted and then having wished him good luck, told him to keep his gob shut and deny I was ever there, I departed. It was the last time I saw him.

I then set out on another of those interminable wartime train journeys having cadged a lift to the nearest station from the good doctor. He was a potential obstacle and not one I could overcome with threats or money. In the end, it was easy. It turned out he had attended the site straight after the crash and had seen who was there. I simply had to suggest royal embarrassment and he took the point.

It took the best part of a day to get to Turnhouse and then I still had to get to Dungavel. Fortunately, Hamilton was there and he drove me himself, mainly to limit my contact with anyone on the airfield. It was probably wise in the circumstances.

He dropped me off in the late afternoon and left me to it having let me in. I found somewhere to lie down and promptly went to sleep.

It was light when I awoke. For a moment I couldn't decide whether it was still afternoon or morning but after a look outside I realised it was morning. I must have slept for a good twelve hours.

I went in search of sustenance and was happily frying more eggs and bacon when I heard car doors slamming. It didn't take Menzies long to find me.

"Breakfast?" I said.

"Why not. It might be the only thing we get to eat for some time." That sounded ominous. "The cat is truly amongst the pigeons now. And the pigeons are running for cover."

"What on earth does that mean?"

"Well, from a position of dictating the future of the war, we are now pawns of the very establishment we were trying to bring down. With Hess and Kent dead we have no chance of resurrecting the plan. They were essential to establishing the consensus between the two countries. And our allies are falling over themselves to get away from the steaming turd."

"What about the King? Can't he say something?"

"Like what? My late brother was negotiating with the Germans and I am here to tell you it was a success. The Germans agree, but we can't prove it so if you would all like to raise your glasses and drink to peace. No chance. Not least because the Germans wouldn't buy it themselves given that they appear to be winning."[223]

"So, what now?"

"We have one last chance. Get back to the crash site as soon as you can. Talk to everyone. But do it discreetly. My contact in SOE tells me there was something fishy going on. He wouldn't

---

[223] The battle of El Alamein, generally regarded as something of a turning point for the British Army was still some weeks away.

elaborate but he alluded in general as to how they, SOE, might consider terminating a troublesome and outspoken but high-profile person. Their favourite idea is an aircraft crash shortly after take-off. Apparently, and these were his words, to the layman, the perfect sabotage is an aircraft disappearing without trace over the Atlantic. In reality however, if one were to need to dispose of someone more publicly important, there needs to be wreckage and bodies to allay any doubts."[224]

---

[224] Assassination in this way was and is by no means impossible or unprecedented. In November 1942, General Sikorski was a passenger on a Lockheed Hudson bound for Montreal when both engines failed on take-off. He survived but both the US and British governments declared the incident sabotage. In July 1943, Sikorski was again taking off from Gibraltar when the aircraft crashed in thirty feet of water killing all on board except the pilot who contrary to usual practice had put his lifejacket on over his parachute. The enquiry decided the reason it crashed was jammed elevators but could not say why they jammed. The enquiry decided it was an accident, but his widow refused to speak to Churchill again. At the time of course, the Poles had become a thorn in the British side, largely because Britain was reneging on its entire reason for going to war and had agreed that Russia could keep at least some of Poland.

Chapter 59

I gave it some thought as I headed north again. It didn't shock me particularly. The idea of rubbing out inconvenient but influential persons was nothing new. Julius Caesar, Jesus, the Twins in the Tower, various other Royals, Perceval[225], Lincoln. The list was pretty comprehensive. Churchill, I had no doubt, wouldn't baulk at a few deaths to add to the thousands so far. For the greater good he would tell himself. Personally, I didn't even need that excuse. If you were in my way as I made my exit, I wouldn't hesitate to hurl you into the firing line if it meant I could escape it. It wasn't personal.

In this case though, how? How did one bring an aircraft down at a specific moment? That comment at the end. No elevator. It had made me jumpy then and it was sure as hell making me jumpy now.

I assumed it was Goyen who made it as he would have been flying. But why?

It took me a long time to get back up to the crash site. On the way past, I decided to see what the locals knew. Being Scots, they would have made damn sure to find out as much as possible and sure enough they did. It didn't take me long to find one of the first men on the scene, Special Constable Will Bethune.

He was a thoroughly reliable, solid middle-aged Scotsman. As a thoroughly unreliable, past middle age Englishman, I realised that to get any information I would have to win him over. I was wondering how to go about this other than dressing up in my Wing Commander's uniform, but it was entirely unnecessary. As soon as I mentioned that I was an official investigating officer for the RAF and was deeply concerned about the death of a member of the Royal Family he was on my side. Well, that and the rather expensive single malt I happened to give him.

"Weel sir, I wisnae first thar of course. Those bluidy farmers were thar but even they wisnae first. Thar bluidy pongos were thar. Twar a bit odd how they got up thar so quick. I saw them on

---

[225] Spencer Perceval was the only British Prime Minister who was assassinated. He was shot dead in the House of Commons Lobby on 11th May 1812.

thar way back doon. They tried to persuade me not to gae up 'cos it war pointless as thee were all deid. They were of course. Deid."

"What regiment were they?"

"Nae idea. Nae badges. I spoke to thee officer. He wis the one who said not tae gae up. I thought it wis odd though. When I got up thar, thar were nae guards, just the bluidy farmers rooting aboot like pigs. He wis reet though. They wis all deid."

"Well, that's very interesting."

It was of course. How the hell did the army get up there so fast and before the locals? That sounded suspicious all by itself. Unless they knew of course. My innards froze at that thought. What if they were still watching?

"Thar wis money everywhere as weel," he added as an afterthought. "Foreign. From the Duke's briefcase. The strangest thing though. I counted fifteen bodies. Everyone said thar wis fifteen crew. So, they wis a' deid. But then thee gunner turns up in hospital next day. So then thee said thar wis fourteen deid and one survivor. But I know thar wis fifteen. I made sure. Three times I counted. Thar wis definitely fifteen."

"That's very strange. You know these government officials. And as for the army."

We both rolled our eyes to the ceiling at that. Bloody army.

I left him to it at that, cursing the soldiers. He would never know. I set off for the crash site.

It took me some time to get there. The car only got me so far and then I had to walk. It was easy enough to find. There were still wisps of smoke from the smouldering wreckage. When I got there, a lot of it had been covered up which was odd as well. What was the point? It wasn't as though anyone could see it. It took me a moment to work it out. The aircraft was white, something only used for diplomatic or neutral flights. To Sweden. Officially they, or rather we, were going to Iceland which was a military flight. As I thought it, I smelt a large rat. Who knew and what did they know? There would have been quite a few who knew of the decoy mission, not least because it involved a member of the Royal Family. The more I thought about it, the more I wondered. The aircraft must have been specially painted because 228's Sunderland's were all camouflaged. Then why fly it over to Invergordon. A real flight to Iceland with a member of the Royal Family on board would have departed from Oban. My blood ran cold.

I looked around me. Were the bastards watching? Surely not. And did they even know I had been onboard. How could they? And if they did, what then?

I ambled around the wreckage wondering and looking. The wrecked cockpit was obvious. I lifted the tarpaulin and stared in. I don't know why really. It had clearly been cleaned up a bit but there was still quite a lot of blood everywhere and worse, it stank of fried beef. I stared through the windscreen for a while, seeing what Goyen would have seen, reliving those last seconds of life. 'No elevator'. Why had he said that?

I turned round and walked back through the field of wreckage looking at the pieces. The tail was one of the largest pieces which I suppose was what protected us when we landed. I pulled a couple of the pegs out that were holding the tarpaulin down and threw it back as far as I could. The elevators themselves were more or less intact as were the cable runs, at least as far as where the fuselage had broken off. I got down on my knees and crawled down under the remains peering in the various holes. I got as far back as the rear access hatch that had broken off. I looked inside and was just scratching my head when I saw it. It was just a burn and I nearly dismissed it as such. It was the cable though. It was snapped. But not snapped. A closer look showed it had a clean break in it. It looked odd and when I lifted both ends, I realised there was a gap. It made no sense, except for the fact it was sitting in the wreckage on the hill. My blood ran cold again as the implications sank in.

They had tried to kill us. In fact, they had largely succeeded. The main players were both dead, just a couple of witnesses left. I didn't hang around any longer[226].

---

[226] In the Spring of 1943, Charles de Gaulle was due to fly to Glasgow from Hendon. On take-off, the elevators failed. Investigation afterwards discovered that the control rods had been eaten through with acid. They blamed the Germans, but this happened at a time when Churchill had come to see de Gaulle as a nuisance to be eliminated. He survived obviously, but Anglo/French relations particularly with de Gaulle were permanently fraught.

Chapter 60

I needed to tell someone. Menzies for preference but someone. I headed back down the track away from the wreckage. I had been going about twenty minutes when I saw some air force uniforms coming my way. I stopped and let them come to me.

"Hello Sir," said a Flight Sergeant, dying to ask me what the hell I was doing there.

"Hello Flight Sarn't. What are you chaps doing up here?" I asked turning his silent question back on him.

"Come to clear the wreckage sir. Just a preliminary survey. Took us a while to get here y'see. Come from Carluke."

That terminated our conversation. It was only as I drove away that what he said sunk in. Carluke? Why would a clearance unit from so far away be sent to clear a wreck here? In fact, it was strange that it was to be cleared at all. Most mountain wrecks were left in situ. It wasn't like they were in the way. But then this one was a little different. And then something else struck me. I had seen a letter at Turnhouse referring to the clearance of the wreckage of Hess' aircraft. Something about the unit coming from Carluke.

As my Father once said, the most unlikely coincidences do occur citing the case of the rifle lost in the desert and its original owner finding it years later. But this was more than a coincidence. This was deliberate use of a unit based much too far away.

I got back to Dunbeath in record time and grabbed the telephone praying Menzies would answer. Thankfully he did.

"It was them."

"My God in heaven. I didn't think they would have it in them."

"What now?" I said, hoping that he would propose a long holiday somewhere warm. There was a long silence.

"That journalist? What was his name again? Carrow was it?

"Nancarrow."

"That's it, Nancarrow. He was on our side as I recall. Wrote a book on your squadron. Dollan wrote the foreword.[227]"

---

[227] This must be Fred Nancarrow, a leading and respected aviation journalist from Glasgow who covered both Hess' flight and the Kent crash.

234

"That is all correct."

"Get hold of him. He covered the night Hess got here and I think he wrote something on the crash. He may be our last chance. Then, get to Balmoral. See Marina[228] and tell her we will do something so that it wasn't for nothing."

It occurred to me that we had already had several last chances and that eventually one of them might be, how shall I put this, fatal. To me at least. That wasn't a chance I particularly wanted to explore.

In the meantime, I decided that the best thing to do was find something decent to eat, something to drink and somewhere soft to sleep. This I did. Thus, next morning I awoke full of the joys of spring. Well, nearly.

I drove to Glasgow. It felt like I was driving forever. The roads were terrible, the traffic was horrendous, and the accents were unintelligible. I eventually found the offices of the Herald and made a nuisance of myself until they let me in. I found Fred's office.

"Harry my boy! What brings you here?"

"We need to talk. Away from here. Kent." The raised eyebrows said it all.

"Understood. I am committed this afternoon but how about this evening? Dinner. On me."

"Excellent. Where?"

"Come with me. I'm going for a trip with 228 around the islands. I'm sure their mess will entertain you suitably until I get back."

"Even better."

He clattered around his office for a few minutes collecting bits of paper and pencils and other random items before we left. I drove him to Oban which also took forever. It was lucky really because it gave me a chance to fill him in on all the ugly details. He had been in on it to some degree for a long time and in fact Menzies certainly had had plans to use him after the joint Stockholm announcement. Obviously that had gone to pot but it didn't matter quite yet.

---

[228] Princess Marina was Kent's wife.

The mess was open, the bar was open, Fred and I partook of a couple of very pleasant single malts and then some junior oik dragged him away for his trip. I ordered another and then ambled outside and down to the water to watch them depart. I realised I had no idea where they were going but it presumably wasn't a long way away.

The Sunderland's engines burst into life and it floated slowly away. I watched it turn and accelerate across the bay and get airborne, climb slowly away, pass the point at which my previous Sunderland flight had abruptly ended and become a speck in the distance. I went back to the bar.

Chapter 61

There are moments in life where one is completely paralysed, unable to function on a basic level. They can last moments or much, much longer. I have had many such moments, the only caveat being that apart from a moment of paralysis my legs have a mind of their own and can usually be relied on to act by removing me from the scene.

On this occasion however, no such thing occurred. An officer came into the mess with a stunned look on his face.

"Lost another one!" he exclaimed to no one in particular.

"Another what?" I replied as none of the few people there felt able to comment.

"Another Sunderland," he said giving me a puzzled look.

I knew straightaway. I almost daren't ask.

"Not the one that took off earlier surely?"

"That's the one. Crashed near Tiree. Mayday[229] call picked up said they were out of fuel. No survivors."

My blood was running cold so often now I was beginning to wonder if I was turning into a reptile. How? How did it run out of fuel? Even then, how did it crash? Most aircraft would glide after a fashion and whilst the Sunderland was nothing like a high performing Spitfire, surely it could have landed on the water? Surely it could?

I stood at the bar, glass in hand, hoping it was all some kind of nightmare from which I would shortly emerge. The officer was still wittering on about the crash but whilst I was aware I was answering and nodding occasionally I knew I wasn't taking any of it in. Not that that mattered really. Eventually he gave up and sought better company. This seemed to jolt me back to life and having made some excuses I went outside, threw up in the hedge, collected the car and drove away. I wasn't sure where I was going to go but at least it was away from there.

---

[229] Radio call used to signify an emergency. Conceived in the 1920s by a radio officer at Croydon airport, he proposed that as most flights were between Croydon and Le Bourget the word 'Mayday' or 'm'aider', help me, would serve. It has been in use ever since.

Turnhouse again. I lay on my bunk in the mess. I had seen Hamilton who had arranged for a driver to take me to Balmoral the next day. I have tried not to describe too many wartime journeys as they were all dull but this one really took the biscuit. It rained. The roads were empty. The landscape was bleak but worst of all was the stomach-churning twists and turns along the tiny road to Balmoral.

I arrived feeling suitably glum and the Footman of the Horse Trough or someone let me in and showed me to my quarters. Clearly I wasn't the only visitor because I could hear someone in the next-door room and as these most definitely weren't fit for royal visitors I could only assume I wasn't alone.

I stared out of the window for some time wondering how it had all come to this. My biggest concern was how to extricate myself from the mess and more importantly remain alive. I supposed it wasn't a bad thing to have some royal support. Assuming I did of course.

Dinner was a tediously formal affair. I was seated some way away from the action with some ancient fossil on one side who couldn't hear a word I said and a mute and tedious Guards officer on the other. At least I discovered who my neighbour was. Lt Colonel William Pilcher, Grenadier Guards. I knew that name of course. He had signed the safe conduct letter for Hess. What he was doing here was a mystery. I did at least manage to collar Princess Marina before everyone retired and offer my sympathy.

"Thank you, Wing Commander. Were you the one who drove him to the meeting at Craigiehall?"

"Yes ma'am. If I may, can I add my condolences. I didn't know him well, but our short acquaintance was an interesting one."

"I am not surprised. George was like that. He liked you of course. He said you were a rogue. Are you?"

"Oh no ma'am," I replied with a hint of a smile.

"Of course not," she replied smiling. "He was. It's sad that the special mission never came off. I shall have some sort of memorial set up for them both. You know they stopped the King visiting that injured airman in hospital? They moved him out of the way. It won't stop you know. Ever. I hope you enjoy your stay here, however long it might be."[230]

I bowed my head and she moved on. I decided it was a good time to make myself scarce, especially as there was a distinct lack of other entertainment. As I left, I found Pilcher heading the same way.

"What brings you here?" he asked.

"Hess," I said without thinking about it. He raised his eyebrows.

"You know all about it then?"

"Of course. I was there for most of it."

"Well, I wouldn't tell too many people if I were you. They," he said gesturing behind us, "got me to sign a safe conduct letter in the King's name for him. Proper Catch 22 I find myself in now. Oh, they've made it comfortable enough, the cottage that is, not this room. But I think I may be here some time."

"Why?"

"Disgrace of course. Lose my commission. Probably everything. Reduced to selling buttons or some such I shouldn't wonder. Even the King can't stop them. But he can keep them at arm's length here. At least that's what they are saying. Good night sir."[231]

---

[230] See Appendix.

[231] Colonel Pilcher was 'kept' in Scotland on the Balmoral estate for the rest of his life apparently. There is however no evidence to confirm this.

Chapter 62

And that was that. To all intents and purposes, the case was closed. I didn't return to London for some time. I stayed in Scotland on Hamilton's estate. Menzies deemed it safer and to be honest so did I. It also meant I needn't go near a front line again.

Epilogue

17th August 1987.

"The British Military Authorities in Berlin announce the death of Prisoner Number 7, Rudolf Hess, the last remaining occupant of Spandau prison. He killed himself by hanging himself using the wire cord on a lamp. He left a suicide note."

I know none of this is true. My contacts on the inside tell me MI5 set up an operation using the SAS to finish the business once and for all.

They murdered Hess and Kent. They murdered Sikorski. They tried to murder de Gaulle. They finally murdered Prisoner Number 7, the man known as Rudolf Hess but whose identity is unknown.

Ask Thomas[232].

But more importantly, get the files from the Royal Archives at Windsor. But of course you can't.

I don't have long left I imagine. I have lived an interesting and much too exciting life. I have lived through unimaginable wars and done unimaginable things. And I have seen first-hand what powerful people do to you, the man in the street. They do it in your name, but they do it for no one but themselves.

Ask yourself this. When I look at my government now, and it doesn't matter which one it is or what era you are reading this in, do I think they are capable, honest, competent people who have my best interests and those of the common people as their goal?

Or do I think they are self-seeking, power hungry maniacs bent on keeping it all for themselves and their elite friends?

THE END

---

[232] This is presumably Dr Hugh Thomas, author of 'The Murder of Rudolf Hess'.

Editor's Note

The Times, September 15th 1988.

Obituary.

Air Vice Marshal Sir Harry Francis Alexander Flashman MC.

Passed away peacefully in his sleep at home in London after a long and eventful life. Educated at Rugby, he left under something of a cloud to go to Sandhurst from where he joined the 1st Bengal Lancers. After several years service on the North-West Frontier, he applied for and was accepted into the Royal Flying Corps. On his way home he was caught up in the events surrounding the assassination of Archduke Franz Ferdinand and arrived in England as war broke out.

After qualifying as a pilot, he served on the Western Front throughout the war gaining the MC. After the war, he served in various government roles behind the scenes in England and in Germany. When war broke out again, Flashman was involved with the Intelligence services as well as flying operationally with the RAF and was active throughout the Battle of France and the Battle of Britain.

Rumoured to have been involved in the strange arrival of Rudolf Hess, the Deputy Führer, in 1941, he is then hard to pin down for some time. There are occasional official mentions of him serving in France again after D-Day and up to the end of the war. He was knighted in the Victory honours.

His family insist he retired in the early fifties but there are several unconfirmed stories of 'Alexander'[233] and his presence in Korea, Malaya, Aden, Cuba, the United States and at home in official but unacknowledged roles up until the early eighties.

He is survived by his son Frederick and daughter Victoria, his wife having predeceased him in 1982.

---

[233] The authors of Double Standards refer to an undercover source known as 'Alexander'. Coincidence?

Appendix 1

Churchill's Speech to the Commons, 10th December 1936

Nothing is more certain or more obvious than that recrimination or controversy at this time would be not only useless but harmful and wrong. What is done is done. What has been done or left undone belongs to history, and to history, so far as I am concerned, it shall be left.

I will, therefore, make two observations only. The first is this: It is clear from what we have been told this afternoon that there was at no time any constitutional issue between the King and his Ministers or between the King and Parliament. The supremacy of Parliament over the Crown; the duty of the Sovereign to act in accordance with the advice of his Ministers; neither of those was ever at any moment in question.

Supporting my right honourable friend the Leader of the Liberal party, I venture to say that no Sovereign has ever conformed more strictly or more faithfully to the letter and spirit of the Constitution than his present Majesty. In fact, he has voluntarily made a sacrifice for the peace and strength of his Realm which goes far beyond the bounds required by the law and the Constitution. That is my first observation.

My second is this: I have, throughout, pleaded for time: anyone can see how grave would have been the evils of protracted controversy. On the other hand, it was. in my view, our duty to endure these evils even at serious inconvenience, if there was any hope that time would bring a solution. Whether there was any hope or not is a mystery which, at the present time, it is impossible to resolve. Time was also important from another point of view. It was essential that there should be no room for aspersions, after the event, that the King had been hurried in his decision. I believe that, if this decision had been taken last week, it could not have been declared that it was an unhurried decision, so far as the King himself was concerned, but now I accept wholeheartedly what the Prime Minister has proved, namely, that the decision taken this week has been taken by His Majesty freely, voluntarily and spontaneously, in his own time and in his own way. As I have been looking at this matter, as is well known, from an angle different from that of most honourable Members. I thought it my duty to place this fact also upon record.

That is all I have to say upon the disputable part of this matter, but I hope the House will bear with me for a minute or two, because it was my duty as Home Secretary, more than a quarter of a century ago, to stand beside his present Majesty and proclaim his style and titles at his investiture as Prince of Wales amid the sunlit battlements of Carnarvon Castle, and ever since then he has honoured me here, and also in wartime, with his personal kindness and, I may even say, friendship. I should have been ashamed if, in my independent and unofficial position. I had not cast about for every lawful means, even the most forlorn, to keep him on the Throne of his fathers, to which he only recently succeeded amid the hopes and prayers of all.

In this Prince there were discerned qualities of courage, of simplicity, of sympathy, and, above all, of sincerity, qualities rare and precious which might have made his reign glorious in the annals of this ancient monarchy. It is the acme of tragedy that these very virtues should, in the private sphere, have led only to this melancholy and bitter conclusion. But, although our hopes to-day are withered, still I will assert that his personality will not go down uncherished to future ages, that it will be particularly remembered in the homes of his poorer subjects, and that they will ever wish from the bottom of their hearts for his private peace and happiness and for the happiness of those who are dear to him.

I must say one word more, and 1 say it specially to those here and out of doors—and do not underrate their numbers—who are most poignantly afflicted by what has occurred. Danger gathers upon our path. We cannot afford and we have no right to look back. We must look forward: we must obey the exhortation of the Prime Minister to look forward. The stronger the advocate of monarchical principle a man may be, the more zealously must he now endeavour to fortify the Throne and to give to His Majesty's successor that strength which can only come from the love of a united nation and Empire.

Appendix 2

The 'Roaring Twenties'

As so often in human history, war breeds death and destruction but also fosters technical innovation and invention. The twenties were no different except in that the boom was driven by American money and the development of cars, telephones, movies, radio and multiple electrical goods. There was also a move away from the formality of previous decades with people wanting a more practical and enjoyable existence. This heralded the 'Jazz Age' and the accelerated consumer demand drove the beginning of the age of celebrity, of sports heroes and movie stars.

The consumer boom was also driven by the recovery from war, a war which unlike the Second World War was fought over a relatively small area and thus the infrastructure damage was limited. Four years of deferred spending helped and despite a brief recession in 1919-20, thousands of soldiers returning and entering the labour force and a construction boom helped.

Europe did not recover as quickly as the US, but once US money started flowing into Europe this soon changed.

Perhaps the biggest change was the advent of mass production especially in the car industry. By 1927, Ford had sold 15 million Model Ts. Close behind though was radio which allowed mass broadcasting and thus mass advertising, and cinema which brought cheap entertainment to the masses.

Almost every part of society was affected and improved. With thousands more cars available, people needed roads to drive them on and places to go which boosted construction, maintenance, oil and tourism with hotels, restaurants and shops proliferating.

The 1920s also saw the emergence of the power of women. Having been drafted into 'mens' jobs during the war, women didn't want to give up their new found freedom and driven by a young generation cynical about their elders grip on society and eager to over turn the constraints of the nineteenth century, they began to dress how they wanted, work where they wanted, do as they wanted and whilst it would be wrong to pretend it was some sort of female utopia, it was the beginning perhaps of the climb to equality – and of course many men realised that the real consumers in the world were predominantly female and provided for them as such.

One event that perhaps symbolised the era was Lindbergh's first non-stop solo flight across the Atlantic from New York to Paris in 1927. The Spirit of St Louis took just over 33 hours to make the crossing. France awarded him the Legion d'Honneur but his arrival back in Washington was accompanied by a fleet of warships and aircraft. President Coolidge awarded him the Distinguished Flying Cross.

Of course, it couldn't last. On October 29th, 1929 the Wall Street stock market collapsed precipitating world-wide depression. Millions were suddenly unemployed and the knock on effect of the cessation of the flow of money led to hyper-inflation in Germany – and thus to the rise of the Nazis and ultimately the Second World War.

Appendix 3

Clarence Hatry

Clarence Charles Hatry, (1888-1965) started life as in insurance clerk in the West End of London. Having already made and lost a considerable sum in the silk industry, he bought a reinsurance business from its German owners in 1914. He paid £60,000, reorganised it and sold his interest for £250,000. The Great War was simply an opportunity for him and it is said he finished the war as a Director of 15 companies.

In 1924 his Commercial Corporation of London failed but somehow, successive bankruptcies didn't stop him. Starting again he invested in photography, cameras, vending machines and office rentals.

In 1929, investors threw money at his General Securities Ltd, the chairman of which was Henry Paulet, 16th Marquess of Winchester and his other limited companies. This led to what was his greatest project, a steel and iron merger creating the $40 million company United Steel. He claimed he had contacted Norman at the Bank of England for further financing but he was refused a bridging loan. At this point however, he was caught borrowing on worthless paper. Having tried to persuade Lloyds Bank to help, it was discovered he had been issuing fraudulent stocks by printing the certificates twice. An alert clerk spotted the discrepancy.

At this point Norman informed the stock exchange that Hatry was bankrupt and trading in his shares was suspended. The shock precipitated an ever increasing share sale culminating in the Wall Street Crash.

In December 1929, Hatry was tried at the Old Bailey and found guilty. He was sentenced to 14 years in prison, two with hard labour. After a month of breaking rocks, he was moved to making mail bags. He was released after nine years.

After his release, he returned to the business world buying Hatchards bookshop in 1939. He died in 1965 aged 76.

Appendix 4

The Reichstag Fire

As with so many of the events described in these pages, the Reichstag fire has elements of farce, tragedy and chaos all rolled into one. Adolf Hitler was sworn in as Chancellor at the end of January 1933 but without an overall majority. At this point he held about a third of the seats. This didn't really suit the Nazis aims which required absolute power. As things stood, the President, Hindenburg, could if desired remove the Chancellor. To that end, Hitler asked the President to dissolve the Reichstag and call an election for the 5th March. One of his aims was to allow use of an Enabling Act to end democracy and have government by decree. Previously this power had been used in 1923 to end hyperinflation. Enabling Acts were supposed to be used in an emergency only and required a two-thirds majority to pass.

The Nazis campaign claimed that Germany was on the verge of a Communist revolution, a not unrealistic claim, and the only way to stop it was to increase the size of the parliamentary Nazi party so that in turn they could pass an enabling act to ban the Communists.

The scene was thus set for the 27th February. The Berlin fire department was informed at about 9pm of the fire but by the time they arrived the fire was well established and although they extinguished it by 11.30pm, the building was gutted. An immediate inspection discovered numerous bundles of firelighting material in the ruins.

Hitler was informed and arrived with Goebbels to be met by Goering proclaiming it as a Communist outrage. The Press loudly agreed the next day calling it an act of terrorism and reiterating the danger to the state.

The head of the Berlin Fire Brigade later presented evidence that there had been a delay in notifying him and that the Nazis themselves were involved. He was dismissed and some years later arrested and murdered in prison.

The day after the fire, Hitler requested Hindenburg sign the 'Reichstag Fire Decree' which essentially suspended free speech, press freedom, free association and public assembly and habeas corpus.

A Dutch communist, Marinus van der Lubbe was arrested for arson and claimed he had acted alone. Four Bulgarians were also arrested amid claims they had played a pivotal role in the fire.

Immediately following the fire, thousands of communists were arrested and imprisoned thus skewing the vote on the 5th March in the Nazis favour. Nevertheless, they still only received 44% of the vote although with their political allies they had 52% of the seats which would make it difficult to pass the enabling act. However, with the communists unable to take their seats and the arrest and intimidation of other opposition politicians, the act was passed on 23rd March. Hitler was now a 'democratically' elected Dictator, at least in his eyes.

In July 1933, van der Lubbe was indicted and the trial took place from late September to late December. There was at least some attempt at a proper hearing and consequently only van der Lubbe was convicted, the others, especially Georgi Dmitrov successfully defending themselves with Dmitrov not only accusing senior Nazis of their involvement but cross-examining Goering in court and frankly making him look ridiculous.

The judge felt that whilst he thought there was a communist conspiracy, there was not enough evidence to convict all the defendants. Van der Lubbe was sentenced to death and guillotined a couple of weeks later.

Hitler was furious and all treason trials would now be heard in the new People's Court, something that became synonymous with death sentences.

At the Nuremberg trials, General Franz Halder said that at the Führer's birthday dinner in 1943 Goering stated that 'the only one who really knows about the Reichstag building is I, for I set fire to it'. Goering denied it at his own trial.

It is almost impossible at this distance to tell what actually happened. Few records survive and any that do are just as likely to be forged as real. As with all dictatorships (and probably most democracies!), the truth is what they want to tell you, so it is unlikely we will ever know what really happened. What cannot be denied however is that, whatever the real story, the result allowed the Nazi takeover of Germany. Whether Germany would have taken a different course otherwise is also open to debate although I suspect Hitler would have bided his time and found another way to impose his rule.

In July 2019 a document was found in Hannover's court archives in which an SA man, Hans-Martin Lennings stated that on the night of the fire, he and his SA group drove van der Lubbe to the Reichstag where they found it already on fire.

In 1967, a West Berlin court overturned the 1933 verdict and changed the sentence to eight years in prison. In 1980, another court overturned it again but was overruled. In 1981, another court changed the verdict to 'not guilty by reason of insanity'. Only in 2008 was van der Lubbe pardoned using the 1998 law that anyone convicted by the Nazis was not guilty.

Quite what good any of that does van der Lubbe is debatable. It does however highlight Germany's continuing struggle with its past – and perhaps with its future in an EC without Britain.

Appendix 5

Instruments of Repression
SA, SS, Gestapo

The 'Sturmabteilung', Storm Detachment or Brownshirts was the Nazis original paramilitary organisation. Its primary roles were protection at Nazi rallies, disruption of opposition group rallies generally fighting their own equivalents and intimidating anyone else who disagreed with them at a time when Germany in particular was awash with former soldiers and paramilitary organisations. The term 'Brownshirts' derives from their uniform colour, chosen mainly because a large shipment of shirts intended for colonial troops in Africa was bought by a Freikorps unit which via a convoluted route became the supplier for the SA. Life is of course bound by such trivia.

The group expanded with the party as it rose to prominence and gained notoriety and perhaps fame with some of its well reported battles at the Hofbräuhaus in the early 20s. With the failure of the 'Beer Hall Putsch' in 1923, the organisation was banned.

While Hitler was in prison, he instructed Ernst Röhm to rebuild the SA as he saw fit. In 1925, Röhm resigned as he couldn't see the point of the legal reconstruction Hitler and others were proposing. For the next few years, the SA was essentially pointless. It survived on royalties provided by its own 'Sturm Cigarette Company' until 1930 when Hitler assumed command and asked Röhm to return. By January 1932, the SA had 400,000 men. By January 1933, there were two million men, many times the size of the official German army.

The power of the SA alarmed the Reichswehr (Army) and the party leadership. Made up of largely working class men, the middle classes preferring to join the SS, it was estimated that a large majority of new recruits were former communists. As Röhm began demanding more and more power, especially military, his opponents in the SS began plotting his and the SAs downfall.

Hitler was concerned that the SA had the power to overthrow him and even in Nazi Germany the real power lay with the industrialists that had backed Hitler and the Army who viewed the SA as untrained thugs, probably not too far from the truth. With Goering, Heydrich and Himmler feeding him false information about Röhm's proposed coup, it was inevitable that matters would come to a head.

Hitler ordered all SA leaders to a meeting in Bad Wiessee where they were arrested. Most were executed. Röhm was given the chance to shoot himself which he refused. Two SS officers did it for him. The 'Night of the Long Knives' restored 'order'. From here on the SA was largely used to persecute the Jewish population and largely disappeared on the outbreak of war

The 'Schutzstaffel' or Protection Squadron was initially a hall security unit for meetings that became Hitler's personal guard. It was formally founded in 1925 as a sub-section of the SA but with the accession of Himmler to its command in 1929 it began expanding and its transformation to an Aryan elite. Slowly but surely it became the dominant instrument of the state, taking over most police functions and after the suppression of the SA effectively the Nazi military. They were responsible for the concentration camps which were initially at least for political opponents and expanded into the extermination camps for the 'Final Solution'. The SS became a separate army alongside the Wehrmacht but still with the supposed elite connotations. It is probably true to say that whilst its members saw themselves as such, the other military services and the civilian population came to regard them as the arrogant, cruel extremists they were.

As the tide turned against Germany, the SS were the most fanatical defenders and would frequently fight to the death – although they weren't averse to letting others fight to the death for them, using the threat of execution to make sure that happened. When the war finished, many tried to escape knowing full well that all that awaited them was the hangman's rope, a fate that was almost merciful to people who deserved none.

Many Nazis fled to South America, notably Argentina, after the war. Himmler and Kaltenbrunner were caught with Himmler committing suicide (although doubts have been expressed about this), Kaltenbrunner being hung. Eichmann was found in Buenos Aires by Israeli intelligence (Mossad) in 1960. He expressed no remorse whatsoever and was hung. Mengele, the notorious doctor who carried out the most terrible experiments on human beings, drowned in 1979 in South America.

Only about 2000 SS concentration camp personnel were brought to trial. Many thousands got away and were never required to pay for their crimes. The Nazi hunter Simon Wiesenthal whose organisation was instrumental in tracking down some of them speculated that the 'ODESSA' organisation was real and assisted in many escapes. It is unproven but it is likely that there were at least some organisations that helped.

The Gestapo, Geheime Staatspolizei, was formed in 1933 and to a large degree took on many of the roles and employees of the national criminal police with which it merged in 1936. It was a secret force and as such carried out the instructions of the regime with regard to suppressing dissent and arresting and torturing those who objected. Probably the major difference to other police forces was the exemption from judicial review. The Gestapo therefore operated above the law.

However, the most interesting thing about the Gestapo is how relatively small it was and how if you stayed out of its view you were very unlikely to come into its orbit. It relied heavily on the willingness of the population to inform on each other, so much so that many Gestapo offices spent significant time sorting out credible denunciation from the nonsense or vindictive. Population compliance therefore was crucial. The idea that the Gestapo had eyes and ears everywhere was ridiculous but believed because, as with most human communities, fear is infectious. A few demonstrations of what would happen to you if you were caught was enough to scare entire populations into submission. There is a theory that the whole idea of the Gestapo being omnipresent was a post war construct to justify the actions of certain sections of the community.

Of course, the Gestapo in common with much of the German state focused on specific groups so the average German citizen was highly unlikely to find themselves a target in the first place.

Even more interesting is that as humans, we all like to think ourselves above this sort of behaviour, that we would somehow behave differently, especially in Britain where because the population never had to deal with the Nazi regime, there is a lingering superiority, an attitude that so much happened because other European countries surrendered. There have been several books and television series exploring the great 'What if...' and most I would say arrive at the same conclusion, ie that we would have behaved in exactly the same way. At the time of writing (2020), it is interesting to note first of all how many people are willing to 'shop' their neighbours for perceived transgressions of rules that are similar to those of a police state, second how willing the police are to enforce those rules regardless of explanation, third the ease with which supposedly liberal politicians accrue powers unheard of in a democracy and are very reluctant to part with them, fourth how easily cowed and scared the populace are by state media, and fifth how debate or contradiction has been closed down.

Personally, I don't want to live in that country and it will be interesting to see in a few years what comes out in the wash. If we are allowed to even do the wash.

Appendix 6

The Abdication Statement

'At long last I am able to say a few words of my own. I have never wanted to withhold anything, but until now it has not been constitutionally possible for me to speak.

A few hours ago I discharged my last duty as King and Emperor, and now that I have been succeeded by my brother, the Duke of York, my first words must be to declare my allegiance to him. This I do with all my heart. You all know the reasons which have impelled me to renounce the throne. But I want you to understand that in making up my mind I did not forget the country or the empire, which, as Prince of Wales, and lately as King, I have for 25 years tried to serve,

But you must believe me when I tell you that I have found it impossible to carry the heavy burden of responsibility and to discharge my duties as King as I would wish to do without the help and support of the woman I love.

And I want you to know that the decision I have made has been mine and mine alone. This was a thing I had to judge entirely for myself. The other person most nearly concerned has tried up to the last to persuade me to take a different course. I have made this, the most serious decision of my life, only upon the single thought of what would, in the end, be best for all.

The decision has been made less difficult to me by the sure knowledge that my brother, with his long training in the public affairs of this country and with his fine qualities, will be able to take my place forthwith without interruption or injury to the life and progress of the empire. And he has one matchless blessing, enjoyed by so many of you, and not bestower on me, a happy home with his wife and children.

During these hard days I have been comforted by her majesty my mother and by my family. The ministers of the crown, and in particular, Mr Baldwin, the Prime Minister, have always treated me with full consideration. There has never been any constitutional difference between me and them, and between me and Parliament. Bred in the constitutional tradition by my father, I should never have allowed any such issue to arise.

Ever since I was Prince of Wales, and later on when I occupied the throne, I have been treated with the greatest kindness by all classes of the people wherever I have lived or journeyed throughout the empire. For that I am very grateful.

I now quit altogether public affairs and I lay down my burden. It may be some time before I return to my native land, but I shall always follow the fortunes of the British race and empire with profound interest, and if at any time in the future I can be found of service to his majesty in a private station, I shall not fail.

And now, we all have a new King. I wish him and you, his people, happiness and prosperity with all my heart.

God bless you all.
God save the King!

Appendix 7

Duke of Windsor's Tour of Germany

Against the advice of the government the Duke and Duchess visited Germany in October 1937. The Government objected on the grounds that the tour would be used as propaganda by the Nazis which of course it was. The Duke was certainly perceived as being sympathetic towards the Germans but another reason for going was to take the Duchess on a pseudo-state visit.

They were received in a similar fashion to a Head of State and whilst much of the tour was taken up with factory visits in accordance with its supposed aim of highlighting the socio-economic position of the working classes, they were also wined and dined by many of the senior Nazis, culminating in the Duke taking tea with the Führer at his mountain retreat in Berchtesgaden whilst the Duchess was entertained by Rudolf Hess.

British diplomatic staff were forbidden from helping and public opinion seemed to be that the tour was in poor taste, albeit this seems to stem more from a view that it disrupted the new reign of George VI.

The trip itself was meant to be followed by another to the USA but following the Nazis execution of two communist party leaders a week after the Windors departed, popular opinion swung against them and it was cancelled.

The Duke most definitely had sympathy for the regime and this had been encouraged by the visit, not least because he was accompanied by various minor German relatives. All his conversations were recorded by the Nazi security services so they were well aware of his views and more than capable of using them. What is therefore interesting is what the position would have been had the Duke still been King. Whilst he may well have not undertaken the tour, his political position is unlikely to have changed. It is often ignored, but even a brief look at the Royal Family's ancestors shows that they are probably more German than British. Of course that doesn't imply support for the Nazis but before their crimes became obvious, it would have been easy to argue for appeasement and some kind of alliance, especially when one remembers the position of most European governments with regard to their Jewish populations and indeed their own working classes along with the then recent memories of the Great War.

Appendix 8

Haushofer

Karl Haushofer was born in 1869 to a family of artists and scholars. He attended the Munich Gymnasium but on graduation joined an artillery regiment. Marrying in 1896, he had two sons, Albrecht and Heinz.

1903 saw him appointed to the Bavarian War Academy and in 1908 he was sent to Tokyo to study the Japanese Army. Returning in 1910, he became ill with a lung disease and was given a three year sabbatical during which he completed his doctorate on Japan's military strength and founded a geopolitical monthly publication.

With the outbreak of war, he served throughout commanding a brigade and retired as a Major-General but like many, severely disillusioned. He returned to academia and at this point met Hess who became a devoted student. Haushofer believed that Germany's lack of geographical and geopolitical knowledge was a major cause of its defeat and this became his area of study.

It is said that it was Haushofer who came up with the idea of 'Lebensraum', living space, and Geopolitics, the relationship between a nation's economics, politics, resources and geographical location. Of course, Germany's unique position in central Europe, its limited access to natural resources and its lack of food growing potential meant that it was fertile ground for these theories to take root. Expansion east would solve all these problems for a growing population by taking over food producing land directly east of Germany and seizing the oil producing areas to the south-east. The obvious problem with all of this was what to do about the people that lived in those areas? This is where the Nazis came in. By essentially declaring everyone east of them as sub-human, they could take their land and resources for the Aryan race and deport, enslave or destroy the indigenous people.

Hess was deeply influenced by Haushofer and whilst he was imprisoned with Hitler, developed and expounded his theories which they then published as 'Mein Kampf'. I say they because there is a school of thought and a certain amount of evidence that it was Hess that wrote large parts of 'Mein Kampf'.

On their release and return to politics, their theories steadily gained traction especially with the financial turmoil of the early 30s and the rest is history.

Haushofer's wife was half jewish and so she and his children were categorized as 'Mischlinge', essentially mixed German and Jewish. Hess helped to obtain German Blood Certificates' for them to circumvent the race laws and restrictions. As the war continued and with the disappearance of Hess, Albrecht Haushofer became more and more opposed to the regime and it would appear became involved with the resistance movements. After the bomb plot of July 1944 failed, he went into hiding. He was caught in December 1944 and imprisoned. As the Russians overran Berlin, the SS began executing almost anyone that wasn't SS. This included Albrecht on the night of the 22nd April. His brother Heinz discovered his body on 12th May.

Karl and Martha Haushofer went into the woods near their home and committed suicide in 1946 having left a note for their son Heinz.

Appendix 9

Sir Stewart Menzies

Major General Sir Stewart Graham Menzies was born in 1890, second son of John Menzies and Susannah West Wilson, daughter of ship owner Arthur Wilson of Tranby Croft, scene of the 'Tranby Croft' affair when a Guards officer, Lt Col William Gordon-Cumming was accused of cheating. The presence of the then Prince of Wales, later Edward VII guaranteed it would become a scandal. Flashman refers to it in 'Flashman and the Knights of the Sky' as occurring just after his Father met Mary of Teck and his Father also refers to it in 'Flashman and the Tiger'. There was an ugly court case with the Prince called as a witness.

His grandfather, Graham Menzies, made a fortune from a whisky distillery cartel and his parents became friends of Edward VII. It was rumoured that the King was his father. John Menzies managed to waste much of the family fortune and died in 1911. Menzies had just left Eton in 1909 from where he joined the Grenadier Guards. He fought through the first years of the Great War but was discharged from active service after being seriously injured in a gas attack.

At this point he joined Haig's counterintelligence unit and after the war ended, MI6. Admiral Hugh Sinclair became Director General in 1924 and in 1929 he made Menzies his deputy. When Sinclair died in 1939 Menzies took over as 'C'. It is worth noting that Churchill did everything in his power to oppose his appointment.

Rumours abound about his involvement with the peace party but very little is provable. He worked closely with Churchill on Ultra with Bletchley Park coming under his jurisdiction and as a result MI6 expanded enormously, all of which brought him into conflict with Churchill's pet rival, SOE. When the war ended, he reorganised SIS for the coming Cold War and took over much of SOE which presumably gave him a measure of satisfaction.

Probably the worst mistake he made was not reviewing how SIS agents were recruited. He oversaw the recruitment of agents like Kim Philby, who, although not unmasked until after Menzies retired, was a classic example of British prejudice at its worst.

Menzies reputedly recruited from a very narrow section of society, those who were upper class former officers and recommended to him or known to him personally. An intelligent communist such as Philby would have found it easy to get in and the subsequent scandals later on for the most part involved upper class, Cambridge or Oxford educated officers.

After 43 years in military service, Menzies retired in 1952 at the same time as he married for the third time. He died in 1968.

Appendix 10

Evian Conference

This conference was held between 6th and 15th July 1938 on the initiative of US President Roosevelt to address the 'problem' of German and Austrian Jewish refugees. It is interesting first of all to note that the Western nations considered it a 'problem'.

Thirty two nations were represented and there were twenty four other observers from various interested organisations, including Golda Meir (fourth Prime Minister of Israel from 1969-1974) who was attending from British Mandate Palestine, a subject that merits a book all by itself. Suffice to say the League of Nations mandate lasted from 1920-1948 after Britain and France had divided the entire Arab area in 1916 with the collapse of the Ottoman Empire, promised support for a Jewish Homeland in Palestine in 1917 and watched as both Arab and Jewish nationalist movements rose to violent prominence. The 1947-1949 Palestine war ended with the division of the land between the new State of Israel, Jordan and Egypt but the problems have never gone away. Meir was not permitted to speak, only observe.

When Hitler heard about the conference he said if other nations agreed to take the Jews, he would help them leave.

Prior to the conference, the US and Britain agreed that Britain would not mention the US failure to fill its immigration quotas and the US would not mention Palestine as a destination for Jewish refugees.

The Conference expressed sympathy for the Jewish population in Germany but did what many conferences do and portrayed itself as 'just the beginning', thereby setting the scene for further conferences. Given what was going on in the world and particularly Europe at the time, delegates like Golda Meir must have wondered what would cause the world to act. The conference did establish the 'Intergovernmental Committee on Refugees' whose purpose was to approach governments with a view to developing opportunities for permanent settlement'. As a vehicle for doing nothing whilst appearing to do something that takes some beating. Consequently, the committee was ignored and achieved nothing.

All that said, between 1938 and 1940 Britain and the US accepted about 40,000 refugees each, Australia about 15,000 (although their delegate stated that they had no racial problem and did not want to import one) and South Africa only taking those with relatives already resident. Canada essentially refused.

France stated that they were already saturated with refugees and most other nations agreed.

The Dominican Republic however bucked the trend and said it would accept 100,000 as did Costa Rica.

The overall problem was not helped by serious disagreement amongst Jewish organisations and even David Ben-Gurion himself opposed Jews being allowed into Western Countries albeit mainly because he hoped the pressure of thousands of refugees would force Britain to open up Palestine and presumably further hopes of a Jewish nation.

The consequences of this failure are well known and whilst the holocaust was by no means the conference's fault, it meant that the Nazis couldn't remove their Jewish population but still didn't want their presence.

When Hitler was allowed to occupy the Sudetenland and subsequently other parts of Czechoslovakia 300,000 Jews became stateless which rather puts into perspective the numbers allowed into Britain and the US. In May 1939, the British Parliament issued a white paper barring Jews from entering Palestine or buying land there.

In 1975, Golda Meir described her outrage at her ludicrous status at the conference, unable to sit with the delegates despite the people under discussion being her people.

In 1979, former US Vice President Walter Mondale made the following statement:

'At stake at Evian were both human lives – and the decency and self-respect of the civilized world. If each nation at Evian had agreed on that day to take 17,000 Jews at once, every Jew in the Reich could have been saved.'

Personally, I think his maths is something of an underestimate particularly because it ignores the large Jewish populations persecuted in the rest of Europe, but the principle is correct. The whole conference also rather confirms that aside from Germany many if not most nations at the time considered the Jews as a 'problem' rather than as a people whose homes were in Europe. Politicians have a lot to answer for.

Appendix 11

Jewish Emigration

Flashman is referring to the MS St Louis, a German liner captained by Gustav Schröder that set sail from Hamburg in May 1939 bound for Cuba with 937 Jewish passengers. Although the passengers held valid visas, all bar 28 were refused entry. Schröder then sailed to Florida where the US government, specifically Cordell Hull, also refused entry and instructed the coast guard to shadow the ship and prevent it being run aground, something Schröder considered. He next tried Canada but the Director of Immigration, Frederick Blair, persuaded Mackenzie King not to assist. (In 2000, Blair's nephew made an apology to the Jewish people for his Uncle's actions).

Returning to Europe he docked in Antwerp. Negotiations ensued and agreement was reached to disperse the passengers amongst England, France, Belgium and the Netherlands. 288 disembarked and were shipped to England, 224 went to France, 214 to Belgium and 181 to the Netherlands.

Records are incomplete for many reasons, but it is estimated that of those who remained on the European mainland, around 250 died in the holocaust. The story is told in a book 'Voyage of the Damned' by Gordon Thomas and was the basis of a film drama in 1976 of the same name.

Schröder was supposed to make another transatlantic voyage but the declaration of war interrupted this and he ended up getting to Hamburg via Murmansk on 1st January 1940. He never went to sea again being assigned a desk job.

After the war, he worked as a writer and attempted unsuccessfully to write his own story. He was exempted from de-nazification on the testimony of some of his surviving Jewish passengers. In 1957 the German government awarded him the Order of Merit and he was rightly praised for his actions. In 1993, he was posthumously honoured at the Yad Vashem memorial in Jerusalem with the title 'Righteous Among the Nations'.

Appendix 12

Venlo

Venlo is one of those strange but true intelligence incidents that border on the farcical and achieve nothing whatsoever, an argument that is occasionally used to question the value of the intelligence services. I have described both the British agents in the footnotes and the only German of interest is Major 'Schaemmel', otherwise known as Sturmbannführer Walter Schellenberg who worked for the Sicherheitsdienst reporting ultimately to Himmler and Heydrich.

Who decided on the Venlo operation is lost in the mists of time but it would appear the Germans had got wind of various peace proposals and decided to act on one. Why this one it is hard to know. A German refugee called Fischer had contacted the exiled Catholic leader, Karl Spiecker, in the Netherlands. Spiecker was apparently in contact with British Intelligence and a meeting was arranged with Payne-Best.

Various meetings took place with a number of apparently German officers who supported a plot against Hitler appearing. It would seem that none of them were who they said they were, including possibly Fischer. As the meetings continued, Schellenberg began to take a personal interest and attended as Major Schaemmel. The final meeting occurred on the 8th November when Schaemmel promised he would bring a General to the meeting scheduled for the next day.

That evening, Georg Elser's bomb blew up thirteen minutes after Hitler had left the Bürgerbräukeller in Munich killing seven people. When he heard about it some time later, Hitler apparently ordered Schellenberg to arrest his contacts and bring them to Berlin for questioning.

Consequently, next day at 4pm when Payne-Best, Stevens, Klop and Lemmens/Flashman arrived at the Café Backus, a brief gun battle took place fatally wounding Klop and the other three were herded into cars and driven across the border and on to Berlin. They were questioned and denied any knowledge of the bombing and Elser claimed he was working alone. That is the most likely scenario.

Payne-Best and Stevens were held at the Gestapo headquarters in Berlin before being transferred to Sachsenhausen. They were moved to other camps during the war finishing in Dachau. As high profile prisoners, in April 1945 they were taken from the camp with 140 others and were heading for the Tyrol when the US Army caught up with them. There is some speculation about what the fate of these high profile prisoners would be, with some suggestion that they would be used as bargaining chips by senior Nazis.

Quite what the point of it all was is unknown. The Germans claimed to have deceived SIS and by linking the operation to the bombing in Munich used it to incite public resentment of Britain. This seems plausible but so miniscule in the grand scheme of things as to not be worth the planning involved. The British were seeking peace on numerous levels but why they thought a couple of lowly 'German' refugees would be able to assist that is open to question as well.

Probably the worst thing was the detention of the two agents for over four years but that was hardly a major coup. Like so much in war, it is an example of far too much effort expended for so little gain.

Appendix 13

Supermarine Spitfire vs Messerschmitt Bf109E

'I should like an outfit of Spitfires for my squadron'.

This quote is attributed to Adolf Galland, one of Germany's leading fighter pilots in reply to Goering's asking what his fighter pilots needed to win the Battle of Britain. Goering was apoplectic. But the real question is, was he right? Galland believed the Spitfire was a better defensive fighter because of its manoeuvrability.

The question has been asked countless times and has defenders on both side of the debate. But James Holland's book 'The Battle of Britain' settles it for me at least.

Both aircraft were a product of their generation. Bombing had become steadily more deadly since the end of the Great War and nations needed some form of defence against it and high-performance fighters were the answer. Germany had been held back by Versailles of course but had a number of leading manufacturers and designers, Messerschmitt being probably the best known and arguably the best designer amongst them. Britain had held itself back but again fortunately had some superb companies and designers, R.J.Mitchell the foremost. Between them they changed the art of air fighting.

The Spitfire almost never made it. The prototype first flew on 5th March 1936 with Mutt Summers at the controls and the Air Ministry ordered 310 in June 1936. Supermarine were too small for the order and Vickers dragged their heels releasing plans to sub-contractors. The problems were eventually overcome and the first Spitfires entered service with 19 Squadron on 4th August 1938.

Direct comparisons are quite difficult largely because not many pilots flew both the Spitfire and the 109, but James Holland's is pretty comprehensive. First, the maximum speeds were virtually identical. In theory the Spitfire could out turn the 109. But, as Pilot Officer Tom Neil, a Battle of Britain Spitfire pilot, said, 'Who gives a bugger about turning? You don't need to turn. All you need to do is go like a bat out of hell, catch the other fellow, fire your guns and disappear. These things the Me109 did very, very well. It could catch us and it could run away from us, almost at will'.

Why was that?

Three things. Supercharger, fuel injection and electric variable pitch propeller, none of which the Spitfire had. The 109 supercharged engine could accelerate the aircraft much quicker than the Spitfire. The fuel injection allowed the 109 to go into a negative 'g' dive under power whereas the carburettor fed Merlin would produce a 'rich cut' where the engine was essentially flooded. This only lasted until positive 'g' returned but it was vital seconds lost. The Spitfire also only had a two-speed propeller meaning it was inefficient compared to the constantly variable 109 propeller. Small differences but they all added up.

Two captured 109s were test flown at Farnborough and the first result of that was the replacement of the Spitfire propeller.

The wing loading was also significantly different. The Spitfire wing was somewhat bigger than the 109 and created more drag to overcome. In basic terms, less drag meant better acceleration and speed. It did have a downside and that was its aerodynamic stall speed being much higher than the Spitfire. To counteract this the 109 had slats on the leading edges that extended automatically and flaps on the trailing edges. This assisted the pilots on take-off and landing but for the inexperienced pilot, take off in a 109 was potentially lethal – and proved so for many.

This difference in wing design is what gave the Spitfire its better turn rate – in theory. In practice, a good 109 pilot could use the autoslats in the turn by slowing down and allowing them to deploy thus making it better than the Spitfire. On top of that, Farnborough tests had also shown that Spitfire and Hurricane pilots were reluctant to turn too tightly because if they did stall and then spin, both types were difficult to handle whereas the 109 was easy to recover from the stall.

That said, both RAF and Luftwaffe accident statistics were broadly comparable. The one real advantage of the Spitfire over the 109 was that as a benign aircraft, leaving aside the stall characteristics, an experienced pilot couldn't do much more with it than a new one. With the 109, experienced pilots could make it do all sorts of things, but new pilots found it difficult. In the Farnborough tests it was found the Spitfire pilots very quickly got used to the 109.

Finally, to armament. Spitfires had eight wing mounted .303 Browning machine guns firing 1200 rounds per minute. They had 300 rounds for each gun and thus 15 seconds of continuous firing. For the guns to be really effective, the target had to be at the convergence point of the ammunition. The bullets themselves did not explode so relied on hitting something important or the pilot. Holland quotes a 74 Squadron report that they fired between them 7000 rounds at a Dornier 17 and it carried on flying. .303 bullets hitting the skin of an aircraft create a .303 hole going in and the same coming out.

109s were armed with a mixture of machine guns and cannon. A standard fit was two machine guns on the engine cowling with one cannon in each wing. The advantages were threefold. First of all, aiming the machine guns meant pointing the aircraft at the target. Second, both guns had 1000 rounds each, or 55 seconds of continuous firing, nearly four times as much as the Spitfire and thirdly, a cannon shell hitting a target exploded taking the target with it. Holland also quotes another RAF pilot, Allan Wright, who saw a Spitfire hit by a cannon shell in the cockpit. It blew up. The canopy disappeared as did the pilot.

To me the answer then is clear. If you put the same pilot in a Spitfire and a 109 with equal experience in both, the 109 would win every time.

Appendix 14

Dunkerque

As I allude to in the book, Dunkerque was the latest in a long list of heroic disasters caused largely by political cowardice and military incompetence on a grand scale. On May 10th 1940, the German army crossed the borders invading Belgium, The Netherlands and France. By the 21st May the BEF was trapped.

For reasons that will remain forever unknown, Hitler ordered his armies to halt. Had he not done this, he would possibly have achieved what he aimed to do, knock both France and Britain out of the war.

The logistics of Dunkerque are staggering, but it would not have been possible without a number of things. First, a heroic defence of the perimeter by thousands of French and British troops, many of whom gave their lives and still more accepted imprisonment albeit they would not have expected it to be for over four years. Second, more or less unfettered control of the Channel by the Royal Navy. Third and largely dismissed (and as alluded to in the book), the RAF fighters defending the skies over Dunkerque and the surrounding areas. Fourth, the east mole without which it would not have been possible at all as around 200,000 men embarked from here and fifth, the weather, which played its part in restricting German bombing.

Just over 338,000 men were evacuated leaving all their equipment behind. The casualties were immense. 68,000 British soldiers were killed, wounded, missing or captured. Six Royal Navy destroyers and nine other large vessels were sunk along with another 200 ships of varying sizes. 145 RAF aircraft were shot down.

In simple terms, Dunkerque happened because Britain and France were still fighting the Great War. The aging Generals simply could not or would not contemplate the possibility of mobile warfare on such a scale. In truth, it was also partly because Guderian and Rommel (both much younger) were prepared to take truly hellish but calculated risks, surmising correctly that resistance would collapse if all appeared lost. In practice that meant allied troops finding they were already in German held territory, albeit held by a few tanks. Confidence plays a big part in military endeavours and the Germans had bags of it whilst the French and British had the stuffing knocked out of them almost immediately and all was pretty much lost from that point on.

In numerical terms, the Germans should have lost. At the start of the battle, the Allies had roughly 14,000 guns, over 3500 tanks and at least 300,000 vehicles. The Germans had 7000 guns, 2400 tanks and 120,000 vehicles. The only area where the Germans were numerically superior was aircraft with approximately 5000 compared to the Allies 3000.

One of the biggest factors was communication. The Germans had modern radio communications and used it effectively. The Allies didn't and suffered accordingly as with the Germans moving so fast, their information was way out of date when they got it. The other was air superiority although Dunkerque proved that bombing moving ships was extremely difficult.

It is interesting although ultimately pointless to speculate on what might have happened if Dunkerque had not been a success. Britain without an army wasn't entirely toothless as to invade, the Germans still had to get past the Navy and Air force, and invasion was something Hitler clearly hadn't seriously considered given the half-hearted planning after Dunkerque. He assumed Britain would surrender and he probably had good reason to think that. Without Churchill, I suspect there would have been an armistice along the lines I have mentioned in the book. What course Europe would have taken then is also an interesting albeit equally pointless debate.

Appendix 15

This was their Finest Hour

Churchill was many things but perhaps his finest quality as a wartime politician was his ability to inspire through words. He did it many times, often in the darkest days when there was little to cheer and much to be concerned over. This was one of his finest, especially the last paragraph. I have reproduced it here because I like it. Most if not all of his major speeches are available online in written format and many can be heard as original recordings.

18th June 1940

"I spoke the other day of the colossal military disaster which occurred when the French High Command failed to withdraw the northern Armies from Belgium at the moment when they knew that the French front was decisively broken at Sedan and on the Meuse. This delay entailed the loss of fifteen or sixteen French divisions and threw out of action for the critical period the whole of the British Expeditionary Force. Our Army and 120,000 French troops were indeed rescued by the British Navy from Dunkirk but only with the loss of their cannon, vehicles and modern equipment. This loss inevitably took some weeks to repair, and in the first two of those weeks the battle in France has been lost. When we consider the heroic resistance made by the French Army against heavy odds in this battle, the enormous losses inflicted upon the enemy and the evident exhaustion of the enemy, it may well be the thought that these 25 divisions of the best-trained and best-equipped troops might have turned the scale. However, General Weygand had to fight without them. Only three British divisions or their equivalent were able to stand in the line with their French comrades. They have suffered severely, but they have fought well. We sent every man we could to France as fast as we could re-equip and transport their formations.

I am not reciting these facts for the purpose of recrimination. That I judge to be utterly futile and even harmful. We cannot afford it. I recite them in order to explain why it was we did not have, as we could have had, between twelve and fourteen British divisions fighting in the line in this great battle instead of only three. Now I put all this aside. I put it on the shelf, from which the historians, when they have time, will select their documents to tell their stories. We have to think of the future and not of the past. This also applies in a small way to our own affairs at home. There are many who would hold an inquest in the House of Commons on the conduct of the Governments—and of Parliaments, for they are in it, too—during the years which led up to this catastrophe. They seek to indict those who were responsible for the guidance of our affairs. This also would be a foolish and pernicious process. There are too many in it. Let each man search his conscience and search his speeches. I frequently search mine.

Of this I am quite sure, that if we open a quarrel between the past and the present, we shall find that we have lost the future. Therefore, I cannot accept the drawing of any distinctions between members of the present Government. It was formed at a moment of crisis in order to unite all the Parties and all sections of opinion. It has received the almost unanimous support of both Houses of Parliament. Its members are going to stand together, and, subject to the authority of the House of Commons, we are going to govern the country and fight the war. It is absolutely necessary at a time like this that every Minister who tries each day to do his duty shall be respected; and their subordinates must know that their chiefs are not threatened men, men who are here today and gone tomorrow, but that their directions must be punctually and faithfully obeyed. Without this concentrated power we cannot face what lies before us. I should not think it would be very advantageous for the House to prolong this debate this afternoon under conditions of public stress. Many facts are not clear that will be clear in a short time. We are to have a secret session on Thursday, and I should think that would be a better opportunity for the many earnest expressions of opinion which members will desire to make and for the House to discuss vital matters without having everything read the next morning by our dangerous foes.

The disastrous military events which have happened during the past fortnight have not come to me with any sense of surprise. Indeed, I indicated a fortnight ago as clearly as I could to the House that the worst possibilities were open; and I made it perfectly clear that whatever happened in France would make no difference to the resolve of Britain and the British Empire to fight on, if necessary for years, if necessary alone.

During the last few days we have successfully brought off the great majority of the troops we had on the line of communication in France; and seven-eighths of the troops we have sent to France since the beginning of the war—that is to say, about 350,000 out of 400,000 men—are safely back in this country. Others are still fighting with the French, and fighting with considerable success in their local encounters against the enemy. We have also brought back a great mass of stores, rifles and munitions of all kinds which had been accumulated in France during the last nine months.

We have, therefore, in this Island today a very large and powerful military force. This force comprises all our best-trained and our finest troops, including scores of thousands of those who have already measured their quality against the Germans and found themselves at no disadvantage. We have under arms at the present time in this Island over a million and a quarter men. Behind these we have the Local Defense Volunteers, numbering half a million, only a portion of whom, however, are yet armed with rifles or other firearms. We have incorporated into our Defense Forces every man for whom we have a weapon. We expect very large additions to our weapons in the near future, and in preparation for this we intend forthwith to call up, drill and train further large numbers. Those who are not called up, or else are employed during the vast business of munitions production in all its branches—and their ramifications are innumerable—will serve their country best by remaining at their ordinary work until they receive their summons. We have also over here Dominions armies. The Canadians had actually landed in France, but have now been safely withdrawn, much disappointed, but in perfect order, with all their artillery and equipment. And these very high-class forces from the Dominions will now take part in the defense of the Mother Country.

Lest the account which I have given of these large forces should raise the question: Why did they not take part in the great battle in France? I must make it clear that, apart from the divisions training and organizing at home, only twelve divisions were equipped to fight upon a scale which justified their being sent abroad. And this was fully up to the number which the French had been led to expect would be available in France at the ninth month of the war. The rest of our forces at home have a fighting value for home defense which will, of course, steadily increase every week that passes. Thus, the invasion of Great Britain would at this time require the transportation across the sea of hostile armies on a very large scale, and after they had been so transported they would have to be continually maintained with all the masses of munitions and supplies which are required for continuous battle—as continuous battle it will surely be.

Here is where we come to the Navy—and after all, we have a Navy. Some people seem to forget that we have a Navy. We must remind them. For the last thirty years I have been concerned in discussions about the possibilities of oversea invasion, and I took the responsibility on behalf of the Admiralty, at the beginning of the last war, of allowing all regular troops to be sent out of the country. That was a very serious step to take, because our Territorials had only just been called up and were quite untrained. Therefore, this Island was for several months particularly denuded of fighting troops. The Admiralty had confidence at that time in their ability to prevent a mass invasion even though at that time the Germans had a magnificent battle fleet in the proportion of 10 to 16, even though they were capable of fighting a general engagement every day and any day, whereas now they have only a couple of heavy ships worth speaking of—the Scharnhorst and the Gneisenau. We are also told that the Italian Navy is to come out and gain sea superiority in these waters. If they seriously intend it, I shall only say that we shall be delighted to offer Signor Mussolini a free and safeguarded passage through the Strait of Gibraltar in order that he may play the part to which he aspires. There is a general curiosity in the British Fleet to find out whether the Italians are up to the level they were at in the last war or whether they have fallen off at all.

Therefore, it seems to me that as far as sea-borne invasion on a great scale is concerned, we are far more capable of meeting it today than we were at many periods in the last war and during the early months of this war, before our other troops were trained, and while the B.E.F. had proceeded abroad. Now, the Navy have never pretended to be able to prevent raids by bodies of 5,000 or 10,000 men flung suddenly across and thrown ashore at several points on the coast some dark night or foggy morning. The efficacy of sea power, especially under modern conditions, depends upon the invading force being of large size; It has to be of large size, in view of our military strength, to be of any use. If it is of large size, then the Navy have something they can find and meet and, as it were, bite on. Now, we must remember that even five divisions, however lightly equipped, would require 200 to 250 ships, and with modern air reconnaissance and photography it would not be easy to collect such an armada, marshal it, and conduct it across the sea without any powerful naval forces to escort it; and there would be very great possibilities, to put it mildly, that this armada would be intercepted long before it reached the coast, and all the men drowned in the sea or, at the worst blown to pieces with their equipment while they were trying to land. We also have a great system of minefields, recently strongly reinforced, through which we alone know the channels. If the enemy tries to sweep passages through these minefields, it will be the task of the Navy to destroy the mine-sweepers and any other forces employed to protect them. There should be no difficulty in this, owing to our great superiority at sea.

Those are the regular, well-tested, well-proved arguments on which we have relied during many years in peace and war. But the question is whether there are any new methods by which those solid assurances can be circumvented. Odd as it may seem, some attention has been given to this by the Admiralty, whose prime duty and responsibility is to destroy any large sea-borne expedition before it reaches, or at the moment when it reaches, these shores. It would not be a good thing for me to go into details of this. It might suggest ideas to other people which they have not thought of, and they would not be likely to give us any of their ideas in exchange. All I will say is that untiring vigilance and mind-searching must be devoted to the subject, because the enemy is crafty and cunning and full of novel treacheries and stratagems. The House may be assured that the utmost ingenuity is being displayed and imagination is being evoked from large numbers of competent officers, well-trained in tactics and thoroughly up to date, to measure and counterwork novel possibilities. Untiring vigilance and untiring searching of the mind is being, and must be, devoted to the subject, because, remember, the enemy is crafty and there is no dirty trick he will not do.

Some people will ask why, then, was it that the British Navy was not able to prevent the movement of a large army from Germany into Norway across the Skagerrak? But the conditions in the Channel and in the North Sea are in no way like those which prevail in the Skagerrak. In the Skagerrak, because of the distance, we could give no air support to our surface ships, and consequently, lying as we did close to the enemy's main air power, we were compelled to use only our submarines. We could not enforce the decisive blockade or interruption which is possible from surface vessels. Our submarines took a heavy toll but could not, by themselves, prevent the invasion of Norway. In the Channel and in the North Sea, on the other hand, our superior naval surface forces, aided by our submarines, will operate with close and effective air assistance.

This brings me, naturally, to the great question of invasion from the air, and of the impending struggle between the British and German Air Forces. It seems quite clear that no invasion on a scale beyond the capacity of our land forces to crush speedily is likely to take place from the air until our Air Force has been definitely overpowered. In the meantime, there may be raids by parachute troops and attempted descents of airborne soldiers. We should be able to give those gentry a warm reception both in the air and on the ground, if they reach it in any condition to continue the dispute. But the great question is: Can we break Hitler's air weapon? Now, of course, it is a very great pity that we have not got an Air Force at least equal to that of the most powerful enemy within striking distance of these shores. But we have a very powerful Air Force which has proved itself far superior in quality, both in men and in many types of machine, to what we have met so far in the numerous and fierce air battles which have been fought with the Germans. In

France, where we were at a considerable disadvantage and lost many machines on the ground when they were standing round the aerodromes, we were accustomed to inflict in the air losses of as much as two and two-and-a-half to one. In the fighting over Dunkirk, which was a sort of no-man's-land, we undoubtedly beat the German Air Force, and gained the mastery of the local air, inflicting here a loss of three or four to one day after day. Anyone who looks at the photographs which were published a week or so ago of the re-embarkation, showing the masses of troops assembled on the beach and forming an ideal target for hours at a time, must realize that this re-embarkation would not have been possible unless the enemy had resigned all hope of recovering air superiority at that time and at that place.

In the defense of this Island the advantages to the defenders will be much greater than they were in the fighting around Dunkirk. We hope to improve on the rate of three or four to one which was realized at Dunkirk; and in addition all our injured machines and their crews which get down safely—and, surprisingly, a very great many injured machines and men do get down safely in modern air fighting—all of these will fall, in an attack upon these Islands, on friendly soil and live to fight another day; whereas all the injured enemy machines and their complements will be total losses as far as the war is concerned.

During the great battle in France, we gave very powerful and continuous aid to the French Army, both by fighters and bombers; but in spite of every kind of pressure we never would allow the entire metropolitan fighter strength of the Air Force to be consumed. This decision was painful, but it was also right, because the fortunes of the battle in France could not have been decisively affected even if we had thrown in our entire fighter force. That battle was lost by the unfortunate strategical opening, by the extraordinary and 283nforeseen power of the armored columns, and by the great preponderance of the German Army in numbers. Our fighter Air Force might easily have been exhausted as a mere accident in that great struggle, and then we should have found ourselves at the present time in a very serious plight. But as it is, I am happy to inform the House that our fighter strength is stronger at the present time relatively to the Germans, who have suffered terrible losses, than it has ever been; and consequently we believe ourselves possessed of the capacity to continue the war in the air under better conditions than we have ever experienced before. I look forward confidently to the exploits of our fighter pilots—these splendid men, this brilliant youth—who will have the glory of saving their native land, their island home, and all they love, from the most deadly of all attacks.

There remains, of course, the danger of bombing attacks, which will certainly be made very soon upon us by the bomber forces of the enemy. It is true that the German bomber force is superior in numbers to ours; but we have a very large bomber force also, which we shall use to strike at military targets in Germany without intermission. I do not at all underrate the severity of the ordeal which lies before us; but I believe our countrymen will show themselves capable of standing up to it, like the brave men of Barcelona, and will be able to stand up to it, and carry on in spite of it, at least as well as any other people in the world. Much will depend upon this; every man and every woman will have the chance to show the finest qualities of their race, and render the highest service to their cause. For all of us, at this time, whatever our sphere, our station, our occupation or our duties, it will be a help to remember the famous lines:

He nothing common did or mean, Upon that memorable scene.

I have thought it right upon this occasion to give the House and the country some indication of the solid, practical grounds upon which we base our inflexible resolve to continue the war. There are a good many people who say, 'Never mind. Win or lose, sink or swim, better die than submit to tyranny—and such a tyranny.' And I do not dissociate myself from them. But I can assure them that our professional advisers of the three Services unitedly advise that we should carry on the war, and that there are good and reasonable hopes of final victory. We have fully informed and consulted all the self-governing Dominions, these great communities far beyond the oceans who have been built up on our laws and on our civilization, and who are absolutely free to choose their course, but are absolutely devoted to the ancient Motherland, and who feel themselves inspired by the same emotions which lead me to stake our all upon duty and honor. We have fully consulted them, and I have received from their Prime Ministers, Mr. Mackenzie King of Canada, Mr. Menzies of Australia, Mr. Fraser of New Zealand, and General Smuts of South Africa—that wonderful man, with his immense profound mind, and his eye watching from a distance the whole panorama of European affairs—I have received from all these eminent men, who all have Governments behind them elected on wide franchises, who are all there because they represent the will of their people, messages couched in the most moving terms in which they endorse our decision to fight on, and declare themselves ready to share our fortunes and to persevere to the end. That is what we are going to do.

We may now ask ourselves: In what way has our position worsened since the beginning of the war? It has worsened by the fact that the Germans have conquered a large part of the coast line of Western Europe, and many small countries have been overrun by them. This aggravates the possibilities of air attack and adds to our naval preoccupations. It in no way diminishes, but on the contrary definitely increases, the power of our long-distance blockade. Similarly, the entrance of Italy into the war increases the power of our long-distance blockade. We have stopped the worst leak by that. We do not know whether military resistance will come to an end in France or not, but should it do so, then of course the Germans will be able to concentrate their forces, both military and industrial, upon us. But for the reasons I have given to the House these will not be found so easy to apply. If invasion has become more imminent, as no doubt it has, we, being relieved from the task of maintaining a large army in France, have far larger and more efficient forces to meet it.

If Hitler can bring under his despotic control the industries of the countries he has conquered, this will add greatly to his already vast armament output. On the other hand, this will not happen immediately, and we are now assured of immense, continuous and increasing support in supplies and munitions of all kinds from the United States; and especially of aeroplanes and pilots from the Dominions and across the oceans coming from regions which are beyond the reach of enemy bombers.

I do not see how any of these factors can operate to our detriment on balance before the winter comes; and the winter will impose a strain upon the Nazi regime, with almost all Europe writhing and starving under its cruel heel, which, for all their ruthlessness, will run them very hard. We must not forget that from the moment when we declared war on the 3rd September it was always possible for Germany to turn all her Air Force upon this country, together with any other devices of invasion she might conceive, and that France could have done little or nothing to prevent her doing so. We have, therefore, lived under this danger, in principle and in a slightly modified form, during all these months. In the meanwhile, however, we have enormously improved our methods of defense, and we have learned what we had no right to assume at the beginning, namely, that the individual aircraft and the individual British pilot have a sure and definite superiority. Therefore, in casting up this dread balance sheet and contemplating our dangers with a disillusioned eye, I see great reason for intense vigilance and exertion, but none whatever for panic or despair.

During the first four years of the last war the Allies experienced nothing but disaster and disappointment. That was our constant fear: one blow after another, terrible losses, frightful dangers. Everything miscarried. And yet at the end of those four years the morale of the Allies was higher than that of the Germans, who had moved from one aggressive triumph to another, and who stood everywhere triumphant invaders of the lands into which they had broken. During that war we repeatedly asked ourselves the question: 'How are we going to win?' And no one was able ever to answer it with much precision, until at the end, quite suddenly, quite unexpectedly, our terrible foe collapsed before us, and we were so glutted with victory that in our folly we threw it away.

We do not yet know what will happen in France or whether the French resistance will be prolonged, both in France and in the French Empire overseas. The French Government will be throwing away great opportunities and casting adrift their future if they do not continue the war in accordance with their treaty obligations, from which we have not felt able to release them. The House will have read the historic declaration in which, at the desire of many Frenchmen—and of our own hearts—we have proclaimed our willingness at the darkest hour in French history to conclude a union of common citizenship in this struggle. However matters may go in

France or with the French Government, or other French Governments, we in this Island and in the British Empire will never lose our sense of comradeship with the French people. If we are now called upon to endure what they have been suffering, we shall emulate their courage, and if final victory rewards our toils they shall share the gains, aye, and freedom shall be restored to all. We abate nothing of our just demands; not one jot or tittle do we recede. Czechs, Poles, Norwegians, Dutch, Belgians have joined their causes to our own. All these shall be restored.

What General Weygand called the Battle of France is over. I expect that the Battle of Britain is about to begin. Upon this battle depends the survival of Christian civilization. Upon it depends our own British life, and the long continuity of our institutions and our Empire. The whole fury and might of the enemy must very soon be turned on us.

Hitler knows that he will have to break us in this Island or lose the war. If we can stand up to him, all Europe may be free and the life of the world may move forward into broad, sunlit uplands. But if we fail, then the whole world, including the United States, including all that we have known and cared for, will sink into the abyss of a new Dark Age made more sinister, and perhaps more protracted, by the lights of perverted science.

Let us therefore brace ourselves to our duties, and so bear ourselves that if the British Empire and its Commonwealth last for a thousand years, men will still say, 'This was their finest hour.'"

Appendix 16

Park, Dowding, Leigh-Mallory and Bader

Four names that I grew up with, heroes even especially because of my interest in aviation and particularly in the Battle of Britain. Bader was probably the most well known, particularly once Paul Brickhill's 'Reach for the Sky' was made into a film but it also rather hid his character. Bader himself realised that people assumed he was more like the actor Kenneth More who portrayed him. In fact, he was a strong, overbearing and hard swearing force of a man. As a leader and fighter pilot, particularly one that had overcome the trauma of losing his legs in a flying accident in 1931, albeit one that was his own fault, these were probably admirable traits. As a contemporary, he was probably the proverbial pain in the neck.

During the Battle of Britain, Bader commanded 242 Squadron at Coltishall and then at Duxford in 12 Group. The squadron had suffered badly in France and it took someone like Bader with his contempt for 'red tape' and unnecessary rules and regulations to turn it round. Even the film shows Bader's frequent clashes with higher authority.

Somewhat frustrated by 12 groups proximity to the Battle of Britain but with Park holding it back, Bader along with Leigh-Mallory promoted the controversial 'Big Wing', a formation of between three and five fighter squadrons that in theory would inflict large casualties on bomber formations.

Leigh-Mallory was a career RAF officer having himself fought as a pilot in the Great War. After the war he remained in the fledgling RAF and worked his way through the ranks such that in 1937 he was appointed to command of 12 Group and promoted to Air Vice-Marshal.

Hugh Dowding was also a career officer having joined the Army in 1900. He transferred to the RFC in October 1914 flying with various squadrons before rising to more senior commands. He clashed with the RFC commander, Hugh Trenchard after the Somme battle because of his view that combat pilots needed time to recuperate from continual operations. Commissioned into the RAF after the war, he was largely responsible for the introduction of the Spitfire and Hurricane into Fighter Command. Appointed to head Fighter Command in 1936, he was due to retire in June 1939 but stayed on as the international situation deteriorated. He was also responsible for the introduction of the integrated defence system that included radar and the observer corps but most importantly the intelligent use of the information provided at RAF Bentley Priory in its Operations Rooms.

During the early part of the war and the Battle of France, Dowding quickly realised that sending fighter squadrons to France was simply squandering scarce resources. He clashed frequently with Churchill who whilst probably realising he was correct, had to be seen to support the French. Dowding managed to limit the RAF deployment and at least kept his Spitfire squadrons in Britain although they did fly missions over France during the battle.

Fortunately for Britain, serving under Dowding and in command of 11 Group was Air Vice-Marshal Keith Park. Park was a New Zealander and joined the New Zealand Army before going to sea. When the Great War started, he returned to his artillery battery as an NCO and was present at Gallipoli before transferring to the British Army and serving in France. Blown off his horse he was certified unfit for active service but after training at Woolwich he joined the RFC. After squadron service and a number of kills he commanded 48 Squadron in France. Commissioned into the RAF he served in various roles before being appointed to 11 Group.

Park was a popular 'hands on' commander, frequently visiting his squadrons and pilots in his personal Hurricane. He was both strategically and tactically astute and together with Dowding, it was their ability to do what was necessary to win, or probably more correctly not lose, that allowed Fighter Command to defeat the Luftwaffe in its attempt to gain air superiority over Britain.

These then were the men who were leading the 'Few'.

Park and Dowding worked well together, did not casually throw away their men's lives, fought when necessary to achieve the aim which at the time was to stop Britain being invaded. If they had a flaw, it was that they had little time for internal politics and in-fighting, something that in my opinion only reinforces their greatness as leaders, but it left them easy targets for the likes of Leigh-Mallory who was jealous of their success and together with Bader and the Big Wing concept tried to undermine them as far as possible. The Big Wing concept was flawed in that it took too long to form up by which time the enemy had done its job. Consequently 12 Group were frequently late to the battle leaving 11 Group to do the job themselves and often confused the defence controllers flying into 11 Group's area.

Once the battle was all but 'won', Leigh-Mallory managed to convince the air ministry that if Dowding and Park had been more aggressive they might have been victorious in the battle rather than just avoiding defeat. He made no allowance for the reality of supplies of pilots and aircraft and the potential for catastrophe if his 'Big Wing' had been caught by swarms of 109s even if this was unlikely. Park's objections to the Big Wing probably contributed to his and Dowding's downfall. Both were replaced in late 1940 with Park becoming AOC 23 Group and Dowding sent to America.

Leigh-Mallory took over 11 Group and began fighter sweeps over France. These were ineffective with the RAF losing four aircraft for each German aircraft destroyed and having virtually no effect on ground targets. 500 pilots were lost.

75 Squadrons were kept in Britain in 1941 carrying out these operations. They would have been more use over Malta or Singapore where small numbers of obsolete fighters were expected to achieve the impossible.

The final verdict should be left to those that really knew. An overwhelming majority of airmen thought that Dowding and Park were right.

Appendix 17

Amy Johnson

Amy Johnson was born in Yorkshire in 1903. Eldest of three sisters she gained a BA in Economics from Sheffield University. She was working for a London solicitors when she started flying as a hobby and gained her aviators certificate on 28th January 1929 and her pilots 'A' licence on 6th July the same year. She learnt at the London Aeroplane Club under the tutelage of Valentine Baker who served through the Great War becoming a civilian instructor post war. He was also the co-founder of the Martin Baker Company and as test pilot was killed in an accident in 1942 leading James Martin to refocus the company on designing ejection seats.

Amy also became the first woman to obtain a ground engineers 'C' licence and was a friend of Fred Slingsby of Slingsby Aviation. He founded the Yorkshire Gliding Club and Amy was an early member.

Amy bought her first aircraft with help from her father, a de Havilland Gipsy Moth she named Jason. In 1930 she was propelled to worldwide fame when she flew solo from Croydon Airport to Darwin, Australia in twenty days. She was awarded the Harmon trophy and a CBE in the Birthday Honours list that year.

In Jason II, a DH80 Puss Moth, she became with her co-pilot the first crew to fly to Moscow in one day. They continued on to Tokyo setting a record time for the journey.

Marrying Jim Mollison in 1932, she set another solo record for London to Cape Town. Together in 1933 they flew to New York as Jim was going to attempt a distance record to Baghdad. Low on fuel they crash landed in a drainage ditch and were both thrown clear. Recovering they were granted a ticker tape parade in New York.

The Mollisons flew from Britain to India in record time in 1934 and in 1936, Amy regained her Britain to South Africa record as well as being awarded the Royal Aero Club gold medal. In 1938 the Mollisons divorced.

Just after the outbreak of war, Amy joined the Air Transport Auxiliary. This organisation flew all types of aircraft around the country and had 166 female pilots at its height including Diana Barnato-Walker who flew around 80 different types of aircraft and became the first holder of the world airspeed record for women flying an English Electric Lightning T4 at Mach 1.6 or approximately 1250mph.

On 5th January 1941, Amy flew an Airspeed Oxford from Prestwick to Blackpool and then she was supposed to go to Kidlington near Oxford. In poor weather, she found herself over the Thames estuary and possibly low on fuel. Whatever the reason, Amy bailed out and somewhat unluckily landed in the water.

She was spotted descending by a convoy including HMS Haslemere which made a rescue attempt. Ropes were thrown but Amy was unable to reach them and disappeared under the ship. The Captain, Lt Cmdr Walter Fletcher, dived in to try reach Amy but himself succumbed to the cold. He was rescued by the ship's lifeboat but died in hospital some days later.

In recent years it has been claimed that Amy was shot down. An AA gunner claimed she was contacted twice and failed to give the correct identification code. They opened fire and the aircraft dived into the estuary.

Amy's body was never recovered.

Appendix 18

Hess' Flight

The flight of Rudolf Hess is a lingering mystery of the Second World War, at least amongst the curious. However, for me at least, it is still relevant even now. This is because whatever the truth of it, the actions of those in power are not only questionable but because they are not subject to public scrutiny, they can treat the population with utter contempt. This 'we know best' attitude is still prevalent but because much of the world is a democracy, whatever that means, politicians can hide behind largely meaningless elections and claim it is all the will of the people.

I am not for a minute advocating we vote in a dictator, but I do believe the world as a whole is at something of a crossroads and the appalling lack of honesty from governments of all nationalities and all political leanings is in my opinion something that if not at least considered will have unintended consequences.

To bring Hess back in, the big question is why did he do it? I read 'Double Standards' for the first time some years ago. I have since read it again and then dissected it and made extensive notes for this book. What strikes me, as it presumably struck the authors, was that the official story makes absolutely no sense at all. Why would the Deputy Führer of a nation that, at the time at least, was in the ascendent, fly the long way round to Scotland, bail out, ask to see the Duke of Hamilton and claim he was meeting a peace group if at least some of that wasn't true or at least what he believed?

Why also didn't Churchill use Hess as propaganda? He barely mentioned him publicly until 1943. But why haven't all papers and documents relating to the flight been released into the public domain? As the authors state, what possible effect could their release have eighty years after the event unless there really is something to hide?

I have had a lifelong interest in aviation and the flight itself interests me. My career in aviation has spanned the end of the navigation by radio beacon era into the global positioning system era making navigation, even for the weekend pilots relatively simple. However, it has a broad correlation with the car satnav problem where the satnav sends drivers on unsuitable routes because it saves a minute failing to account for other potential problems, such as whether the road itself is suitable. As the systems get cleverer, so the operator has to think less and less until the day they are lost.

The same applies in aircraft. Our weekend flier programming the GPS enters Waterloo near Brussels instead of Waterloo in London and because he is starting from Dunkerque the two are in precisely opposite directions but more or less the same distance away. He takes off on the opposite runway to every other time he has done so because the wind is unusual today and turns left as normal then climbs through the cloud layer into the sun. Here there is nothing to navigate by, apart from the sun of course (ask the average teenager to point in the general direction of north using the sun and see what happens) and so he follows the line on his GPS, not noticing that he is flying exactly 180 degrees in the wrong direction. Implausible? I don't think so.

The point I am making is that navigation is difficult and in 1941 in wartime conditions with little in the way of electronic or radio aids and slow aircraft with variable and largely unknown wind speeds, it was dreadfully so. Hence why, possibly, Amy Johnson got lost and ended up dead like so many pilots through history. And hence why Hess' flight was a carefully planned expedition and not one where he would have made the deviations claimed afterwards and so readily believed. The Double Standards theory is far more believable, not least because it is so much more achievable. Following the Kalundborg radio beam, a signal at Alnwick and again at Dungavel makes more sense. Equally, why go to all that trouble if all he was trying to do was get to Britain? Far easier to take the short route across the channel and find somewhere to land or bail out in spite of the air defences.

I have discussed Hess the man in the previous book in the series and the more I read and think about it, Hess strikes me as not only the power but the brains behind the throne. I don't have the space to discuss all the anomalies here as there are so many but if you are interested, read Double Standards. I have included some of the events in my story and tried to portray them as accurately as possible. Anecdotal evidence from those who briefly saw Hess where he shouldn't have been wouldn't stand up in court, but what reason would these people have to make these things up? Why for example would the anonymous lady mention the presence of Messerschmitt fuel tanks at Dungavel and indeed the presence of the 'Duke' and not Hamilton but Kent? She had absolutely nothing to gain. Why would Squadron Leader Day claim he had seen Hess and then the Duke of Kent?

And then of course there is Kent himself. He is the only member of the Royal Family to have been killed on active military service since about the fifteenth century and yet virtually nothing has been said about it. Most people if asked who indeed was the last royal to be killed are more likely to come up with Henry V or Richard III.

As for the flight... see below.

Finally, what became of Hess? Again there are so many anomalies.

If the truth is what the government said, then why the odd performance at Nuremberg? Why the letters claiming he had lost his memory and that he couldn't see his wife? Why could he only respond to subjects she initiated? Why didn't he recognise former colleagues like Goering? Why also did Lord Moran, Churchill's personal physician, in the words of a psychiatrist, (Moran wasn't a psychiatrist) wish himself onto the three-man board that assessed Hess' ability to stand trial and why did only he recommend he not stand trial on grounds of insanity, the outcome of which would have been his detention in a high security unit in Britain? Was he drugged or brainwashed or both? (The CIA programs in the 50s proved comprehensively that western governments were more than capable of this sort of behaviour).

Why was Hess' stopped from speaking at his trial after ten minutes when he was allowed twenty? How when he arrived at Spandau prison did he spontaneously recover from paranoid schizophrenia or whatever mental condition he was supposed to have?

If it wasn't Hess, then who was it and what became of the real Hess? The Double Standards authors (and I) place the real Hess in the aircraft that crashed on Eagle's Rock as the extra body, again an anomaly that has been brushed conveniently under the establishment carpet. If he wasn't in it, then what happened to him? Was he also brushed under the carpet?

Who was the double?

The problem with this is who would agree to be the double, but it doesn't take too much to invent plausible scenarios. The Germans had a word for it. Sippenhaft. It meant your whole family becoming responsible for your actions and punished accordingly. Or, you could admit to whatever it was you were accused of guilty or not and accept the punishment on the promise your family would be left alone. Obviously, you would never know if that actually happened, but human hope is a powerful driver. Few people go gladly to their deaths and the vast majority would cling on to the scenario where if you accept the situation now, things could change in the future. It isn't hard therefore to construct a position where you impersonate someone on the understanding that something beneficial would accrue to you or other people. Time leads to acceptance. Stockholm Syndrome or something similar may come into play. Life in prison is better than life outside you believe.

One of the most recent examples of this sort of behaviour was inflicted on the guards on the Berlin Wall or Iron Curtain. Guards generally patrolled in pairs. Usually the pairs consisted of one married and one younger single guard. If one of them decided to run for it, the other was expected to shoot them. The theory was that the married guard would never run because of the reprisals against his family and the single guard wouldn't run because the married one would definitely shoot him to prevent the same thing.

The double goes to Spandau, a harsh, colourless regime. Prisoner Number 7 appears to try and make the best of it by reading but stays rather aloof from the other inmates. He wrote numerous letters but refused visits from anyone until 1965 when he allowed his lawyer to visit. It was only in 1969 that his wife and son were permitted to visit because Hess thought he had a terminal illness.

Hess denied the existence of the sequel to Mein Kampf on the grounds he would have known about it. The manuscript dated from 1928 when Hess was Hitler's secretary and like Mein Kampf, parts of it appear to have been written by Hess.

All the other prisoners, all of whom were serving life sentences, were eventually released. Whenever this was requested for Hess, it was vetoed by the Russians, any of the four controlling powers being able to do this. The accepted story is that the Russians had wanted Hess to be given the death sentence, plus Spandau was in West Berlin so when it was their turn to provide the guards, it meant they had a small presence in the West.

It seems likely however that the British just used this as a convenient excuse. After 1948 when the Russians left the command set up for Germany, the other three could have simply stopped the Russians from entering West Berlin. In 1957, a request was made for Hess' release that the Russians did not veto. The British stepped in on the grounds that the Russians must have forgotten to do so and the prisoner wouldn't be able to cope with life outside. The British talent for cruelty is at least as developed as the Germans.

The secret rules for Spandau stated that if any of the four powers withdrew, the prisoners would be returned to the power that initially held them, in this case Britain. Britain, therefore, could simply have declared the prison closed and taken Hess back to Britain. So why didn't they, instead spending vast amounts of money on one frail old man for twenty-one years after the last of the other prisoners was released. The British were so concerned about Hess and his health that in 1965 they opened a new military hospital that had a maximum-security Hess suite where he would be taken for medical treatment. He was a hypochondriac, but who wouldn't be if it meant you got a change of scenery for a day or two?

Wolf Hess started a 'Free Rudolf Hess' campaign in 1966 after the last of the other prisoners was released. Hess himself refused to ask for release on humanitarian grounds, so his supporters had to try and campaign on the grounds that the sentence was unjust. Margaret Thatcher's private secretary replied to Dr Seidl, Hess' doctor and supporter in 1979, saying that 'the British Government, together with the US and French, have for the last twelve years expressed themselves in favour of the unconditional release on humanitarian grounds. The Prime Minister has asked me to assure you that the British Government for its part is continuing to press for agreement among the four powers for his release.

I should say, however, that in HM Government's view, the arguments which you put forward relating to Hess' trial and conviction are likely to reinforce the Soviet Union in their opposition to Hess' release and make it less likely that they will reconsider their firmly held position'.

So, what was the difference in 1957? And if any of that were true, the British could simply take Hess to Britain and let him go.

At the same time, there were increasing calls for Hess' release from highly placed individuals. Airey Neave, former Army officer and present at the Nuremberg trials was among them. After his murder by the IRA, his widow continued to campaign for his release. Other notable voices included former PM Alec Douglas-Home, Jewish journalist Bernard Levin, Lord Shawcross (British Prosecutor at Nuremberg) and even Simon Wiesenthal who considered he should be released on medical grounds.

In 1969 Hess was diagnosed with a duodenal ulcer, potentially life threatening at age 75, and agreed to a visit from his wife at the new hospital. Among many oddities about the meeting, Ilse Hess (his wife) commented that his voice was lower than it used to be. Most male voices get higher with age.

There was another odd episode in September 1979 when it was rumoured the Russians would agree to release. Hess was rushed to hospital and the British Director phoned Ilse to say Hess was refusing urgent prostate surgery. Ilse and Wolf whilst concerned refused to allow surgery as well. Surgery did not take place and Hess miraculously recovered. All discussion of the incident was forbidden when Wolf visited Hess and any written mention was confiscated. The story leaked to the press and the British government dismissed it as 'speculation'. Of course, whilst in hospital, Hess was effectively on British territory. And if he died during an operation?

All of that paled into insignificance in 1987. On 17th August the British announced he was dead. After a post-mortem, they stated that Hess had hanged himself in a small hut in the grounds that he was allowed to use. He had gone for a stroll and the American warder accompanying him had been called away for a telephone call, in itself slightly odd. When he returned, he said, Hess was lying in the hut with an electrical cord from the lamp tight around his neck.

Revival was attempted but he was declared dead. The cause was reported as 'Suspension'. On 19th September an official report said that he hanged himself from a window latch. A suicide note was found. There was no inquest.

Wolf Hess had recently managed to persuade the Directors that when his father died, his body would be handed over rather than cremated and scattered in secret, the original agreement and what happened to those who were executed at Nuremberg. On 20th August the body was flown by the RAF to a USAF base near Munich and handed over. Wolf and Dr Seidl arranged a second post-mortem.

A year after the death, an eye-witness came forward. Abdullah Melaouhi had been Hess' nurse since 1982. On the day, he was recalled to the prison and after various issues getting in, finally reached the scene. Along with the warder, there were two US soldiers – who shouldn't have been there. The lamp was still plugged in and there was no flex attached to the window latch.

Melaouhi states that the 93 year old Hess would have been physically incapable of killing himself in such a way. Not many 93 year olds would be. He also says why there? If after all these years he had decided to end it, why not do it in his cell at night?

The warder, Jordan's testimony has never been made public and he never spoke about it.

Melaouhi accompanied Hess to the hospital. He says that the Directors opened a bottle of champagne and that a British officer told him to keep his mouth shut and asked him to sign a document. On leaving he went to the police and reported a murder. In the following weeks he says he was called numerous times and warned not to say anything. The West Berlin State Prosecutor opened a murder file but the death was on foreign territory and so he had no jurisdiction.

The only other statement about the incident was given by Lt Colonel Tony le Tissier, a British officer who wasn't actually there and whose statement is therefore legally inadmissible. Le

Tissier says that Hess looped the lamp cable around his neck and then slid down the wall to tighten it. Jordan then removed it – and plugged it back in if Melaouhi is to be believed – and raised the alarm.

Le Tissier implies that Melaouhi knew the two American soldiers/orderlies. He also expresses astonishment that Melaouhi could think he had witnessed a state sponsored crime. Melaouhi has never said that, but all accounts suggest that he was a frightened man.

The first post-mortem gave the cause of death as suspension. But, and it is a big but, there is no mention of any marks on the neck. Dr Spann who carried out the second noted straight marks on Hess' neck, marks that must have been there at the first examination. These marks are consistent with death by strangulation or throttling which closes the carotid arteries, but not suspension which closes the windpipe and generally leaves a 'V' shaped mark. It is almost impossible to commit suicide by strangulation because unconsciousness would release the pressure. And as for a frail 93 year old reaching the high window, attaching a lamp flex and then slumping down the wall with enough pressure to hang himself – I leave you to judge.

Wolf Hess believes the suicide note left is a forgery although possibly based on a 1969 letter written when he thought he may die. There are numerous anomalies again.

The investigation into Hess' death was at the very least sloppy if not utterly unprofessional. Spandau prison was destroyed, literally, six weeks after Hess died.

After a television report raised questions, a Scotland Yard review was carried out. The police officer involved told Labour MP Rhodri Morgan that the investigation was incompetent. He subsequently came back to him worried and Morgan believes the officer was warned off. The British Director of Public Prosecutions reviewed the evidence and decided there was no basis for further investigation, it wasn't in the public interest and was covered by Public Interest Immunity. This is a government procedure for a state cover up and is used if the interests of the state are likely to be 'compromised'.

Why?

In 1987, it was reported that in the interests of Glasnost and German-Soviet relations, President Gorbachev was going to agree to release Hess. Melaouhi claims that on hearing about this possibility, Hess said that 'the English will kill me'.

If it was true, the British could veto it themselves, but of course the next time the Russians were in their guard month, they could simply walk away and the British would look foolish.

Wolf Hess believes that Prisoner Number 7 was his father. He also believes he was murdered by the British Government to prevent him revealing the details of the peace document from 1941. Were that to be revealed, thousands of families would ask why? They might even sue and want compensation.

The Double Standards authors clearly have numerous contacts in high places, some of which are adamant that a British Security Services team of some kind executed Hess. They have stated that contacts in the CIA and Mossad have confirmed this. The British Government's reluctance to talk about it confirms rather than denies it. But then that is the way of governments.

I only have to watch a politician squirm on television to know they are lying. None of them are capable of giving straight answers, preferring to obfuscate. I cannot think of a single one that I would trust with my wallet, my wife or my car.

What do I think about it all?

I think something very unusual happened on the night of the 10th May 1941. I think it was carefully planned but that something catastrophic went wrong. Whether the establishment set a trap (a possibility suggested in Double Standards) will never be known. How and why it went wrong will also remain unknown. But go wrong it did. From there on, everyone was trying to make the best of it to further their agendas. Plans were made on the hoof.

The biggest conundrum is why a negotiated peace was never publicly discussed. Britain had just been soundly beaten and the Battle of Britain aside, was hardly winning elsewhere. What was Churchill's reason for carrying on the fight? The German regime was distasteful, but they hadn't yet resorted to mass murder. They certainly were no worse than our charming allies the Russians and a cursory look at most pre-war regimes in Europe doesn't make one feel a deep and desperate desire to help them. And given the British governments position on Jewish emigration we can hardly say that had anything to do with it.

Churchill beggared the British economy and effectively ended the Empire of which he was so proud he mentioned it lasting a thousand years. He did this knowingly. Of course, it is almost a crime in the UK to consider Churchill as anything other than a national hero.

Personally, I'd ask the legions of the dead, once they had read the peace agreement and been told what the alternative outcome of years more war would be, whether they thought it was worth it in 1941, whether they thought their lives were worth sacrificing for the vanity of a few powerful men. But I can't.

Appendix 19

World War Two
What was the point?

Almost anyone will tell you it was to defeat the murderous Nazi scourge, to save humanity from a vile dictator. But if that were really true, why didn't the American and British forces continue to confront the Russians? The Cold War was a confrontation of sorts but more than that it was an acceptance that the western allies had neither the means nor the will to do so. History on the whole now accepts that the Russian regime was as bad if not worse than the Nazis. The targets were different of course and in fact had little basis in logic, but in 1937-38 alone, around a million people were killed in the purges. The total figure is hard to ascertain but a conservative estimate would be 5-6 million. That figure is broadly the same as the death toll from the Holocaust.

The question still remains then. Why did the west not attempt to remove this vile dictator?

There is no answer really. Britain was exhausted, financially and materially. There is some evidence that British troops in Normandy after D-Day were reluctant to push hard against the somewhat more fanatical German troops. One can see why. After years of war and hardship, the thought of losing your life in a ditch in France had little appeal, especially if it could be left to the fighter bombers or the artillery. It is easy to forget this was a citizen army with more to live for than die for. I do not intend that as a criticism in the slightest. There were many, many acts of heroism and sacrifice but reality is different and I doubt I would have felt any different. Age of course compels one to examine the motives and beliefs of those in charge and generally find them wanting – and certainly not people one would give one's life for.

The Americans must have had similar feelings. What on earth was a GI from the Midwest doing fighting in a field in France? There is a classic scene in Spielberg's film 'Saving Private Ryan' where the officer, Captain Miller, following the death of one of his men in what seems such a pointless way, tells his men that he was a teacher in real life. To my mind it is one of the most poignant scenes in a film with many – and it is a film that, in my opinion, in its realism sums up the futility of war whatever the cause.

To return then to my original point, what was the point? And having answered that, the next question is, was there another way?

The peace group thought so, but what would that peace have looked like? And did it just shift the battle to somewhere else?

Obviously it is hard to know with any certainty, but the peace proposals that were discussed in various circles were probably broadly accurate in what a deal would have looked like. Britain retained its Empire, Germany controlled Europe. Western European nations became German satellites but almost certainly with some form of supervised autonomy. Eastern Europe was invaded. Without the losses from the Western Front, it is possible the Germans would have defeated the Russians. It is worth noting again that Hess outlined what Europe would look like after an exhausting war with the communist border on the west coast of the continent and Britain bankrupt. The only part he got wrong was the location of the border which only fell where it was because of American intervention. The enormously expensive Cold War followed as well as numerous Communist v Capitalist proxy wars like Vietnam or Korea. It was another forty plus years before the Communist state imploded.

Would the holocaust have happened? In my previous book I argue that Hess was a moderating influence albeit still antisemitic, but as we have seen, most of the rest of the world was hardly in a position to judge. Russia may well have experienced a holocaust of its own – but then they managed their own even without German help.

The answer then is probably that the world would still have been different, just maybe with less of the slaughter. But then who knows?

Appendix 20

Hamilton: Libel Cases

Much has been written about the Duke of Hamilton albeit not recently. Firstly, I should state what I think although my opinion is just that, opinion and carries no weight whatsoever.

The Duke strikes me as a thoroughly honourable man faced with an impossible situation. He clearly wasn't alone in his opinions on peace proposals, but he seems to be more or less the only one who suffered publicly. Anecdotally, an outraged woman slapped his face at a society party. Of course, the British public were not aware of the extent of the peace group, the proposals and how high in society the group reached.

More and more people expressed their anger leading to two libel cases. In February 1942 Hamilton sued the London District Committee of the Communist Party and the authors, publishers, printers and distributors of an article in 'World News and Views' over allegations that he had plotted with Britain's enemies, knew Hess before the war and knew about the flight. A fine case of hypocrisy if ever there was one.

The case was settled when some, but not all of the defendants issued a public apology. Hamilton asked only for costs.

In 'Double Standards' however, the authors state that one of Hamilton's statements read out by his barrister claims that 'when he was informed that a German airman named Alfred Horn was asking to see him, he thereupon went with his interrogation officer to interview him'. The implication is that he went immediately. The official line is that he didn't go until the following morning, but the evidence in the book suggests he did go straightaway, so is this a clever use of language to avoid perjury?

Later in 1942 Hamilton sued in the American courts a journalist called Pierre van Passen whose book 'This Day Alone' published in 1941 described the Duke as a British fascist who had plotted with Hess. This was also settled out of court.

These cases appear to reinforce the case for Hamilton not being part of the peace group. However, again as stated in the book, there is more to it. His submission in the first case was approved by the Air Ministry and the government in the form of the Home Secretary pressed for him to drop the cases stating that his reputation had been cleared by the statement in Parliament.

In the American case, Hamilton again asked for costs. He received £110 which did not cover his costs, ie he was happy with a compromise. He also received $1300 in instalments and the offending passage was removed. He claimed $100,000.

Of course in the American case, calling Hamilton a fascist was about as far from the truth as it was possible to get. He certainly wasn't that but by objecting to that he could remove other comments as well.

There is one other case that did not go to court. The Daily Express edition of 13th May 1941 headline read 'Boxer Marquis Dined With Hess'. The article said he had met Hess several times. Hamilton's solicitor met the editor, Godfrey Norris, and it seemed that the Express would print a retraction. However, at a second meeting, the solicitor arrived to find Norris in a meeting with Beaverbrook. Norris then declared that Sinclair's Commons statement was false and the Express would defend its claims in court. Hamilton backed down. Beaverbrook of course was very well informed.

It seems clear that Hamilton, in trying to do what he thought was right, was caught between a rock and a hard place and despite being powerful himself, was powerless against the kind of opposition Churchill could summon. Had the peace group succeeded, history would be very different and Hamilton's role would have been eclipsed by Kent.

Appendix 21

Death on Eagle's Rock

As I mentioned above, the Duke of Kent was the first member of the Royal Family to be killed on active service for 500 years. His only memorial is a cross at the accident site placed there by Princess Marina. He is not mentioned at the RAF museum at Hendon or the Imperial War Museum at Duxford.

Officially, a Short Sunderland flying boat took off from Invergordon and a few minutes later crashed into a hill called Eagle's Rock killing all but one on board. The accident report blames the pilot – a not unusual occurrence in military and civil accident reports through the entire history of aviation.

A recent example is the Mull of Kintyre crash of an RAF Chinook in fog that killed numerous intelligence personnel as well as the crew. The initial inquiry failed to establish a cause, but two senior officers overturned this and declared the cause was gross negligence on the part of the pilots. As a professional pilot, I found this disturbing at the time and I doubt there is a professional pilot anywhere that isn't at least aware that if it all goes pear shaped, one would need to defend ones actions in court to people that weren't there. A little like the military enquiries that have dogged the British Army and Royal Marines in recent years that take little or no account of the reality of battlefields which, unless you have been on one (I haven't) I doubt you can appreciate and have no equivalent in ordinary civil life.

The verdict was overturned some years later, gross negligence being a verdict that says the pilots deliberately endangered their aircraft and how two desk drivers reached that conclusion about two men who were experienced special forces pilots and had no history of taking risks is beyond me. It is possible they made a mistake, but as the report also states, they had been flying for over 6 hours and on duty for 9. In a military aircraft in difficult conditions that is plenty to cope with and I would guess that fatigue played a significant part.

Back to Eagle's Rock, the entire story was brushed under the carpet for years and forgotten about until the author and researcher Robert Brydon realised that there were significant anomalies in the story.

His basic questions were these. 'How did a crew handpicked for the job crash into the hill? And, 'What exactly was a flying boat doing over land in the first place?'

His investigations quickly uncovered many oddities. First, the flight was officially going to Iceland. 228 Squadron were based on the west coast. Why did they not depart from the west coast? It would have been simpler for the royal party to drive over to the west coast. Second, why, if they were lost, or had changed the flight plan as claimed by the official story, did they not follow standard procedure and climb?

It is almost impossible to believe they were lost given the crew on board, so the idea as posited by the air ministry that they turned inland and descended into cloud is utter nonsense. These were professional pilots who knew the area and the performance of their aircraft. They were also aware of the weather reports that said they only had to go a bit further north to find clear skies. (Former WAAF, Dorothea Grey is on record as saying that the Oban civilian meteorologists that provided the weather reports were immediately drafted into the RAF – and therefore subject to the Official Secrets Act or its equivalent).

Even the official reports don't really make sense. Sinclair's statement in the Commons omitted to say that the engines were discovered by the Maintenance Unit that cleared the wreckage to be at full throttle with the propellers in coarse pitch. The aircraft was therefore climbing when it hit the ground, not descending as the report says.

This same maintenance unit, the same one that cleared Hess' Me110, were also ordered to completely clear the wreckage from the site. This was supposedly to prevent people collecting macabre souvenirs. But the areas is littered with aircraft wrecks. It was a complete waste of time removing them from such a remote area. There may be another reason for this though. The wreckage was covered with tarpaulins, in itself unusual as the bodies had already been removed. Unless of course the authorities didn't wish it to be known that the aircraft had been repainted white. Which made the flight a neutral flight rather than a military

308

flight. Flights to Iceland were not neutral, those to Sweden for example were.

Other anomalies include the body count. Fifteen bodies were recovered from the site. Initial reports said that everybody onboard had died. Telegrams were sent. It was only when the tail gunner turned up alive that the authorities realised something was amiss. Then they changed their story to fourteen dead and one survivor. More than one person would have counted the bodies. The most unlikely scenario is that they miscounted, so we have an extra body.

The Double Standards theory then is that the Sunderland took off from Loch More having collected Hess, misidentified the valley below and crashed in the climb, and this fits much better than the official version. The inconvenient survivor was subject to military discipline. He was not called to give a statement to the inquiry, the only time he publicly said anything was in 1961 and he said he couldn't remember anything. His statement however did deflect attention from Princess Marina and her family's first visit to the crash site.

There is far more detail in the book, most of it simply reinforcing the view that, all in all, this was a thoroughly inept cover up of something. We will never know what. I will leave the final words to Princess Marina who erected the only memorial to the Duke. It mentions his 'Special Mission'. As the authors say though, what was 'special' about a morale boosting trip to Iceland? On the other hand, a flight to somewhere neutral with the Deputy Führer on board? That would be special.

IN MEMORY OF
AIR CDRE H.R.H. THE DUKE OF KENT
K.G., K.T., G.C.M.C.,G.C.V.O.
AND HIS COMPANIONS
WHO LOST THEIR LIVES ON ACTIVE SERVICE
DURING A FLIGHT TO ICELAND ON A SPECIAL
MISSION

THE 25TH OF AUGUST 1942
'MAY THEY REST IN PEACE'

Printed in Great Britain
by Amazon

87477091R00180